PINNED TO A TREE, A SPEAR THROUGH HIS CHEST, WAS THE BODY OF BUFFALO BILL.

Blood was dripping from his lifeless mouth. His body was riddled with bullet holes. Standing next to the corpse was a pair of NVA soldiers, smiling at each other and talking cheerfully.

Marlin Beckwith planted his heels in the mud. He fired a burst from the rifle at his waist and walked the bullets up the body of the soldier on the left. Before he had a chance to take out the other soldier, another rifle sounded and the second NVA fell to his knees.

Simmons came crashing out of the jungle. When he saw Buffalo Bill, he stopped in his tracks.

"Where's Hoppy?" Beckwith demanded.

"They took him," Simmons said. Then he jerked his head up and stared at the impaled body of his murdered friend.

"They didn't have to do it, Sir," Simmons whispered, tears in his eyes. "They didn't have to stick him to the tree like that. He was already dead. They just did it for fun."

"We'll get 'em, Simmons," Beckwith assured him. "We'll get 'em and we'll get Hoppy back too." Undisguised hatred burned in the Lieutenant's eyes. "We'll make the bastards pay."

THOSE WHO DARED

JIM SIMMEN

ZEBRA BOOKS
KENSINGTON PUBLISHING CORP.

ZEBRA BOOKS

are published by

Kensington Publishing Corp.
475 Park Avenue South
New York, NY 10016

First printing: January, 1990

Printed in the United States of America

Dedicated to those men in Vietnam who stood toe to toe with death — and spat in its face.

I want to thank Irving Warner for challenging me to write this book and for the invaluable help he provided. I want to thank all my friends who labored through my first writings and came away with smiles of encouragement, this includes Gloria Grandau, Marty Loken, Penny Rennick, Ruth and Dave Shapiro, Bill Couturie, Virginia Heiner, John Bowers, and Bernie Edelman. My family's encouragement during this process was invaluable. And thanks to my son, Russell, for keeping me home.

Chapter 1

Three Huey helicopters dropped out of the sky above the flooded rice field between the American base camp and the village of Binh Phuoc, and just before making contact with the ground, heeled back. The wind from their blades flattened the rice plants and whipped up water like sea breeze from a cresting wave. Two sleek Cobra gunships made a fast and low pass over their heads and swooped over the huts of the small village, ready to unleash their bittersweet fury on anything that hinted of hostility.

Foot soldiers jumped out of the open doors of the Hueys and ran to the nearest berm and either fell on their bellies or knelt on one knee and crouched down to protect themselves from any incoming rounds they might not hear in the moment of loud confusion.

Half a mile away, a cluster of Vietnamese worked in knee-deep water with their pants rolled up above their knees and their shirts rolled up above their elbows. They stood up straight and with the back of their wrists moved the tan straw brimmed hats from their eyes so they could see better.

Once the helicopters were unloaded, they quickly departed. When it was quiet enough for the soldiers to hear that they were not under attack, the platoon leader, Lt. Marlin Beckwith, stood up and signaled for the men to follow suit. As the soldiers gained their feet now with grunts of pleasure, Marlin looked contentedly at the base camp and smiled. In its scuzzy way, it provided all the creature comforts that a man could eke from this miserable swamp land in the Mekong Delta. Just the thought of a cold beer made his mouth water. Marlin signaled the first squad leader, Jaime Rodriguez, to start towards the camp. The rest of the men formed a file and nearly as possible followed in his footsteps. Rodriguez did not take the easier path atop the rice berms but sludged through the muddy water to minimize the chances of triggering a booby trap.

The platoon filed around the camp's long perimeter which was protected by pyramids of concertina wire and an open mine field. Fifty five-gallon barrels filled with dirt and piled two on end hid the camp from view.

The platoon crossed a shallow irrigation ditch and then onto the muddy road that ran through the village of Binh Phuoc, population approximately 8,000. Hootches fanned out on both sides of a clay road that was shaded by coconut and palm trees and sundry other plants growing like fungus in the humid climate. The soldiers on the road exchanged curious stares with musk ox and civilian alike, ready to disintegrate both of them if need be.

Pushed off in a ditch next to the front gate was a smoldering American deuce and a half truck that had been hit recently by a Russian-made recoilless propelled grenade as a hole was blown out of the engine compartment the size of a basketball hoop.

The men in the third platoon did not waste energy asking questions, but dragged their exhausted bodies through the metal gate held open by an alert Military Police guard who stood to one side wearing a shiny white helmet and green poncho rain gear.

Once inside, the soldiers slung their rifles over their

shoulders, broke out of formation and headed for their platoon tent. Medics came forward with a stretcher and immediately relieved Squad Leaders Gatz and Wilson of Private James Hutch who had been shot in the right thigh. Hutch was whisked off to the battalion medical station with a lot of exaggerated motions and shouts of urgency. The Military Police just as quickly, but much more quietly, took away the two Vietnamese prisoners in black pajamas who walked directly in front of the Lieutenant.

Ninety-five percent of the base camp was made out of sandbags. They covered the ammunition caches, and surrounded the 105 howitzer artillery battery at the east end of the camp, and protected each platoon tent. The eight machine gun bunkers sat behind sandbags as did the platoon bunkers where the men sought protection during mortar attacks.

On the way to the officer's tent, Beckwith stopped at Supply and picked up two cold beers and his mail. As he headed down the wooden walk, he guzzled the first beer and threw the empty container in a bullet-riddled eight-inch artillery casing used to catch garbage. He clutched at the mail. It just made him smile knowing that he was about to share a few moments with his family and friends back in the States.

When he entered the tent, no bodies were sacked out asleep on the half-dozen cots; the mosquito nets were in place and the footlockers pushed under the bedding.

Beckwith placed his M-16 against the wall, took off his back pack and dropped it at the foot of the cot, flung his helmet on top and breathed heavily at the sudden relief. He lifted the mosquito net from his bed and flung it over atop itself and sat down.

He quickly flipped through the letters to see who they were from. The familiar handwriting on each identified the writer before he even had to read the return address. There were three letters from his girlfriend, Roxeanne, one from his mother and father, a letter from his old buddy Hal in California, another from his mother, and a package wrapped in brown paper. He opened the package first. It was filled with chocolate chip cookies from home. Marlin quickly wolfed down a handful, barely tasting the delicious walnuts hidden inside.

He stuffed another cookie into his mouth and opened one of the letters from his girlfriend. He read the salutation, *Dear Marlin,* and smiled. He lifted the letter to his nose and sniffed the sweet perfume that flooded him with happy memories. He read the last line, where she said she loved him, and set the letter aside. He'd read the rest later when he had time to relax and enjoy the thoughts from home, but now to clean up.

He quickly undressed, wrapped a towel around his body, slipped his feet into the shower clogs covered with dust and walked out the squeaking screen door to step into a small stall shower, the door only large enough to cover his midsection. He draped the towel over the back wall and opened the valve to a fifty-five gallon barrel overhead.

It was just barely warm, heated by the weather, but it made him feel euphoric. He splashed his body with water, turned the valve off, slowly lathered up the soap and worked the dirt and smells of the jungle to the surface, washed his hair and rinsed off. He wanted to do it again, but he had learned to conserve the water for the next guy.

As he was toweling off, a soldier drew closer. Beckwith recognized him as one of the company commander's runners. Before the man could speak, Beckwith said, "Don't tell me. The Old Man wants to see me now."

10

"Yes, Sir, as soon as you get out of the shower."

"Will do."

The soldier hesitated a moment, his brow furrowing. He seemed nervous, uncertain of his next move; finally he blurted out, almost innocently, "Did you bring back any souvenirs, Sir?"

Beckwith stopped for a moment, looked at the man curiously and said, "I'm not into collecting ears, soldier."

"No, Sir. I mean, pistols or rifles?"

Beckwith started to dry himself off again, more slowly, "There are plenty out there, go get your own."

"I'm always back in camp, Sir."

"Well, that could be rearranged. I could talk to the Old Man about it when I see him."

"I don't really want them that bad, Sir, but I'd pay you good money for one."

"Shut the fuck up before you make me mad, soldier. Tell the Old Man I'll be there in a heartbeat."

As if shocked by a bolt of electricity, the soldier turned and left. Beckwith finished drying and returned to the room. The clothes he had thrown on the floor were already hardening up and smelling rotten. He could never smell himself in the field, but once he took off the clothes and held them away from his body even for a few minutes, the stench amazed him, especially after taking a shower. He stuffed the dirty clothes into a laundry sack, feeling like he should wash his hands again.

It started to drizzle, and by the time he put on a fresh uniform, it was coming down hard. He strapped his .45 around his waist, rolled the sleeves of his shirt above the elbow, and donned a soft jungle cap, then stood tall and pulled the bottom of his shirt down hard under his pistol belt.

He stepped outside and stayed on the wooden platforms. The rain seemed to be colder than normal and turned his uniform sticky.

At the C.O.'s tent, Marlin walked up the front steps, opened the screened door, and walked inside. The door slammed shut on springs. The sound startled the C.O. who was stooped over a table in front of a line of radios next to a man with earphones on.

The C.O. stood up, smiled, and walked towards Beckwith with his hand out. He was a medium-sized man with blond hair that reminded Marlin of a porcupine with a crewcut. Captain Rice's jungle fatigue pants were tucked into his boots, the dog tags clinking outside the T-shirt. The C.O. was responsible for four platoons, over 150 men. Although he was only twenty-three years old, the job was known to make an old man out of the youngest. This was his second tour in Nam, his first having been spent in the field as a platoon leader.

Captain Rice shook Beckwith's hand enthusiastically. "Good to see you again, Beckwith. Things are getting pretty hairy out there now, aren't they?"

"Yes, Sir."

"What did you do with the prisoners?"

"The MPs picked them up as soon as we entered the gate."

"Good. They might have some information about the enemy build-up that could help us stop them dead in their tracks."

"I wanted to shoot the sons of bitches myself."

"Uh huh," he said quickly. "How are your wounded?"

"Hutch was shot in the thigh. It looked like the bullet missed the bone. I suppose he'll be out for a few days."

The C.O. wrinkled his face. "Nasty. Well, he is in good hands now. How the hell did it happen?"

When Beckwith explained about the sniper, the C.O. kept nodding his head and saying, "Yes." When

Beckwith finished, the C.O. asked, "You see any NVA?"

"Negative. All local VC. Sir. What was the message you had for me?"

"Oh, right. I have some replacements for you. Three men in all. They are in your platoon area right now."

"I guess I should thank you for that."

His lips formed a wry smile. "There is a reason . . . You are going to need them, Beckwith. I want you to take your platoon up to the Ben Luc bridge on the east fork of the Vam Co River. This is the only bridge that connects the Delta to Saigon. I want you to search the traffic for enemy supplies moving either way. You will work with a Coastal Riverine Squadron located near the bridge. They can ferry you to wherever you need to go."

"What's going on up there?"

"Not much, but the Air Force is having a field day north of Saigon with whole companies of NVA soldiers being caught in the open."

"And we're to stop them from attacking Saigon!"

"That's the plan."

"Any date set for the attack?"

"The Vietnamese lunar New Year is coming up in about six weeks and our intelligence expects it to happen before then, if it happens at all. The rainy season will be slacking off after that," he took a deep breath, "my guess is before Tet."

"How long should I expect to stay at Ben Luc?"

The C.O. handed Beckwith some maps. "Here. You better take these before I forget. They cover Ben Luc and Saigon. You might need them before I see you again."

Beckwith smiled as he took the maps, folded them in squares about chest size and asked, "How long?"

"A week. Maybe two. Depends upon what is going

on in the area and if the NVA make a move. I'm driving the other platoons slowly towards your position. They might chase something your way."

"When do we leave?"

"At dusk the trucks will drive you up north. I want you to set up in an ambush along the river tonight and tomorrow dig yourself in at both ends of the bridge. If they blow that sucker up, it will definitely cut the Delta off from Saigon as far as road traffic, so no fuck-ups."

He ignored the threat. "Anybody else at Ben Luc?"

"There is a 155 mm artillery battery there as well as a battery of eight-inch guns. Some ARVNs and a Green Beret, Captain Crystal. He's your contact."

Beckwith stood up, drained his can of beer and flipped it into the wastebasket at the end of all the radios. "Two points," he said as he tipped his hat at the C.O., stuffed the maps into his shirt, and started to leave.

"Good luck, Beckwith. I'll probably see you at Ben Luc as the other platoons move closer to your position."

"Thanks."

Without turning, Beckwith headed out the door, down the steps and around the side, and headed for the third platoon tent. The rain had increased in intensity and he hunched his shoulders over to keep the maps dry. He looked up from under the brim of the dripping hat and saw that the sides of his platoon's tent were rolled up except for the mosquito netting. He hopped up the two steps and ran inside. A lane down the middle of the tent divided the bunks in half.

The men were in various stages of taking showers and securing their gear and cleaning it. Dog tags rattled and shower clogs smacked the floor.

It smelled like a locker room after a sweaty, humid, southern football game, reeking of victory.

As soon as Larry Gatz saw the Lieutenant, he asked,

"I don't want to ask no foolish question, Sir, but how long we got back at camp?"

Larry was a tall, muscular black man whose skin shone in the humidity.

"Five hours. Be packed and ready to move on to Ben Luc."

There were groans and cheers at the news and Beckwith moved towards the new men in sweat-soaked uniforms who stood in a circle in the middle of the tent. They were smoking and watching.

As Beckwith approached, he eyed them as fresh meat. Their eyes were wide and their heads jerked around at the slightest sound as if they were about to be ambushed. Their duffel bags were propped up against their legs.

When Beckwith drew close enough, one of the new recruits called the others to attention. The tent grew silent for a second and then grew loud with laughter.

Beckwith said, "At ease, men." He chuckled. "We don't do that over here."

There were some guffaws inside the tent as the chatter started up again and the rest of the platoon resumed their activities.

As the men relaxed, Beckwith introduced himself and shook their hands.

Immediately Allen wanted to know where the latrine was. When Beckwith explained, Allen took off at a trot. Fosdale was a porker of a man with a bulbous nose, and Norman Justice, a country boy, judging his accent. Fosdale had eyes that never seemed to stop moving, and he gave the impression of not listening.

The Lieutenant did not care how they looked, but did wonder how they would perform under fire.

Beckwith sat at the end of Hoppy's cot and told the two men to take a seat.

"Hoppy?" Fosdale asked, as he sat at the end of a cot

across from the Lieutenant.

Beckwith looked over his shoulder at Earl Moss, nicknamed Hoppy, who was a pale man with a round face and freckles and short, light blond hair, turning almost white.

"Yeah," Beckwith said, "Hoppy here acts like he's been goosed by a water buffalo every time he hears a sound louder than a firecracker. Comes right off the ground."

Hoppy smiled, almost apologetically, and returned to reading a letter that he hunched his shoulders over.

Beckwith said, "Lots of nicknames go around over here, but it is all in good fun."

Justice asked, "Lieutenant, Sir, what happened to that truck out the front gate?"

"Truck?"

"Yes, the one that was on fire."

"Oh, right. The truck. It looked like an RPG hit it."

The private started to shake his head and said, "Was . . . anyone killed?"

"I don't know, but I should hear soon."

The new boy nodded.

"Now, let me assign you to your squads."

When Allen returned, working on his zipper, Beckwith assigned Fosdale and Justice to the fourth squad. Allen went to the third. The Lieutenant did not tell the new men that they were replacing men recently killed or wounded. He was sure they would find out soon enough.

Men were writing letters, reading mail, drinking beer; some napping. Given enough time, they'd all be sacked out.

Kraus said, "Lieutenant, the beer?" he was putting on his pants in a hurry.

"Right, Kraus." The Lieutenant turned to the new men, "My radio operator says he just saved my life and

16

I owe him one. Why don't . . . ? Suddenly there was the sound of a mortar round exploding. The volume was about the same as outgoing artillery which sounded like a piston thrusting, but this sound was shattering.

Hoppy bounced in the air like a bunny as someone shouted, "Incoming!" and immediately the tent began to empty out the back door to where the platoon bunker was.

Beckwith pushed the new men in front of him and got them moving down the aisle.

Heads kept popping up in the air as the men jumped over something. When it was Beckwith's turn to jump, he saw what they were jumping over. There was the big body of the fourth squad leader, a black man weighing near to 250 pounds and nicknamed Buffalo Bill, down on his hands and knees with his arms full of letters, and still reaching out for more that he had just dropped in the commotion.

Chapter 2

The camp's siren shrieked as Beckwith helped Buffalo Bill to his feet. As the aisle was now blocked, men started to jump over cots on both sides of the squad leader. Marlin joined them.

Finally Buffalo Bill stretched his body over his cot, stuffed the letters under the pillow, and ran to catch up to the others.

Marlin ran out the back door, jumped off the two stairs onto the wooden walk, spun to the right and dashed through the alley of sandbags into the bunker.

The four-foot-long tunnel turned to the right and became total darkness. Men pushed each other to the back until the ones who were against the back wall started to squeeze back.

Buffalo Bill finally came in swearing and cussing and demanding an unprecedented amount of elbowroom.

The incoming rounds, which could not have totalled more than a dozen, stopped.

When you could hear only the sound of people catching their breaths, the high-pitched sound of a fart broke the silence, followed by the booming of the camp's artillery as it fired back at the VC.

A second later someone hollered, "Castillo, you are supposed to digest your food—not ferment it! Let me out of this rotten place!"

Bodies started to squirm and push against each other and some of the men began to laugh.

Buffalo Bill could be heard, "I ain't lettin' any of you assholes out of here. Steppin' all over my letters."

"Hey, man, those letters aren't going anywhere. You could have picked them up later."

"They weren't your letters, Honkie. They were mine."

"Buffalo Bill, this is your commanding officer," Beckwith pleaded.

"I let you out, Sir, but not these other assholes."

"It smells like mustard gas," Kraus hollered, trying to hold his breath.

"Castillo blew a hole in his pants."

When the fumes finally reached Buffalo Bill, he hollered, "Whhhoooooeee. That is the smell of death itself. I'm gone."

The hole unplugged and the bunker emptied faster than it had filled.

By the time the men staggered back into the tent, Beckwith looked at Private Fosdale, who was trying to smile, but his bulging eyes were giving away the nervousness.

Beckwith returned to Hoppy's cot and said, "Your first mortar attack, Fosdale. Usually the VC don't hit anything, but it is that ten percent of the time that makes everyone run."

"How often does that happen, Lieutenant?"

Beckwith shot out a spurt of air. "Too often. You can never get a good night's sleep in this camp, no matter what."

"Don't they usually follow up with a ground attack?"

"I wish they would. The dinks might be stupid but they are not crazy. They would have to cross a mine field with machine guns strafing them, and by then everyone would be on the berm shooting them in the wire."

The front door slammed and Beckwith looked up to see the Old Man's messenger come running down the aisle and hollering his name.

"Yo," the Lieutenant replied as he stood up.

"The Captain wants to see you, Sir. Pronto."

"I'm coming." He shook his head and followed the messenger back to the Old Man's radio shack.

The C.O. was standing in the middle of the tent with his hands on his hips, his face red with anger. As soon as he saw the third platoon leader, he pointed his finger at him and said, "I want you to find those sons of bitches this time, Beckwith, and wipe them out. You hear me? Find those mortars and destroy them."

"Fuck," Beckwith whispered to one side.

"I want you to search the jungle northeast of camp and root out those bastards if you have to chase them all the way to China."

"Are you sure that is where the firing came from?"

"Number four machine gun on the berm radioed that he saw the muzzle flashes coming from that direction."

"Maybe the artillery will pick them off."

"I want you to follow up and find out."

Beckwith felt disgusted, "Did anyone get hurt?"

"No, the rounds did not even land inside the camp, but that is not the point."

Beckwith shook his head. "What about Ben Luc?"

"You're still going, but I want you to skirt the treeline first. The trucks can pick you up down the road when you come out of the jungle. I want you to leave now."

"Hey, the VC have been firing at us since the war began."

"Well, we won't find them sitting in camp either."

"My men have been in the field without a break for

20

three weeks now, Sir. They are so damn exhausted they can hardly keep their eyes open during an ambush at night. They're hurting and could really use a few hours of rest."

"Now."

"Yes, Sir."

Beckwith stormed back to the platoon tent, stepped inside and hollered, "Put it all away, men. We are going to find those bastards and hang them by their nuts. Now."

There was nothing but groaning from the tent as disbelieving faces registered shock.

Beckwith shouted out the Old Man's orders again and finished with, "I want you in formation in ten minutes. Move it."

Footlockers were slammed, cards thrown, towels snapped, letter pads folded as curses filled the air.

"Ten minutes," Beckwith repeated before he slammed the door.

He trotted back to his own tent, emptied out his rucksack onto the floor, stuffed the dirty clothes into the laundry sack, crammed a couple of clean changes of clothes inside the rucksack, all the clean socks, shaving kit, unread letters and closed it up. He donned the flack jacket, the rucksack, helmet, picked up the M-16 and returned to the platoon tent to roust out the slower men onto the road.

When heads were counted, all twenty-seven men were there. He had Buffalo Bill's squad go to supply to draw more ammunition. When they returned, the men broke formation and picked over the supply of LAWs, incendiary, concussion, fragmentary and M79 grenades, claymores, machine gun bandoliers and boxes of M-16 rounds. They were like kids planning for a Fourth of July celebration.

When everyone had their fill, Marlin had them fall

back in formation and checked them out quickly, then gave the signal for Cox and his squad to move out.

Cox assigned Hill as point man and the squad started to file out the front gate. Beckwith and Kraus followed behind the first squad. The Vietnamese Chieu Hoi and the artillery forward observer went with the platoon sergeant Roberts.

The guard at the gate asked, "Leaving so soon?"

The cussing and cursing shot back at him made him laugh.

"Spread the hell out," Beckwith hollered before they got too far down the road and into the jungle where silence was a strict rule.

"Those gooks picked on the right platoon this time. I could strangle every one of them with my bare hands," Kraus said.

Beckwith knew what he meant — another hot afternoon walking through the miserable jungle searching for holes, traps, trip wires, pungi stakes, swatting mosquitoes, and after being so close to enjoying a cold beer at the club and relaxing.

Before Beckwith waded across the first canal, he looked down to make certain that his pants were tucked into his boots. He didn't want any leeches crawling up his legs. As he waded into the water, he thought, *So much for a clean uniform.* It was too damn much work anyway.

Across the rice paddies and into the jungle that was so thick you could not see your own feet, and when you could see down that far, you saw that your feet were under the water or sinking in the slimy mud.

Lieutenant Beckwith knew better than to follow a man-made trail. There was always the possibility that one of the villagers was a VC who would sneak from his work in the field, move ahead of the third platoon, and set a booby trap at one of the gates, bridges, or across a path. The difference between life and death for the point man would be detecting or tripping one small, thin piece of wire concealed somewhere under the thick leaves or sunk in the mud. Whichever Vietnamese set the trap would never be told upon by his or her fellow villagers. If they did, at night they would pay for their sin, and the following day there would be at least one less straw hat working the field.

The thick jungle was usually safer. They crossed the suspected area of attack and continued deeper into the greenery, taking breaks hourly, treating each moment as if it could be their last, feeling extra hateful for the few moments of rest that the VC had taken from them.

Kraus was one of the few men in the platoon who did not smoke cigarettes, but when it came to burning off leeches, he always lighted up.

The leeches were thicker in the canals than in the rice paddies. It was during a rest period after such a crossing, Kraus raised his pants above the knee, drew his boot up to his crotch, and found a leech on the fatty part of his calf where he always seemed to find one. He smiled, removed a cigarette from its small C-ration packet and without placing it in his mouth, lighted a match under the cigarette tip and held it there. He let it torch until he knew it was securely lighted, then shook it out, flicked the ashes off the tip and drew his head real close to the leech and applied the flame to its yellow, slimy back.

There was the sizzle, the squirming as the leech removed its sucker from the skin and fell to the ground. If the cigarette touched the leech too hard it would go out, so Kraus applied just the right pressure.

As Marlin watched with disgust, he said, "Kraus, I know you leave the bottom of your trousers out of your boots just so you can fuck with those little things during break."

23

Kraus lifted his head, smiled and flatly denied the accusation.

"Kill the son of a bitch," Marlin said.

Kraus poised the cigarette over the second leech, just like a doctor would a scalpel, and said, "I will."

Marlin hated the sizzling sound. It just gnawed at him.

"Let's get started," Marlin said as he stood up and signaled Spielberg, the man ahead of him, to get moving. The giant-sized leaves made it impossible for Marlin to see the man ahead of Spielberg.

As Beckwith drew deeper into the jungle, he not only listened for strange sounds not made by his platoon, like the distant breaking of a branch or the loading of a round in the chamber of a rifle, but he walked with his nose testing the air as well. The jungle had the sweet scent of rotting vegetation, and Beckwith sniffed for the smoke of a stray campfire or food cooking. It was just something else to be aware of that might save a man's life.

All his senses were alert as he moved through the jungle, watching, listening, smelling, and waiting.

The third platoon's radio squawked and a voice came over the speaker. "Bravo three-six, this is three-five. Over."

Beckwith dropped his rifle from the ready position and held it in his left hand. As Kraus moved towards him with the receiver in his outstretched hand, Beckwith wiped the rain and mud from his face with his forearm, grabbed the receiver and pressed the transmitting key and said, "This is three-six. Go."

"Hold up a second, I think we have a problem back here."

Beckwith recognized the voice of his platoon sergeant, two-thirds of the way back in the column. He had a hand-held transreceiver to communicate. Beckwith saw the men behind him starting to draw closer so he signaled for them to get down. He crouched next to Kraus and watched as Castillo signaled Jesus Perez, the rifleman in the second squad. Perez extended an open hand at Thomas White who gave a thumb's down sign to whoever was behind him. Beckwith could not see that far. It was all green jungle with the sound of rain beating submission into those who dared.

"Jesus Christ, Kraus," Beckwith said to the radioman, "stop the point element up there, will you."

Kraus knew better than to leave the Lieutenant's side for very long. He walked forward and caught up to Spielberg directly in front of him and who was about to disappear into the greenery, grabbed him by the arm and pulled on his shirt to get down.

Spielberg hissed at the point man in front of him. When Randy Emmal stopped and saw what was going on, he crouched on one knee, buried the butt of his M-16 into the mud and leaned on the barrel.

When Beckwith heard the squelch sound coming from the radio, he knew he was about to get a message and grabbed for the receiver. He watched it as the sound came out, "Six, This is Five."

Beckwith replied as soon as he heard the sound of the receiver button being released, "Go."

"Yeah, we got problems." The Platoon Sergeant knew better than to say too much over the radio, either his exact location or what the problem was. The VC could be listening and somehow, someway, take advantage of the information; they always did. The Sergeant continued, "You better come back here."

As Beckwith stood up, he signaled for his men to stay put and he started back down the line of his platoon. He was supposed to have thirty-four men, but he was losing them faster than they could be replaced and it pissed him off.

He could only see two or three men at a time; the remaining stayed hidden in the jungle.

"What's up, Sir?" Gatz asked Beckwith as he passed.

"I'll tell you as soon as I find out," Marlin replied.

The men looked tired, almost beyond description. Marlin knew it was due to the contact the previous night. Keats and Kramm were stretched out on their rucksacks still on their backs. Most of the men looked too disappointed to show interest in why the column had stopped and the Lieutenant was moving to the rear. Beckwith continued back until he came to Sergeant Roberts crouched on one knee next to Hyde and Hill, both men in the fourth squad.

The Lieutenant knelt on one knee next to them.

Kraus squatted with his back to them, watching the jungle.

Beckwith asked, "What's the problem, Sarge?"

Roberts took a deep breath and stared into the eyes of the Lieutenant. His eyes were full of fear. "I think what happened was the last time we took a break, Simmons, Hoppy and Buffalo Bill did not get the signal to move out. They're not with us."

A jolt of fear ran through Beckwith's body. He looked around instinctively, planning his next move. If it was not bad enough that his men were dying, he was losing track of them now.

"When did this happen?"

"At the last break, maybe ten minutes ago."

"We'd better get back there and find them before they go running off in the wrong direction, get themselves lost or —"

"They won't be captured, Sir," Kraus said. "We'll find them."

"They can't be that far back there," Beckwith continued. He felt like screaming out their names, but nine months in the field had taught him that if Charlie were

26

in the vicinity, he would drop on him like flies on shit.

"OK, Sarge, we'll just keep in file and turn everyone around 180 degrees. Let's go."

As the Sergeant passed along the message that they were turning around, Beckwith moved closer to Hill, grabbed ahold of his elbow and asked, "Hill, what happened?"

Hill was a small, skinny soldier, due mostly to his allergy to eating C-rations. The only things he could eat from the brown boxes were the crackers, cheese and fruit. Everything else made him physically sick to his stomach.

"I don't know, Sir. When I got up and started walking, I waved at Hoppy. I could have sworn I saw him getting up when I signaled."

Hill looked at the hand squeezing his elbow.

Beckwith's knuckles were turning white.

Hill continued, "I never looked back again until just a while ago. Then I noticed no one was behind me. I don't know what happened to them."

Even as Beckwith chewed on Hill's ass about checking over his shoulder every so often for the guy behind him, he knew it was not entirely Hill's fault. The only sleep the third platoon had been getting at night for the last few weeks had been an hour or two at a time and that while they were cramped behind a paddy dike or in a foxhole filled with water or behind some bushes overlooking a trail in ambush. If they engaged the enemy, they got even less sleep. No, Beckwith knew the problems his men were having staying awake and keeping sharp.

"Do you think you can find the way back?" Beckwith asked Hill.

"I think so. There was that canal about ten minutes back. We moved into the jungle from there and took the break. It should be easy enough."

27

"Just stop if you have any doubts, and be careful. Charlie might have been following us, so don't think that the first movement you see is friendly. Got it?"

"Yes, Sir."

Beckwith tried to calm his own nerves about the lost element. Buffalo Bill was one of the men back there — one of his best. The man was all guts. Standing just over six feet tall, and although he was the squad leader, he carried the M-60 machine gun for that squad. If any of the men would stay calm, it would be he. Beckwith had his doubts about Hoppy, who really did not belong in the field. Hoppy was always too scared. His mind short-circuited under pressure, wandering, thinking about home. Simmons would do all right, complain, but he was not afraid to kill if he had to. Buffalo Bill would take care of them.

Beckwith hoped that when they figured out that they were lost, after the initial search, they would stay right where they were, form a small protective perimeter in case they were attacked and wait.

The thought made Beckwith breathe a little easier. His basic emotion was that of fear. He felt like he were almost abandoning some of his men; something he never would do consciously under any circumstances.

About that time the radio clicked on again.

"Three-six, this is Bravo-six. Over."

It was the Old Man.

The Lieutenant grabbed the receiver from Kraus and replied. "This is three-six."

"I've been monitoring your last transmissions. You need some help?"

"Negative on that. Everything is under control. I'll give you a situation report in a few minutes. Over."

"OK, but remember, I can call in artillery any time you want."

Even the thought of artillery now made Beckwith

28

cringe. That was the last thing he wanted, even if he engaged the enemy. With his platoon divided, there was the possibility that an artillery round would land on one of the lost men. No matter what, until the platoon was intact again, there would be no heavy guns or even air support for the third platoon.

Beckwith no sooner got everyone turned around and moving, slightly, then he heard the sound of rifle fire. The first bursts were from an M-60 machine gun, probably from Buffalo Bill, he guessed; then he heard the sound of the Russian-made AK-47 rifle firing, lots of them firing on full automatic. It was a higher pitched sound and a bit faster than the M-60 and slower than the M-16. It had not taken the Lieutenant nor any of his men very long to distinguish the sound.

Marlin could hear the rattling of the M-60 machine gun and then heard it grow quiet. He hoped that it was only a misfire and Buffalo Bill was clearing the gun.

Beckwith signaled Hill to start moving in the direction of the sound at a faster pace.

Chapter 3

Beckwith ran up to the point position, passed Hill, and ran in the direction of the fading sounds. The M-60 machine gun was quiet, with only sporadic fire from a lone M-16 rifle followed by the thunderous return of AK-47s crackling. Marlin whipped the tree branches and leaves away from his face and looked up and saw blue sky streaming through the treetops. He knew he was nearing the canal and even closer to where they had taken their last break. He began to look around for signs of the exact positions — clumps of leaves that had been sat upon, discarded candy wrappers, toilet paper or cigarette butts.

Under normal conditions, Beckwith hated when his men scattered such garbage; it just left a trail for the VC to follow. C-ration cans were the worst as they could be turned into booby traps; but under the circumstances, he craved for a sighting.

When the jungle started to thin out as he remembered it doing near the canal, he looked ahead and saw a picture that made him stop in his tracks. There pinned against a tree by a long spear through the chest was the drooping body of Buffalo Bill. Blood was dripping from his mouth. His body was riddled with bullet holes; his green, muddy fatigues were saturated with blood.

Standing right next to the body were two NVA soldiers smiling at each other and talking cheerfully.

They heard Marlin before they saw him and started to raise their rifles from their waist to their shoulders.

Marlin planted his heels in the mud, hugged the butt of the rifle under his arm and held his breath to steady his aim. He fired a burst of automatic fire from his waist and walked the bullets up the body of the soldier on the left. Before he had time to move his rifle on the other soldier, another rifle sounded and the second NVA fell to his knees.

Beckwith let his lungs collapse and dropped to one knee as he scanned the area for more NVA soldiers. Kraus, panting, came alongside and leaned against a tree.

"Are there any more?" Kraus asked.

Before Marlin had a chance to answer, they both saw movement to the right and out of the jungle walked Simmons, who ran up to the body of Buffalo Bill, grabbed hold of the spear with both hands and pulled on it. Simmons was a hefty man, but only half the size of Buffalo Bill. Aaron was having a hell of a time. When he finally yanked the spear from the tree, the body fell to one side, dragging Simmons along, both of them toppling to the ground.

Beckwith ran up to the pair and helped Simmons to his feet. The soldier was looking at Buffalo Bill with eyes big enough to bowl.

Beckwith knew the best medicine for Simmons now was to get him thinking. He asked, "Where is Hoppy?"

"They took him," Simmons replied as he jerked his head in the direction of the canal and his arm straightened out like a railroad crossing signal.

Beckwith's heart sank to his bowels and he felt a wave of anger again. "Son of a bitch," he whispered.

Simmons said, "They didn't have to do it, Sir." There

31

were nearly tears in his eyes. "They didn't have to stick him to the tree like that. He was already dead. They just did it for fun."

"We'll get 'em, Simmons. We'll get 'em and we'll get Hoppy back too."

Beckwith raced towards the canal using the barrel and butt of the rifle to make a path. He felt the sting of a bite on the back of his neck and knew what it was. He had knocked a red ant from its nest in the treetop and it had landed down his shirt. Beckwith slapped at the ant with the force that would nearly knock out a man, smashed the small pest into a bloody mess just as it sunk its teeth into his skin and was tearing the flesh away.

As soon as Beckwith reached the canal, he saw movement to the left. At the same time someone from the opposite bank started firing at him. Marlin dove behind a tree and Kraus landed right next to him. The firing from the opposite bank got heavier.

Beckwith got on the radio, "Three-five, move the men up on line around to the left. We've got to stop them from crossing the canal."

Hill started firing, all too close.

"Watch out for Hoppy," Beckwith warned. "He's over there somewhere."

Hill nodded his head without taking his eyes from the rifle sights.

There were half a dozen sampans in the water to the left and suddenly one of them started to move to the middle of the waterway.

The craft was about twelve feet long and two feet wide, with half a dozen uniformed North Vietnamese soldiers aboard wearing their distinctive French colonial style helmets.

All eyes riveted on the sampan. Kraus started to aim his M-79 in their direction when Beckwith stopped him with a hand on the barrel.

Beckwith got on the radio, "Three-five, there is a sampan full of NVA soldiers that you should come upon any moment now. Don't fire at them until you know for sure that Hoppy in not with them. If he isn't, blow 'em out of the water."

The reply was two clicking sounds over the radio.

As the sampan reached the distant bank, three NVA soldiers firing automatic weapons marched from the treeline towards the sampan, laying down a base of fire to cover their comrades.

When the sampan rammed into the slithering mud and the men started to unload, Hoppy did not stand up.

Gatz started the firing with a LAW, a light antitank weapon. The recoilless propelled rocket hit the bow of the sampan, exploded, and scattered wood, metal, bodies and muck. Bodies twirled, rifles cracked and grenades exploded. The rest of the platoon joined in with hand grenades, M-79 grenades, small arms and machine gun fire.

Beckwith watched with a quivering grin on his face as the sampan disintegrated and the bodies sunk into the mud. He saw the muzzle of an NVA rifle blazing from the opposite side, took aim at the source of the green tracers and fired one well-placed round into the enemy's helmet.

The opposite bank grew quiet. Hill jumped to his feet and started running towards the other sampans no more than a hundred feet away. "I'll get Hoppy back," he screamed.

Beckwith and Kraus waited with their rifles aimed at the jungle, ready to lay into any place from where the muzzle of a rifle fired.

There was no firing, only the sound of Hill sloshing through the muck.

When Hill reached the sampan, Sergeant Roberts ran from the treeline to help him free it from the slime. When it floated free, Hill jumped aboard and worked his way to the bow as Roberts gave the craft a final push and joined him. With their rifles at their feet, they paddled across the short waterway.

When the sampan rammed the opposite shore, Hill disembarked and held the bow steady as Roberts worked his way forward and jumped ashore. They both disappeared into the jungle.

Realizing that the platoon had better catch up, Beckwith ran from his cover towards the remaining sampans. When he reached them, he stopped, turned back towards the jungle and called out, "Gatz, bring your squad down here and move across."

Men scrambled from the treeline.

Beckwith saw the other squads coming towards him and signaled with his upraised hand for them to stay put. If they all bunched up, one grenade could take them all out. Spread out, they would have a better chance.

But his arm signaling was the giveaway.

Not all the NVA had left; there was still one in a swaying treetop way up there watching, picking out the target that would end all pursuit, the one target that would make him a bit richer man if he survived, for taking out a platoon leader was money in his pocket. All American officers had bounties on their heads.

The American officer did not need shiny bars on the hat or on the shirt collar for the NVA to pick out. The leader had his arms waving and the radioman right next to him.

Before the NVA soldier made another move, he checked his route of escape. At his feet was a tunnel down the hollowed-out tree that led all the way underground. Once he popped off the platoon leader, he would drop down the hole and be gone. The Americans would never figure out where the fire was coming from. He clicked off the safety on the rifle and took aim. The tree was swaying slightly and it made it a bit tricky, but not that much. He aimed for several seconds until he got used to the motion and just as the tree began to sway his rifle back to the leader, he fired.

The round threw chips from the sampan in Beckwith's face and his arms protected his eyes in a reflex.

Kraus read the situation immediately as he spotted the muzzle flash in the tree. He fell to one knee, brought the M-79 grenade launcher to his shoulder and fired.

When the round struck the treetop, leaves and limbs scattered as the dead weight of the soldier dropped out of the bottom of the disintegrating treetop and somersaulted into the water.

When Beckwith saw what had happened, he looked at Kraus and at the smoking grenade launcher and said, "I owe you another one, Kraus."

"Just put it up on the board, Sir." Kraus smiled. "I'll drink it later."

It was the first relaxed smile of the day.

"Let's get on the other side," Beckwith said.

Just as the Lieutenant's foot touched the far shore, he heard the sound of a single explosion. It was not very far away, and was coming from where Hill and Roberts had disappeared into the undergrowth.

As each squad reached the far shore, the Lieutenant directed them into the protection of the greenery, which now had become their ally.

When they were all hidden, Marlin ran to where he thought Hill and Roberts had gone and the rest of the platoon fell in line behind him.

A hundred yards down the trail and the source of the mysterious explosion dissolved. Hill was sitting down in the mud with Roberts' head lying across his lap. Roberts was in a state of semiconsciousness. His body and face were a mass of blood.

When Beckwith drew nearer, he looked over Roberts' body and saw that his right foot was missing. All that remained was a mass of chipped bones and gnarled flesh.

There was a big hole in the ground where Roberts had stepped on the mine; the small crater of mud was already filled with water.

Beckwith hollered, "Doc, you better get up here."

Just as fast as he spoke a soldier with a bulging back pack moved forward and began to attend to Roberts.

"You better give him a shot of morphine," Beckwith said.

"That is exactly what I was planning on doing."

They both knew that as soon as Roberts recovered from the shock of the situation, he would start to experience the pain of having a foot blown off.

"Looks like you are going to beat me home after all," Beckwith said to Roberts.

"It is that good, huh, Sir?"

"Yeah, you'll be in warm sheets and having a nurse play with you before the day is over."

Roberts did not hear him. He started to fade into the agony of the pain.

Beckwith looked to see where the trail led through the jungle, but he would go no farther. He was certain that there would be more booby traps ahead, and he was not about to sacrifice more men — but he was not about to give up on Hoppy either, not by a long shot. He vowed on the spot he'd make every one of those sons-of-bitches NVA regulars pay in blood for what they had done.

Beckwith took the receiver from Kraus and called the company commander. "Bravo-six, this is three-six.

I need a medevac here ASAP."

"Where are you located?" Bravo-six answered.

Beckwith gave the coordinates and said, "We'll move out in the rice paddy and mark our position with smoke when we see the chopper coming."

"You need some help?"

"Right now I need a dust-off."

"Roger. What is the body count?"

Beckwith thought of the two men he and Simmons had taken out, the bloody mess of bodies back at the sampans, the one in the jungle, one in the tree. "At least eleven." He never mentioned his own casualties over the radio.

"I am going to send a couple more platoons into your area as blocking forces."

"OK, but watch out. They have one of our men with them. Don't bring down the heavy artillery. You could be raining it in on our own."

"I understand. I'll give you all the support I can. I want him back as much as you do."

"I forgot if I told you, but those gooks were North Vietnamese regulars, not the local Viet Cong."

"That is what we have been looking for. Good work."

"Yeah," Marlin replied as he returned the receiver back to Kraus.

With Roberts anesthetized and carried by two men, and the body of Buffalo Bill positioned in the same manner, Beckwith started back towards the canal. He would recross the channel and walk the few hundred yards back to a rice paddy they had skirted.

Beckwith knew if Hoppy were not recovered very shortly, he would be removed from the field of engagement and interrogated about the objectives of the Americans, their bases, ammunition caches, methods of operations, immediate goals. If Hoppy did not answer, or probably even if he did, the torture would begin. The Lieutenant cringed at the thought. It was one thing he dreaded more than death itself, being captured by the enemy. He knew that Hoppy had to feel the same way.

Marlin had to act fast, before too much security was placed around the POW and before the NVA realized what a prize they had captured.

When the platoon moved back past the dead NVAs at the canal, Beckwith gave Gatz's squad the assignment of stripping the ammunition and weapons from the bodies.

As the second squad started its work and the rest of the platoon waited to recross the canal, Larry Gatz looked around to see if anyone was watching. Satisfied that he was unobserved, as his men removed the weapons and ammunition from the bodies and slung them into the water, Larry removed the knife from his scabbard, knelt over one body, pulled on a heft of hair, twisted it and sawed it off with the drawn knife. When the hair came into his fingers, he took the Bible from his shirt, placed the hair in the center, closed it and placed the book back in his shirt. He'd fix it later. He looked around to make sure no one had seen him, removed the rifle from the side of the soldier and threw it over his shoulder.

When he was finished, he and his squad crossed the canal and joined the platoon as they quickly moved forward.

Once the third platoon reached the rice paddy and stopped to reconnoiter the area, Beckwith called Simmons over. Aaron's eyes had shrunk back to normal, but they were still red and somewhat wet, yet his mouth was set and determined.

"What happened back there, Simmons?"

"That crazy Hoppy never told us you was moving out. Buffalo Bill got real mad at him and Hoppy wanted to go back to base camp. He didn't want to go no farther. Said he was going back to camp. Buffalo Bill wanted us to all sit tight but Hoppy started to take off down the canal and he got stuck in the mud. Buffalo Bill went to stop him. When they were in the open, a whole bunch of them NVA stepped out of the jungle. Buffalo Bill started to mow into them, but they shot him apart. Buffalo went down fighting. Hoppy fell to his knees in the mud and his arms flew up in the air. I seen it all. I started to fire my rifle and got a few of them, but there were just too many and they started after me and that is when I took off into the jungle." He stopped a moment to catch his breath. The telling was relieving some of the tension. "When I heard that they were not following me, I snuck back and shot that one right after you fired. Buffalo Bill was already dead, they didn't have to pin him to the tree like that. No how."

They are savages, Marlin thought, and they just knocked off one of my best men. "Thanks, Simmons."

"Did I do all right, Sir?"

"You did just fine, Simmons. Just fine."

"Thank ya, Sir." It was important for him to hear that.

"Go ahead and get back to your squad. We'll get 'em all next time."

"Yes, Sir," Simmons replied as he turned and crept back into the jungle.

Beckwith sent Doc and the first squad into the open rice paddy with Roberts and the body of Buffalo Bill. Impatient and nervous, he waited in the jungle with the rest of the platoon to provide security.

Beckwith got on the horn again. "Bravo-six, this is three-six. Over."

When he was about to try again, the reply came. "This is Bravo-six."

"Make sure you call me when the friendlies are in place. I want to have an idea where I could drive the NVA if I get another chance. Also, I don't want to go walking on my own troops hidden in the jungle. My men are a little jumpy now."

"Roger. They are on their way now. From your position, where are the NVA headed?"

Beckwith had already checked his compass. "On a 150 degree course."

"Got you. Out."

The "whopping" sound of the distant chopper approaching lightened the load on Beckwith's mind. For years later that sound would bring a smile to the Lieutenant's face and make him a very happy man, just the sound, and he would not understand why everyone in the world did not have the same feeling.

He watched as Rodriguez removed a smoke grenade from his suspenders, pulled the pin and threw it out to one side. When the cannister popped and hissed out smoke, Marlin took the receiver from Kraus and said, "Skate Force, this is three-six, do you see smoke?"

The reply came, "Indeed I do, and if I my eyes are not playing games with me, it is the same color as an angry bull's eyes."

"That's us, Skate Force. Come on down."

Chapter 4

The medevec helicopter was identical to a Huey transport chopper except it was painted white with a large red cross on the closed door. Inside there was no door gunner. As the helicopter started to waver towards the rice paddy, Beckwith heard a message over the radio. "Three-six, This is Skate Force. Is this a hot LZ we are coming into?"

Marlin grabbed the receiver from Kraus and replied, "Negative on that." However, curiosity made him look at the treeline that leaned threateningly towards the rice field and he added, "At this time."

"Such a confidence builder," came the reply over the radio mixed with a lot of static that almost sounded like rifles firing.

The Lieutenant stared at the careening ship on its final approach and had an odd feeling that something was missing—it was the pair of Cobra gunships that usually flanked all the Hueys, but not the medevacs.

"Heard you guys have one lost out there," came the voice over the radio.

"Affirmative."

The thought made Beckwith angry, and he looked up at the helicopter until it got so close that he could see the two pilots wearing sunglasses, in fresh uniforms with bubble helmets, like in a fish bowl. Beckwith

41

guessed that one of them was the man that he had been talking to. They both seemed to be relaxed, but attentive to their job.

When the chopper landed, the noise level was on the range of a steel plant. The door flew open, two medics carrying a stretcher jumped into the water and splashed up to Roberts who was on his feet and supported under both arms by Jaime Rodriguez and Salvador Castillo. The medics relieved the two soldiers of Roberts and laid him on the stretcher which they had set atop a berm, and just as quickly moved him aboard. After the body of Buffalo Bill was slung alongside of Roberts, the two medics jumped inside. The body bag would come later.

The door closed and as the roar of the engines increased in volume as the ship started to lift from the water. Beckwith gave Roberts and the entire medevac crew a clenched-fist farewell.

Castillo stood up, then dropped dead in his tracks onto his knees and started to grope around the field with both hands extended. He finally came up with a pair of glasses, wiped them quickly on his shirt and replaced them on the bridge of his nose and around his ears.

"He's always dropping those glasses," Marlin said as he stared at the confused soldier.

When the sound of the rotors had disappeared and Rodriguez and his men had rejoined the platoon, Marlin called the squad leaders together and assigned Douglas Ivy, third squad leader, as acting platoon sergeant and had Kenny Keats, the only redhead in the platoon, take Ivy's squad. It was a tossup between Ivy and Gatz to take Roberts' job. They were both Spec 4s, the highest rank amongst the enlisted men, but Gatz was a better fighter, and Marlin just couldn't afford to lose Gatz right now when the platoon was so low on men and so many of those remaining were inexperienced. He put Ken Hyde in charge of Buffalo Bill's squad.

Beckwith gave Ivy the hand-held transreceiver which had been used by Roberts. The radio was bloody, or was it only mud? In either case, Ivy wiped it off quickly and moved back down the line of men to where Roberts usually performed his job, away from the Lieutenant but ready to take over in case of an emergency.

With news of the changes circulating through the platoon as the squad leaders returned to their positions, the Lieutenant took out the map, got on the radio and called the C.O. "Bravo-six, this is three-five. We are ready to move now."

"Good. Did you draw any fire?"

"Negative."

"Three other elements are moving into your area on foot. I want you to skirt the treeline you are in, move north and stop at the next canal system."

Beckwith sighed at the realization that the entire company was coming his way. They might root Hoppy out yet. "Sounds good."

"Keep me posted if you hear or see anything."

"Roger. Out."

Marlin knew the mission at Ben Luc was probably being cancelled because of Hoppy's capture. He did not even want to remind the Old Man. Beckwith handed the receiver back to Kraus and said, "Let's get back on Hoppy's trail."

Beckwith studied the map and pinpointed the canal the Old Man was referring to. He realized if the other platoons engaged the NVA and started them running, the NVA might try and retreat down the canal. Marlin would be waiting. It was just a guess, but that's what it was half the time anyway in the jungle.

Jesus Perez walked point. No flank security was posted as it was just too thick and Beckwith was a bit paranoid about losing another man.

Beckwith tested the air with his nose. There were no scents of fire in the area, no smells of villagers or village life. Funny how his nose could distinguish such smells in the steaming jungle and not even smell himself or his men.

The move through the jungle was tense and unnerving. Marlin knew the NVA were close and might be waiting for him to move into their ambush. He wouldn't know until the jungle exploded with gunfire. After a mile walk, the platoon came to a stop. Beckwith moved forward and stopped alongside of Perez.

"Good," was all that Beckwith said as he looked up and down the still water of the narrow channel, similar to the one where Hoppy had been captured, but now some distance north.

It was late enough in the afternoon to set his men in a line ambush for the night. The first position was the farthest from the water—that way the NVA would have a harder time rolling up the ends of his platoon if they attacked from one of the flanks. It could happen if he strung them out in a straight line.

If the NVA came from the left, it would be a less effective ambush, but still the men would not have to shoot over each other's heads to protect themselves.

Kraus, Thuy, the Vietnamese Chieu Hoi, and the artillery forward observer, Arnie Mosby, nicknamed Stove Pipe, cleared out a small area for their field of fire in both directions along the canal and set out the claymores. They would be the closest position to the water.

Beckwith made his way to each station, briefed the squads on the situation—in what direction they should set out their claymore mines, where the other men were in relation to their own position, where they should look for the enemy to approach from. He listened as the squad leaders explained who would stand watch at what time and whom each man would awake to relieve him. Beckwith relayed the password given by the C.O. — "Fire-fly." Usually passwords were not necessary, but with so many friendly elements in the same area, it was not a bad idea. No C-4 would be used to cook the C-rations that night and no smoking. The NVA might smell them both.

When he got to the fourth squad's position, Paul Truskowski's legs spread across the entire cleared out area. Paul could barely fit comfortably anywhere. He was half an inch from getting a 4F deferment. At six feet, five and a half inches, he felt like he had all the problems of a tall man without any of the benefits.

Marlin stepped over Paul's legs and as he crouched next to him, was asked, "Sir, what do you think will happen to Hoppy?"

"What do you mean?" Marlin asked as he steadied himself against a tree.

"If we don't get him back."

Beckwith gulped and looked at the dark silhouette of a man he could tell was looking at him and said, "I suppose they will torture him and kill him . . . Gives you something to think about before you give up, Truskowski."

"I'll never give up, Sir . . . Do you think we will get him back?"

"I think we have a good chance . . ."

"But some of us might die looking for him?"

"And if we stayed right here for the rest of the year some of us would die as well. Just think of yourself out there, Truskowski. It makes all the sense in the world that way. If you were out there, we'd be doing the same. It is just part of the job of being a soldier."

"Yes, Sir."

"This is a team effort. A hero would end up a dead fool without anyone covering him. Remember that. We are all in this together and when one falls behind, we all stop to help him along. That is rule number one."

"Yes, Sir."

"Any more questions?"

"No, Sir."

Marlin looked at the other men in the fourth squad and when their interest seemed more in what they were eating than in the conversation, he returned to his own site and before it got too dark, ate. It was ham and crackers, fruit cake and peaches. He would save the cigarettes for the next day and the gum for later that night.

Watch would be an hour at a time. Beckwith would start, then wake Thuy, who would wake Arnie who would wake Kraus, then start all over again.

As Kraus stretched his body out on the damp ground and leaned his head on his helmet, out of the path of insects, field mice, and rats, Beckwith said, "Kraus."

"Yes, Sir?"

"When you wake me up to stand watch, make sure I am awake before you fall off to sleep. Talk to me and make sure I know where I am. OK?"

"Sure, Sir."

Those words assured the Lieutenant.

Before it got too dark and quiet, Beckwith called up the Old Man and asked, "Did you get any information out of the prisoners I brought in this morning?"

"Negative. Their papers checked out and they were released."

One man wounded and the damn VC are released. "Out," was all that Beckwith said as he set the transmitter back in its cradle. He stared at it for a second, waiting for the Old Man to say something else, but it was quiet. Just as well, it would only make him madder if the Old Man tried to explain.

Doc did not have to stand watch, since he was officially not a part of the war.

The first hour for Marlin went fast. He was tired, but still energized from the day's tension.

When he awoke Thuy, the Vietnamese slithered to his feet and nodded for Marlin to go to sleep. Thuy was a good man. He used to be a VC, but it was only because he had been forced to join the local fighting force as a youngster. When his parents were killed by the VC for being sympathetic to the Americans, with no more family to protect, Thuy switched sides. He had been with Beckwith now for four months and had proven his reliability and worth in the field on more than one occasion. He was indispensable to Beckwith as an interpreter. Without him, the only way Beckwith had of talking to the locals was, "VC number ten. GI number one. VC?" and point around like, "Where the fuck are they?" It was easier to shoot 'em.

Marlin laid back on the soft leaves he had prepared for a ground cover, set his helmet under his head, pulled the poncho liner and rain gear over his body, and fell asleep that fast.

"Sir . . . Sir."

Beckwith felt someone tugging at his shirt. He sat up and grabbed for his rifle.

Kraus said, "It is me, Sir. Are you awake?"

It was pitch black and Beckwith felt a chill from the damp ground. He was also feeling kind of sick to his stomach. "What?" he repeated.

"It is your turn to stand watch."

"Right," it all started to come into focus now. "Right.

I'm awake, Kraus," he whispered. He blinked his eyes, but still could not see any clearer. His eyes were still used to sleep more than they were to being open.

Beckwith could not stand up and stretch and yawn and go pour himself a cup of coffee to help stay awake. He had to stay in the same spot, not move, just keep his eyes open and . . . and stay awake.

"Do you want me to talk to you any longer?" Kraus asked.

"No. I'm awake. I got it."

"Good night, Sir."

"Kraus, when you wake me again. Make certain. OK?"

"Sure, Sir."

Kraus's poncho could be heard ruffling as he stretched out on the ground.

The thought of the NVA out there moving around made Beckwith think himself a little more awake.

He checked his watch. The two dials glowed at five minutes to one. Kraus had mobilize him five minutes earlier than he was supposed to.

Marlin would not check each position to see if the men were awake. The jungle was too thick and the men too keyed up for him to go crawling up to them in the night. One of them might shoot him.

Beckwith picked up the starlight scope and looked through it down the canal. God, it was clear, almost beautiful. What a night for an ambush. When the rain clouds cleared, the sky shone bright with a half-moon. With the help of the starlight scope that magnified the existing light by 400 times, it was even brighter. Although the scope turned everything green, any type of movement could be detected and the outline of men moving easily picked up, often like small dots on a computer. Just looking for the movement kept Beckwith awake. He set down the scope and all turned to darkness.

He leaned his head back on a tree and sighed. The image of his girlfriend, Roxeanne, flashed to mind. He could just see her standing in front of the french window in her bedroom, stretching her long legs on tiptoes. The glow of the morning sun making her nightgown transparent, her warm curves showing through, her long blond hair flowing down her back. He could almost smell the perfume of her soap, just like on the letter.

It was a dream and he could feel his mind floating back into sleep. Beckwith shook his head. It helped for a second. He still hadn't read her letters yet, and it was too dark now and too dangerous to turn on his flashlight. He looked over at the other ambush positions. Still he could see no one. He yawned and craned his neck and exercised the muscles around his mouth.

He reached into his shirt pocket, removed the package of gum he had saved from the previous meal, opened it and jawed it. The sweet taste added to his sense of reality.

He thought of the NVA and how they were multiplying in his area of operation as fast as cockroaches. He knew they had to be stopped before they hit Saigon. It would be a moral victory for them to take over the city. It would prove to the American people back home the strength and determination of the enemy, a reality that no politician wanted to face.

The thought of killing the NVA helped keep Beckwith awake.

Now if he could only get Hoppy back. Poor Hoppy. Beckwith knew little about the homely country boy from South Dakota. Hoppy had a gap between his front teeth. Marlin guessed that as a younger boy Hoppy had been shy and certainly not very bright, more harmless and caring, probably a hard worker but not athletic. A country boy whose country had plans for him other than farming.

The sound of M-16 fire broke the night silence and then the return fire of AK-47. Soon it stopped. It was not a major battle. Maybe recon fire. Maybe an ineffective triggered ambush. Maybe nothing.

Usually there was more artillery fire at night, but now the big guns were quiet, a silent requiem to Hoppy.

The sky to the south lighted up with flares, their small parachutes gliding to the ground.

Soon there were more flares and the sound of more gunfire being exchanged.

Beckwith drew closer to the radio to listen but no messages were being relayed.

By the end of Beckwith's watch, the firing had ended and raindrops were starting to drizzle on the leaves. The air smelled of dew.

Beckwith awoke Thuy and moved back under the protection of the jungle. It started to rain harder and Beckwith put his poncho over his head and fell asleep leaning against a tree.

Kraus talked Beckwith awake at five o'clock and took the Lieutenant's place up against the base of a tree where it was still warm and somewhat dry. Kraus quit moving as soon as he pulled the poncho liner over his face.

The sky hinted of the coming daylight.

Beckwith did his stretching exercises in place and felt more rested this time and somewhat comforted by the approaching light.

Around six o'clock Beckwith would call up the C.O. and give him a situation report. He consoled himself that the ambush had nearly ended without incident.

Beckwith grabbed his rifle and crawled to the edge of the trail so that he could see better down the canal. What he wouldn't do for a cup of coffee.

He looked in both directions. No movement, not even a ripple on the water. He turned around to look for the other ambush positions, but the men were too well hidden. He just hoped they weren't all sleeping, but he was not about to check. He'd caught Jaime Rodriguez's squad sleeping one night and reamed them out good, but he knew there was nothing he could do about it. It was their lives. If Marlin threw a sleeper out of his platoon, he would just be a man shorter. They were already too low to bust, and could care less. If he worked them harder they would fall asleep sooner.

He looked down the canal to the left and strained his eyes wide open. By the end of his watch it would be full daylight. This was the easiest time to stay awake, watching the sun come up.

He'd eat some ham patties and crackers in about an hour, maybe warm them up with C-4. He'd save the can of fruit for the heat of the day. He sighed at the realization that another ambush was about to end and he had not engaged the enemy; that was good, but Hoppy was still out there.

The next hour was spent on his belly, straining his eyes awake, looking to the left and right, wondering about the men, wondering about Hoppy and trying to stay awake. The trees quit dripping but he could not stand up and remove his poncho.

Minutes before he was to mobilize the platoon, he looked to the right and there was movement, out of nowhere. His head dropped forward onto the ground and his chin struck the mud and bounced back upright.

He became totally alert, picked up the starlight

51

scope, slid it through the bushes and scanned the area. What he saw made him gasp for air.

It was the NVA all right, three of them. There was one person with them who was not an NVA. He was taller than the others and his head was bowed way forward and his arms seemed to be tied behind his back. Beckwith could not make out Hoppy's blond hair, but he was almost positive who it was.

Beckwith was thrilled. He clenched his fist and shook it excitedly. He could feel the warm adrenalin charging through his veins. He grinned and whispered, "This is it."

Chapter 5

Although Beckwith's reflex was to start throwing out lead, his better judgment told him that the odds of hitting the NVA without hitting Hoppy were so minute that it would only increase the enemy's chances of escape, and make it more dangerous to follow. Instead he decided not to act until he was absolutely positive that his efforts would rescue Hoppy. He figured he would get only one chance.

As suddenly as they had appeared, the NVA soldiers crouched down and disappeared into the earth, first one, then two, Hoppy, and the final soldier.

At first Marlin thought they might have just crouched down to rest, but when they did not appear for a while, he knew something was wrong. Suddenly it hit him, "Tunnels." He turned on his side and stood up at the same time and said, "Kraus . . . Kraus, get everyone moving."

Kraus was on his feet in seconds with Thuy and Arnie right alongside him.

"What's wrong, Sir?" Stove Pipe asked.

"I just spotted Hoppy with some NVA soldiers and it looks like they dropped down into a tunnel."

"Wake everyone up," Beckwith commanded in a loud whisper. "Have them pull the claymore mines in and fall out on the canal trail."

Sounds of abandoning the ambush position echoed through the jungle as Kraus rumbled through the greenery. It was only a matter of minutes before the last man appeared on the trail and the anxious Beckwith gave the hand motion to follow him at point. If he was too cautious it would take him too long to get to the tunnel, so he trotted. He realized he was making the same mistake as Roberts had done when he had chased after Buffalo Bill's killers back at the canal the previous day. It was not good tactics, but his instinct would not let him take the slower path.

Son of a bitch, he kept thinking. Tunnels. That's why the NVA have been so elusive. They have been living like moles under the ground.

Two hundred yards down the canal Beckwith started sniffing around the area for signs of a tunnel. When the other men drew close to him, he said, "Kraus, tell Ivy to get the first and second squads to set up security around us. Have Gatz's and Keat's squads help us look for the tunnel. I know the entrance is right in this area."

With rifles in the port arms position, half a dozen men joined in the search, kicking at the muddy soil and brushing aside the branches while the other two squads fanned out in a large circle and watched for enemy movement.

"Look here," Rodriguez said.

Beckwith ran over to where Rodriguez was standing and looked down a hole with a dozen or so pungi stakes set in the mud at different angles.

The trap was easy to spot, old and not camouflaged. Beckwith had seen hundreds of such traps and not once had any of his men fallen inside. It was not deep enough nor sharp enough for a man to die in, but it was enough to cause infection and keep a soldier out of the field for a couple of days. "Yeah," was all Beckwith replied, his voice reflecting his disappointment. "The entrance is right in this area . . . Keep looking."

The men formed on line and worked the first ten yards bordering the canal; if the entrance to the tunnel were set any deeper into the brush, Beckwith would never have seen Hoppy drop down into it from where he had laid in ambush.

"You sure this is the area?" Kraus asked.

"I'm positive," Beckwith replied.

"And they didn't just crouch down and crawl?" Gatz asked. "Maybe they snuck away and you just thought you saw 'em go under."

"Look for a trap door. Kick the mud around. Check the stumps," Beckwith replied. It was already too wet to check for footprints.

"Got something here," Gatz said just as fast.

The Lieutenant walked over to where the squad leader was kicking aside a stand of grass. Gatz stooped down and raised a hatch cover and threw it to one side. He and the platoon leader looked down the shaft about six feet deep. On the left side could be seen a black hole.

Hill walked over, looked down and said, "I'll go down and find him, Sir."

Beckwith looked at the sinewy black man who was just the right size. Half of the men in the platoon were too big to even squeeze their shoulders into the tunnel.

"I go too," Thuy said.

Beckwith said, "You don't have to."

"I know," Hill said.

Beckwith was not going to argue with them. He knew that he did not have time to call in the professional "tunnel rats" from Dong Tam. It would take them too long to fly down and by then Hoppy could be miles away.

"You won't need your back pack, helmet or rifle.

Take off all your gear except for your pants, T-shirt and boots."

With Hill stripped down to the bare essentials, Beckwith said, "You can use my .45," as he removed the pistol from its holster and extended it towards Hill. Hill took the handgun and checked to make sure it was loaded.

Beckwith had a flashlight on the back pack which he used sometimes at night to read a map, and then by letting only a sliver of light creep through his fingers held over the face of the glass. As he handed it to Hill, he said, "Use this sparingly. The VC don't use flashlights down there so if they see one, they'll know who it is."

"Why should I bring it then?"

"They have false tunnels that dead-end in booby traps. Sometimes there are snakes and spiders. They all know about 'em."

Hill took the flashlight.

When Thuy was down to his cammies, Stove Pipe came over and offered him his .45 as well. Thuy took it aggressively.

Both men stood in front of Beckwith for a final inspection.

Beckwith nodded his head and said, "Good luck." He was proud of his men. They always came through in the clutch.

"How about the dog tags?" Hill asked.

Beckwith looked at the two tin tags around Hill's neck. Often they were the only means to identify a body that was badly blown apart or burned. There was a little notch in the tags and it was said that the notch was fitted between a dead man's teeth and smashed into place so that it would not be separated from the body. Beckwith finally replied. "Stick 'em in your back pocket. They won't make any noise."

56

Beckwith gave Hill two extra .45 clips. Arnie gave Thuy some extra ammunition as well. Both men stuffed grenades into their thigh pockets.

Beckwith said, "Remember, we are after Hoppy. Don't go after the entire North Vietnamese Army."

"We don't have enough ammo," Hill said and smiled.

The first smile of the day came earlier than normal. Marlin felt a surge of pride for both men.

"Stay cool," Beckwith said.

Hill was going to have to be lowered on a rope by his feet as there was not enough room at the bottom of the hole for him to go down feet first, bend over and slip into the entrance of the tunnel.

Gatz held the rope as Hill looped it around both of his legs and crawled to the entrance of the hole, took a deep breath, and started to slink over the edge.

When the blood began to rush to his head, he extended his hands, holding the flashlight and the pistol ahead of him and used his elbows to prevent his body from striking the walls of the shaft. He twisted his neck backwards so that he could see where he was going.

Entering the tunnel was the most dangerous point. If the NVA suspected they were being followed, one of them would be waiting to grease the first part of Hill that showed in the tunnel. It would be his head, an easy target from a few feet away.

Hill tried to slip his head and .45 inside the tunnel at the same time so that he could at least take a shot at whatever he saw as soon as he saw it. The gun was too close to his face and not pointed in the right direction, and he was lucky that no one was waiting for him.

When he peeked the flashlight into the tunnel, it was empty as far as he could see. He turned it off. As his feet came down, he used his elbows to pull his way inside. Before he tucked his legs into the shaft, he removed the rope from his legs while he still had the chance; soon he would be too cramped to even reach backwards.

He moved forward five feet and stopped. God, it was quiet. The sound of his breathing was magnified so much that he worried about it being heard.

It stank down there too, of blood, shit and sweat. The air was so stale it almost made him want to throw up, but he held it back and tried to breathe through his mouth.

When Thuy entered the cave behind him, the small Vietnamese sounded like a bulldozer rolling up a wall of earth.

Hill started breathing harder and faster as his fear intensified. It was almost impossible to get out now; he could not turn around in the tunnel. He would have to wait for Thuy to be pulled back up, feet first, and then himself raised back upside down. He did not know how he would get that rope around his ankle again. The thought nearly panicked him, but then he thought of how Hoppy must feel and found consolation in the fact that he could blow the shit out of the NVA that were with Hoppy.

He started to crawl forward, stopped, listened to Thuy behind him, flashed his light ahead and saw where the tunnel took a turn. There were no hanging wires nor spider cobwebs between him and the corner so he turned the light off and started wriggling down the tunnel. Both of his shoulders were touching the sides when he moved. He had to keep his neck stretched and lowered so that his head did not bump the roof of the cave.

He knew Hoppy was probably having a hell of a time at it.

Hill did not want to get the .45 and the flashlight so dirty that they would not function properly, which meant that he had to place more of his weight on his knuckles, and it hurt. He stopped and pressed the sides of his legs against the walls, lowered his head and looked back between his legs. When he flashed the light in Thuy's face, Thuy squinted and turned his head to one side.

Hill quickly turned off the light. He did not want to screw up Thuy's night vision, but Hill just had to make sure. If he were shot, Thuy would have to drag him out backwards by his feet.

The first turn was to the right. Before Hill made it, he stuck the flashlight and his head around the corner to look. Unfortunately the tunnel sloped downward. As he crawled down, the blood rushed to his head and made him feel dizzy. His knees began to ache and the sweat dripping from his forehead began to sting his eyes. The temperature inside the hole was rising.

He stopped a moment, panting, wiped the sweat from his brow and continued. He was making so much noise breathing that he reminded himself of a bull ready to charge. His heart beating sounded like it was going to pop out of his chest.

The distance to the next turn was about twice as far as the last and it felt like he had sunk another fifty feet deeper under the earth. The air was becoming more stale, the stink stronger, and now the cave was pitch-black. It felt like there was not enough oxygen in the air to keep a man alive.

When the walls of the tunnel began to squeeze Hill's shoulders together, he felt almost like his mind was going to explode with fear. In order to calm himself, he made believe that his girlfriend Loretta was squeezing him the way she used to do whenever she got mad. She was strong and she used to just put her arms around his and try to lift him off the ground. It almost felt like that, Hill thought as the muscles behind his neck started to sag. He stopped and rested his hip against the sides of the tunnel, then leaned his shoulder into it and dropped his head.

He blinked and swore he could hear his eyelashes batting.

"You OK?" Thuy whispered.

"Shhhh," was all Hill replied as he panted, lifted himself back on his knees and continued crawling. He could feel his knuckles growing thin. His pants were torn at the knees and he could feel the dirt sawing at his skin. He guessed that there was an ample amount of blood caked with mud.

The next turn was to the left and if Hill guessed right, parallel with the canal. He thought about it for a moment and wondered if he were not headed back towards where Roberts had stepped on the land mine. He wondered if those NVA might have set it just before the whole lot of them snuck underground.

If he ran into them now headed this way, what a fuckin' mess. To shoot one of them would set up a roadblock in his path and he would have to start crawling ass backwards.

Just let me find Hoppy and take him out of this place, he prayed. When and if he found Hoppy, he'd make sure that Hoppy followed this time. No way was Hill going to leave him behind again. Hoppy would follow one way or another, dead or alive. Damn Hoppy. If Hill ever asked Hoppy to give him a can of peaches for a can of lima beans, and if Hoppy refused, Hill swore right then and there that he would kill Hoppy dead on the spot, with his bare hands.

When Hill shone the light down the next finger of the tunnel, he could tell that his luck had run out. There were two caverns off the main tunnel from which flickering light from a candle was shining. He could see the movement of shadows within and it made his heart crash against his chest cage.

Hill crawled down to the first side entrance and before he did anything, he stopped and listened to the conversations within. He was almost positive that they could hear his breathing and heartbeat from within, but from the relaxed and casual tone of the conversation and the sounds of utensils being clinked, and cups of tea sipped, he guessed they were unaware of his presence.

He had a tremendous decision to make at this moment. If he entered the cave with his .45 blazing, if Hoppy were not there, he would be up shit creek without a paddle. All the noise would certainly alert the other soldiers in the tunnels, which would put him and Thuy on the defensive. They would have to turn around and go back.

Hill tried to remember the twists and turns he had made so far. He couldn't. They were lost.

He decided that before he barged into any camp and started firing, he had to be certain that Hoppy was there to rescue. At the same time, he knew he could not stick his head in every cave to look around.

There was another reason for his fear of passing these two caves. Once offensive action was taken further down the tunnel, if he had to return this way, he knew he would have to shoot his way through. He hoped that he could hear Hoppy say something right now. To go further could be surrounding himself. He listened for nearly a minute. No Hoppy.

He took a deep breath and slipped forward. He noticed that the entrance ran up and to the left. He could not see any of the men inside. He waited at the second entrance the same amount of time and passed that one.

There was a silence from the chamber. Either he was making so much noise or else those inside the chamber had stopped all movement to listen.

61

Someone called out in Vietnamese.

Hill froze.

Thuy responded loudly in Vietnamese. That made all the Vietnamese inside laugh, from both caves.

Thuy pushed on Hill's ass to get him going faster.

At the next intersection, Hill turned to the left and soon came upon another fork in the tunnel.

Hill crept down to the left and shone the light down the shaft. About thirty feet ahead he saw that it ended. He held his breath and carefully looked in front of him for any signs of a booby trap.

He did not dare go further down that tunnel.

"Pssst. Back up," he told Thuy.

Thuy had to crawl backwards and when he reached the fork, he had to move ass backwards into the tunnel they had come from, and far enough back for Hill to fit. Hill moved his rear end into the tunnel, twisted his shoulder around and started back down the right fork headfirst.

When they passed another cave with light coming from it and were far enough away not to be heard, Hill whispered, "What was in there?"

"There were two VC sleeping in hammocks. I think they were both wounded."

Hill flashed the light ahead and saw something sparkle. His .45 came up from the ground and pointed at the light, but by that time Hill had enough time to figure out what he was looking at—water.

He advanced slowly, watching the pond ripple with the breaths of air. It marked the end of the tunnel.

Oh, shit, he thought. He knew what it was from the stories he had heard about the tunnels. It was a water trap. Not meant to drown him, hopefully, but used by the VC to stop poisonous fumes from contaminating the entire tunnel system. Such traps were supposedly near many of the entrances.

It consisted of a hole in the ground filled with water and with the ceiling of the cave projecting underwater. That way no poisonous gases could pass. The only way to get through was under the water and out the other side, only a matter of feet away.

Hill knew that on the other side might be a chamber with an NVA soldier waiting to blow his head off.

He did not know how long he would have to stay underwater and how far he would have to move to get to the other side. His heart felt like an apple in his throat. He lost no time worrying about it. He just might lose his nerve.

He would slither into the water and grope his way forward.

He placed his face inches from the water and took a deep breath. It stank of urine but he realized there was no other way.

Chapter 6

With exaggerated care, Hill held the .45 out front, took another deep breath and looked at the flashlight in his left hand. Realizing the water would destroy it, he set it aside, exhaled deeply, stuffed his lungs with air and dipped the pistol into the water and slid in behind it.

The water was warm, body temperature, and tickled his skin and slowly seeped between his lips. It tasted so foul he clamped his mouth tighter, and puckered up his nose and lips about as tight as he could squeeze.

With his body totally submerged, he was still upside down, so he worked his legs under his body and found that he could crouch in a low crawl. It took so long to get his feet under him that he was afraid he was going to run out of air so he tried to hurry. He raised the hand that held the flashlight above his head, felt the roof of the hole only inches away and duck-crawled forward. His finger tips searched the slimy roof for an exit.

Suddenly he felt his hand slip away from the mud and fly into the open air. At the same time he uncoiled his legs, lunged forward and stood up, spitting out water, gasping for air and blinking his eyes open.

In the fraction of a second it took his mind to register, he saw a small perfume bottle lamp with a lighted candle squashed into its top. It was shaded by a long brown leaf and the light from the candle shone on the faces of four astonished Vietnamese squatting around a serving of tea. There were two NVA soldiers in khaki uniforms and two women in black silk gowns with their hair tied in a bun behind their heads, like they had just gotten out of the rice fields.

As soon as the two NVA soldiers saw him, they leaned back in their cross-legged position and reached for their AK-47 rifles, set behind them against the cave wall.

Hill aimed and fired into the right rib cage of the one closest to him. The force of the bullet slammed the body against the wall. Hill was deafened and stunned by the concussion of his own firing, but it did not slow down the other NVA soldier who now had the weapon in his hand and was swinging it in Hill's direction. Hill guided the pistol to his new target and fired again, this time striking the man's chest. The force of the bullet literally picked up the man and slapped him against the chamber wall.

Hill studied the fallen bodies to decide if he should pump another round into each, but neither of them moved and there were large holes where the .45 slugs had ripped into their flesh and enough blood to satisfy his curiosity about their well-being.

Hill aimed the pistol in the direction of the two women who had moved closer together but apparently had no weapons to reach for. One of them looked so much like the pretty girls he had seen at the markets. She had a soft, round face with pretty brown eyes that looked so full of fear and pain that Hill wanted to feel sorry for her. Her long fingers were raised to her mouth. As the girl trembled, Hill started to relieve the pressure on his trigger finger. He couldn't bring himself to kill two attractive women. He could not do it.

Something grabbed his pants leg and he let out a howl of terror. He did not mean to make the noise, but the air was forced out of his lungs in such a way that the noise bubbled out. In spite of all that he had been through, he felt embarrassed when he realized it was Thuy tugging at his pants leg trying to pop up out of the water from behind him. Then he felt anger and wanted to kick him. Instead he jumped up out of the water and crawled over beside the two dead NVA soldiers, still keeping his pistol trained on the two women prisoners.

As soon as Thuy stood up, he remained in the waist-deep water dripping wet, looked at the two dead men, then at the women. He pointed his pistol at the cute girl and asked in Vietnamese, "Where is the nearest exit?"

She bowed her head meekly.

Thuy shot her right in the throat. She was blown against the wall, her arms flying out at both sides; an astonished look on her face quickly turned to terror and then nothing.

Hill was shocked. He knew that the girls were VC and that at night they were as dangerous as any man — but still, they were women.

The remaining girl held her head in the cup of her hands. Thuy screamed at her. "Where is the exit?"

She replied, "You can go to the left. It is about a hundred meters away."

"Are there any more?"

"They are all over."

"Do you know where the American prisoner is?"

At first she looked perplexed, then she just nodded her head.

Thuy said, "Get us out of here."

"But Hoppy?" Hill asked.

"We will both die down here along with Hoppy if we

66

do not leave. There are too many NVA soldiers around here and now that they know we are here, they will come looking for us."

When the reality of being hunted sunk into Hill's brain, he realized he did not want to die unknown in a cave. His body might not ever be recovered. For now he had tried hard enough.

Thuy shoved the prisoner into the tunnel leading from the cave and said, "If you are lying, I will shoot you through the asshole."

When her feet disappeared into the darkness, Thuy followed.

Hill was about to crawl forward when he saw in the corner of the chamber a small jar and inside the jar a small green snake, about five or six inches long. Hill recognized it right away. It was a bamboo viper. The men in his platoon called it "One-two-three," the number of steps a man would take before falling over dead from its nervous-system-attacking venom.

Hill took a hold of the jar and looked to see that Thuy was already out of sight. Hill thought of the helpless feeling of getting shot in the ass. He'd like to leave the snake in his trail, as it was accustomed for the VC to do when they thought they were being followed; but he was not sure how he could do it and escape its attack himself. Once he was inside the tunnel, he could not turn around and just drop it. He decided to hang onto the jar until the opportunity came for him to do just that.

Hill tucked the jar into his shirt, shuddered at the coldness of the glass and the nearness to death it held, and crawled on his bleeding knees to catch up. Now that their position was known and he was pulling up the rear, he felt vulnerable and impotent. He could not fire between his legs and barely look back. It was dark and he didn't have a flashlight to see. The noise of the girl and Thuy crawling became his security. When the cave began to rise, he became consoled as well.

A shot rang out and Hill sprawled out on his belly, but when he felt the glass press against his stomach, he kept the pressure of his body from breaking it. When another shot was fired, Hill could see the muzzle flash outline Thuy's backside. He felt for the jar, found it and ran his hand around the glass to check for cracks. It was OK.

He wondered what the hell had motivated him to drag the snake along. Nothing scared him more.

When Thuy began to move forward again, Hill followed close behind and looked to where a small flicker of light shone from a cave to his left. Inside was a NVA regular in bandages with a bullet hole through his head. The body was still twitching.

When Thuy stopped again, Hill's head ran into his butt. He withdrew slightly and asked, "Why are you stopping, Thuy?"

"We're getting out of here."

Hill sighed. His heartbeat was sounding like the rolling of a drum. He looked backwards between his legs and saw that no one was following just yet, but he could hear voices back there.

When Thuy crawled forward, squeezed out of the tunnel into the exit hole and stood up, Hill stared at the legs in front of him and felt a claustrophobic feeling for the first time and crawled right up to them, waited until they disappeared, then pulled, squeezed, arched his back and stood up into the hole.

He looked up another two feet and could see Thuy standing there looking down at him. Hill placed the .45 in his pants, took the jar from his shirt and placed it on the ground next to Thuy's feet, raised both hands above his head and went to grab hold of Thuy's extended fingers with his right hand.

Hill could hear the NVA behind him crawling down the hole, ferreting their way after him. He took Thuy's hand, flexed at the knees to help him hop out of the hole. Suddenly he heard the sound of a gun go off and his right leg felt like a baseball bat had slammed into it. He could feel himself falling to his knees and at the same time in horror he braced himself with his elbows from falling out of the grasp of Thuy. Another shot rang out and he looked down to where it tore into the side of the cave only inches away from his bleeding leg.

Thuy still had hold of his right hand, but when his leg went, he had fallen and now Thuy was on his belly still holding on but taking more of the weight. Hill transferred all his weight to his good leg, raised up and was hoisted upward.

He slid across the grass and lay face down. The burning in his leg was starting to spread up to his thighs. It was an excruciating pain, but not painful enough for him to forget that he was fighting for his life. He rolled over on his back and looked to the sky and realized nothing, nothing in the world had ever seemed so bright, so beautiful, so free as the sky itself. The fresh air and the sound of the wind invigorated him. The sound of leaves made him forget the sound of his pounding heartbeat.

Hill crawled back to the side of the hole and took the jar that somehow had remained intact, removed the top and shook it upside down into the hole.

When the snake fell down the hole, Hill flung the jar down after it, crawled back a foot or two from the hole, took a grenade from his left pocket, pulled the pin and waited.

Suddenly the voice of a man screamed from the hole. Hill let the handle on the grenade fly, held it for the count of one thousand one, one thousand two as the fuse inside burned towards its last two and a half

69

seconds, then he lobbed the grenade into the hole and rolled back.

Within a second of striking the ground, it exploded. The ground shook, and a geyser of mud and smoke flew in the air from the tunnel.

As the debris was settling. Hill said to Thuy, "Get the Lieutenant."

"Where do you think he is?" Thuy asked.

"He is still on this side of the canal," Hill panted. "He is probably a few hundred yards up the canal . . . a ways. Get him."

"What about you?" Thuy asked.

"I'll stay here and make sure nobody else comes out of the tunnel. You go get the Lieutenant and take the girl with you."

Hill knew that the NVA would not stop their fighting because one entrance had been sealed. He remembered what the woman prisoner had said about there being many more in the area.

Thuy looked down at Hill. "I could carry you back with us?"

"It is not that far; hell, the platoon is probably on their way right now. I'd slow you up too much, and then they would get a shot at both of us."

Thuy said, "You know there are many exits in this area from those tunnels. Many exits. The NVA will be coming out of them now like ants."

"I know that. That is why I want you to get the hell out of here and let me watch this hole by myself. I know what I'm doing. Get." He moved the barrel of his pistol in the direction for them to flee.

Thuy hesitated a moment, then realizing that Hill was right, pushed the VC who was watching with a gawking mouth down the trail and got her running.

As they disappeared behind the trees, for the first time Hill looked down at his leg. There was plenty of blood all right. Lots of blood, but what the hell did he expect getting shot. When Hill looked up and saw that he was alone, he crawled back over to the cave and looked down. There was the definite smell of gunpowder mixed with burnt flesh and blood. The entrance appeared to be sealed. He doubted if anyone would be coming out of this one, but he knew they had not given up. They would be coming up from somewhere.

Hill decided to crawl back into the jungle for cover. He tried to stand, but the pain in his right leg was excruciating.

He rested, panting until the pain subsided, and finally looked down at his injured foot. The boot was turned to one side, resting on the ground in an odd fashion, as if it was almost detached from his leg at the bloody calf.

He pulled himself on his elbows over to the bushes only a matter of feet from the burned-out hole and took his last grenade in one hand and the cocked .45 in the other, listened to the sounds of the jungle and waited.

He knew that the Lieutenant had probably heard the sound of the first grenade and was on his way, but it would mean more time that he had to remain alone.

Hill could feel himself sweating and it made him thirsty but there was not water to be had. That was the first thing he wanted as soon as he was found, some water. He looked at the canal, the red-tinted water. That would do. His body was on fire, burning up. He thought of the water trap and felt nauseated.

There was the sound of troops approaching.

Hill came to his senses and could hear the NVA soldiers moving around him. He saw the movement of a helmet for a brief moment as it disappeared behind a tree. They were not killing him and he wondered why. Suddenly he knew what they were doing. They were using him for live bait.

He set the pistol down and went to pull the pin from the grenade, but the pain was so overwhelming that he blacked out.

When Hill awoke, he could hear Beckwith and the platoon returning. It was not a loud sound of crashing through the jungle, it was the far-off rattle of a canteen, the slapping of pants legs, the shifting of a back pack on someone's shoulders, the sound of a cracked branch. He could not hear the rifles and the M-79 grenade launchers or the LAWs, but he knew they were cocked and ready to fire; he also knew that the NVA were waiting in ambush.

Hill felt helpless, but, he decided, not for long — dead or alive, not for long.

He thought of crawling back into the hole, but that would be an easy receptacle for an NVA grenade. He thought of moving to the canal, but he knew what would happen to him then. He would be shot again, if not in the same leg, the other one. The thought of more pain in the same leg was almost unbearable.

What he would do was exactly what he was doing right now, remain still so that they thought he was still unconscious; at that they would not be able to use him. He remembered Melon, a fellow from his platoon who had been shot by the VC and left for his comrades to try and rescue. Four of his fellow platoon members had been killed trying to crawl forward.

But Hill would not give the NVA that pleasure. He would not use his fellow platoon members like that. He still had the cocked .45 in one hand and the grenade with a pin in it in the other hand. He would just wait and when he heard the sons of bitches getting real close or trying to make him feel pain to cry out, he would roll over on his back and plug the closest son of a bitch wherever he could and toss that last grenade into the biggest concentration of NVA that was around him and fuck the rest. They were not going to use him.

They were coming, he could hear them. He didn't care. As far as he was concerned, he could not hurt anymore than he already did. He could hurt from a different wound, but he knew in his mind that he could not hurt anymore. Big fucking deal. What is one more hole, and if it was through the heart, he would not even be around to feel it. He was not going to drag any of his platoon members into the terror and pain that he was experiencing. It almost made him stronger knowing that he was defying the enemy.

The platoon was getting closer and at the same time Hill could hear the NVA soldiers surrounding him. He did not give a shit. Let them play their silly little game, he'd show them how to end it. He heard the leaves around him rustling and he knew that now was the time to turn. He knew for sure he would get one of them, at least one. He opened one eye and could feel the presence around him, see the outlines of cloth move through the branches.

He took one deep breath, slowly, to give him strength against the pain of moving. When his lungs were full, he rolled over onto his bad leg and the pain that shot up through his backbone made his head scream out. He whipped the .45 around in front of him with his finger pressing down on the trigger and pointed the pistol at the closest man-sized target.

Before he could pull the trigger, he heard someone say, "Spread the fuck out. What do you think we have here, a goddamn circus carnival? They throw one grenade around here and we all go home in the same body bag."

The tension in Hill's neck relaxed and his head dropped back onto the ground and splashed in the mud. He started panting. He could hear his hand sloshing in the mud and turned his face to see that the .45 in his hand was flopping around like a fish out of water, sending off small tremor waves across the wet ground.

He looked up again and there was Doc, with his famous morphine needle coming down on him, talking bullshit like he always did, telling Hill that the wound was not that bad and he had seen worse on a football field back home in high school.

"You're going to the hospital," Doc told Hill.

Before Hill fainted, he knew he would never see any of his platoon again.

Chapter 7

"Bravo-six, this is three-six. Over." When there was no answer, Beckwith tried again. "Bravo-six, this is three-six."

After listening to static for a moment, Marlin turned to Kraus and was about to tell him to change the radio frequency to the medevac station when a reply came over the small speaker, "This is Bravo-six. Go."

"We need another dust-off," he spoke almost threateningly.

After more static and a long pause that made Beckwith feel uncomfortable, the answer came. "Roger."

Beckwith continued, "We also captured a prisoner, a young Vietnamese woman." Beckwith looked at the girl, whom he guessed to be about twenty years old and whom Thuy was still guarding with his pistol. She was barefoot, all skin and bones. Her muddy black clothes shivered in the heat of the day. Her face was streaked with dirt and her black hair clung like cobwebs to her neck and cheeks.

"Are you sure she is a VC?" the C.O. asked.

Beckwith smacked his lips and replied. "They pulled her out of a tunnel full of North Vietnamese soldiers."

"Well, good. I am sure she knows some information that our intelligence section will find interesting . . . I don't want anything to happen to her before they get a chance to question her."

Marlin huffed at the repetition of the old phrase. Feeling indignant that the Old Man had turned loose the last prisoners, he wondered if the same would happen to this one.

"What were you doing down tunnels?" the C.O. asked.

Beckwith took a deep breath and answered, "I didn't have a choice. I spotted Hoppy going underground. I thought it was the best decision at the time to send two men down after him."

There was a long pause before Captain Rice answered. "You're not qualified to go under the ground like that, three-six. You should have called in the 'rats' from Dong Tam. You are lucky you did not lose more men."

The word "more" grated against Beckwith's nerves. He answered, "I thought of calling them up, but I was afraid if I waited much longer Hoppy would only get that much farther away from us."

"Well, did it work?"

"Negative."

Another long pause. "You are lucky, three-six . . . I want you to proceed onto Ben Luc, today, and continue your original mission as planned."

The Lieutenant could feel his anger rising almost like a heat wave through his body. He replied, "But what about Hoppy?"

"I haven't forgotten; but if the NVA are moving him north, they will have to cross the Vam Co River, either by boat or across the bridge. You can try and intercept him at that point."

Marlin pressed the send button on the radio, "I just can't leave him out there."

"I'll have the other platoons sweep the area."

"But what about us?"

"That is an order, three-six."

Marlin slowly felt the heat in his head subsiding as his anger gradually cooled down. Maybe he was being a bit paranoid, overanxious. Maybe the C.O.'s caution was warranted. "Roger," he replied.

"When the dust-off comes in, I will send in three other choppers to move you to a new location. There will be an MP on board to take charge of the prisoner. When you are on the ground again, call me on the radio and I will tell you where and how you will proceed from there."

Marlin wondered what the hell the Old Man was up to now. Seemed like he was always moving him around, in and out of danger, like a pawn in a chess game. "Why don't you have the choppers bring us right onto Ben Luc, Bravo-six?"

"Just do as you are ordered, three-six. I don't want to explain everything to you over the radio . . . and I am sending some artillery your way to help you walk out of there."

Beckwith scowled at Kraus who was watching him talk. Beckwith replied bitterly, "Do you think it is necessary?"

"Artillery is not going to hurt any of those tunnels, unfortunately. We have tried before. The only results have been accomplished with 500-pound bombs and those are not available in this district."

"But I don't want artillery."

"I don't remember even asking you. It is coming your way. Figure out where to put it."

Marlin knew where he wanted to put it. He replied, "Roger. I'll let Stove Pipe take over."

"Any KIAs?"

Beckwith looked at Hill who was semi-conscious with his head bobbling like a street junkie and babbling about being surrounded. He was in no shape to talk. Beckwith looked at Thuy and asked, "How many did you kill down there?"

Thuy thought a moment. "Hill shoot two of them and I shoot three. Then we threw a grenade in the hole just as we get out."

Beckwith relayed the message.

Before the C.O. signed off, he said, "You just keep that prisoner safe."

"Roger. Out." Marlin figured she'd probably be home for supper after a slap on the back of the hand.

Beckwith sighed and felt a moment of relief. He looked around at the tangled vines close to his face and realized his platoon would be safer sitting in the middle of a snake pit. Since Hill and Thuy had not crawled out of the same tunnel they had entered, Beckwith knew the place was crawling with exits, which meant the NVA might pop up again and set more booby traps or lay another ambush. He had had enough of both within the last 24 hours.

Kraus had already switched the radio frequency and handed the receiver to Arnie, who accepted it graciously and said, "I'll walk you out of here on a path as safe as Moses walking through the parted Red Sea."

Beckwith heard the distant boom of the cannon being fired, listened to the humming which eventually turned to a whistle as it flew closer.

Beckwith cupped his hands over his mouth and hollered for everyone to hear, "Incoming!" He did not care if the whole North Vietnamese Army heard him now. At this point the danger of artillery hitting one of his own men was more serious than the NVA knowing where they were located.

He looked up at the treetops and watched.

When the whistle grew almost loud enough to touch, it turned to an explosion that left behind a white, puffy cloud suspended in the air. As the split cannister somersaulted to the ground, it broke branches and landed in the mud with a thud.

Arnie pointed his compass at the smoke and took a reading on its position. He got on the radio again, gave the compass direction and said, "Halo Four, drop fifty yards, to the right one hundred yards . . ."

Beckwith interrupted him, "I want a time fuse on those high explosives."

Without a delayed fuse the artillery would rip to shreds the treetops but little of its destructive power would reach the ground. With a delayed fuse, the jungle canopy would set off the artillery round and by the time it broke through the top branches and nearly reached the ground, it would explode at waist level. If Charlie were trying to hide in ambush or set a booby trap, what remained of the evidence of such foul play would probably go undetected.

Arnie continued, "Give me five H.E. with a half-second delayed fuse."

The cannons in the distance started to boom and soon the whistle of their approach could be heard. Beckwith crouched down behind a tree and hugged his helmet while the five rounds rumbled the ground and sent trees crashing against each other.

Just as the last rounds exploded, Arnie got back on the radio and said, "Add fifty yards and repeat."

When the next burst of artillery saturated the ground, with smoke and the smell of sweet gunpowder in the air, Beckwith rousted his platoon and headed after it.

Ken Hyde and Kurt Fosdale lifted Hill to his feet, placed his arms over their shoulders and carried him between their interlocked hands.

"Add fifty and repeat," Arnie said over the radio.

It was easier walking through the jungle after the artillery had ripped it apart and a lot safer. This time as the platoon stretched out in a line and moved forward, their thoughts were more on the danger of the incoming rounds than of Charlie's presence.

When the daylight of the rice paddy shone on their faces, the artillery was called off, and each squad moved forward into the open field and took cover behind the rice berm about fifty yards apart, the space it took for a helicopter to land.

Beckwith switched to Skate Force's frequency and found out that the C.O. had already dispatched the helicopters. Beckwith gave the coordinates of the landing zone and told them to watch for the smoke.

Hill was moaning in a state of semiconsciousness. He had lost a great deal of blood, and the foot was in bad shape as the bone had been penetrated.

Marlin scanned the treeline for enemy activity and saw none.

"I think I hear 'em," Kraus said.

They all listened with their ears perked to the wind. Doc said. "It's the mosquitoes buzzing."

Kraus said, "Screw you, Doc. It's the choppers."

They all listened, holding their breath.

It was them, all right, and the sound grew louder and then the line of four choppers appeared above the trees about four miles away, as pretty as a reprieve for a man on death row.

Kraus popped a smoke grenade, set it on the berm so it would not go out underwater, and stood back as it puffed out a cloud of green smoke that the choppers immediately turned and swooped down towards.

The first chopper was a medevac. As soon as it landed, Doc, Kraus and the Lieutenant helped Hill aboard and without further delay, ran in a wide arc around the tail prop. If one of them ran into the spinning blade he would be sent home in a milk shake cup.

When they reached the open cabin of the second chopper, the door gunner, wearing the same brand of sunglasses as the pilots and with the same bulging communication helmet, sat behind his M-60 machine gun mounted to the floor, his index finger ready to squeeze off an automatic burst. There were no greetings as he kept his eyes riveted on the treeline.

Inside, Castillo and Spielberg were aboard, sitting in the one long seat like anxious passengers aboard a bus, their job as riflemen ceasing until they landed again. The only ones permitted to return fire in the helicopter were the door gunners.

The VC woman was aboard and handcuffed to a Military Police guard in a clean uniform and shining helmet.

Doc jumped in first, then Kraus and Beckwith about the same time. Beckwith did not even get seated when he could feel the chopper swoop up and forward and the sound of the props whop the air and whip the rice plants in circles with their downwash. He made sure he was totally inside, looked to the treeline for muzzle flashes, then looked forward between the two pilots and out the front windshield that extended from behind the pilots' heads all the way down to their feet. It was truly a spectacular view, but it also made them the same kind of target. The skids on the ship cleared the treetops by only a few feet.

"You know where you are dropping us off?" Beckwith screamed at the pilot.

The man in the copilot seat turned his head around and hollered back, "Sit down and enjoy the flight . . . No time for refreshments. We'll be landing shortly."

The strip of jungle they flew over was no more than a mile wide, with more unattended rice paddies on the far side. There were no signs of enemy movement, no fire fights in progress and no workers in the fields.

Placing his arm on Kraus's shoulder, Marlin took a seat next to the open door.

The higher they rose, the safer Marlin felt, and the safer he felt, the more he smiled. The wind blowing into the open doorway was a refreshing relief for his sweaty body.

Beckwith looked at Kraus, who was a total mess. The mud was caked on his clothes in different layers of color. His face was smeared with mud and camouflage stick, especially around the eyes. The only two things clean about Kraus were his rifle and his teeth which were glistening white.

Beckwith hollered at Kraus, "Can't beat this, Kraus. I don't know why the hell you'd want to get out of the Army and become an auctioneer. You'd be bored to death."

"I hope I get the chance to die that way then," he hollered, "it would be a pleasure compared to this shit."

As Beckwith smiled, he looked at the band on Kraus's helmet that held the camouflage cover in place. It was the only place where Kraus could display his personal feelings about the war. Written in ink and traced over several times was the phrase, "If you can't eat it, drink it, or fuck it, kill it."

Marlin looked over at Castillo and Spielberg who were holding their weapons by the handguards with the butt plates on the deck.

Spielberg looked depressed, with his head low between his arms. Gary was one of the smarter men in the third platoon, and Marlin just shook his head and smiled as he recalled Spielberg telling how he had screwed up all his tests getting into the Army so he would not have to come to Vietnam. Maybe he wasn't all that smart.

Castillo was the youngest man in the platoon, having enlisted the day he was eighteen years old. Salvador could barely see beyond his nose. He had the M-60 machine gun so that he could just spray whatever he shot at and even then he was always missing.

Beckwith looked out the door at the open rice paddies and stretches of jungle. It was loud inside the chopper, but the breeze felt refreshing. His thoughts turned to Hoppy. He knew that Hoppy was still down in the tunnels, probably being shuffled around so that he would not be found. It was too early for him to be questioned and tortured. The NVA were still in a great deal of danger themselves. Beckwith knew there was still time.

As quickly as they had risen, they dropped from the sky and towards a familiar-looking rice paddy.

Beckwith had a feeling it was going to be a hot LZ this time. Otherwise, why would he be getting off here?

When the ship was no more than twenty feet off the ground, the gunner on the left side opened up with his M-60 machine gun. The noise startled everyone. The machine gun started bouncing on its swivel and spitting out brass. Smoke filled the compartment as well as the smell of gunpowder. The gunner on the right joined in the firing.

When Marlin felt the Huey careening, he looked out the open door at the treeline, but there was too much smoke swirling around inside to see if they were taking on fire.

The chopper hovered about six feet off the ground and the pilot made a quick turn of his head. He had lost that silly grin and all coolness. "Jump!" he hollered at the same time that he jerked his clenched fist and extended thumb in a tight ball at Beckwith.

Maybe the pilot felt like he did not want to sink into the mud and risk getting stuck, maybe he did not want to spend the extra moments it took to land completely, maybe he took a round and was losing control. Not the time to ask questions.

"Jump," Beckwith relayed the message. Everyone stood up like they were leaving a house afire.

Beckwith was the first one out on his side, and as he hit the water, he looked to see if Kraus was going to jump right on top of him. The helicopter was no longer directly overhead and Kraus landed in the water several feet to his right.

Spielberg and Castillo hit the water about the same time and sank to their knees in the mud on the other side. Doc ended up rolling in the water when he hit the paddy.

Marlin was on all fours in the water, he stretched forward and half-floated towards the rice berm running parallel with the jungle. Castillo and Spielberg lined up alongside of him and watched to see where the door gunners were firing. The choppers created so much confusion that it was impossible to understand what was happening.

All eyes rotated from the treeline to the choppers and back to the treeline waiting to see and hear what was going to happen next.

The helicopters swooped forward and disappeared over the next stretch of trees, and with them the sound of their blades, motors, and guns.

Soon the whole scene turned quiet.

Beckwith was the first to speak, "Crazy, damn pilot. Some of those guys are totally out of control. Jump," he whispered, "Jump my ass."

Kraus looked over the top of the berm and at the same time asked, "Were we taking on fire coming in, Sir?"

"Hell if I know. The way that pilot acted we sure were."

"I don't see anything, and I never heard anything."

"Well, we can't stay out here. They'll be lobbing

mortars on us in no time. Let's get back into the jungle."

Beckwith looked to a squad of men that were in the helicopter behind him, and they were fifty yards to his left huddled against the rice paddy berm like him.

He caught the attention of Hyde and signaled him forward. Hyde crawled over the berm and kind of floated through the water on his belly towards another berm perpendicular to the jungle. About ten yards behind him came Fosdale, then Justice, then another. Beckwith waited for Hyde and his squad to enter the treeline before he followed, all without incident.

When they were all within the protection of the foliage, Beckwith turned to Kraus who was smiling and said, "That Old Man don't give us a break no how."

"He's not happy unless we are pinned down."

"Kraus, pass the word to spread out."

The Lieutenant got on the radio again.

The Old Man's first comment was, "Was it a hot LZ?"

"About as hot as a melted ice cream . . . What the hell was that all about?"

The C.O. did not answer the question. "OK. Three-six. How is my prisoner?"

"I didn't kick her out of the helicopter for her stinking breath if that is what you mean . . . The last I saw of her she was handcuffed to an MP and flying your way."

"I want you to proceed to checkpoint Lima."

"No more eagle missions, I hope."

"Negative . . . You're in this war to make contact, three-six, not to sell shoes . . . One-six and two-six are moving into the area of operation you just left."

"How about the trucks?"

"Sorry. They are being used elsewhere."

Marlin shook his head at Kraus, then said into the

85

radio, "Roger. Will proceed."

Beckwith returned the receiver to Kraus and said, "Always fucking with us . . . Let's get moving. We have a long way to walk before it gets dark."

Chapter 8

When night settled on the wetlands, as each man in the third platoon climbed onto the road leading to Ben Luc, he stomped the mud from his pants, spread out along the grassy berm that lined both sides of the road, and collapsed on his rucksack or flak jacket for a rest.

Beckwith knelt in the middle of the road, unsheathed the starlight scope and scanned the area, first in the direction of the bridge. In the distant were dim lights, the candles of a community glowing in cartoon-like silhouettes. More hootches along the banks of a river, the water fizzling like the tips of a sparkler. When the bridge finally came into view, it was unlighted and appeared only as a dark outline.

To the right of the bridge, rice paddies stretched back toward the jungle too far away to be of concern. On the left, in the middle of all the glitter of water, closer to a hundred yards was the dark shadow of a lone Vietnamese hootch.

The rain was starting to fog the scope. Beckwith had had the same problem before, and every effort to clean it had made the visibility only worse. He knew it would only be a matter of minutes before the scope would be nearly useless unless he got it out of the rain.

He thought of moving towards the bridge, but did not want to risk it at night; too many friendlies in the area and too little known about their exact positions, and it was no secret that the ARVNs were notorious for setting booby traps around their camps and firing indiscriminately at anything that moved. Marlin did not want to lose any of his men by sheer stupidity. Besides, sometimes he got a better night's rest in the field when the VC did not know exactly where he was and could not harass him. Oftentimes bridges and camps were the nightly targets of mortar barrages and no matter how ineffective the attack might be, if it accomplished nothing else, it kept men awake.

The Lieutenant moved towards the dark shadow of the nearest man on the road, found White, and grabbed him by the arm as he looked about for his squad leader. "Gatz," he whispered, almost too loudly.

"Here I am, Sir," came the reply as a poncho ruffled and a body stood up and drew closer, a big body.

Beckwith handed Gatz the starlight scope and pointed in the direction of the hootch. "That's where I want you to take us."

Gatz took a look through the scope, grunted, and returned the scope to the platoon leader.

"I ain't no fool, Sir, but what do you want me to do?"

"Just lead us to the hootch, safely."

"No problem."

While Gatz herded up his squad and got them moving, Beckwith rolled up the other squads behind him, the men somewhat out of order. To make certain that everyone was following and no one was going off on his own, Marlin used the starlight scope to count the bodies as they strung out along the top of a rice paddy—they appeared as black silhouettes surrounded by green light, reminding him of beasts of burden, stooped, dragging, balancing, fading. All twenty-two of them.

Beckwith returned the starlight scope to its case and

trailed behind the file until the man in front of him came to a stop. At that point Marlin stepped off the berm and sloshed through the rice paddy water until he had passed all the men and reached the hut, then he stepped back onto firm ground and entered the doorless hootch, once again stomping his feet.

The room was lighted by a solitary candle perched in a candleholder made from a coconut. The residents were huddled against the back wall, in a tight group like a family portrait. The two children were drawn up against a nervous mamasan whose mouth quivered, exposing even in the dim light black teeth from the betel nut.

She kept bowing her head and chattering in her native language. She hugged the shoulders of the two boys towards her and shot glances at the encircling soldiers. The kids acted excited, like they wanted to play.

When the headquarters element was all inside, Thuy started to question the old lady in a high-pitched chant. Beckwith took out the flashlight from his pack and with fingers spread over the glass to restrict the light, walked into the adjoining room following the spot of light with his eyes. Hammocks hanging in the two far corners cast eerie shadows across the walls; Beckwith walked over to a footlocker, opened it, and used the tip of his rifle to move the clothes around. He dropped the top shut and checked another trunk. The same harmless clothes, no hidden uniforms or weapons. He flashed the light around his left arm at a tall dresser in the corner and saw the outline of a person crouched behind it against the wall. Reflexively, Marlin whipped his rifle at the body, applied pressure on his trigger finger and waited for the person to make a hostile move.

When the person stayed crouched and quivering, Marlin drew closer and said, "Get up."

The Vietnamese stood up and exhaled a lungful of air and reached towards his face.

When Marlin realized the guy was only shading his eyes from the light, he sighed in relief and said, "Who are you?"

The fingers covering the face slowly slid down the cheeks to reveal the long eyelashes and deep brown eyes of a very attractive woman.

"My name is Lisa," she said slowly in English. "Le Thi Phuoc."

The fact that she was not a man and speaking English startled Beckwith. He still held the light right in her eyes. She blinked and turned her face to one side. She did not have the rounded head of a Vietnamese, but a much longer face with high cheek bones and soft brown skin. Her hair was not black, but a soft brown, slightly curled and bleached at the tips by the sun. She was a good three inches taller than the tallest Vietnamese, yet she was dressed like a native in black pants and a white shirt.

Marlin began to relax, almost gawk as he pointed the light on her chest which was full, rounded, and stretching the buttons.

"You speak English? What are you doing in here?" he asked.

"I was frightened and hiding."

They stared into each other's eyes for a moment. When Marlin noticed her lips quivering, as if reading his mind she licked at them to stop the trembling.

Finally he said, "You better get in the room with the others." He waved his rifle in the direction for her to move.

As she walked into the kitchen ahead of him, Marlin ran his eyes down her long curvy legs and marveled at the slimness of her waist.

When the two of them entered the room, Kraus,

who had taken the lid off a large rice pot, had his arms up to his elbows inside of it. He smiled at the young woman and asked, "Where did she come from?"

"She was hiding," Marlin repeated almost foolishly.

Doc, who was sitting at the table starting a game of solitaire, said, "If I had to guess, I would say she is half-French."

Lisa drew closer to her mother and stood behind her.

As Kraus removed his hands from the rice bowl, he grabbed hold of its rim with both hands, ready to pull it over.

"Don't spill that," the Lieutenant said.

"But there could be grenades buried in here," Kraus replied as he relaxed against the pot.

The Lieutenant looked at the old mamasan, the two kids and Lisa. Then he looked at Thuy and asked, "What did you find out from Mamasan?"

"She is not friendly to the VC."

"Does she know anything about Hoppy?"

Thuy shook his head as he twitched his nose.

Marlin looked back at Kraus, "Negative. We are going to spend the night here, not destroy the place."

Beckwith decided to avoid further controversy, and to set his mind at ease, continued checking out the hootch. He moved to the back wall of the room where the kitchen utensils were stacked and saw bowls and a small blade used for cutting fish. Although it could be used to slit someone's throat, he was not about to confiscate it.

Stove Pipe asked, "Do you want me to bracket in our position for artillery in case of an attack, Lieutenant?"

"Sure, Stove Pipe, but no marking rounds, just on your map."

"I'll give the coordinates to the battery in Ben Luc."

Marlin did not answer as he was staring at the Christian pictures on the wall that reminded him of the saintly pictures his mother hung in their home.

He looked to the hard floor and saw sandals lined in a row, then looked up again at the slots in the bamboo siding wide enough for a rifle barrel to fit through.

The bomb shelter in the corner was like a bee's nest. He crouched to look inside and saw where the tunnel made a turn. He really did not want to go inside, but when he thought of Hoppy, he crawled forward and with the flashlight pointing the way—just to set his mind at ease. It was empty but for a small drinking cup.

When Beckwith crawled back out, he said to Thuy, "Tell them that we are going to spend the night here in this kitchen and not for them to worry. We will leave in the morning."

When Thuy explained in Vietnamese, the mamasan seemed concerned, but somewhat relieved. So did Beckwith. He often gauged his own physical danger from the reaction of the Vietnamese around him. He trusted those instincts, sometimes almost beyond reason.

"You ought to make Thuy your platoon sergeant the way you rely on his advice," Kraus commented.

"Kraus, it has been a long day. Shut the fuck up."

Beckwith returned outside, moved the men forward and placed a squad at each corner of the hut and showed them in what direction to set their claymores. There was plenty of space under the awnings for the men to stay dry when it rained and adequate protection in the moat around the house in case of an attack.

Beckwith finished his rounds and returned to the kitchen. Lisa had gone into the next room with the rest of her family. He was disappointed, as he enjoyed looking at her, but at the same time he did not want to invade her privacy.

Thuy and Kraus bedded down on the floor.

Marlin removed all his gear and shirt, sat at the table and smoked a cigarette, removed his boots and socks, massaged his feet and talked with Doc and Stove Pipe, who had the first watch. Finally, exhausted, he laid the liner on the ground and used his flak jacket as a pillow to fall asleep. He would stand third watch.

When Marlin felt someone tug at his shoulder and call out his name, he felt like he was coming out of a coma, like he had been drugged and was now barely alive; the only way to maintain his life was to reach for it. He looked around the room and saw some bodies scattered around the kitchen with poncho liners covering them, packs next to them and rifles nearby. He shook his head, rolled his neck in a wide circle to maintain his state of consciousness, sniffled, threw the poncho liner off his shoulders, stood up and stretched. "Thanks, Kraus."

"You sure you're awake, Sir."

"Positive. You can go to sleep."

No sooner said than Kraus was on the ground alongside his radio and covering himself with the liner. "Good night, Sir."

"Yeah. Good night."

Marlin looked at the table. Doc's scattered cards were still there; so was Stove Pipe's radio, canteen, and map. A brown, dried-up coconut was in the middle of the table next to the nearly burned-out candle. Marlin knew what was inside. He retrieved his drinking cup from the pack, sat at the table, lifted the top off the coconut, removed the small pot inside and poured himself a cup of tea. He set the pot back under the coconut, took a sip from the cup, walked to the doorway and looked outside. As it happened so often at night, the skies had cleared and the enlarging moon lighted the fields. It was a beautiful sight. The breeze was cool and refreshing. He inhaled deeply the sweet air, returned to his pack, took out the starlight scope and scanned the area. There was no unfriendly movement coming from any direction.

As he put the scope away, his thoughts returned to Hoppy. He wondered if he were still alive. He almost pitied him if he were. Then he started to play the "what if" game. What if he hadn't taken a break just when he had the day that Hoppy was lost . . . what if he had made certain that all the men were moving by having Roberts personally check . . . what if he had discovered the missing men sooner or had run back faster or . . . It was a stupid game. The NVA following them might have taken on the whole platoon and wiped them out in an ambush. Who knew, in such a war? Marlin shook his head and just made up his mind to do as good a job as he could. Whatever happened, he'd teach those NVA soldiers a lesson for messing with his platoon and taking Hoppy. He sipped from the cup again.

He heard the explosion of incoming mortar rounds in the distance. He could not tell where they were landing, just far away and to the north. He was content where he was.

He finished his tea, put on his helmet and flak jacket, picked up his rifle and went outside to make the rounds around the hootch to see how his men were doing.

At the first corner, Gary Spielberg was leaning against the wall of the hootch with his M-79 laid across his lap, three men stretched asleep beside him.

Beckwith knelt beside Spielberg and asked, "Seen anything?"

"A quiet night, Sir . . . This place can sure be pretty when there's no firing going on and it quits raining."

The Lieutenant half-chuckled, "And when it is night

and cool, and nobody is shooting at you . . . Having trouble staying awake?"

"No. I feel pretty good. I was kind of thinking about my dad's ranch back home. Funny how a guy can remember all the pretty things and not the cow shit."

"And when you think about the cow shit, it doesn't even smell."

Speilberg wasn't stuttering and it made Marlin relax as well. Marlin looked at the other three men on the berm stretched out asleep next to Spielberg and said, "Stay tuned and don't let anyone sneak up on you."

"Yes, Sir."

At the next position, Mark Allen was awake. He had already been nicknamed "Zipper" because he was always taking a leak and having trouble with his zipper. Beckwith had picked up the name just as quickly.

As he was new, Beckwith took the opportunity to explain to him, "If you see anything move out there, shoot it. Don't fire the claymores unless you have to."

"Sir, we were told in training to fire the claymores first."

"Forget it. Around here the VC will reverse the direction of the claymores, then stand up. They're hoping you'll blow your own face off when you detonate it. Just to be safe, shoot the son of a bitch first or throw a grenade at him. Use the claymores only if you see a line of men running at you, and stay low when you detonate it."

Allen asked, "How about the people inside? Can we trust them?"

"Yes," he replied, almost threateningly.

There was a moment of silence in which Beckwith felt his defenses up.

"OK."

Beckwith got up and moved toward Gatz's position.

Gatz looked both ways to make certain that no one was coming his way and none of his men were awake. He removed the knife from its scabbard, opened his Bible to the page with the hairs inside, placed the knife across the pages to hold the book open, and lifted the last strands of hair from the Bible that he had gotten back at the canal during the day. It was awkward doing it in the dark and the fact that his hands were so big and sticky did not make it any easier, but the brightness of the moon reflecting off the white paper helped. He removed half a dozen hairs from the bundle and set them on the page, then removed another half dozen, twisted them like thread and tied them around the large bundle of hair like he was tying up a sleeping blanket. He tied the other end of hairs with the other threads of hair, then placed the bundle on the cover of the Bible, and sawed off the loose ends of the hair at both ends with the sharp blade. He could hear the Lieutenant coming his way. He lifted the small package of hair into his hand, looked at it real close, smiled and placed it in the Bible as a marker.

Almost everyone leads at least one secret life.

When the Lieutenant arrived, Gatz talked to him in a warm and comforting tone.

Ken Hyde was awake at the last position. He was the only man who challenged the Lieutenant with the password, "Fire."

"Fly," said Marlin as he approached cautiously. Hyde did things by the book and even Marlin was not going to challenge his ways. Ken was an excellent squad leader, a man who worked hard, but very quiet and withdrawn. After a brief stop to make certain that all was OK, Marlin returned to the hut.

Marlin sat down at the table, studied the map under the candlelight and memorized the new radio frequencies, then removed the letters from his rucksack that he had not had a chance to read yet. They were all wet and had to be carefully opened and removed so as not to tear them apart. Then he laid each out on the table in a stack and read each of them under the fading candlelight. The words and the scenes created in his mind seemed so distant and so removed from his life, but the smell of the letters flooded his mind with memories. In a way he felt saddened. He enjoyed the thought of the mail, but the contents were like from another planet. The daily routine of his family, the prank-playing of his friend Al, Roxeanne's studies and her family. He loved them all, but at the same time he felt confused, resentful.

Marlin's hour was up. He awoke Stove Pipe and went off to sleep as soon as his head touched the helmet.

Chapter 9

By the time the platoon returned to the road the next morning, the pounding rain had ceased.

Merchants and shoppers rushing off to market were scattered along the steaming road elevated about ten feet above the rice paddies. The platoon fell in stride behind an old, barefooted man wearing shorts and a buttonless shirt and dragging along a large pig by a rope tied around its neck. The pig kept turning its head and oinking at the point man. Kurt Fosdale kept turning around and looking at the Lieutenant for an order. Beckwith just waved him forward.

On the left side of the road another Vietnamese herded a small flock of ducks with a long stick, chattering and jabbing at the lead duck to keep it out of the tall grass. Several oxen, with their heads bowed and necks flexing like on a death march, drew rickety carts loaded with sacks of rice and loose hay; the wheels of which were lopsided and ready to fall off. Several other Vietnamese, men and women alike, carried rice and firewood on what looked like an old-fashioned scale with their shoulder the fulcrum. They were all headed for the bridge, a formidable structure of American ingenuity and achievement, truly an example of modern design, but totally out of place.

The bridge must have been a hundred yards long,

with a sweeping approach to it on both sides. Two arching spans were supported in the middle by a single tower leg that set on a broad pier in the middle of the river. Vertical and diagonal braces about every thirty feet reinforced the structure that looked strong enough to hold the weight of a train and tall enough for a large-sized freighter to pass under.

The river was a hundred feet wide, brown and silty, moving so slow it was hard to figure out which direction it was headed until floating sticks and branches were observed going to the right.

The near bank was lined with scrub brush that bordered the rice fields; the far shore was cleared back from the water line, with several sand pans pulled on high, the scattered village of Ben Luc in the background.

Where the road started to rise from the level ground on the opposite shore was an ARVN compound that appeared like an ant hill with small firing ports pointing in every direction. On top of the mound was a heavily sandbagged watch position. The whole camp was surrounded by rows and rows of wire. The only person visible in the camp was a nursing mother in a small courtyard area, sitting on a stool and surrounded by a dozen or so feeding chickens.

Across from the ARNV compound and a bit closer to the bridge was a two-story cement tower similar to a lighthouse with a small opened door overlooking the road and one small window half way up. A weaponless ARVN soldier in shower clogs leaned his chair against the tower, picking his teeth with a piece of straw. When the platoon was halfway across the bridge, the ARVN turned his head and spoke into the doorway.

Out stepped a tall American in a clean jungle uniform and helmet strapped in place, flak jacket zipped up to his chest and rifle at the port position. He came towards the third platoon with a smile on his face. The whole file stopped to look in bewilderment at the man.

The soldier looked at Kraus, turned with a snap in his direction, eyed the Lieutenant next to the radioman, stopped in front of the platoon leader, popped to attention and saluted, "Sir. Sergeant John Hillerman reporting, your new platoon sergeant, sir."

The whole platoon was absolutely silent.

Beckwith wiped the sweat from his brow and massaged his forehead at the same time. As he whipped his dripping hand to one side, he said. "Sarge, if you ever salute me again over here, I'll bust your face open."

The Sergeant dropped his salute along with his shoulders, acting genuinely hurt and confused.

Kraus said to Hillerman, "The Lieutenant does not like to be singled out. Makes him feel like a big bull's-eye."

Marlin sneered at Kraus who was now smiling, turned his attention back to Hillerman and extended his hand to the Sergeant and introduced himself. As they shook hands, Beckwith said, "Welcome aboard, Sarge." It sounded like he left his enthusiasm somewhere back at Lisa's hut.

Another American stepped out of the same doorway in the tower. He was a tall, muscular-looking man. His pants were tucked into his shined boots, his T-shirt blowing free, a green beret on his head cocked to one side.

Marlin guessed the Green Beret to be his contact and said, "Excuse me a minute, Sarge. I'll be right back."

As Beckwith walked around Sergeant Hillerman, he looked at the Green Beret and noticed a beer can in his hand. In the room behind him, a young Vietnamese girl stooped over a bed, smoothing the sheets. Her long, black, shiny hair cascaded over her back and over the camouflaged Army fatigues that were tailored to hug her tight little butt.

The American waved with his free hand. "You must be the platoon from Bravo Company I heard was headed our way."

Beckwith replied, "That's right."

"I'm Captain Crystal." He touched his green beret. "Special Forces. You want to come inside for some coffee or something?" He saluted with the can of beer.

"I'd like to get set up first, Captain. My men have a lot of digging in before nightfall."

"There's an ambitious man for you," Crystal said over his shoulder. He turned back to the Lieutenant, "Tell you what, we got ourselves some unused bunkers at both ends of this bridge that you could use, save you some digging . . . We didn't dig 'em especially for you, but they will serve the purpose while you are here. You interested in looking?"

"Sure," Beckwith nodded. "Anything is better than busting ass filling sandbags with entrenching tools." In spite of the Green Beret's sarcastic tone and egotistical attitude, Beckwith started to like him.

When Marlin turned around and made the motion of snapping a stick, the men in the platoon moved from their file position and scattered to both sides of the bridge, took off the rucksacks and sat down, some on the railing, others on their packs. Out came the cigarettes as they eyed the Captain's honey who had come to the door to watch.

"Sarge," Beckwith said to Hillerman. "You stay here with Kraus and take charge of the platoon."

"What should I do?" he asked nervously.

"Nothing . . . just nothing. If you have any questions, ask Kraus."

While Hillerman eyed the men nervously, the Captain pointed out the two bunkers nearby.

"Come on," the Captain said, "I'll show you the other two."

Beckwith and the Captain recrossed the bridge and stopped at the far end. Marlin looked down at one of the bunkers he had noticed when he had first crossed the bridge but to which he had paid little attention. It was about six feet down the hillside. All that could be seen of it was its top and entry hole.

"Here is one of them," the Captain said. "They're all about the same size. Looking up and down the river and maybe a bit across the bridge."

Marlin turned to one side and slid down the hill standing up, stooped over, ducked inside, and crouched his way to the firing ports. The view was like the Captain had said, but some of the village of Ben Luc was visible as well. As he grunted his approval, he said, "It's obvious who dug out these bunkers. They are about two feet too short, but they'll do just fine."

The Captain, who had slid in right behind him and was sitting on an ammo box, lighted a cigarette and asked, "How long you expect to be around?"

Marlin turned around and knelt on one knee, resting his back against the sandbags and using his rifle to steady himself. "Probably long enough to dig out another two feet. How long you been here?"

"This is my second tour. After my first I took my old lady to Hawaii for 30 days. I returned as a captain."

Beckwith wrinkled his brow in admiration.

The Captain accepted the lack of enthusiasm with a shrug of his own.

Beckwith eyed the sagging roof and the dry, compacted floor. "I'll take 'em. Now let's get out of here." He slipped out of the entrance and walked back up to the bridge, then asked the Captain, who was right behind him, "You seen much action around here lately?"

The Captain guzzled the rest of the beer and threw the can down the hill, "Fuck, with these ARVN monkeys. If I stepped into the bushes, one of them would shoot me in the back or try and pork me up the yanger. No. I stay here, adviser, liaison, intelligence. Fuck the patrols. When I go to Saigon I don't even tell them I'm leaving. They might try and ambush me up the road." He laughed, nervously. "But the important thing is I understand them." He pointed to his head as if he were about to shoot himself. "If the VC attack, they'll shoot back; but if the VC want to skirt their position, it is all right for you Americans to go after them."

Beckwith looked back down at the bunker, "One thing about your Ruff Puffs. They know how to dig in."

"They are in this war for the duration. When it ends, so does their enlistment."

"You know what, Captain, I don't really give a shit about the ARVNs, let alone want to work with them."

When the Captain shook his head somewhat forlornly, Marlin asked, "You heard anything about a POW?"

The Captain puffed out his cheeks. "American?"

"Yes."

"If I did, I couldn't guarantee the information wouldn't get you in trouble; but no, I haven't."

"He is one of my men and that's who I'm looking for."

"What happened?"

As Beckwith explained, he started back across the bridge. When he finished the story, he said, "We are supposed to tag up with a riverine squadron. They will move us around and help us patrol the area. Our intelligence has it that Hoppy is headed north right now."

"The riverine squadron is to the west about two hundred yards," Crystal pointed downriver to a small dock berthing a variety of small boats next to a sandbagged camp area. He continued, "They're a crack outfit. The trail along the river is safe, as long as a Vietnamese is walking about ten feet in front of you."

"I'd better get down there. Thanks for the bunkers. Saved us a lot of work."

"No problem." He rubbed his hands as if he were ready for another beer. "That's what I'm here for, to help out."

When Beckwith reached Kraus's position, Hillerman sighed in relief.

The Captain veered towards his woman waiting at the door, her outstretched right arm resting on the jamb, her left hand cupped around her hip.

Beckwith moved to the bunker right off the side of the road across from the cement tower. He looked inside to see that it was dry. Satisfied, he removed his pack and set it atop the sandbags, then had Kraus call together the squad leaders.

Stove Pipe strutted over to Beckwith's position first. He said, "I'm on my way, Sir."

"Where are you going, Stove Pipe?"

"I'm to report to an eight-inch battery in Ben Luc, down the road a ways."

"Nice having you," Beckwith said as he stood up. "Come back anytime."

Stove Pipe chuckled, "I might be back sooner than you expect. Can't tell in this crazy war, but good luck."

"Same to you."

As Stove Pipe hefted his radio and started walking, a jeep approached from the village and picked him up, turned around and took off back down the road.

When the squad leaders were all together, Marlin introduced them to the new platoon sergeant and got down to business, "Rodriguez, you and Gatz take the two bunkers at the far end of the bridge. There is one on each side of the road. You can't miss them. I don't

104

care who takes which. Once you get settled in, I want you to take turns checking out the vehicles and wagons coming across. Look for Hoppy as well as any weapons under all that straw and rice and keep each other covered . . . Sergeant Hillerman, I want you to stay across the bridge with them as well."

"Ivy, you take back your third squad again. You and Hyde take the bunker across the road from me." He pointed to the left of the tower. "It will be kind of tight in there, but I want somebody on watch at all times. The only reason you should be in the bunker anyway is to sleep or to take cover during a mortar attack . . . This bunker right here," he pointed at where he was sitting, "will be headquarters . . . Get going . . . I want all the weapons broken down and cleaned, the bunkers reinforced."

As the men started to turn, Beckwith said, "Sergeant Hillerman, I want to talk to you for a moment."

Beckwith indicated for the Sergeant to sit down beside him on the sandbags. As the Sergeant nervously complied with the order, Marlin said, "Sorry about the shaky start there, Sarge, but I've had a lot on my mind lately."

"That's all right, Lieutenant. I'm sure in a short while I'll understand."

"Yes," he agreed solemnly. "Where are you from, Sarge?"

"Huntsville, Alabama."

"How long you been in the Army?" Beckwith withdrew a pack of smokes and gave one to the Sergeant. As he lit them, Sergeant Hillerman replied, "Eight months now."

Beckwith said, "The platoon sergeant you replaced had six years in service . . ."

"I know, Sir. I'm a 90-day wonder." But he said it proudly.

Beckwith knew it was a school for bright soldiers who wanted to become leaders fast. The Army was hurting for platoon sergeants, about as much as for platoon leaders, and had a special school at Ft. Benning to push them through.

"As long as you know where I am coming from, Sarge . . . You got your work cut out for you. I'll be up front most of the time when we move and you will pull up the rear. Sometimes I will have to split the platoon. At that time you will be in charge of the other half. If anything happens, to me, you are in charge of the whole circus . . . Kraus, my radio operator," Beckwith looked at Kraus who had taken the radio off and was dialing it atop the bunker. Kraus nodded his head at the Sarge. Beckwith continued, "He knows the frequencies for all the helicopters and artillery and medevacs in the area. They are on the back of his radio. If anything happens to you, Ivy is in charge, but by that time I guess you won't be worrying about it . . ."

Sarge chuckled, nervously.

"What did you think of the Old Man?"

"He seemed very professional."

"He didn't even tell me you were coming. I guess that is the way he is." Marlin turned to Kraus, "Call up the Old Man and tell him three-five arrived."

Kraus nodded his head.

Beckwith continued, "I'm going to break you in fast, Sarge. I want you to make contact with the Riverine Squadron and cruise the river with them. You can take the interpreter Thuy along, as well as the third squad . . . Give you a chance to check out the countryside during the day. As you will find out soon enough, most of the fighting takes place at night."

As Hillerman nodded his head enthusiastically, Beckwith said, "Now go move in with the men and keep your ears open."

As the Sarge stood up and forced himself not to salute, he turned and marched across the bridge. Marlin just shook his head.

Two Vietnamese boys approached the Lieutenant's position tentatively. They were carrying a metal tub and slung it down at their feet. It was full of ice and bottled soda. One of the boys asked, "GI numba one. You buy a coke?" They both smiled.

Marlin recognized them as Lisa's brothers and smiled. He was definitely thirsty and the thought of a coke instead of the lukewarm canteen water was appealing. "You don't have any glass laced into those sodas do you?"

The older boy replied, "GI numba one. Coke, numba one." His disarming smile was contagious.

"Sure," Marlin replied.

The boy quickly picked up a bottle, opened it, and handed it to the Lieutenant. It was ice cold. He guzzled half of it down and set it alongside a can of cheese and crackers. Beckwith dug into his pocket and handed the boy some piasters.

Kraus, Thuy and Doc were quick to follow the Lieutenant's example.

The kids made their rounds and returned to bunker with an empty pot of melting ice. The tall boy stood there and watched.

"Why aren't you in school?" Beckwith asked, but it sounded more like a command.

The boys giggled. The taller boy replied, "We don't go to school. Too many VC."

Beckwith looked at him and said, "What's your name?"

"Mark."

The name made him smile. "Is that your Vietnamese name?"

"Yes. It is my name."

"Mark, can you read?"

"Nooooo."

"I can see you can count all right. You did give me my change, didn't you?"

"GI numba one." He dug into his pocket and pulled out some change as his brother drew closer to help him arrange the coins in a line of value.

"What do you want to do when you grow up?" Beckwith asked Mark.

Mark shrugged his shoulders and dropped the change into Marlin's outstretched hand and said, "Fight VC."

The kids laughed and pushed each other.

"GI have C-rations?" the younger boy asked. He stepped forward, right hand out, left arm still in the position of attention. His crooked teeth pointed every which way. He was barefoot, bowlegged, wearing briefs and a short-sleeved shirt without buttons. It looked like a pot had been placed over his head the last time he had gotten a haircut.

Beckwith picked out the can of fruit, set it aside and tossed him another can without looking at the label.

Beckwith said, "Hey."

When Mark looked at him, Marlin flipped him a can of cheese and crackers.

"GI numba one," Mark said.

Beckwith asked, "Do you know anything about an American who was captured here a while ago by the North Vietnamese? Blond hair, heavy-set, a little shorter than I am."

The boys stopped playing and withdrew from him in fright. There was one last clamping onto the can of C-rations by the younger boy, but recess was over. The chattering grew in pitch as they scooped up their belongings and fled down the road in an effort to overtake each other.

108

It was not until they were far away that they began to chatter and push each other and become playful again.

Watching them flee, Beckwith said, "You'd think I had just signed their death warrant."

"If they talked, maybe you would," Thuy replied.

Kraus added, "The little sons of bitches are probably VC anyway. Go tell the neighbors how many men are in the platoon and what kind of weapons we have."

"Let's get started," Beckwith said. Both comments were depressing.

Captain Crystal walked out of the tower with a cold beer in his hand and approached Beckwith. When Marlin looked at him as if he were interested in what the Captain might have to say, the Green Beret said, "I think I might have some information about your POW that would be of interest to you, Beckwith. Why don't you come along to my office."

Beckwith nodded to the Captain and then turned his eyes to the pretty little Vietnamese girl who stepped into view from behind the Captain. She did not look like she belonged in a war, but as a centerfold for a girlie magazine. She flashed her white teeth in a smile and moved her hip in a wide circle.

"Sure. I'll be right along," Marlin replied.

As Marlin stood up, he smiled to himself. How some soldiers always got the good assignments, even in Nam, while others ate shit for their entire tour. Like Hoppy, the poor son of a bitch. Marlin wondered what was going on with him right now. He wondered if he were still alive, was talking his head off, or quiet.

He promised himself if he ever . . . ever got back on Hoppy's trail again, no matter what the Old Man had to say, he would stay on the trail until he either recaptured Hoppy or died trying. It was that simple.

Chapter 10

One of Hoppy's constant companions, a guard by the name of Hoang Tran, who spoke English with a French accent, spat out a mouthful of rice in Hoppy's direction. The man laughed and spoke loudly to his companions who were stretched out on cots with different parts of their bodies covered with blood-soaked bandages. It was an underground hospital with half a dozen occupied cots lining each wall.

Hoppy did not like to make eye contact with the NVA soldiers as he could feel so much hate emanating from them. He knew that each wounded man in the tunnel blamed Hoppy for his misery and would enjoy taking vengeance out on Hoppy at any moment.

The cave was so narrow that Hoppy could not sit up straight and his neck was crunched forward. He could not pick up the rice with his hands tied behind his back; he was literally starving to death. His stomach felt like it was tied in knots and it was growling constantly. He looked down at the scattered kernels lying in the damp soil, then at Hoang Tran who pointed to the rice with an outstretched hand holding a pair of chopsticks. "Eat," he commanded.

Already Hoppy was learning to follow Hoang Tran's orders. Although the thought of mouthing what the Vietnamese had just spit out was revulsive,

Hoppy thought of the moisture in the kernels of rice and it made his mouth drop open.

Hoppy decided to go for it. He bent forward.

When his chin reached the ground, his nose sniffed at the rice and reacted to the acidic smell of piss and stale blood in the mud. He gagged and lifted his eyes almost reflexively, looked at the scowling face of Hoang and started to breathe through his mouth to avoid the smell. His tongue licked out to delicately lift the rice from the contaminated dirt, but before it reached the first large lump of rice, he felt a hand press at the back of his hair and shove his head into the ground. He tried to close his mouth, but his jaws bit into the contaminated soil. He moved his tongue to the back of his throat so that he would not have to eat the dirt, but now the clay was shoving the tongue even farther back and choking him. He could feel the clay squeeze between his teeth and seep to the palate, taste the tainted saliva trickle down his throat. Since his nose was buried in the mud as well, he could not breathe. He squeezed his eyes closed and tried to free his head, but he was in such a cramped position there was no power in his movements. All he could do was wiggle his shoulders and moan.

As soon as the hand released the back of his head, he came up spitting, panting, and retching. When he opened his eyes, he saw Hoang Tran reaching out towards him with a knife in his hand. Hoang looked diabolic, his eyes sparkling with hate and his lips curled in a grotesque manner. Hoppy tried to move his convulsing head backwards but the knife was faster and it came at his face and penetrated his right cheek. Hoppy could feel the cold steel clink against his opposite jaw. The pain shot through his skull and made him see stars. He drew his head farther back and the knife slipped out of his flesh, leaving a hole from which blood began to stream. He bent forward, mouth open, and used his tongue to stop the flowing blood from choking him. Red spots streamed onto the floor.

Hoppy looked up at Hoang Tran and saw him laughing. The tiny soldier called out in Vietnamese for everyone to look. Faces on the cots smiled as Hoang Tran spoke in Vietnamese and stared at Hoppy, pointing his knife and waving it.

All of Hoppy's hate was directed at Hoang Tran, a wiry dink with sunken cheeks and pointed chin, hair always groomed no matter what. His piercing black eyes were the most dreadful part of him, always forewarning of hateful gestures to come.

Hoang Tran pointed to his wounded companions on the cots and said. "If you think these men are hurt, wait until you get to North Vietnam. You will wish you had died back there at the canal."

Hoppy's mouth was in a world of pain, more than his cramped legs and back had ever been. There was nothing in his entire existence on this earth to prepare him for this experience.

He remembered from basic camp that if captured, according the the Geneva Convention, he was to state only his name, rank, service number and date of birth. They hadn't even asked him yet. They had been treating him like a disobedient dog, beating him at their pleasure.

Hoppy bent his head forward and pressed his tongue against his cheek as the blood flowed onto his pants. He moved his head to one side so that the blood would hit the ground, but soon it puddled up and flowed in a small stream towards him. He tried to move away, but Hoang Tran saw the movement and lifted the knife threateningly and wrinkled his brow.

Hoppy caught his breath and stayed still. Up until now, the tunnels had been the most cramped and putrid experience in his life. Now the pain in his mouth was worse.

In his effort to get away from Hoang Tran, Hoppy had wiggled closer to one of the cots. The bedridden Vietnamese, whom Hoppy thought was too weak to move, sat up on one elbow and punched out at Hoppy's face. It was not a hard blow, but compounded with the bleeding cheek that pulsed out his lifeblood with each heartbeat, it felt like the force of a sledge hammer.

Hoppy fell over on his right side and lay there a moment, out of the reach of everyone. He looked down at his knees, at the blood caked in mud from so much crawling. It felt like he could not stretch them out if his life depended upon it.

He had no idea that his platoon had nearly caught up to him. He had heard the shots in the tunnel, but they sounded so distant and muffled he thought they were just the popping of a fire. He had also heard the slight rumble of the artillery, but it did not even set loose dirt from the roof of the caves.

He thought of the first time he had been shoved down the tunnel. He had to admit it was the most terrorizing moment. If he had been the first one to go down, he would have put up more of a fight as he would have felt they were burying him alive. To make it worse, once he got inside, they tied his wrists to his knees and when he moved he had to drag his knees in short crawls. It caused a chafing at the wrist and knee that added to the misery of every movement.

He looked around with one eye at the underground hospital lighted by bedside candles atop pop cans. The Vietnamese could waddle around like

113

ducks, but he had to crawl. He felt only hatred for them all.

Hoppy wished he had been shot like Buffalo Bill. All of this would have been over by now. He thought back to the canal and he saw once again all those NVA standing in the treeline with their rifles on him. Without thinking he had dropped his rifle. It had been a reflex, a costly one; one that he would regret for the rest of his life, however long that would be.

The thought of home was the one thing that relaxed him. He remembered how the Lieutenant used to tell him not to think of such things because it would make him sleepy and relaxed, now Hoppy hoped the Lieutenant was right. Maybe he would awake and it would all be over. Maybe it was a dream. He did not have a girlfriend to think about. He thought of his father and felt almost ashamed of his fear. His father had been so proud of him the first time Hoppy had come home in uniform. When he thought of his mother his mouth began to drool for her cooking. Hoppy had an insatiable craving for cherry cobbler pie and his mother had a recipe that made the cherries just dance around in his mouth.

Thoughts of home, of the past came so pleasantly that they relieved the pain for the duration of his concentration; but there were always the North Vietnamese soldiers to bring him back to reality with their savagery.

The Vietnamese girl stood naked before the ARVN soldier. She hung her head against her chest and trembled, but not from the cold. She was still a virgin and did not want to be molested, nor did she want to be tortured to death. The thought of her experiencing both within a very short time made her almost hysterical.

The guard was not much taller than she, but his arms rested away from his sides. His stocky chest heaved with each breath as he inspected her. She could tell that it was only a matter of a command that separated him from his lust.

The room was dark but for a small cork-sized hole in the wall that shed a spot of daylight. The room had one chair and a drain in the floor. There was an array of tools on one wall — a whip, a towel, several small truncheons and a pair of wire cutters and some rags. In one corner there was a three-foot-tall pot, often used by the villagers to catch rain water. A pulley hung from the ceiling. The girl surmised that all of these things were used to twist her flesh, crack her bones and tear at her nerves.

The air smelled like puke and filth.

Barefoot, she could feel her toes cooled by her own urine. Terror so overwhelmed her that she couldn't control her bowels. A steady dribble ran down her leg.

The guard smiled.

She was a VC all right, just like her parents had been fighting the French. There was no chance of her going to the other side because there was no other side, only the Americans, and she had seen what horror they had reigned on her country and the thought of life with them after the war made her wish death itself.

Her arms were tied behind her, duck-wing style, and her wrists bound together. As long as the guard kept his distance, she would not move. If he tried to attack her, she could always kick him between the legs. That was her plan.

The steel door to the cell opened letting in a flash of light. She shied from the glare and pulled her

115

right shoulder closer to her face. An overhead bulb lighted the room.

Her shoulders hunched forward and her eyes looked to see who had entered — two men. One was much taller, and American officer. The Major was well-groomed, wearing a starched uniform with no weapon, carrying only a brief case. There was an urgent look on his face as he inspected her with scrutiny, almost like a physician would a patient before an operation.

The other man was a Vietnamese captain. He was smoking a cigarette in a black filter. He had a small grease line moustache, his black hair pressed against his scalp.

There were two soldiers behind the American, wearing MP helmets. They were about twice as big as the Captain and a bit shorter than the tall American; they both had pistols in their holsters.

Men's eyes had never seen her naked before and now five pairs stared at her. She looked down at her tiny breasts and her soft, small patch of pubic hair and then back at them. The two MPs and the Vietnamese guard were still looking at her body.

The Major and Captain were locked in conversation, in English, a language she did not understand.

The American seemed concerned and polite, but defiant, his eyes penetrating. The Captain seemed to be dodging questions, on the defensive, and when at all possible, groveling to the American.

Finally the Captain turned to her and in Vietnamese asked, "What is your name?"

The question stunned her. The staring eyes, total concentration. She felt overwhelmed and averted her glare.

The American shook his head in disappointment and sighed loudly. The Captain started to move his

116

hands in circles and speak in an apologetic tone.

The Major sighed, turned, and walked out the door. The two MPs finally took their eyes off her and followed.

The steel door slammed on its squeaking hinges.

The Vietnamese Captain's disposition turned 180 degrees. He looked at her with contempt, revulsion, disappointment, disdain. He popped the cigarette out of the filter, dropped it on the floor and ground it into the cement, his hands shaking.

Without taking his eyes off her, he spoke to her in Vietnamese, "Young lady, I am not going to go through the regular procedure of offering you rice and tea for your knowledge and proceed to become more physical the more you hold back ... My American friends are very interested in what you might know and I most anxious to show them how competent I am. There are two questions that I want you to answer for me. Where are they bringing this American soldier that was captured and what is the specific mission of the NVA in the Long An province? If you cooperate and answer my questions, I will let you become a part of the Chieu Hoi program and be repatriated in another district. For all that your villagers will think, you were killed and no harm will be done your family. The more you do not cooperate, the more harm will befall you first, then your family. It is that simple. I want the answers.

"We will start out with the location of this Earl Moss. Where is he being taken? Tell me."

The girl hung her head in refusal. Her body began to convulse with weeping.

"Vong," the Captain said to the guard.

She had decided to kick him between the legs if the drew closer, but her crying further weakened her body and when he moved quickly towards her all she could do was retain her balance.

The first punch to her womb sent a sharp pain through her body as if her insides were tumbled and stretched. She flew back against the wall, her hands striking the cement, then her head. Her shoulders and neck throbbed with pain as she slid to the floor.

Vong came at her with lightning speed and kicked her in the same spot. There was no room to absorb the shock and the foot sunk deeply.

When Vong withdrew, the Captain asked again, "Where are they bringing the prisoner?"

As she panted in silence, she watched the Captain. He was becoming frustrated quickly and his anger was growing. He pointed to the water canister and shouted at Vong.

Vong straddled her legs, lifted both her feet and bound them tightly together with a stretch of wire. The pain nearly made her pass out.

Vong dropped her legs and took the hook from the pulley hanging from the ceiling, placed it between her ankles and hoisted her off the ground.

This time she did pass out.

When she awoke, she was dangling from the rope upside down. It felt like her legs had been cut off at the ankle and she looked to see her feet already twice the size as they normally were. Rags protruded from her nose and made her gag for air through the mouth.

She turned her head to see the Captain sitting in a chair reading a book by a small light on a stand that had not been there before. When she caught his stare, he beamed one of the most sinister smiles she had ever seen. He stood up, placed the book on the chair and moved towards her.

His crotch stopped at eye level. If he drew any closer she would bite him.

118

"What is your name, young lady?" he asked in Vietnamese.

She shook her head defiantly.

Vong grabbed her by the hair from behind and began to pour water from a small pitcher onto the rags sticking from her nose. She started swallowing quickly, a drop at a time.

He asked again.

She took advantage of the silence to gasp.

More water was applied to the rags.

At first she thought that she could keep up with the water, but after hours of questioning, the blood rushing to her head, her body in pain, more punches to her body, across the face, more water, she could swallow no more and the water began to seep into her lungs and choke her.

Her body began to twitch and flip around on the end of the rope out of control. She could not breathe. Her heart felt like a sledge hammer striking an anvil with each beat, louder and louder and louder until it struck with such force that she could feel her body exploding with pain — but only for a second. She could feel herself becoming detached from her body and knew that she was dying; but it was just as well, the pain was going away. She was dying a martyr, and it made it easier.

When the Captain saw that she was dead, he looked at Vong with disgust and turned and walked into the other room where there was a radio on a table next to where another guard sat. The guard stood up and the Captain sat down. He cranked the dial and finally got ahold of the American Major. He wiped his brow with a handkerchief.

He spoke in English, "Yes, Major. The girl finally

talked."

After a pause, he continued, "Yes. Yes. Private Hoppy is being transported to Hanoi for propaganda purposes . . . Yes . . . Yes . . ." The Captain looked at the guard watching him and with the back of his hand brushed him away. The Captain had been with the war now for eight years and knew all the answers. "They will be taking the prisoner to Saigon first and from there to Cambodia on the Ho Chi Minh trail . . . She says that the North Vietnamese soldiers are in her province to recruit more troops to join them in the attack on Saigon . . . No dates yet . . . Her name? Her name is Tri Von Dong. I think she was ashamed to talk in front of you. I knew she would talk for me. We are going to repatriate her in the Chieu Hoi Program. She will do just fine. Thank you, Major. Thank you. If you need my assistance again, just call me."

When he hung up the phone, he sighed with relief. It was easy to satisfy the Americans. That would be the end of her. If need be, he could always find another woman to question if the Americans demanded to see her again. It was that simple.

Chapter 11

About two hundred yards down the road on the left-hand side, on the outskirts of Ben Luc where the houses started to touch each other, was a two-storey building with a French-looking facade. The wooden deck out front had curved, arched moldings between four posts; and on the second storey porch, with similar scrolled molding, was a wrought-iron rail from which hung a white sign in black letters— LAUNDROMAT.

They did laundry, all right. They hosed 'em down.

Captain Crystal's office was a whorehouse.

Beckwith figured it out when he listened to the wooden planks squeak under his footsteps and looked inside through the opened shuttered window and saw four Vietnamese girls sitting at a table alongside a bar. From the way the girls dressed, it was obvious their clothes had not been hand-sewn by their grandmothers, but more like imported from Paris, as was their perfume. The girls were smoking, drinking coffee, doing their nails or preening themselves in sensuous manners.

Beckwith followed the Captain and his woman across the wooden deck, with Kraus and Gatz following close behind and craning their necks in all directions at the feisty girls. Gatz found comfort in touching his Bible beneath his shirt. He saw this as a war zone against sin and followed his platoon leader proudly.

Kraus was walking half an inch taller. It was the first time in weeks he left the radio behind with the rest of the platoon, at the command bunker with Hyde, and it felt good. Hillerman was gone on his patrol and it was time to relax, and in a whorehouse to boot.

Inside, the establishment was definitely in the stage of catching its breath. There were a couple of GIs sitting at square tables and bending very close to their female Vietnamese partners, talking quietly, intimately, and in all probability, not about the laundry.

Two ARVN soldiers with glasses of beer in front of them sat at a table nearby watching the Americans. They seemed stiff and uptight, somewhat fascinated and proud at what they were watching.

The amazing thing about everyone was that they were so damn clean.

Marlin had to squint to see as it was so dark compared to outside. The bar itself ran the entire length of the left wall in a horseshoe shape with patches from the different American and Vietnamese units pinned to the wall above the display of liquors. Another bold sign above the bar read, VC HUNTING CLUB. In smaller letters, *members only.*

A rainbow-colored juke box in the far corner was playing "Hey Jude"; beside it was an idle pinball machine, twinkling in a way like the women nearby, ready to be played.

The four girls smiled at the Captain and his girlfriend, eyed the Lieutenant and his men. The girls were pretty in their individual ways; but like most Vietnamese women, flat-chested, short, and broad in the shoulders.

As soon as Beckwith and his party sat down, one of the girls stood up and moved over to the table, her high heels clicking on the wooden floor almost theatrically. She was not bad-looking, a bit too made up and her face too round, but with very nice legs and a dress that revealed the top of her breasts. She stopped next to Kraus, set her hand on his shoulder, and when he looked at her, she asked, "You souvenir me tea?" She batted her eyelashes like a woman would in a 1930 movie and smiled, hopefully.

In spite of the growing pineapple in his pants, Kraus felt embarrassed in front of his friends. He gulped and looked at the Lieutenant, "Sir?"

Marlin chuckled at the sight of Kraus so flustered.

The Captain laughed, "This is where I found my Honey. They have nothing but the best here. Including the food. Relax and I'll buy you breakfast."

Kraus was still looking at the Lieutenant who gave him the thumbs up sign. Kraus acted shocked, glanced back at the girl and said, "Not right now, but thanks."

She looked at Gatz who seemed to be fuming under the collar. The Lieutenant just nodded his head. She said, "Cheap Charlies," and whipped around back towards her friends.

"What is there to eat here?" Kraus asked.

For the first time the Captain's girl spoke, "Anything you wan', GI."

Kraus looked around nervously. "I . . . I guess I'll have myself a steak and onions and mushrooms."

Beckwith asked, "What does Uncle Sam think of

this place?"

The Captain replied proudly, "The Military Police send a doctor over here once a week and have the girls checked out for any jungle rot."

"They don't close down the place?" the Lieutenant answered with genuine surprise.

"Sure. Sometimes. If the men get too drunk or carry their fighting into the streets, the MPs come here and nail the doors shut; but in my two years here, I've never . . . never seen it closed down for more than a week. The GIs start screaming about dirty clothes and pretty soon the boards are pulled off and the place is bulging at the seams with stinkin' fatigues. It is the waiting to get them clean that gets the GIs into trouble . . . You ought to see this place around sunset—hopping. No band, but the juke box blares away . . . Here, Honey." He balanced on the two back legs of his chair, dug deep into his pocket and handed his girlfriend a fist of money, "Go play a couple of songs."

She stood up, turned and started strutting her stuff and watching over her shoulder to make certain that everyone was watching.

"They got showers and a steam room out back too, but upstairs . . ." He pointed his thumb over his shoulder at some green doors across a landing, "That's where all the inbalance in trade is snowballing."

American posters of the Beatles, racing cars, girls in jungle fatigues, and cartoons decorated the wall to the second floor.

One of the doors on the top floor swung open and out staggered a GI rolling up his sleeves and stretching tall like a bugling elk. The girl behind him seemed as sober as a revolutionary.

The shuttered windows overlooking the street

were open and Beckwith asked, "Aren't you worried about someone throwing a grenade inside?"

"My Honey says the mamasan here pays off the VC to stay away, and from what I understand, it is a walletful each week, but it works. Never bomb once. Even the Military Police can't provide that kind of protection. A man can drink himself unconscious here at night and not have to worry about waking up in the morning in any other place than right where he passes out."

It sounded like a voice of experience, and it was spoken proudly.

"Louie, Louie" blared over the juke box. The volume was turned up as the record played.

"They love this one," the Captain smiled. "I got this record for them myself when I was in Hawaii."

Beckwith shrugged "OK. Enough about this place. Now what did you have to tell me about Hoppy?"

"Let's order breakfast first, OK? I'm starving."

Since the Captain would have it no other way, a waitress was summoned. From the sweet smell of her perfume and the way she dressed, she was holding down more than one job. The Captain ordered ham and eggs, over easy. The third platoon would have nothing to do with eggs. They ordered the same as Kraus—steak, mushrooms and onions.

When the waitress left, Beckwith asked, "What's this information you have for me?"

"Right," the Captain said as he leaned forward. "I have a source of information. That is the information. I'll introduce her to you." He sat back comfortably in his chair, "Let's find out." He looked over to where the group of girls were sitting and saw that his girlfriend had joined them. He shouted, "Honey."

125

She turned around to look.

"Get Mamasan."

When she scowled, he said, "Chop. Chop." He smacked the back of his hand into his open palm.

She twirled her hair over her shoulder, turned, and walked through a swinging door and soon returned with an older woman right on her heels.

Mamasan wore an embroidered, silk gossamer gown over light pants. She was older, just out of the reach of most GIs' fantasies, which made her job that much easier.

As the Captain bid her forward with a waving arm and introduced her to each man, she smiled and bobbed her head ever so slightly.

The Captain got right to the point, "Mamasan, the Lieutenant here had one of his men captured by the VC. You heard of any prisoner taken in this area?"

She looked confident, calm and bowed her head at Beckwith. She was not pretty, but seemed to have something the others were lacking—wisdom, common sense, a bit of diplomacy—whatever it was, it was mature and not mixed with betel nut.

"What does this American look like?" she asked.

When Beckwith described Hoppy briefly, she inquired, very businesslike, "How much is it worth to you, Lieutenant?"

"Worth?" he asked. The question caught him by surprise, but he kept his cool. She was a professional.

The Captain broke into the conversation. "You can discuss that with me later, Mamasan. Just give the details to the Lieutenant."

Mamasan said, "I have heard of no American prisoner captured in this area, and I have seen none. I will inquire and there is the possibility that

126

something could be arranged, if it is at all possible to find this man. It is a very large, confused country now with many separate engagements occurring everywhere."

The front swinging doors flung open and all heads turned to see four American troopers coming inside.

The Captain smirked and spoke out of the side of his mouth, "Here comes the artillery."

Kraus said, "Son of a bitch."

"What do you have against those guys?" the Captain asked, almost disbelieving. "They've probably pulled you out of more than one bind since you've been here."

The Lieutenant smiled, "Just like brothers fighting, that's all."

"The lazy shits are always complaining about the weather or the work," Kraus said, "but they get three hot meals a day and sleep in a dry bed every night. No wonder they're so fuckin' fat."

The Lieutenant was well aware of the rivalry between the two fighting elements. Whenever his platoon got around the artillery, they did not just win money in a card game, they beat the artillery. They did not win an arm wrestling contest, they blasted the bastards. In reality, it was probably a draw; but mix the two elements and it was like making home brew — you could never forecast the results, but you knew it was going to be strong.

The four artillerymen walked past the table and eyed them and their weapons smugly. The tallest of them said, "The only gun you need in here is tucked behind your zipper, unless ya gotta squat."

His friends laughed in such a way that made the juices brew in Kraus.

"What's the tall one's name?" Gatz asked the

Captain.

"I think his name is Arnie."

"Asshole."

If it had not been for the food, Gatz would have left right then.

The Captain said, "They're a bunch of good guys. They pack this place sometimes. No lie."

Breakfast was served and it was as good-looking as a Raquel Welch poster. No twists of sliced orange or parsley, but cooked red meat.

The Captain got wound up drinking his beer and the war stories started flowing.

The good food caught Beckwith and his men by surprise and in spite of their morning rations of Cs, they chowed down wolfishly. Gatz was the first to clean his plate.

The artillerymen were already on their second round of draft and getting loose. Arnie slung his head towards Marlin's table and asked his friends, "I wonder if these guys are the ones that we supported all night long."

"They look too clean to me," the other man replied.

Walking down the stairs was a laundry girl with her face buried in an armful of white, balled-up bedsheets. She was in shower clogs and held her arms with the balloon of sheets out to one side to see where she was going.

Marlin looked at her and recognized her as Lisa. He formed her name on his lips without saying anything.

Kraus had his mouth full of steak and nodded his head towards her as if he recognized her as well.

The Captain said, "That's Lisa, the laundry girl, as cold-hearted as a Viet Cong. She won't go down for anyone, no matter how much they offer her."

Lisa walked right past the table of the artillery-men and disappeared into the laundry room.

When another beer was served the Captain, he said to the waitress, "Put the breakfasts on my tab . . ." He looked at Beckwith, "How about that, a tab?"

The back door swung open and back came Lisa with a stack of folded sheets. She headed back up the stairs.

As she passed the beer-guzzling artillerymen, Arnie leaned back in his chair and reached out towards her. He had his timing down perfectly so that she was trapped by his touch. She put her back to the wall and hid behind the sheets.

He released her arm and thrust his hand between her legs to grab the inside of her thigh. At that, Lisa threw the sheets at him and retreated out of his reach. Her eyes refused to blink as she gasped in horror at the now soiled sheets, one of them having knocked over a glass of beer and soaking up the suds.

Arnie laughed uproariously and eyed the infantry-men's table wickedly.

"Leave her alone," one of his friends said.

"I'm just having a little fun with the whore," Arnie replied.

Mamasan came through the swinging doors and saw the sheets on the floor and began to scream at Lisa in Vietnamese. Lisa went to her knees and reached for the sheets with her right arm trying to stay out of Arnie's reach.

Arnie was chugging his beer.

Lisa pulled in a few sheets without the man trying anything. Then as she reached for the last two sheets on the table, mamasan turned and walked away. At that, Arnie thrust his right hand out and locked his grip around her wrist. He laughed and slowly started to pull her closer.

Beckwith could feel his blood starting to boil.

The Captain looked at the empty plates and said, "Let's get the hell out of here."

As Arnie started drawing his left hand over Lisa's thighs and explaining how they felt to the entire bar, Lisa kicked and fought with her clenched fists, but it only made Arnie laugh louder.

Beckwith turned to Gatz and said, "I think that is about enough, Gatz. Close down the place."

Gatz was reliably efficient. He was so anxious to get to the other table that he knocked over his own chair as he stood up.

Gatz was about the size of Arnie, but madder. He weighed in at 240 pounds. If he could have eaten more he would have pushed 300, but there is just so much weight that a man can put on from eating C-rations every day. He set the Bible on the table next to his. The junk box started a new song, "Soldier Boy." It was Gatz's favorite.

Gatz rumbled forward like a mechanized twin forty tank, lifted up the artillerymen's table by one leg and flung it against the back wall. Glasses, plates, and wood shattered.

The three men at the table fell over in their chairs as they tried to clear the mess, but Arnie had pushed himself back and wisely set Lisa to one side. She stood as stiff as a board, her brown eyes glaring.

As soon as Arnie's hands were free, he took a swing at Gatz. The fist sunk into the side of Gatz's jaw, and pushed his neck around.

That made Gatz smile.

Nobody in the room was bigger than Gatz; Rodriguez and White in full uniform drew closer to his weight. Gatz had a Christian heart but a gladiator's mind. He loved to destroy and prayed to God that he was doing right.

He picked up Arnie by the shirt collar in his left hand, cocked his right arm back like a train piston and shot it forward into the hard spot on Arnie's face where his sunglasses usually rested.

From that day forward, Arnie's sunglasses would rest on the bridge of his nose cocked to the right. The fight that ensued would have made any soldier proud, but was all too short for Gatz.

Arnie got in two good blows, one to the rib cage and another to the face, but they only added to the mess in the whorehouse.

By the time "Soldier Boy" finished, the juke box was the only thing in the room that was not broken. When the record slipped back into its sleeve, Gatz polished off Arnie with two consecutive left jabs to the chest and a right to the jaw that sent the artilleryman crashing into the bar and slumping to the floor. The fight was over.

Gatz returned for his Bible being held by the disbelieving Kraus and walked out the front door grinning. There he found the Lieutenant and Captain face to face.

The Captain said, "I'm gonna kick your ass out of those bunkers."

Beckwith replied, "You're gonna have to shoot us out because we aren't moving." They drew closer and in spite of their rank were about to tangle if it were not for Gonzales.

Gonzalez came jumping up onto the wooden porch, panting and pointing back to the bridge, "Lieutenant," he said, "Lieutenant. The new platoon sergeant has run into some fire . . . It sounds like he got himself into a big one."

Beckwith and the Captain stopped shouting at each other and listened. They heard the distant sound of a grenade exploding. Beckwith and his men started running back towards the bridge.

Chapter 12

When Beckwith reached his bunker at the bridge where he had left his radio, he swung inside, and saw the startled Hyde sitting there on the cot with the receiver to his mouth. Marlin grabbed the radio and said, "Three-five. Three-five. This is three-six, over."

Waiting for an answer, he bent over and looked through the firing port downriver hoping to spot some signs of Hillerman's fighting.

The sound of static came over the radio, followed by the voice of the Platoon Sergeant. "This is three-five. We are under attack . . ." His voice rattled with fear. The sound of firing could be heard in the background.

Beckwith envisioned the patrol being overrun by VC.

Beckwith asked, "Where are you?"

"About a mile or two downriver."

"Fuck," Beckwith stammered. He pressed the send button. "Is that as close to your exact location as you can tell me?"

"I . . . I . . . think so."

Every time the Platoon Sergeant transmitted, the sound of firing almost drowned out his voice.

"Well. How many of them are there?"

"I don't know for sure. I think there must be at least twenty, maybe more."

"Keep your ass down and I'll be there with some help." Marlin was about to run back out the bunker when he heard, "What do we do until then?"

Beckwith pulled the receiver closer to his mouth and said, "Don't stand up and play John Wayne, but shoot the bastards. Understand me? Shoot the fuckers. We'll be there in no time."

"Phew." Beckwith did not want to rattle the Platoon Sergeant any more than he already was, but the question just blurted out. "What the hell did you get off the boat for?"

"I saw some movement and went after it . . . I think they are charging."

Beckwith dropped the radio and popped his head out of the bunker. He saw Gatz standing there and said, "Gatz, make contact with the Riverine Squadron and see if they can give us a lift back downriver to help out Hillerman."

Gatz took off on the run.

"Cox," Beckwith hollered to the squad leader who was sitting on the rail of the bridge with his rifle resting at his side, smoking a cigarette. Cox stood up, picked up the rifle and trotted towards the Lieutenant.

Beckwith said, "You and your squad stay behind to keep an eye on the gooks crossing the bridge. I doubt if Hillerman's skirmish is some type of distraction to blow up the bridge, but since that is our prime mission, you'll have to cover for us."

Cox nodded his head.

When the PBR landed on the muddy bank below the bridge, the reset of the platoon, numbering eight, moved down the trail towards the water's edge for the pickup.

The PBR was a duck hunter's dream for camouflage, with machine guns hanging from it like Christmas tree ornaments—thirty feet long, low draft, and heavily armored.

No sooner did the last man swing his feet onto the deck than the patrol boat roared its engines, swung back and around, and lurched forward, coming up on step as quick as a shot-at duck.

Gatz and his men were nearly all washed up against the transom by the mounting g's. As they recovered and got used to the speed, they instinctively started to check their weapons—wiping them off, squirting oil into the chamber, touching the grenades on their pouch, patting the LAWs, knowing that any defects in the equipment could create instant panic.

The boat was staying as close to the center of the river as possible, boiling the water under its bow.

Beckwith stood up and moved forward to the coxswain's den and stood alongside the tall fellow with a flak jacket over his bare chest. His hair was short and contrasted with the length of his face. Marlin asked, "What the hell happened to my men?"

The coxswain shrugged his shoulders. "We saw some movement along the river's edge and my men opened up with some reconnaissance fire. The sarge hollered to be dropped off." The coxswain shrugged his shoulders. "We don't give a shit. He could get off anywhere he wanted. We thought he was going all the way, but what the hell . . ."

"Yeah. This is his first patrol."

"Green . . . huh? Shit!" He rolled his head.

Beckwith got on the radio again and asked Hillerman to throw out some smoke.

Red smoke drifted above the tall grass lining the river about a mile away. The problem was that it came up in two spots, about a quarter of a mile apart. Beckwith called over the radio, "I see red smoke, but I see it coming from two locations. How many did you throw out?"

As Beckwith listened for a reply, the first sound over the radio was machine gun fire. Half a second later, the echo of the weapon could be heard faintly above the roar of the engine.

Hillerman replied, "That's me."

"Which one? . . . I said there are two smokes out there. WHICH ONE IS YOU?" Beckwith was shouting now.

"What do you mean, which one? I threw out only one . . . Well, I'll be a son of a bitch, red smoke is coming from the treeline right where those people ran into it."

"Try another color."

Beckwith waited and soon saw two green smokes arise above the elephant grass about the same time.

"Fuck it," he said to Kraus.

"They got you pegged," he said into the radio transmitter. "I'll come from the middle and for God's sake's don't shoot at me. Tell the rest of the patrol about us coming from your right. Don't shoot us."

Beckwith knew that once he got close enough to see and hear the sound of the firing and pinpoint the location, he would know his own men, but two identical smokes would be totally confusing to a gunship, and as far as the VC knew, that is what was coming after them.

Beyond the tall grass along the banks of the river in the distance could be seen the treetops of the jungle. A few tracer rounds ricocheted into the air.

Beckwith pointed to the river bank where he wanted to be dropped off. The coxswain did not slow down, just returned the bow in the direction of the pointed finger, raced up to the shoreline and at the last second, came off on the throttle. The PBR mushed into the water and as its backwash lifted the boat high on its wave towards the bank, the coxswain threw the boat in reverse and stopped it right on the money.

Beckwith held the map of the area in his left hand. He had circled in black crayon the grid where the Platoon Sergeant was located and written down the coordinates on the plastic cover. Even if he were hit, that was enough information for any of his men to call in artillery, medevac or gunships.

The Lieutenant was first ashore with Kraus right behind.

He was not sure yet exactly where the enemy was, but as soon as he could pinpoint their location, he would call up Ben Luc for some high explosives to saturate the area. He thought of Arnie on the floor of the bar back in the whorehouse and it made him smile. Arnie would love it if he knew they were out here so soon.

By the time the patrol was fifty yards into the head-tall grass, all firing had stopped. It was quiet but for the swishing of grass. The sweet smell of burnt powder filled the air. Beckwith could feel his clothes starting to exude moisture already. The sweat stung his eyes and blurred his vision. He hated the fucking tall grass. It was full of spiders and snakes and cut off all air from circulation, making it feel like a stale sauna.

Beckwith stopped, knelt down and got on the radio again. "Three-five, this is three-six."

When the Sarge answered, the Lieutenant replied, "I want you to try something new this time. When I tell you, I want you to fire three shots on

137

automatic. Then stop."

"What for?" came the tense, quiet reply.

"Just do it, Sergeant."

"Affirmative."

"Now."

As Beckwith listened for the rounds, he watched Kraus. When the bullets cackled, he pointed in the direction he thought it was coming from and Kraus shook his head.

Beckwith spoke into the hand receiver, "Gotcha. I think I know where you are now. We are coming closer."

The grass thinned out into a rice paddy. There lay the patrol stretched out along a rice berm about a hundred yards perpendicular to the jungle.

It didn't look like Hillerman was in much trouble. Beckwith saw the last man, Who Do, was on his back smoking a cigarette, and Kramm, a few men forward, was chowing down on a can of Cs.

But it was unfriendly territory all right. About a hundred feet from the treeline, raised tall on a bamboo pole and fluttering in the breeze, was a VC flag—a yellow star centered between rectangular patches of blue and red cloth.

When Beckwith waved, Hillerman came out of the prone position onto his knees. Beckwith signaled him to get back down and started to crawl closer along the side of a berm.

Marlin stopped by Who Do, who threw a cigarette butt into the paddy. They both watched it sizzle. Beckwith panting, Who Do looked like he was on the point of snoozing.

"Afternoon, Sir," Who Do said.

Gulping to hide his fatigue, Beckwith asked, "Any casualties?"

"They're fuckin with us. That's all."

"What is the body count?"

"Maybe some chickens. I don't know. I was pulling up the rear and really did not see anything. I fired a few rounds into the treeline like everybody else, but I didn't see anything."

"OK. Don't get too relaxed though."

Beckwith did not stop and talk to any of the other men. He crawled all the way to where Hillerman was lying and stopped. Hillerman was hyperventilating, sweat soaking his face, the muscles twitching. Beads of sweat dripped from the hair beneath his helmet.

"All right," Beckwith said, "You can relax now, Sarge. I'm in charge. What are you up against?" When Hillerman pointed at the flag, they both looked over the berm together at the treeline. It was so quiet you could hear a bird fart.

"We followed them through the tall grass and came upon them as they were headed into the jungle. I don't know. Maybe they circled around and are behind us."

"I think I would have seen them if they were back there. Six to one that flag is booby trapped . . . Let's get into the treeline first . . . Check around for ammo caches or whatever. The boat is back there waiting for us. We don't want to stay too long."

"Roger."

"I'll go up there first," Beckwith said. "You pull up the rear. Good work." He was not totally positive it had been handled all that well, but no one was hurt and that was an accomplishment in itself. The Sarge was drenching wet and looked like he could gulp a dozen Valiums just to feel normal.

When the platoon leader entered the treeline and stood up, he waited for the next man to come

139

forward. It was Jesus Perez. Marlin pointed for him to move through the foliage in the direction of the flag.

The Lieutenant knew that if any VC were around, they would be in the vicinity of the flag, which if booby trapped, he wanted to disarm and make it one less piece of explosives that the VC could use against him.

As they moved forward, even though the Platoon Sergeant was no more than a hundred feet back, Beckwith called him up on the radio. "Three-five, this is three-six." He could hear his own voice coming over the radio in the rear of the column.

"This is three-five. Go."

"First of all, turn down your radio."

Beckwith waited a moment and continued, "I'm going out and check that flag. I want you to cover me. Got it?"

"Roger."

Beckwith nodded to Kraus and signaled Perez to crawl forward.

They got to within thirty yards and stopped to look more carefully. Beckwith saw at its base a hole dug into the clay bank and covered with straw.

Beckwith asked, "See that cave, Kraus?"

"Yes, Sir."

"I'm going to throw a grenade to detonate whatever is inside it."

Beckwith removed his rucksack and laid the rifle on the berm, and as he calculated the distance to the flag, removed a grenade from a thigh pocket on his fatigues. He popped the pin, discarded it to one side, studied the distance to the flag again and threw the grenade, falling to the ground as he followed through.

When the grenade exploded, it was obvious from

140

the volume of the roar that it had not set off any other explosives.

The three men poked their heads up and looked at the cloud of smoke dissipating around a leaning flagpole.

When it was clear enough to see the hole again, the scene had changed—projecting from the cave was the butt end of a U.S. 105 artillery round.

"See that, Kraus?" Beckwith asked again.

"Sure as a dink in the wire, Sir."

"Let's all try it this time," Beckwith said.

Rodriguez was already to go, but Kraus had to take off the radio and set it to one side.

Tensed, they each held a grenade in their hands. Beckwith gave the command, "Pull the pin. Throw."

The three grenades crossed each other's flight paths on the way to the target, hit the ground, rolled and exploded, sending up a skyscraper of dirt and debris into the air, obviously having set off the artillery round.

When the air cleared, Kraus and Perez were smiling. "We got that sucker that time," Perez said.

Beckwith agreed by nodding his head.

The flag was nowhere to be seen.

They left their equipment in place, dragging only their weapons, and crawled closer to the dissipating smoke.

There was a huge hole in the ground all right, just where the flagpole had stood. Half of the sheared pole was thrown off to one side, a few shreds of the flag scattered about.

Beckwith smiled at Kraus, "One less booby trap for us."

As they looked back into the treeline for signs of enemy movement, they stood up and started to walk back towards their equipment.

"Lieutenant," a voice shouted from the treeline.

Beckwith, Kraus and Perez crouched down and turned towards the sound of the man hollering.

There standing at the edge of the treeline was Hillerman.

Hillerman walked out into the paddy about ten feet towards them, stopped and knelt down. He bent over and stood up with a piece of wire in his hand and said, "Look what I found."

The wire was stretched out towards Beckwith's position. He had not seen it on his way out as it was on the other side of the berm and under the water.

Beckwith got to his feet and shouted, "No."

Hillerman ignored the shouting and said, "I found it." At the same time he grabbed hold of the wire with both hands and before anyone could stop him, he pulled on it.

His movement was so sudden that Beckwith did not have time to duck. All he could do was to continue to shout, "No," but it was too late.

As Hillerman reared back and stretched, halfway between them, but closer to Beckwith, came another explosion.

The Lieutenant was just rolling backwards with his legs spread out when he felt a stinging in the groin.

He hit the paddy and rolled in the mud as if it would help him escape the pain or more flying shrapmetal; finally he stopped on his back, spread-eagled.

He raised his head and looked down at his crotch to see a red, bloody mess. His pants were torn apart and the band of his underwear was showing. The blood ran up it like it was a sponge.

"Doc," he hollered. "Doc." He envisioned the grenade having snipped off his balls and the thought made him wish that it had penetrated his skull.

He dropped his head back into the mud and did want to touch himself. "Not the balls," he kept repeating. "Not the balls."

Doc was there in a flash and kneeling over the Lieutenant.

As soon as Beckwith saw him, he said, "Not the balls, Doc . . . Not the balls," he kept repeating.

Doc leaned closer to the Lieutenant's crotch and slowly started to remove some of the fragments of cloth embedded in the blood.

Beckwith watched the expression on Doc's face as the man worked. Marlin did not want to look at his own flesh torn apart. He was afraid to find out.

"Do you want a shot of morphine?" Doc asked.

"I want to know first."

Doc turned around and removed from his bag a pair of scissors and started to cut around the burnt-out zipper. He cut out the material in squares and discarded them.

By now the men in the platoon had come up and were starting to gather around.

Beckwith saw all the staring faces and said, "What the fuck are you guys doing? Spread out. The war's not over just because I drew some blood."

The words made him angry and the faces scattered.

"Hillerman," Beckwith hollered. "Take charge."

Kraus said, "You'll be all right, Sir."

It did not help.

"How many got it?" Beckwith asked.

Kraus replied, "You're the only one, Sir . . . They must have booby trapped the booby trap."

The pain was right there in his balls.

Doc cut the pants around the thighs and then up

the side. He cut off the shorts at the seams and laid them back down between Beckwith's legs, pulled out a swab of cotton and began to absorb the blood and look more carefully for its source.

"Nah," Doc finally said. "It missed you by a good half inch." Cut through the gracilis muscle, that's all. It is only a superficial wound."

"What's a gracilis muscle?" Kraus asked for Beckwith, still not wanting to look himself.

"The muscle in the inner thigh, right next to the genitals. There's a pencil-sized hole from the shrapmetal."

Beckwith, who was now sweating like a triathlon athlete at the end of the race, suddenly felt chilled, then relieved. "My nuts are OK?"

"Yeah. No problem. Missed you by a half inch."

"Thanks, Doc. You don't know how happy that makes me feel."

"You don't look very happy."

Marlin's smile quivered. "I am, though. I really am." A pencil-sized hole did not make sense for all the blood that Marlin was losing, but he knew that was Doc's way of relaxing the wounded.

"We better get you out of here and dry you off. You don't want to get this wound infected, and it is already dirty. Do you want some morphine?"

"Nah. I feel great."

Doc said, "This one's sending you to the hospital."

The Lieutenant sighed and dropped his head back. The helmet felt like it was floating. Not now, he thought. I have to find Hoppy. Hillerman will take over the platoon. Not now. The sweat was just flowing from him like a waterfall. He could even feel it soaking into his wound.

"Where is the closest hospital?"

"Saigon."

"Shit."

After Doc bandaged him up and covered up his midsection, the Lieutenant's equipment was divided between the men.

He tried to walk, but the direct pressure made his whole leg streak with pain. Gatz and Allen lifted him in a fireman's carry. Beckwith sat on their crossed hands and put his arms around their shoulders. He felt ridiculous being carried, but there was nothing he could do about it.

When they reached the river and boarded the PBR, before they took off, Kraus said to Beckwith, "Sir, I hope this does not mean that you won't be back to our platoon when you recover."

Beckwith just shook his head. He knew that if he stayed in the hospital too long or if he were medevaced to Japan, when he returned, he would be treated almost like a new recruit and placed in Vietnam wherever there was a need for a platoon leader. He probably would never see any of his men again.

When the patrol boat shot forward with full throttle, the pain in Beckwith's groin made him not care about anything.

Chapter 13

A white medevac helicopter came speeding down the river trying to stay over the water, but because of its weight and speed made wide banking turns around the curves.

When the coxswain of the PBR caught sight of the chopper, he drew back on the throttle and settled the boat into the water. It rocked on its own waves, forcing most of the men to hold onto the gunwales to prevent them from falling over. The coxswain gave the engines just enough power to stop the PBR from floating back downriver.

Hillerman got on the radio, identified himself and told the pilot to come in closer.

The helo slowly approached the boat, its blades kicking up a rainstorm of water and slowly drowning out all other sounds other than its own.

With the Huey directly over the PBR, a litter was tossed from the side door and slowly belayed to within reach of the boat. Kraus and Gatz pulled it to the deck right next to the engine compartment where Marlin was sitting holding onto his helmet and grimacing his face in pain at the swirling winds which made his efforts to remain motionless nearly impossible.

When Kraus and Gatz took hold of Marlin's

arms, he balanced himself against them, skipped closer to the litter, and lowered himself slowly onto the blankets, laid his head back on the pillow and grabbed hold of both sides. Kraus buckled a single strap across his belly.

Marlin looked up helplessly at the concentrating faces attentively doing their jobs.

When Kraus looked up and raised his clenched fist above his head, the litter rose into the air. Beckwith held onto the runners of the litter and kept his head up so he could somehow feel more in control of the situation than he actually was.

When the last guiding hands released his carriage, the chopper slowly began to rise and move away from the boat. The intense sound of its blades over the water slackened, the spindrift stopped and Marlin turned his head from the PBR to the helo as it lifted higher. As he watched the line to his litter draw up tight against a pulley attached to an extended pole, two attendants reached out, pulled him inside and just as quickly slammed the door shut.

The chopper lifted higher, lurching forward. The Lieutenant's stretcher was precariously placed on the top rack on the lee side of the ship. Still strapped in, he looked out the small window to his left and watched the PBR make a donut in the water and speed ahead towards the bridge.

Beckwith looked for Hillerman, but he was nowhere to be seen. Marlin was worried about the Platoon Sergeant as well as his men. If Hillerman listened to Kraus and played his cards right, he would be all right; but if the bridge were hit, the third platoon could be in a world of shit.

Hillerman was not a bad man, it was just that he did not have the experience. Given time, seasoned to the sneaky, dirty rotten war he had volunteered for, he would straighten out and become the conniving, distrustful, suspicious platoon sergeant that stayed alive. But it would take time.

The helicopter leveled off at about a thousand feet and followed the highway north. The city of Saigon came into sight—blanketed with a thin layer of smog. It was flat, like unleavened bread, without a skyscraper on its horizon.

Suddenly the helicopter started to fall back towards the earth.

Beckwith felt panic because he knew he wasn't there yet. He sat up on his elbows and shouted to the medics, "What's wrong?"

"Got to pick up some more casualties," hollered one of the men as he threw his cigarette on the deck and stepped on it.

The thought of dropping into a hot LZ right now frustrated Marlin. He didn't have an M-16 or even a .45. He was as helpless as a kid, and now in a Huey, one of the biggest, slowest targets in Nam.

As the chopper dropped from the clouds, he looked outside to see where it was landing. On the road, off to the left was a demolished jeep with civilians milling about. The Military Police with their white helmets were pushing back the Vietnamese to make a landing zone. The sight of friendlies made the Lieutenant relax.

When the helicopter touched down, the right door swung open, bringing with it the loud sound of the twirling blades, the swirling of grass and dirt. The medics jumped out with a fresh stretcher and soon returned with it full—a soldier with his right leg blown off. What remained of the shattered bone dangled from beneath a blanket, blood soaking the fabric liner. The man choked with pain, mumbled, whimpered, screamed out. He was placed in the rack across from Beckwith.

Marlin felt lucky to have his minor wound.

When a rifle was fired, Marlin turned his head out the window and saw an MP waving a pistol over his head; the residents were scattering off the highway, the destroyed jeep smoldering on the road.

Marlin wondered if one of the civilians might run forward and throw a grenade into the opened door of the chopper. There was nothing he could do about it if someone tried and there was no place to hide.

Beckwith licked a drop of salty perspiration from the side of his mouth. "Get going," he said to himself.

The medics returned to the open door and shoved a rubber body bag on the floor between Marlin and the man with the missing leg. The medics jumped inside right behind the bag and sat in the forward seats behind the pilots.

When the door slammed shut, the single engine roared with power and slowly lifted itself from the threatening scene.

The rubber body bag at Beckwith's feet shook with the vibrations of the engine. The two medics stepped over it and started the wounded soldier on an I.V. When they finished, one of the medics returned to his seat while the other turned to Beckwith and asked, "Want a cigarette?"

"Sure," Beckwith wiped the sweat from his forehead and dried his hand on his shirt, but his hand came away even wetter now.

The attendant shook the pack of cigarettes and when three filters popped up, he squeezed them in place and extended them towards Marlin, who took one and set it between his sticky lips. The medic lighted it for him, snapped the lighter shut, placed a small lap-sized pillow under Marlin's head and returned to his seat.

Beckwith inhaled deeply on the filter and looked out the window at the straight road to Saigon, fields of rice, patches of jungle and the growing outline of the city. He laid his head back on the pillow and savored the smoke. He looked at his hand and saw the fingers shaking. He wondered if he were ever going to make it out of this place alive. Sometimes, time seemed to go in reverse, back and forth, or move ahead as if it wore spurs implanted in the ground, never ahead full steam. It dragged its way forward one agonizing moment at a time, even in sleep, so slow, taking with it all memories of relaxation, enjoyment and companionship as Marlin grew up to know it. Changing all the time. Changing him, the men, his outlook, his goals. It was all time's fault, time and the time that crept so torturously slow, not skipping one agonizing moment.

Fear was its only companion. Always ready to lurch on the scene and scare whatever civility existed back into hiding. Fear that grew out of all proportion to life, like a cancer cell feeding on itself, the ever-present emotion in all circumstances. The controller of time. The night watchman that could change a laugh to a scream. Victory to defeat. The emotion that had to be controlled 24 hours of the day, always trying to escape, whipped into submission before it turned everything around it into a living nightmare. Fear that knew no bounds to its running, no escape, only deeper into itself, its only friend, time.

When the helo shut down its motor, Beckwith was panting with each breath. He looked at the door and wondered what would come through next.

The door slammed open and more men in white stretched their arms into the chopper, grabbed the corners of the body bag, dragged it forward until they could pick it up and slid it on the ground.

The man with the blown-off leg was removed next. By now he was so quiet Beckwith wondered if he were dead.

Two hefty attendants picked up Beckwith's stretcher and gave instructions to each other as they moved him to the sunshine, across a helicopter pad and through double swinging doors into a noisy room with half a dozen stretchers with soldiers on them in a close group. In the background were the intense lights of an operating room with white uniforms in masks and hats, wielding knives.

When Beckwith's stretcher touched the floor, an attendant with a clipboard came alongside of him, checked his dog tags and asked, "Where are you wounded?"

When Beckwith explained, the man wrote it down, smiled and said, "You're lucky. Are you allergic to penicillin?"

When Marlin shook his head, the attendant walked on to the next stretcher.

Beckwith looked at the operating table and saw a body slide onto the white paper cover and grabbed at like a slab of meat.

Bodies moved through like an assembly line.

Marlin looked at the man next to him. A hole in his neck was still uncovered. Blood ran down from the hole and soaked the shirt collar. The man looked straight up at the ceiling without moving his neck, his back as straight as a board, not saying a word. Blood was dripping.

Beckwith looked to the right. The man next to him was coming up off the stretcher in a ball, rocking back and forth holding his stomach, his face squished up as if he were in a great deal of pain. Marlin leaned forward and counted seven stretchers. What they all had in common besides the looks of composed pain was an excessive amount of mud and sweat all over their bodies. Blood was dripping on the floor. It reminded him of a slaughterhouse. An orderly moved between the stretchers to mop up the blood.

It took nearly half an hour before Beckwith was placed on the operating table. He pointed to his crotch and half smiled, "They missed 'em." He lay back looking at the intensely hot lights and listened. The first thing they did was cut his pants away at the seams.

One of the nurses hollered, "He has a pocketful of grenades."

It was at that moment that Beckwith realized they were talking about him. He had forgotten to leave the grenades behind. He carried them in the lower pockets of his jungle fatigues as did all of his men. It was the safest spot. If they dangled off the ruck-sack suspenders or the ammunition belt, even with the pins turned over, there was the possibility that their weight could pull themselves free of the pins in a moment of panic and go off.

More shouts and orders, more confusion. Marlin half smiled to himself when he realized that they were afraid of a hand grenade with the pin still attached. Like being afraid of a caged snake. Stupid.

Stripped, a white nightgown was slipped over his arms that reached down to his groin.

Doc's bandage was snipped off and Marlin's hip was stuck with a needle at the same time. His wound was quickly diagnosed, another fresh ban-

152

dage placed over the fresh wound, much smaller.

Marlin's whole world started to become relaxed. When he slipped over onto another wheeled stretcher, he looked back to see the blood-soaked paper on the table being removed and replaced with fresh paper about as fast as another body slid aboard.

Rumbling down another corridor through more doors only to wait again.

When Beckwith's was moved onto another table, his bandages were removed. This time the doctor shot him in the left leg around the wound and continued to work his way around the wound with the needle, then plucked out some metal with tweezers, dropped them into a metal pot and stitched him up.

Beckwith was groggy and felt no pain. He lifted up his head and for the first time looked at the wound. It was not all that bad, as Doc had said; there was a gash missing from his leg that the doctor was stitching together. It was black and yellow.

He laid his head back down on the pillow and moved his hands along the crinkly white paper. He could feel no pain in his lower body now, but he could feel the doctor pulling at the skin on his leg.

"You're going to be all right, soldier," the Doc said.

Marlin did not reply.

In no time he was placed back on the wheeled stretcher, set up with an IV and carted further down the hall. He watched the bubbles in the water make their way up the tube attached to his arm.

He was rolled inside a ward full of beds with GIs wrapped in various sizes and shapes of bandages. Some of the men were quiet and others were talking.

As Beckwith was helped into a bed, he ran his hands over the clean sheets and inhaled their freshness. His leg was only throbbing now. He leaned his head against the pillow, picked it up and tried it again in a more comfortable position. He was exhausted. He fell asleep just about that fast.

When he awoke, he felt someone touching his right leg and he thought of the damn mouse he had caught one night in an ambush nibbling on his shoelace. He nearly came unglued. He bent his leg and pulled it up, and held onto the sides of the mattress as he looked down at the end of the bed to see a woman in a white uniform, with a nurse's headband, both her hands around a face cloth clutched to her breast. Marlin looked down at the end of his bed and saw his exposed foot, the wash pan alongside.

"I'm sorry, I didn't mean to frighten you," she said.

Beckwith ran his hand over his face as if to wipe away his terror and said, "That's all right. I'm sorry for startling you like that . . . I was thinking of something else."

"I was on my rounds giving the men sponge baths. I tried to wake you first, but you were asleep. I decided to wash you anyway."

"Sorry. Go right ahead."

She smiled and meekly moved forward with her face cloth and picked up his leg as if it were a newborn baby's. She squeezed the washcloth in the bowl of water and stroked his leg softly with the lukewarm pad.

"Are you all right?" she asked.

He swallowed hard and blinked his eyes. "Yes," he replied. "I'm OK . . . Yes. Yes."

The young woman bathed him off completely and it was the most wonderful experience that Beckwith had felt in the last nine months in country.

While she worked, he stared at her. He could not help it. Once he tried to break the spell, but when his gaze returned, he could feel his neck leaning forward and his eyes drying up from not blinking.

Her skin seemed so unblemished and soft. Whereas the Vietnamese women were as thin as broom handles, this woman was much taller and so well proportioned. Her breasts were so full, so sensuous beneath the white gown. When she moved her arms, her breasts moved with them.

The smell of her perfume was Hawaiian acacias. It smelled good enough to take a bath in, eat, or just wallow in for hours.

God, it was so relaxing. Beckwith just lay back and felt her hands move the warm cloth over his right arm, washing it, stopping to scrape the mud away. He wished that he were caked in mud. He did not want her to stop.

As soon as her hands stopped touching him, Beckwith fell back into sleep.

It was nighttime and the sounds and feelings of the hospital terrorized Marlin when he opened his eyes. He was sweating, not from the heat, but from fear. He wondered if there were any VC down the hall, coming to get him in the dark, stab him in bed, or slice his throat. It was not impossible. He wondered if there was a trap door under his bed and a VC about to crawl out from beneath the sheets and lunge at him. If he had a fucking pistol

155

he would feel better. This unarmed shit was too much, even in a hospital. After all, he was still in Nam. He was an infantry platoon leader, with a bounty on his head. The VC would know him.

An emergency button glowed on a table beside his bed and Beckwith leaned over and squeezed it until it glowed brighter.

He hoped it would summon the same girl who had given him the bath upon his arrival in the ward, but it was somebody different, a male orderly.

"Could I get a drink of water?" Beckwith asked.

The orderly said, "It is right next to your bed." His tone was not polite. The man was tall and muscular with a mean-looking face. The white of his eyes glowed in the dark.

Beckwith looked over to see a small cream-colored pitcher with a plastic cup inverted over its top. "OK. I see it here. I can get it myself."

The orderly turned and walked out the swinging door and into the darkness.

Beckwith wiped his brow and bent over and poured himself a cup of water and drank it.

Setting the cup back on the table, he pushed the blanket away from his body and looked at his midsection. He was bandaged around the leg. It was clean. He tried to move his leg, but upon tensing the muscles up, he could feel the tightness of the stitches. He didn't want to rip them apart, so he just lay back with his head on the pillow catching his breath.

He looked at the fan circling over his head, then at the other beds on the ward.

His IV had been removed and he was definitely coming down from whatever they had given him for the pain. He was feeling more together right now.

More in charge of himself and his actions and feelings.

Content, he fell to sleep again, but this time much more peacefully.

In the morning an orderly served him breakfast in bed. He sat up and quickly ate the bowl of warm mush with sugar on top, a glass of orange juice and a portion of scrambled eggs with cardboard-texture bacon. The coffee tasted the best.

No sooner was the tray taken away than a doctor came by with a chart and stethoscope, making his rounds. He was friendly and to the point, removed the bandages from Marlin's leg and hummed over the inspection. The wound was black and blue with brown and yellow around its perimeter, some strands of skin charred black. A dozen stitches held it together. Definitely more than a pencil wound, more like the bite from a good-sized dog.

Beckwith's first question was, "How long will I be out now, Doctor?"

The doctor started to secure a new bandage. "I'll keep you here a couple of weeks. If the wound does not heal satisfactorily in that time, I'll send you to Japan."

"How long would I be there, if I went?"

"That would be their decision entirely . . . I've seen men like you come in here and walk the next day. You just have to be careful of infection; but the healing process can take any amount of time. You can try walking any time you want. Just keep the wound clean."

Beckwith nodded his head.

The doctor finished with the bandage and said, "You're lucky."

Beckwith felt it and nodded.

When Marlin was left to himself again, he covered himself with the sheet and sat up. He tried to lift his foot. The pain made him drop it back on the sheet. He tried again and raised it completely off, although it was no more than a quarter of an inch. It hurt, but the pain was not beyond his capacity. If all went well, he would be back at Ben Luc within two weeks. He would work as hard at recuperating as he did fighting the war. He had to get back there. He lay back in the bed and wondered how his men were doing back there. He wondered if Hillerman had gotten back on Hoppy's trail, if the bridge was still intact or if his platoon had increased their body count.

Marlin knew he had it better than Hoppy, even in this condition.

Chapter 14

It was one of those clear nights on the Vam Co River when the moon was nearly as bright as the sun on a cloudy day, and its reflection in the water was enough to make a man think of his girlfriend back home, wish she was here beside him so he could hold her hand, cuddle up to her and talk about the future. The mosquitoes were gone and the sound of crickets and frogs echoed along the shores. A slight sea breeze whiffed from the east and smelled of palm trees, ripe fruit, and flower blossoms.

Perez and White were sitting atop the bunker, watching the river and looking down the road across the bridge.

White flicked his shoulders, twitched his head. "Something happens to guys when they get short, that's all. If it happens to anyone, it's those short guys. I don't want to be reminded. Especially by some half-fried taco shell." He spoke in a half whisper. He shifted his weight on his helmet, the damn round top was slowly working its way up the crack in his skinny ass. He stood up, removed his flak vest, placed it on the helmet and sat back down. It helped, but it was no chaise longue.

Perez said, "If you get shot now there will be

nothing to stop the bullet."

"Shut the fuck up, Wetback." White slipped the rain poncho over his head, but without sticking his head through the hood, used it to form a tent over his body. He pulled out a pack of cigarettes from his pocket, stuck one between his lips and pulled the lighter from his other vest pocket, flipped it open, struck it to light, and set the flames to the tip of the cigarette. As he inhaled, he watched with pleasure as the tip glowed. He held his breath and looked at the lighter still burning. There was a picture of Snoopy engraved on the side of the Zippo. Snoopy was lying on top of his doghouse looking skyward. His speech balloon read, "Fuck It." With pleasure, White thought as he clicked the lighter closed and replaced it in his shirt pocket.

He exhaled into the hollow formed by his arms resting on his knees and looked at the sandbags he was sitting on, but it was too dark beyond the burning cigarette tip. Even the inside of the poncho was wet. He thought of his four-month-old son, Edgar Thomas White. He couldn't wait to get home and meet him for the first time. The thought made him smile.

Perez's voice penetrated White's small cell and fell on damp ears, "I can see a glow of light coming from the bottom of your poncho, White. Don't be stupid, man. You better put that cigarette out. If the Lieutenant were here, he'd be shoving that thing up your ass."

White didn't answer. The cigarette afforded enough light to see now. He looked at his wrist, the skin shriveled and pale from being so wet, then at the trembling hand holding the cigarette. He couldn't even enjoy a smoke before he went to sleep without getting hassled. He raised his shoulders and it felt like he was lifting a soggy tub of washed clothes. Smoke was building up under the hood and he could taste the air getting stale.

Perez said, "If Charlie sees it, he'll put a bullet right in your mouth that would tear out the back of your head."

White took a long drag, held his breath for a few seconds, then as he exhaled, wormed his head back through the hole in the poncho back into fresh air. "Nobody is gonna see nothing," he said a he blew smoke that came out like a breath on fire.

White's appearance silenced Perez. The two of them sat there, side by side, looking out at the river. Curfew had started at sunset. It was quiet. The VC usually did not come out on such brightly lighted nights. It was too easy to see them. They preferred the rainy, dark nights.

White asked, "Why do you think Hoppy jumped the way he did?"

Gatz voice came from inside the bunker, "He didn't jump, he was captured."

White grunted, "When he saw all those gooks pointing their rifles at him, I bet he just heave hoed his rifle and started talking. I know that Hoppy. He didn't have a spine wide enough to hold up his helmet."

"Nah," Perez piped in. "The guy saw it was all over. What could you do with a dozen rifles aiming at ya?"

"I'd a fuck done something," White said. "I wouldn't let no dink capture me."

"You would have died."

"No. I would have wasted a dozen gooks. That's what I would have done. I'd a wasted 'em."

"They would a made a lamp shade out of your belly and used your dong to turn it on."

"I wished your parents drowned swimming the Rio Grande . . . Whose watch is it anyway?"

"It's mine," Perez said. "And I wake you up. You better go to sleep."

"Then I wake you up, huh Gatz?" White asked, raising his voice and speaking in the direction of one of the firing ports.

"Right," came the reply.

White dipped his head under the poncho for another drag from his cigarette and came out just as fast.

Without being asked, Perez said, "When I get out of this mess, I'm going back to school and get my degree."

White withheld a chuckle, "That's where all the damn demonstrators back home are holding rallies and screaming for us to come home. They'd string you up on a flagpole if they ever got a hold of you."

"Why? I want to go home too."

"Yeah, but you ain't and you're killing dinks."

"I don't want to."

"Well you are, you stupid fucker. That's the difference."

"You're getting loud again . . . Yeah, I'm gonna go to college and get a degree and make myself a certified poet."

White said, "Man, they'll drive you out of school in no time. Call you a warmonger. The professors will probably flunk you just because you're over here. They're intellectuals, not killers like you."

Perez became smug. "That's foolish, short timer."

"Cut that shit out."

"What? You got only 62 days left. Everybody in the platoon knows it. You tell everybody every day but when I repeat what you say to me, you get mad."

Gatz broke it up. "Go to sleep, White. It ain't your turn to be up now anyway. You go to sleep or else I'll put you to sleep."

"Fuck you guys, you're not worth talking to anyway. What's gonna happen tomorrow?"

"We're gonna find Hoppy and bring him back home," Gatz said.

"Home?" Perez grumbled. "Some home."

Gatz said, "I'm going to talk to the Lieutenant when he comes back about you two. I'm going to ask him to split you two up. All you two do is argue all day long."

"If he comes back."

"He will."

"I don't want to go to the third squad," White said. "Those guys are praying all the time. They'd drive me crazy. Shoot a dink, pray. Shoot a dink, bless 'em. No. Not the third squad."

"And the first squad are a bunch of fuckin' bloodthirsty cutthroats. They are," Perez said. "It is all that Castillo's fault. No way, the first squad. I heard you got to give blood as soon as you join 'em. They cut your wrist and they all suck it."

"And Cox's squad are afraid of their own shadows now. We'll quit fighting," White said.

"You two guys are loco," Gatz said.

"Good night, Perez," White said. He waited for an answer but heard only the patter of rain. A dark cloud was moving from the south, its outline tipped in white. The breeze was blowing its rain ahead of itself.

"Do you see what I see, White?" Perez asked.

"What? Rain?"

"No. Looks like something floating down the river."

White sat up straight. "No, I don't see it."

"Put out that cigarette and look real hard."

White placed the butt on the sandbag under the poncho and it sizzled out.

"Where?"

"Coming right down the middle of the damn river. I swear."

"What do you want to do?"

"Go get Hillerman," Gatz said as he could be heard moving to get outside.

"Fuck him," Perez said. "He'll probably want one of us to dive in after it."

"What do you want to do then?" White was getting nervous.

"I say we shoot it out of the water."

"But I don't even see what you are talking about."

"It is coming closer."

"How far away is it? . . . Oh yeah," White finally said. "I think I see what you are talking about. It is right in the middle of the river."

"That's what I said."

"It looks like a big old turd from here."

"I guess."

"Do you have a LAW?"

Gatz came grunting out of the exit, wiggling his shoulders past the sandbags. "There are four of them in the bunker," Gatz said as he stood tall to look where they were now pointing.

White said to Perez, "Go down and bring out a couple of LAWs and some concussion grenades."

"What for?"

"Just bring 'em out and I'll show you. Don't start talking now . . . Hurry up."

Willie, who had been sleeping inside, came out with the ordinances in both hands and asked, "Is this what you want?"

"Yeah," White said as he took a couple of LAWs

from him.

Gatz asked, "What do you guys see?"

"There is something floating down the river. We are going to blow the shit out of it before it reaches the bridge."

"Maybe you had better ask Hillerman first?"

"Fuck him," Perez said. "Our job is to prevent this bridge from being blown up and it is my watch. Give me one of those LAWs."

When Willie handed one to Perez, all four of them ran to the middle of the bridge right over the support column and stopped.

Perez pulled the safety pin from the LAW, snapped the two sections open, shouldered the weapon, aimed and as Gatz pointed at the long log, fired.

The flame shot out the back of the tube as the rocket shot towards its target and hit the water short of the floating object. There were a few seconds before the rocket exploded underwater.

By that time Hillerman was right on top of Perez, "What the fuck are you doing, soldier?" he screamed. He did not even know the name of the man he was talking to.

Perez paid him no mind, but said to White, "Give me another one."

Hillerman screamed, "You don't go firing that son of a bitch without my command. That could be part of the Riverine Squadron that you are firing at."

Perez said, "If that was the riverine boat, they'd have shot my ass off this bridge by now." He pulled the pin out of the second LAW and started to cock it open.

Hillerman grabbed a hold of the weapon and tried to wrench it from Perez, but the soldier was not about to let go. He was lighter than the Platoon Sergeant but madder.

Hillerman said to Gatz, "Squad leader, give me a hand."

Gatz's eyes were glowing in the dark. "Perez, you do what the Sergeant says."

As the three men scuffled, White ran to the bridge's edge, looked over and saw the log coming towards the middle support of the bridge. If it was being maneuvered by a man in camouflage, it was headed right for the supporting pier.

White set his M-16 and LAWs on the ground and went for the grenades. He pulled the pin on one of the concussion grenades and threw it at the log. Before it even hit the water he had the pin out of a second grenade and was slinging it out across the water. By the time he had the pin out of the third grenade, the first one exploded and then the second.

Nobody really heard the second one explode all by itself, it took something else with it that sent a geyser of water over the side of the bridge and shook it at its very foundation, literally soaking all of those standing on the middle span and drowning the scuffle between the enlisted men.

White still had the grenade in his right hand with the pin out of it. When he fell to the ground, he clasped it to his chest and held on for dear life.

When the water stopped spraying and the bridge quite shaking, it was as quiet as a funeral. The air was filled with mist.

Perez let out a war cry that sung of victory—such a happy scream.

White did not want to chance placing the pin back into the grenade. He stood up and tossed it far out over the water. When it exploded, it added to the sounds of the celebration.

Perez said to Hillerman, "That ought to earn us a Bronze Star if anything does!"

Hillerman's eyes were glaring, even in the darkness. He took their actions as insubordination and stormed back to his bunker with threats of court-martial.

It made White and Perez laugh, but at the same time they knew that something was wrong with the Platoon Sergeant. He was just too dinky in the head.

Gatz said to them, "OK. You better get back to the bunker and continue your watch."

"But we saved the bridge, man. We saved the fucking bridge," Perez said. "We're heroes."

"Yeah, but you also ticked off the Platoon Sergeant."

"Fuck him," White said.

"He is still the man in charge," Gatz said. "He can bring down the smoke. Let's get back to the bunker."

They grumbled back to their watch position, Gatz went to bed, and Perez and White got back on top of the sandbags. Perez asked, "What a crock of shit, that was. We're damn heroes and the guy is gonna court-martial us."

"I think he sucks through a bent straw, man. The guy is bent."

"I know. If it were not for him, the Lieutenant would still be here and not in the hospital and we'd be all at the bottom of the river now."

"And he's going to court-martial us. Phew. I can't wait for the Lieutenant to get back."

"Suppose he tries something like that on us?"

"What do you mean?"

"I mean if he tries to get us killed or something.

You know?"

"No. I don't know."

"Well you know, we know what is dangerous and what isn't, just like the Lieutenant does. The Lieutenant sends us on some dangerous missions, but they ain't suicide. There is a chance of us making it back all the time, and if anything happens, the Lieutenant will do everything in his power to help us out."

"I know what you mean."

"Suppose the Platoon Sergeant sends us on a suicide mission."

"I won't go."

"Then he could shoot your ass."

"I'd shoot the son of a bitch before he clicked the safety off his rifle."

"Maybe we should do it before he gets the chance. I mean the guy is working with half a deck of cards. He don't know his ass from a tunnel. Under pressure, he'd probably shoot himself. Know what I mean?"

"Yeah. I guess. What do you think we should do?"

"I say we frag the guy. Get rid of him before he gets rid of us."

"Ho-ho-ho-ho."

"Just roll a grenade his way one day and that is the end of it. Nobody will know the difference. It'll look like he blew himself up, or a VC got him."

"I don't know. How long is the Lieutenant supposed to be gone?"

"I heard about a month or two, maybe more."

"Didn't seem like it was that bad. I'd hate like hell to be under Hillerman for that long. None of us would survive."

"That's my point. It's either him or us." After a

long pause, Perez said, "I say it's him."

"When do you think we should do it?"

"I say we give him one more chance. The next time he makes a mistake, he's history."

"Well suppose the next time it is one of us?"

"OK. Let me put it this way. It is either when someone else is shot or when he gives one of us an order and it looks like if we follow it, it will get us all killed. Know what I mean?"

"Yeah, I do."

"Do you think we would get caught?"

"If it comes right down to my life or his, who cares?"

"I wish the Lieutenant were here. We wouldn't be in this big mess. I wonder how long he'll be gone?"

"Probably in the hospital somewhere getting stitched up."

"Probably."

Gatz's voice could be heard, "White, get yourself to sleep."

White stood up and nodded his head at Perez. "One more time, Jesus."

He held his finger up. "It's a deal."

Chapter 15

A black telephone hung on a wall halfway down a long hallway outside the ward where Marlin lay. He got a glimpse of it every time someone came through the swinging doors. Whenever he lay back to rest, he would lay his head pointed in that direction, just waiting for the door to open to watch the expressions on the faces of the patients as they talked. Some openly laughed outright, others were on the point of tears, some hiding against the wall whispering, hunched over like they were hiding something.

Marlin asked one of the soldiers who had just gotten off the phone and was passing the foot of his bed, "Who did you talk to, soldier?"

The man replied, "Home, of course," and looked at Marlin in such a way as to question his sanity.

Home, Marlin thought. Like an out-of-focus camera zooming in on a rifle muzzle, the word itself was frightening. Marlin struggled with the memories of his childhood, pushing them back, avoiding them. The sweet smell of a California morning at his father's lumberyard became so real that it made him shudder. Twisting his head to one side, he struggled to stay in the present. He knew if he let himself melt into the world of wonderful memories, of romances and friends, he might awake and find himself in the hands of a merciless, stalking, smirking VC who would proceed to slowly draw his life from him, savoring every moment of the killing. Nah, he told himself. That's in the field. This is a hospital.

Home was such a distant goal that to think about it prematurely could make it disappear forever. As if Marlin were on a merry-go-round, he had to concentrate on the brass ring and not on the free ride that he would win if he succeeded. To change focus would court certain failure.

That afternoon, after the doctor's call, Marlin's bed was rolled into a private room for officers with only half a dozen beds.

There were two other patients in the room.

The first thing one of the patients said to Marlin when the attendants left was, "They didn't send you to Japan. Too bad."

Marlin replied, "I'd just as soon finish up my tour here and go back home for good."

"Not me," the soldier sat up in bed. "Oh, my name is Ed Kost and the weird guy over there with his head shaved is Greg Rivitt, Airborne, a screaming chicken."

"You're nothing but a big red one from the First," Greg popped back, acting somewhat offended at the cliché.

Ed laughed and said to Marlin, "I'd go there in a heartbeat, and they'd play hell getting me back too. Problem is they didn't shoot me good enough. Where did you get it?"

"Half an inch from my crowned jewels. You?"

"Not quite as unique. In the upper arm. Just grazed me. No bingo."

"Ed, you'd come back from Japan with a smile on

your face," Greg finally spoke up, "and the first day back here little Charlie would wipe it away; probably take your face with it."

That's how Marlin felt too.

"At least I would be smiling."

"Nope," Greg said. "I hate this son of a bitching place and the next place I want to go to is Minnesota. I don't need any breaks. I might not be able to handle this place when I got back."

"Then they'd send you home for good too."

"Bullshit."

"Say, Marlin. Did that Donut Dolly give you a hand job when she washed you off the first day you got here?"

"What are you talking about?"

"You should have told her you were an officer. She gives all the officers a hand job."

"You're full of shit."

They just laughed.

The conversation ran easy as the three Lieutenants shared stories about killing, victory, sex, and booze.

That afternoon a Lieutenant with a Twenty-fifth Division patch on his jungle fatigues came into the room and greeted Ed and Greg and went over to the empty bed across from Marlin and started to pack the belongings out of the small stand.

"How was Saigon?" Ed asked the officer.

"Better than gay Paree."

"Where ya been?" Marlin asked.

The Lieutenant looked somewhat annoyed as he said to Marlin. "Day pass . . . just looking around the city. That's all."

"And now he's headed back to the war," Greg said.

"Have fun?" Ed said.

"I did this afternoon."

"How did you arrange that?" Marlin asked.

Without looking Marlin's way, the officer explained, "They'll give you a day before they discharge you to make sure you don't go tits up on them as soon as you hit the front steps." He stuffed the rest of his belongings into a paper bag and said, "Adios, amigos. Hurry back to the war. I'll need help."

"You going back to your old unit?" Marlin asked.

"No other."

"Good," Marlin smiled.

Marlin did not want to replace a platoon leader who had either been killed or wounded in another war zone, just like he had done with his third platoon going on nine months ago. There was so much friction and learning to do so quickly and emotions ran so high, that he had just as soon return to his old platoon and carry on where he had left off instead of adopting some other Lieutenant's problems. For some reason he felt like he would be safer with his platoon.

When the officer from the Twenty-fifth Division waved as he walked out the room, in the silence that followed, Greg asked, "You used the phone yet, Marlin?"

"No, not yet."

"You ought to give it a try. It's a trip."

"Yeah. I'd just like to be able to get down there on my own two feet."

"Go for it . . . It's just like a radio. When you finish your transmission, you have to say, "Over." Whoever you are talking to has to say the same thing. You got to explain that one to them right away. There is no charge. You got five minutes. After four minutes you will hear a beep. One min-

173

ute after that, if you haven't hung up, you will be disconnected . . . It is all written down right next to the phone, but it takes longer to read the instructions than it does to make the phone call."

Marlin started the healing process by wiggling the toes of his left leg. It was a long way off from his wound, but he could feel the pain even then — the muscles in his inner thigh screaming out a warning to stay away. But he pressed them and continued the exercise until the pain was bearable enough to start bending his knee — sliding his foot up and down the sheet with all the weight on the foot. It made him sweat like he were in a sauna, but that was nothing new in Nam.

The next day he made history of the bedpan by walking to the bathroom, keeping all his weight on his heel. When he got back he walked around the bed, holding onto the rail as a crutch, concentrating as diligently on his moves as he would on throwing a hand grenade. Once around, he got back into the bed, rested a while, and did it again, starting this time on the opposite side and walking around the other way.

As the doctor told him he could take a shower as long as he kept the wound dry, Marlin wrapped some plastic around the leg and taped it to his shaven skin, then slowly stumbled to the bathroom where the single stall shower was located. He turned the water on and adjusted the temperature, bent over and let the water run over his head and shoulders. It felt like he was getting a massage over his entire upper body. He stood up, lathered, rinsed off, then dangled each of his legs under the water.

Bending over was nearly impossible, but the bathing experience was definitely a highlight of his last few days in the hospital. It ranked up there with a cold drink on a sweltering day after pressing through the deep rice paddies, right up there with a good night's sleep without any mortar attacks. By the time Beckwith made it back to his bed, he felt refreshed.

On Friday, he hobbled on his heel down to the telephone with a bathrobe over his nightgown. It was not that cold for a robe but the nightgown was split down the back and he felt embarrassed to go walking around in public bare ass.

He stood against the wall smoking a cigarette. He dreaded the telephone as he knew that his parents would know that something was wrong if they heard from him. He knew that all sorts of feelings, emotions and thoughts might bubble to the surface and screw up with his killer personality; but it was like being at a carnival and not wanting to eat a hot dog for fear of getting sick later. He thought of his dad, who would probably riddle him with questions. Where are you located? How many VC did you kill? What is your mission? He felt nervous just thinking about the questions.

When it was his turn to get on the radio, his palms were sweating.

It would be yesterday and then less a few hours in California.

When he picked up the receiver from its cradle and listened, a male operator asked for the number he wanted to call. Marlin repeated the number and waited, nervously. Marlin did not even know if he wanted to tell his parents he had been wounded as he did not want to worry them any more than they already were, but he knew his mother would work it out of him. His father would take it OK, but his poor mother . . . He wound the cord of the telephone around his right index finger.

He could hear the wires being connected across the world and finally heard the phone ringing. Memories of home made him just about smell sweet lasagna. He could picture the phone on the wall ringing in the corner across from the TV and next to his mother's easy chair, below the clock on the wall-papered partition.

The phone rang again. He knew if no one picked it up by the sixth ring, nobody would be home. It was just that small of a house; even if his folks were in the back yard or out in the garage, more than six rings would be a no-go situation.

The phone rang ten times. After that the operator came back on the line and asked if Marlin wanted to continue trying. Beckwith asked for a little longer. He got six more rings and hung up, forming his lips into a smile for the next man waiting to use the phone.

Now he began to worry. Oh, they just might be at the market or visiting a neighbor or his dad might have had to work late at the yard, his mother visiting friends. Everything was OK.

The weight of the disappointment drove him back to bed and made him not want to try and get out again. Funny how a small thing like that could work on a man — take the steam out of him, almost like losing a best friend.

"You better try again," Ed said after dinner.

"What are you talking about?"

"Phone home, man. I don't know if I can live with you if you don't. Do it."

This time he got through.

He recognized his mother's voice when she answered, "Hello."

"Mom," he said. "Mom. This is your son, Marlin. Over."

"Who is this?"

There was a long pause.

Marlin said, "Mom, you have only one son. It's me. Marlin. Over."

"Marlin . . . Is this you? Marlin? Is this my son? It can't be."

"Mom, when you finish a transmission, you have to say, 'over.' Over."

"Marlin, where are you?"

Long pause.

"Ma. Say 'over' when you are finished. I'm in Nam. Mom. I'm still in Nam and I'm calling to say hello. Over."

"Holy Mary, Mother of God. Are you all right, son? Are you all right? Why are you calling?"

"Say 'over', Mom."

"Over. Why are you calling? Over."

" 'Cause I love you, Mom, and you are the first person I wanted to talk to when I got the chance. That's why. Over."

"Oh, Son. I have been praying for you every day and Father Trestle says a Mass for you boys on the first Friday of each month. Are you sure you are OK? Over."

"I'm fine, Mom. Really. Over."

"Where are you calling from? Over."

Marlin could feel her getting closer. He twisted his finger up through the spires of the cord. "I'm calling from a phone in Saigon. Uncle Sam has it all rigged so we can call home. Isn't that something? Huh, Ma? Over." Marlin was smiling from ear to ear, just pronouncing his mother's name made him glow.

"Where in Saigon? How do they arrange that? Over."

He sighed and let it all out, just like he always

177

did as a kid when his mom started putting the third degree to him. "I got a little bit of shrapmetal in my leg and it is going to be OK. It was just kind of an accident. I didn't even get shot. It was an accident. I tripped over some wire. Over."

"Oh my God. Are you coming home? Over."

"No. I told you. It is just a scratch. I'm fine. I just got to use a phone. That's all. Where is Dad? Can I say a few words to him . . . Over."

"Your father is not here right now. Yesterday his brother Harold passed away. Your father is with your Aunt Margie. Over."

Marlin was startled and didn't know what to say. Uncle Harold was his favorite uncle, one of his best friends. A private in the Army during World War II. The man he wanted to share his war stories with when he got home. A man who would understand. Suddenly he realized that his world was not the only one where death lurked, but at the same time he felt the emptiness that he lived with so often.

He was on his own now, fighting for his own cause, not to impress or better his uncle, just doing it.

There was a silence for a while. Marlin caught his breath. "God. I didn't know that . . ." He had grown so used to suppressing all grief upon seeing dead people that he could not recall any even for his uncle. He felt cold.

There was a beep and it annoyed Marlin. "Mom, that beep means we only have another minute to talk. Then I'm cut off . . . Mom, I love all of you and I am doing just fine over here. Say hello to everyone for me. Give Aunt Margie a kiss and tell everyone home that I love them. Tell Roxeanne I love her. I love you, Mom. Over."

"Son, when are you going to call again? Over."

"I don't know, Mom. This could be it . . . Tell everyone I love them. Over."

"I love you too, Son. Be careful and I am praying for you. Over."

"I know, Mom. I love you. Mom. Over."

"I love you too, Son. But write us a letter. You never write. Goodbye. Over."

"I will, Mom. I'll do exactly as you say. I will. I love your letters. Your cookies are delic—"

The phone went dead.

"I love you all," he mumbled, holding the receiver from his ear and watched as he replaced it back in its cradle, and without looking at the next man in line walked back to his bed. He had worked so hard to get to that phone and he knew it had not been worth it. Hearing his mother's voice made him so homesick that it depressed him. He would like nothing better than to go home now, be home, sitting down to one of his mother's delicious meals, be a part of the whole scene and live like Vietnam had never happened to him. But that was impossible and the impossible is always depressing, especially when it is wished for so badly. Then there was Uncle Harold. He would never see him again.

He would not call home again. He would not call Roxeanne. He would concentrate on going home for good. The only way he could do that is kill every son of a bitching VC in the country; and that's what he felt like doing right now.

Once Marlin got off all the medications and came down completely from all the pain pills, he felt normal but he did not yet have the full control of the leg. His limp had gone down from day to day so that it was only slight by the fifth day.

On the tenth day in the hospital, right after lunch, alone in his room with Greg, as Ed was out on a day pass, he lay there and thought of his platoon.

He was smoking a cigarette, wiggling his toes without pain. He heard a knock at the door and looked over to see a familiar face that nearly knocked him out of the bed. It was a visitor, a friend and a beautiful one at that. It was Lisa, the laundry girl from the whorehouse.

"Lisa," he exclaimed, almost bewildered as he stared at her pretty face, covering himself up with a sheet. "What are you doing here?"

"I came to visit you. It is that time during the day."

"How did you know I was here?"

"I asked your men at the bridge."

Marlin smiled, "How are they?"

"They are fine."

Marlin thought of drilling her with tactical questions, but realized she might not know the answers or want to talk. Instead he stared at her.

She wore a silk lavender dress fitted to her neck, accentuating the fullness of her breasts and slim waist. Her soft brown hair cascaded softly over her shoulders. She smelled of sweet perfume. Although Marlin knew that she was used to working hard, she was so young, only the softness of her skin and wonderful smile came across.

"You are looking wonderful," he exclaimed before he could even think of anything else to say.

"Thank you," she replied, bowing her head and smiling.

"Here," she said. She extended a flower forward. It was an orchid, a red one.

Marlin accepted the gift and inhaled the sweet fragrance, then leaned over and placed it in the water glass on the stand next to the bed. "I want to keep this fresh," he exclaimed. "That was thoughtful of you. . . . What are you doing here?"

She acted embarrassed. "I came to visit you."

"Of course," he laughed. "Of course. My first visitor. Don't you have to work?"

She hung her head again. "I don't work there any longer. It was a bad job. They paid me well but it was no good . . ." She perked up her head and asked, "When will you be back?"

"I hope within a few days. I am feeling much better and can walk around now. I don't think I will be here much longer. Where are you staying?"

Marlin felt lost for words. He had seen Lisa before more as a beautiful body, but as a friend to visit flabbergasted him. He wanted to act friendly, ask her questions, but didn't know about what.

"I have relatives in Saigon. I am staying with them."

"What brought you up here?"

"I told you. I came to visit. That is all." She laughed nervously.

"I feel privileged." He also felt confused. When Marlin looked at her this time, starting to relax, he said, "How are you?"

"I am OK," she replied, lowering her head again. "I have come to do some shopping for my family," she continued. "Is there anything you would like me to get you?"

"I don't know. I have just been thinking about recuperating. I don't know."

"Saigon has many things to buy."

Marlin thought of Greg who was out on a day pass and said, "Maybe I could go shopping with you."

Her head rose and she smiled. "That would be wonderful."

"Yeah. I get a pass before I leave this place to make sure I have recuperated. Maybe you could show me around."

Her eyes sparkled as she held her breath. "When do you think that would be?"

"I expect within the next few days. Will you still be in Saigon?"

"For that I would stay." Her smile was so youthful, so disarming and innocent.

"If that idea doesn't make me feel better, nothing does."

"And you have never seen Saigon?"

"Never, except through the rear sights of a rifle."

She acted upset, maybe offended. Maybe he had aimed at one of her relatives.

"I must be going," she said. "I have many places to go today."

"How can I reach you?"

"I can come each day until you are ready to leave. That way I will know."

"Isn't that a lot of trouble?"

"I am staying close to here. It is no trouble."

"I'll be ready for you."

As Lisa left the room, Ed was at the doorway gawking at her. They both stared at her flowing body sway down the hallway.

When she disappeared around a corner, Ed finally broke the silence, "I'll be a son of a bitch . . . What a doll."

Marlin beamed. "I feel better already."

Chapter 16

When Marlin received his day pass at the nurse's station, he asked to be issued a pistol.

"As far as we are concerned," the nurse answered, "you can visit the PX and the cafeteria on Base; if you get bored, take in a movie. We will expect you back here by supper."

"But I plan to visit Saigon," he answered, "and I'm just not used to walking around without a weapon."

"If you want to see Saigon, buy a pair of binoculars at the PX."

Marlin stared into her black eyes, the consistency of hardened tar. There was no depth there at all. Some men in his platoon were not that callous.

"You're back in the war tomorrow," she said with the tip of her index finger.

He sneered, turned around in disgust, walked out of the door and all the way to the front gate of the Base; then, feeling like he were entering a war zone, he stepped through the chain-linked gate.

He watched the heavy traffic pass in front of him. Where was Lisa? Without any type of hardware on his person, he felt like he were partially naked, or at least missing a weight from his stance that chipped the corner off his confidence.

When he felt a tug at his arm and heard his name spoken softly, he quickly turned around and was face to face with Lisa.

She withdrew slightly, which provided him a better look at her.

"Lisa," he said, "you made it."

"Of course I did. I was waiting for you inside the bus shelter." She half turned, pointing over her shoulder.

When she stretched her arm out, her golden-tipped hair rolled over her shoulders. She was wearing purple silk pants and a traditional Vietnamese dress, the ao-dai, which covered her hips and legs like a slit dress and her upper body like a tight-fitting leotard. The neckline of her dress slid close to her breasts where a small gold chain sparkled against her brown skin. When she turned around, tiny gold earrings set her face off perfectly. She beamed an airy smile at Marlin.

Marlin was speechless. Her eyes were so intriguing, so full of depth and warmth that he found himself just staring at them.

"Let's get started," she said as she took his hand and began to move towards the curb and wave down a taxi.

Saigon was as hectic as any city Marlin had ever visited. Maybe even more so as there was an overabundance of bicycles, three wheel scooters, motorcycles, donkey-drawn carts—all with little regard for traffic signs or keeping any type of order with the few cars that seemed forever stopped and honking their horns in fogs of exhaust.

First they visited the crowded stores on Tu Do Street where Marlin bought a gold necklace with a cross on it for his mother an an ivory etched cigarette lighter for his father.

The place was teeming with activity as vendors flowed out onto the sidewalks to set up their goods for sale. The many American civilians, unarmed GIs, and the Military Police took the edge off Marlin's fear that he might be the object of a lone sniper.

When Lisa asked, "Can I take you to my favorite place in the whole city?" Marlin was more than happy to oblige.

"We need a taxi," she added.

Marlin heralded a French Peugot to the side of the curb and when he slid into the back seat behind Lisa, the driver turned around to ask them where they wanted to go.

Marlin had the gut feeling that the guy was a Viet Cong. Whether it was the scarred face, crooked teeth, sinister smile, or the peeping eyes, Marlin could not tell, but he did not trust the man. As the car revved its engine and slipped from the curb, Marlin looked around the car for something to kill the driver with. There were no bludgeons in the back seat, no ropes. He decided if he had to he would use his bare hands; just wrap his left arm around his throat and gouge out his eyes with his right index finger.

"You're not taking me to the North Vietnamese headquarters, are you?" Marlin asked.

Lisa did not smile, instead, she acted offended. "You are talking dinky dau."

"I'm sorry. I'm still nervous running around the city without weapon. I just have to get used to it."

"I won't take you any place where you can get hurt. I promise."

Marlin saw the driver watching him in the rear

view mirror. He believed Lisa but the driver was no friend of either of theirs.

The taxi ride lasted an uncomfortable half-hour. The traffic was forever stopping and the driver constantly taking back alleys and making sudden movements with his hands.

Lisa finally said, "Here we are."

Marlin looked out the window. He saw a large sign with the words in English, SAIGON ZOO.

He chuckled in surprise, "I don't believe it. In Saigon, a zoo?"

"We even have a panda bear from China," Lisa said. "I love it here. It is so peaceful."

When they stepped out of the car, Marlin paid the driver, took Lisa's hand in his and led her down the wide path into the thick garden of trees, watching over his shoulder until the taxi disappeared.

As they strolled past hanging bougainvillaeas, Marlin asked, "Lisa, where did you learn to speak English so well?"

"I went to St. Mary's Catholic School in Saigon where English is the second language."

"How long did you go to school there?"

"Nearly three years."

"Did you graduate?"

"I had to quit when my second father died; my mother would not move up to Saigon and I had to take care of her. I am still trying to convince her to move here, but she is stubborn. She wants to stay in the country."

Marlin felt like he was more in an arboretum than a zoo as the animal cages were few and far between, but Lisa was like a little kid, excited to search out her favorite animals and show them to Marlin.

186

His leg felt stiff, but strong. The scab from his wound had shrunk considerably, and all the weight lifting machines the hospital provided definitely toned the muscles. They spent the entire afternoon at the zoo, walking, feeding plants to the squirrels and sitting on the different benches holding hands and just talking.

At dusk, Marlin reluctantly heralded a taxi.

As they slid inside, he said, "I'm almost willing to get shot again so I would not have to go back to that hospital tonight."

When Lisa spoke to the driver in Vietnamese, the young boy turned his head and said, "I know of a numba one restaurant."

Marlin smiled at Lisa, "Can't court-martial a guy for not wanting to eat hospital food."

The elevator opened on the eighteenth floor of the Embassy hotel and when Marlin looked out, he felt like he were on the French Riviera instead of in downtown Saigon. Soft music set the mood as he inspected the dining tables spread out over the roof top with maybe a quarter of them occupied by either Americans in civilian clothes or Vietnamese.

Half of the tables were set under an awning near the bar where the majority of patrons were gathered. The other tables were in the open. As it was not raining, Marlin directed Lisa to a far corner table, on the edge of the building surrounded by a waist-level cement wall topped with a metal handrail. It was near the dance floor where a small stage held the stands and chairs for a band.

The maître d' caught up to them and ran a towel over the cover of each chair to make certain they were dry, then helped Lisa into her seat.

"What a magnificent view," Marlin said as he sat down.

The Vietnamese maître d' smiled, "Yes. Do you know the city well?"

"This is my first social visit."

"Let me point out some of the buildings for you then."

The hotel was tucked between the Independence Palace and the Central Market on the corner of Duong Nguyen Duc and Nguyen Trung Trug. The gardens around Independence Palace were lighted as well as the columned, white Palace itself. To the far right of the Palace were the towers of the Catholic basilica, which reminded Marlin of pictures he had seen of Notre Dame. A few blocks away was Tu Do street where the Chase Manhattan Bank and the Bank of America were lighted. MACV headquarters was glowing with lights as well as the American embassy which looked like a bank safe painted white. The Saigon River shimmered in the background.

By the time the maître d' finished his tour, Marlin and Lisa were back at their table, staring at the lights of the city thinning out as they faded into the darkness of the Mekong Delta.

"Thank you," Marlin said.

The maître d' bowed and walked away.

Marlin looked across the table into Lisa's eyes and asked, "Is this city part of the same country I have been in for the last nine months?"

"Yes. The French knew what they were fighting for when they came here."

The waitress came over. She wore a green silk gossamer. She was no taller than five feet, husky and broad-shouldered. "Cocktails?" she asked.

"Certainly," Marlin said. "What would you care for, Lisa?"

"I don't know." She acted puzzled.

"How about a bottle of champagne," Marlin said. "Do you have champagne?"

"Of course, Sir. Would you like the wine list?"

"Do you have a California champagne?"

She smiled, "No, Sir. Only French champagnes."

"That will be fine then." He looked at Lisa, "I guess we haven't been here that long yet."

As the waitress wrote down the order, she asked, "Some hors d'oeuvres?"

"Let us take a look at the menu first." Marlin answered.

The menu was written in French and English and the prices were rather extravagant for a war zone, but there was plenty to choose from.

When the waitress returned with the champagne and glasses, Marlin ordered escargot.

"They are from cans," the waitress warned.

"As long as there is plenty of garlic butter and french bread, from cans will be fine."

Marlin found the buttery appetizers to the consistency of raw oysters, which he savored. Lisa watched him eat them.

For entrees, Marlin ordered curried eel, shrimp egg rolls, rice and vegetables.

"What do you think of Saigon so far?" Lisa asked.

"It is a beautiful city, but I don't trust it."

She nodded her head knowingly.

"There is a war going on here and our intelligence says that Saigon is the next target."

"I don't think so," Lisa said. "It is too big."

Marlin just huffed.

"How did you get over here, Marlin?"

"It was easy, and fast . . . I don't really feel like talking about it now, but let me tell you, I didn't pay for the ticket."

"I hope this war will end soon," she said as she picked up her fork and started to eat.

"I agree but I don't know why it would."

"It is a terrible thing. And going on for so long. It killed my father, one uncle and many of my friends . . . many of them. Only horror stories, all the time."

"Would you want to go to America?"

She smiled. "No. I love it here. It is my home. I do not want to go to America."

"I thought all of Vietnam wanted to move to America."

"Some people here think the opposite, that America wants to move here."

"If all the girls were as pretty as you, I'm sure they would—the male population anyway."

As they ate, the sky to the south, beyond the river, came aglow with flares. Flares that were so consistent and exact and plentiful that Marlin knew they had to be shot from a cannon.

Instead of feeling the horror of a night ambush lighted by flares and possibly being overrun, Beckwith thought of his men at the Ben Luc bridge. Under the circumstances, he felt only pride.

The food was delicious and added to their excitement.

Marlin drank most of the champagne himself and was feeling woozy by the time the meal was consumed.

"Where do you live in America?" Lisa asked.

"Petaluma, California . . . My father runs a small lumber mill there."

"Do you miss your family?"

"Of course. Every one of them."

"You are lucky to have them."

"And I am also lucky to have you."

Her smile revealed her shyness. "My father was a Frenchman, a tall, handsome man. He owned a rubber plantation in the Na Trang district and was killed by the Viet Cong when I was a small child. My mother brought me south to live with her relative in Saigon where I went to school. Mother remarried and moved to Ben Luc."

"And her second husband was killed as well?"

"Yes," Lisa bowed her head. "Mother said that the plantation was beautiful—a two-story white house, swimming pool and lines of tall rubber trees. I hope I can see it someday." More flares popped open to the south and tracers streaked up across the sky as the spotlights of a chopper's beamed down on the ground miles away.

Lisa placed her hand on top of Marlin's to get his attention, to point out the lights of a vehicle moving down the nearby street and looking so small. Marlin took her hand into his. It was trembling.

"What are you so nervous about?" Marlin asked.

"I feel wonderful right now . . . What will they do to you when you show up late tonight at the hospital?"

"Probably send me to Vietnam as an infantry platoon leader."

He laughed, but she stared at him.

"If I rented a room here for the night, would you stay with me?"

Her eyes grew in diameter. The pupils sparkled

like the remaining champagne in her glass. "Won't you get in trouble?"

"Yes, but I'll still end up at the bridge at Ben Luc tomorrow."

Marlin looked at her for an answer and when he saw the coy licking of her lips, he beckoned the maître d' to the table and asked him to arrange for a room.

The room had a radio and TV, a small bar in one of the cabinets, bathroom and fresh, clean sheets. Two paintings of the Vietnamese countryside decorated the walls — one picture of farmers transferring rice from seedbeds to the field, the other of a musk ox pulling a cartful of rice with a small boy sitting on its back and directing the animal with a long stick.

There were no bullet holes anywhere.

French cognac was brought to the room shortly thereafter and when Marlin signed for it at the door, he turned, and began to laugh.

"Why are you laughing?" Lisa asked.

"Because I feel so darn good."

"It is probably the champagne," she smiled.

"No. It's you, Lisa. That's what it is, you."

Marlin set the two glasses down on the top of the dresser and turned the lights out. He stood there for a moment until his eyes got used to the darkness. The light from the window outlined Lisa who was sitting on the bed.

He moved to her side and touched her arm. She turned towards him and opened her mouth slowly.

Their lips touched and their bodies melted together.

They stopped only long enough to shed their clothes and throw the covers back from the bed. Then their lust exploded and their bodies melted together completely.

Marlin felt like he was hurting her when he entered her body. She moaned with each of his thrusts, almost painfully. He found himself wanting to dig deeper into her. The realization surprised him, but it did not make him want to stop. She squeezed him so tightly and gasped air through her teeth like she was enjoying the pain. Both of their bodies began to sweat which lubricated their movements and added to their passion.

When she finally accepted his final thrusts with a satisfying moan, he relaxed against her heaving chest, and just joined in her breathing, holding her snugly around the hips.

They relaxed together, touched each other tenderly, hugged each other, explored each other's bodies, breathed at the same rate, cuddled and fondled, and after another fling of youthful sex, fell asleep in each other's arms, fully satisfied.

Chapter 17

The Huey helicopter was flying so high over the open rice fields that even with Ben Luc in view, Marlin could not make out the bridge as he sat in the window seat with his head close to the glass, squinting to look forward. The river was in sight as well as a line of Highway 4, but no bridge. Standing, he moved forward to the cockpit and looked out the panoramic front windshield. The bridge stood as tall and whole as he had remembered it before his injury. He grinned and sighed at the same time.

Realizing they were flying high, he tapped the pilot on the shoulder.

The captain turned around and looked at Marlin. "What's wrong?" he hollered without removing his helmet.

"I just want to make sure you are going to drop me off at the bridge."

"Geez," the pilot replied, shaking his head, "you'd think you were going home or something. Calm down. We always come in this way."

Marlin shrugged his shoulders. Two weeks and he had already forgotten how high the choppers approached their LZs to avoid ground fire.

At the thought of biting the big one, Marlin's mind drifted from thoughts of Lisa to the job he was about to take over again. The hospital had softened his outlook on life; now was as good a time as any to start concentrating on staying alive again.

When the chopper landed on the road a hundred yards south of the bridge, Marlin slid the door open and looked out. To his surprise, standing there in the tornado-force winds was his platoon sergeant Hillerman.

When Hillerman started to run closer to the helicopter, Marlin waved him off, jumped out and ran in the stooped position towards the Sergeant. Pushing him back a ways, he knelt on one knee, held onto his helmet with one hand and steadied himself on John's shoulder.

When the pilot gave him the thumbs up sign, Marlin returned the gesture and lowered his head as the helo swooped south, blowing a trail of swirling dirt into his face.

When it was quiet enough to hear, Marlin stood up and looked at his platoon sergeant.

Hillerman looked terrible — visibly shaking, the skin on his face sagging, thick sacks having formed under his eyes that were circled with black, and it was not camouflage. His eyes were sunk deep into his skull and glazed with fear.

Hillerman spoke first. "They tried to blow up the bridge again last night."

"What happened?" Marlin asked, looking down the road at the bridge. There was only a pair of Vietnamese about halfway across. He looked at the command bunkers at the far end. One head popped out and looked his way, but Marlin did not recognize the face.

"I don't know. They tried it once before by strapping dynamite to a floating log, but nobody saw anything last night. I was in the bunker sleeping when I heard an explosion that knocked me on the ground."

"Anybody hurt?"

"I don't know what the hell happened to White. I just can't find him."

They started walking towards the bridge.

"Was he on guard duty at the time?"

"Yes, Sir. He was . . . We looked all morning around the bridge, up and down the river banks, but we couldn't find a hair from his head anywhere."

"Anybody else missing."

"No. Perez was standing watch with White. Jesus had some cuts on his arm. It almost looked like he did it to himself. I didn't tell him that, but it looked like it to me. He said it was from shrapnel; I sent him to the infirmary over at the artillery compound."

"What did he have to say about White?"

"He said that White was sitting on the bridge rail and the explosion threw him into the water."

"Did White have a flak jacket on?"

"Yes, Sir."

Beckwith shook his head. A man could not swim a foot with all that gear on and it was too darn much to take off after falling so far. They might not ever find White's body.

"How many men do you have?"

"I got four new recruits while you were gone. So

196

that brings us up to twenty-six."

"You still in the bunkers?"

"Yes, Sir. Boy, am I glad to see you back here. The men haven't been watching for you, but I have. Every chopper that comes within half a mile of here," he smiled wickedly.

"You look like you could use a month's sleep, Sarge. Why don't you take a break?"

"I've been waiting for you ever since you left . . . and I'm sorry too."

"About what?"

"About pulling that wire like I did. I still have dreams about that. I thought I was just disarming the damn thing."

"That is what Charlie wanted you to think."

"I'll never do that again."

"Just make sure none of the new men do it again either . . . Any news about Hoppy?"

"Hoppy?"

"Yeah. Hoppy?"

"No. I don't think so."

By the time the two of them reached the first bunker, more heads were looking their way.

Gatz was the first one to come running over to greet Marlin. Although Marlin retreated slightly at the sight of the huge black man running so fast, he extended his hand in greeting. Gatz took it and nearly squeezed it out of joint he was so excited. "I never thought this day would come, Sir. Am I happy to see you back."

"About as happy as I am to be here, Gatz. How is your squad?"

"They're fine, and you?"

"I feel like a million bucks right now. Really fine."

Marlin heard his name called and looked to see Kraus running across the bridge waving his arms, with some of the other men following him.

Kraus ran up to Marlin, threw his arms around Beckwith's neck and gave him a big hug.

Marlin laughed and said, "Holy shit, Kraus. What the hell are you doing?"

"Lieutenant, it is so good to see you back here. Really." Kraus released the Lieutenant and stood back to look at how he had stained the front of Marlin's clothes with fresh mud.

"You just ruined my whole image," Marlin said as he laughed.

Kraus replied, "That platoon sergeant has been driving everyone nuts around here, Sir."

Beckwith looked for Hillerman, but he was nowhere to be seen.

Ivy tapped the Lieutenant on the shoulder and asked, "How does it feel to be back, Sir?"

"I am about as happy as a pig in his favorite shit hole."

"Stick around a while and you might change your mind," Kraus said. "This place is getting worse all the time."

"I was just worried about them sending me to a different Division somewhere in country . . . Where is my pistol and M-16?"

"They're in our bunker. I tore both of them down and scrubbed them clean with a toothbrush and kept them oiled. The actions on them are like new."

Marlin followed Kraus back to the bunker, shaking hands with his men, rattling off about the hospital and Saigon, about all the nurses, the food and hot baths and saunas. He felt a sense of power being back with the platoon. He never mentioned Lisa.

He stooped as he entered the bunker, sat down on his cot and reached out for the M-16 and checked it quickly, then set it against the sandbag wall behind him. He took the holstered .45 pistol from Kraus's outstretched hands, unholstered it, snapped open the sliding action, let it snap shut, replaced the pistol in its holster and sat down with a satisfied look on his face.

"I missed this pistol about as much as anything in my life," he said as he tapped its case. "If I had it tucked under my pillow in that hospital, I think I would have slept a lot sounder at night."

"I knew you'd miss it; that's why I took such good care of it. Seems like every time I thought of you I cleaned that son of a bitch."

Beckwith stared at Kraus, those nondescript colored eyes, pointed nose and pointed head. Rudolph's shirt was open, dog tags tangling; he was sitting relaxed on an ammunition crate and smelling like a dirty bag of laundry socks.

"Thanks, Kraus."

"It is good to have you back, Sir."

The noise of men talking outside the bunker brought Marlin to his feet and outside; he was feeling taller and more secure now with his weight there, pressing against his hips.

The rain started again and as if being initiated, Marlin let it drench him. He finally was introduced to the new men, two white boys and two black. Barney Bowen was in the first squad, Steve Avezac in the second, Bob Newsome in the third and Abraham Quick with the fourth. Marlin just smiled at

199

them and did not try to read any of the expressions on their faces that held deeper, more troubled thoughts. Usually he studied the new men to figure out ways of quickly identifying them, but with these men, now he just grinned and marveled at the cheerfulness of his platoon living in such squalor. Finally, as if from a bad dream, he said, "You better spread the fuck out. One grenade would get us all."

Although they all smiled as if it was a joke, they did so.

"How is your leg, Sir?" Kraus asked.

"Little sore. I have to take penicillin pills daily and make sure the damn thing doesn't get infected, but it'll be all right. What is going on around here?"

"Let's get inside and I'll brief you."

When they moved back in out of the rain, they both sat down on the opposing cots and Kraus said, "There is still talk of them attacking Saigon, but nothing has come through yet. That seems to be what is on Command's mind."

"It seemed pretty quiet when I was up there. They've been talking about that so damn long, you'd think something would have come of it by now."

"Maybe they were waiting for you to leave before they started anything."

Beckwith chuckled.

"Tet, their religious holiday, is supposed to start this weekend. Something like New Year's for them, and it is the Year of the Monkey. We are going to acknowledge their holiday and let them celebrate for a week without fighting. So personally I doubt that it will happen before Tet. Maybe right after though."

"A truce, huh?"

"Something like that."

"Well, good, I could use another week off. How is the Old Man doing?"

"He was concerned when you got hit."

"Where is he now?"

"A few days ago he moved into the field with the first and second platoons. They found some tunnels with a lot of ammunition stored inside and it caught his attention. They've been out there a long time."

"Yeah . . . Any news about Hoppy?"

"No, Sir."

"You seen the Green Beret around?"

"Oh yeah. He walks around like he has a grenade rammed up his ass and it is about to go off any second. He won't give us the right time of the day."

"How about the laundromat?"

"It is still closed down."

"That old whore promised me some information about Hoppy too. Why don't we get over there and see how mamasan is doing? Maybe I can get her to talk."

"Sir. I think you better get some more supplies first. Things are going to shit around here. Nobody knows what is happening and they are all pissed off at Hillerman. It will be nighttime soon and nobody knows who is to stand guard on the bridge and how to do it. Hillerman's latest plans is to have us stand on the middle pilings at water level. He just told us that this afternoon. We all thought he was out of his mind."

"OK. Maybe we can get over and see mamasan in the morning . . . Why not try and pick up the Old Man on the radio and tell him I'm back."

"I can't seem to pick up Bravo-six, either. Maybe he is still too far away."

"They're OK though?"

"I haven't heard any helicopters or artillery units sent to their aid. I assume they're fine."

"Anything big happen while I was gone?"

Kraus wrinkled his upper lip and shook his head. "White was lost over the bridge last night. That's the biggest so far. Some ambushes picking up a few here and there, but nothing big."

"How about you guys?"

"We are like sitting ducks during the day, but nobody has been hurt except last night." "Good."

"And that is lucky for Hillerman. Everybody thinks he is going dinky dau. He would have called artillery in on Ben Luc if I had let him last night. You should have seen him running around. I thought he was going to shoot one of us. He thought we were under attack and was firing his rifle on automatic at whatever."

"Geez, if he does not calm down, I might talk to the C.O. about him."

"You better, Sir. Hillerman is going buggy and one of the men might shoot him before he gets us all hurt. It could be that serious."

"How about White?"

"Shit, the fucker fell off the bridge with all his gear on. He can't walk on water."

"Yeah. OK. I'll see to things. Try again and see if you can pick up Bravo-six."

Kraus tried but with no success.

202

At dusk, Beckwith and Kraus went to see the Green Beret and listened as the Captain complained about Hillerman throwing grenades at his own shadow and how the Vietnamese were even afraid to cross the bridge during the day for fear of being shot.

Beckwith did not apologize, but realized he had to do something.

He did not stay long. The Captain's cutie was cooking supper and she smiled at Beckwith as if she knew what had taken place in Saigon. The news could have spread that fast.

Beckwith was quick to leave before the topic came up.

It was not until the next afternoon that Marlin got over to the laundromat. Mamasan was about as happy to see him as the Captain had been.

The front door still had the closed sign on it, so the Lieutenant, Kraus with his radio, and Gatz had to walk around to the side door to enter.

The laundromat smelled like stale, spilt beer. The girls were dressed in robes with half the make-up on that they usually wore. They were still smoking American cigarettes and downing the coffee, but sandals had replaced the high heels.

When they saw Beckwith, they withdrew from the mamasan sitting at a table near the quiet juke box. She picked up her cigarette and glared distastefully at Marlin.

Outside of her role as madam, she looked much older and worn. The lines around her jowls were much deeper, her lips cracked, nose streaked with veins, the sacks below her eyes were as thick as orange peels.

"The place is closed down, Lieutenant. This is off limits for you now. You could be reprimanded for even being here."

"I'm here on business. I am still missing a man and you said you might have some information about his whereabouts."

She stubbed out the cigarette. "You don't have the money to make me even want to look."

Beckwith pointed the barrel of the rifle at her face, "And you don't have the brains to cross me."

Maybe it was the good times in Saigon, maybe it was what Marlin feared she might do to Lisa, maybe it was all the time to relax, but the tension just exploded to the surface. He could feel a surge of hate shoot adrenalin into his veins and it made him feel a surge of power. He knew if he shot her, it would be unprovoked; but at the same time, there would be no investigation, just another dead gook.

She could read his thoughts. She said, "I have seen many men die. It really does not matter."

Beckwith used his free hand to brush his chin. As he regained control of himself, he lowered the shaking rifle to his side. "I asked you a question. If you do not cooperate, I'll have you arrested."

Without moving her head, she scanned the room with her eyes, "I have not heard a thing about POWs in this area. As far as I know, there are none."

"Did you ask?"

"My regular links of communication have been broken. You are aware of the NVA buildup."

Beckwith nodded his head.

"There is nothing," she said.

Beckwith glared at her and concluded she was telling the truth.

"Let's get out of here, Kraus. This place is beginning to stink of more than the beer."

Kraus hefted the radio and as they walked out the side door, mamasan was lighting another cigarette and the girls were moving back towards her.

Marlin headed down the road, walking quickly back towards the bunkers which now were becoming like a friendly, warm place to stay, although it was no more than a dry hole underground.

There were not many people on the road. It was time for the Vietnamese to take their afternoon rest.

They were passing a large-trunked mango tree when a rock splashed in a puddle of water beside them. The three men turned their heads and rifles in the direction of the tree.

Lisa stood behind the tree, her lower body hidden, her chest and face exposed, her hands resting on a branch.

When Marlin saw her, his face lit up.

She pressed her forefinger to her lips, picked up another rock in front of her and flipped it at Marlin. He caught it.

As he unwrapped a note around the rock, he looked back at the tree and saw that Lisa was gone. He unfolded the small, torn piece of paper and read:

I KNOW WHERE HAPPY IS.

Beckwith handed the note to Kraus.

When Kraus read it, he asked, "What are you going to do about it, Sir?"

Marlin kept looking in the direction that Lisa had fled, "Tonight we'll visit Lisa and find out what she knows. Let's get back to the bunker and prepare to move out."

Chapter 18

When Hoppy finally popped his head up out of the tunnel and looked around, for the first time since he arrived in Nam eight months ago, he welcomed the sight of the thick jungle with its dangling vines and thick green leaves.

He wiggled his way out of the hole, gained his balance and stretched on tiptoes, inhaling the sweet breeze. He tilted his head backwards and savored the cleansing rain as it ran down his cheeks and into his eyes. He blinked.

As all his senses soaked in the freedom, he felt a stab in the back and turned to see a young Vietnamese soldier thrusting a rifle mounted bayonet at him, then pointing the rifle down a path. The boy was young, probably no more than sixteen years old, and nervous, but Hoppy was so weak that he did not dare to try and overpower him.

"OK . . . OK," Hoppy said as he started down the trail which led to a cleared field of rice. His feet hurt on the grass and he watched where he stepped, but it felt good to stand up and walk.

He inspected the area to see if he recognized where he was. It was all too familiar, but no paths leading to home, no signs of his platoon, no American base.

As he stood there studying the terrain, trying to remember, the guard walked in front of him, and with the bayonet at the ready, poked at his shirt. Hoppy retreated. The guard shouted orders in Vietnamese and this time slashed at Hoppy's pants, repeating the same command.

Hoppy thought the guard was going nuts. The young kid pointed the bayonet towards the canal and then slashed at Hoppy's clothes again. Hoppy finally concluded that he was about to take a bath and the guard wanted him to disrobe.

As Hoppy started to take his clothes off, the guard relaxed and spoke more calmly, nodding his head, but not smiling.

Naked, without further prodding, Hoppy led the way to the water and about thirty feet shy of his target, he came upon a hole in the ground about the size that a 24-inch television might be crated in. At first Hoppy thought it was a latrine, but it did not smell like one and it was empty.

When he tried to walk around it, the guard hollered and pointed inside the hole. Hoppy did not understand.

Hoppy looked at the hole, then into the grass at a bamboo lid with four-inch slots. There were notches in the rim of the hole where the lid could be held in place.

Hoppy began to shake his head. "No . . . Oh no . . . I'm not getting in there."

The guard started panting through his opened mouth. Instead of removing his hands from the gun, he licked at a bead of sweat balancing on his upper lip. The barrel of the rifle quivered.

Hoppy looked at the open rice field before him. It was void of workers. He looked back at the guard who was stretching his neck over his shoulder, the rifle barrel pointed to one side.

Hoppy should have thought of doing this when he was first captured. As if struck by a cattle prod, he started to run as fast as his bare feet and weak legs could carry him.

He heard a shot fired into the air and the shouting of Vietnamese behind him that fueled his adrenalin. He jumped into the rice paddy, the water about knee-deep, and pushed as hard as he could to cross it.

No more than fifty yards into the paddy he heard more Vietnamese shouting and the splash of their pursuit.

He was running out of breath and turned his head to see four Vietnamese with arms flaying, legs hurdling, coming after him.

Still looking backwards, his knees struck a rice paddy berm and he tumbled forward into the water, head first.

Before he had a chance to come up for air, he was grabbed around the legs. With his eyes clenched tight, his nose squished, he was beaten with fists and rifle butts that struck him in the kidneys, back of the head, buttocks, ribs.

He went limp with despair and used his hands to shield his head.

When he was pulled to his feet, gagging, one of the men kicked him between the legs and the pain from all the other blows was minor compared to the wrenching that overwhelmed his body.

In a semi-state of shock, he was dragged back to the hole and thrown inside. He did not fit by a long shot and the butts of rifles mashed at his back and his hands until his knees gave in and he crouched into a small, tight ball that just barely squeezed together. He could feel the lid set in place and crunch him even tighter into the hole.

At first he just lay there in the kneeling position with his head tucked forward onto his chest, his arms extended backwards towards his feet, whimpering, not having the energy to scream as his ribs felt like they were broken.

When he tried to extend his legs to give his neck more room, his back pressed up against the lid and made the move impossible. The thought of wanting to stretch out made him claustrophobic and want to panic.

He was in a perfect spot to hide, from everything except the pain.

He did not even hear them walk away.

After several hours in that position, Hoppy was so cramped he tried to turn over. He moved his left arm around to his right buttock and rolled his right shoulder backwards. As his body twisted, his backbone felt like it was going to come apart and his knee caps explode. He was stuck.

He screamed bloody murder and tried to gain strength to move himself back into his original position, but he couldn't. He was curled into a ball like a puppy with its chain wound around a stake for the first time, losing its voice barking.

He whimpered and moaned and talked to himself slowly back into the kneeling position, abandoning all future plans for a more comfortable position.

The sun beat down on his bare back and made it sizzle. The air he gasped into his lungs felt totally void of oxygen. He had to pant to stay alive.

When the jungle cast its cool shadow over his frying body, he heard a new sound, a buzzing. It was an all-too-familiar sound he wanted to hide from. He silently prayed that the mosquito would not find him.

He heard the change in pitch as the mosquito turned.

When the buzzing stopped, his heart sank with disappointment as he felt the tiny feet tickle his back. He had been discovered. He heard the sound of another buzzing, then silence as the other insect landed. They walked parallel courses, stopping, tentatively searching, silently sticking their stingers into his flesh and filling their bellies on his blood. More mosquitoes came and had their fill of Hoppy.

It was neither sunrise nor sunset, it was feeding time for the bugs. Hoppy did not want to scratch them, he wanted to pull their wings and legs off and crush each individual mosquito between his finger tips. He wanted them to holler out with pain before they died.

He urinated on himself to distract them, but it did not work. It only made a bigger mess of the hole and him.

His mind wandered off. He made sense all the time, but it just skipped around like in a dream.

At first his stomach knotted up and hurt, but as it shrank, he lost the feeling of hunger. As his body fat was slowly consumed, he started to feel himself actually wasting away. He could almost feel his bones being leaked of the marrow to sustain his vital organs.

But he did not want to bake his organs like fish on a drying rack. He needed water the most. He could feel his temperature climbing, like his bodily organs were going on strike and demanding better conditions. If they only knew.

He wanted the lungs to last as long as the heart. His heart almost felt like it were rejuvenated, free. The heart felt good.

The sun was slowly setting, or was it rising? Hoppy was not sure. It was just that he could not remember. He knew that it was not on its full pass over his head.

He could not remember how it was before that. The muscles were so twisted, in so much pain.

For the first time in many mind trips, he could hear someone drawing closer to his position, and it was funny how the new sound in itself was exciting. Footsteps, he remembered now, a person was coming closer. A person. Somebody. He did not want food, he wanted a companion.

When the lid was removed, he could feel his back grow like an accordion, like a hope chest opened after many years.

He heard the sound of the lid thrown to one side and his back popped upward. In the kneeling position, he looked up to see the smiling face of his Vietnamese captor, Hoang Tran, with his slicked-down hair and his smirking face. Hoppy's world was reeling. He touched the cheek. It did not hurt, but neither did the rest of his body. When he looked at the hand that touched his face, there was green puss on the finger tips.

The Vietnamese smiled. "Comrade," he said, "We are ready to talk to you about your war crimes. Do you wish to talk?"

Hoppy was dazed. He did not even know if he was willing to stand up. He did not answer. Instead he placed his hands in the dirt and tried to lift himself out of the hole. He could hardly move. He was exhausted, weak.

Hoang Tran said, "I have come to help you go home, but first you must answer some questions. I have discussed your situation with my superiors, and they said if you cooperate, you will go home. Would you like that? Home?"

"Home," Hoppy whispered. He did not think of the rolling hills of wheat in North Dakota. He did not think of his parents or his brother or the 1951 Chevy pick-up parked beside the barn ready for him to start. He thought of his squad leader, Buffalo Bill, and Beckwith, and the rest of the platoon.

Hoppy opened his mouth and for the first time since he had stopped screaming how long ago, he said, "Home." But his voice was raspy. The vocal chords vibrated and tickled his throat.

He pulled himself into the kneeling position and crawled out of the hole.

Hoang Tran helped him to his feet and with a turned-up nose pointed to the canal a short distance away. "Maybe you would like to wash first."

Hoang Tran handed Hoppy a small bar of lime soap and helped him to the edge of the water.

Hoppy sat down on a log and placed his feet in

the water; his body hungered for the water and the feeling sent a shot of satisfaction through his body. He washed the shit off the back of his calf and off his toes. He worked the soap back up his legs and thighs, feeling his body awakening with pain. His body was weak but his mind raced forward like a car out of control into euphoria, ecstasy.

He looked over his shoulder at Hoang Tran and the young guard standing behind him with an AK-47 at the ready.

Hoppy had a flashback of his original capture at a canal similar to the one he stood in. He thought he was going to be captured again. By reflex, he dropped the soap, plunged into the water and sucked up a mouthful. After the first gasp, his system went on freeze. The volume of his heartbeat picked up.

He could feel his hair being tugged, the glare of sun in his eyes and the feel of mud and slime on his back. He opened his eyes to see the face of Hoang Tran about two feet away. The small mouth opened. He said, "I think it is time we talk."

Hoppy turned over and started wretching the filthy water from his stomach and lungs. He lay there in pain until the probing of the bayonet from his captor made more sense than his sickness.

When he wobbled to his feet, clothes were thrown at him by the guard. Hoppy staggered back to the log, sat down and worked his way into a black pair of pants, the kind a karate fighter might wear, but much lighter in fabric. They came only to below his knees. The shirt was the same color, without buttons, and short at the sleeves.

When Hoppy walked to the top of the canal, the guard shoved him back into the jungle to a large, command-post-type, leaf-shaded canopy.

Hoang Tran was sitting there on a stool behind a table no larger than a typewriter stand. On the opposite side of the table was another stool. Hoang Tran pointed for Hoppy to sit down.

Hoppy walked down the two steps into the hole, leaned on the table and sat down.

"What would you like to eat when we finish talking?" Hoang Tran asked.

"Food." It was all that he could think of.

Hoang Tran smiled, "How would you like a club sandwich with a glass of iced tea? Would you like that?"

Hoppy's mouth started to salivate just at the thought of iced tea. He nodded his head.

"Good, then that is what I will have the guards fix you when we are finished. Just one sandwich though. That is probably all you feel like eating anyway. I know they are taking good care of you . . . Hoppy, since I want to become your friend, why don't you tell me a little about yourself. Where are you from?"

Hoppy knew that according to the Geneva Convention he was not supposed to tell him anything except his name, rank, serial number, date of birth. He knew that, but under the pain and fatigue he felt, he wondered if it mattered.

He said, "My name . . ." It came out so raspy and cracked, that he stopped.

Hoang Tran said, "Let me get a glass of water before you talk. It might help."

Hoang Tran spoke to the guard behind Hoppy and within a few seconds, as Hoppy watched, the guard returned with a green plastic cup. Before he placed it down on the table, Hoppy took it from his hands and guzzled the water. It was lukewarm and like morphine it shot to his head. He could feel his organs fighting for their share.

It was like a pep pill. It woke him up and almost reminded him of the will to live again. As he sat there gasping, he looked at Hoang Tran and realized that now he had something to lose again. The thought was depressing.

Hoppy touched his cheek and could feel the wound awakening with pain.

"Yes," Hoang Tran said, "I will have a doctor look at that wound as soon as we finish discussing your war crimes; but first, where are you from?"

Hoppy did not think it would matter. He said, "I am from North Dakota."

"Would you like to write this all down for me, Hoppy?"

Hoang Tran leaned to one side, opened a brief case at his feet, produced a piece of lined paper and a sharpened, yellow Skilcraft Bonded number 2 medium lead pencil. He placed both of them in front of Hoppy, pointed in his direction for easy pickup and said, "Please write this down."

Hoppy stared at the paper and foolishly believed that without the paper, he would not have to write. He fell on the lined paper and tore it to shreds as he panted and whimpered.

When he was through, clutching the paper to his chest with shoulders hunched high and expecting a

216

beating, he meekly looked up at Hoang Tran who was so calm and patient, the thin face not moving.

Hoang Tran produced another sheet of paper from his brief case and explained as he set it in the same spot as the first, "Hoppy, if you do not write these things down as you promised me, I will not give you that sandwich. And it was very difficult for me to get all the ingredients for that sandwich. I have lettuce, tomatoes, a little ham, not much. The hardest was the mayonnaise. It was all hard, but I knew you would want it just right. Do you understand? I want your cooperation so that you can go home. I want to send you home, Hoppy, but unless you do as I tell you to atone for your war crimes, I will be forced to keep you here. Now try again."

Hoang Tran's English was superb, spoken with a slight French accent, if anything.

Hoppy thought of the juicy lettuce and then of his platoon again and tears welled up in his eyes. He took up the pencil and Hoang Tran said, "There, I understand, but it will not take long. Tell me where you are from, about your family. What the weather is like there. How many people in your town. Things you miss and would enjoy again. All the things that will be yours when you finish and go home. Write them down."

The lack of food had made Hoppy so weak that his hand shook as he wrote. Once he wrote down the first line, "My name is Earl Moss and I am from North Dakota." After that, he knew that it did not really matter how much more he wrote. He was already in territory deep enough to have himself shot as a traitor. He could not go back.

When he finished the first page, Hoang Tran picked up the sheet of paper and slid another piece before him and started to read what was written down. Hoang Tran smiled as he read and said, "Very good. It will be something for you to go home there."

When Hoppy finished the second page, he looked at Hoang Tran and said, "I'm finished." Hoang Tran took the paper from him and read the second sheet. "Finished." He wadded up the papers and threw them on the ground.

"Very good, Hoppy. Now I want you to write about your war crimes. Tell me about the men you fought with and about your missions. I want you to write these things down, then I will give you that sandwich I promised; and of course the iced tea."

When another piece of paper was set before Hoppy, he stared at it.

"Please write, first the name of your unit and your platoon leader's name. When you are finished, I will tear the sheet of paper up like I did the first."

Hoppy stared at Hoang Tran and shook his head. He did not believe him.

Hoang Tran said, "We already know these things, Hoppy. We just want you to write them down. We know that Lieutenant Marlin Beckwith is your leader. We know it. We just want you to write it down. Now, do so."

Hoppy sighed. He thought of the sandwich and then the iced tea. His mind was so weak that he believed that they might even send him home.

When he wrote down the Lieutenant's name, he felt shame, then fear, as if he had signed the Lieutenant's death warrant.

"Very good, now write down the other members of your platoon. There is White and Gatz and Kraus. Just write their names down. We know."

Hoppy did as he was told, and as he wrote, he found pleasure in seeing the names on paper. He was not betraying them, he was seeing them again, all of them, and it brought joy, pure joy to his heart.

He wrote down everything Hoang Tran asked of him, until it came time to write down the mission of his platoon.

Hoppy refused.

His refusal went on for many minutes and Hoang Tran began to show his anger. He threatened and pleaded, but Hoppy would not write further.

Having exhausted his alternatives, Hoang Tran bent over the side of the table, opened the brief case, pulled out a small revolver, sat back up straight in the chair and checked the cylinder to make certain that it was loaded. He snapped the cylinder back into place and looked at Hoppy. He said, "Hoppy, if you do not continue to write, I will shoot you through the top lip. It will probably blow out the back of your throat." Hoang picked up the pistol, pointed it at Hoppy's mouth and said, "Write."

Hoppy could not help it, but he stared at the barrel of the pistol and smiled like an exciting movie was about to pop out onto a screen.

Hoang Tran set the pistol down and looked over Hoppy's shoulder to the guard and said, "Then I will have to place you back in the hole until you want to cooperate with me. Next time, the hole might fill with rain water. A drop at a time."

The thought of being so cramped again and the bugs eating on his back, and having to watch water creep up to his nose wondering when it would get so deep he could not avoid inhaling it, made Hoppy shudder with fear. "Wait," he said. "Wait."

Chapter 19

When Marlin saw Lisa step into the door opening from her bedroom, although he had seen her only a few hours ago at the mango tree, he felt his body relax as he savored her looks, glowing in lovely innocence, like the way she had been in Saigon.

Thuy distracted Marlin by moving along the right wall, his eyes darting back and forth, his rifle at the ready.

Kraus walked up to the table, turned, bent his knees so that the bottom of the radio rested on its lip, worked his shoulders out of the back straps, turned around and held the radio from falling.

Marlin looked back at Lisa. She was wearing black silk pants and a white blouse; the top two buttons were open revealing a small portion of her undergarment. She looked like she had been working in a field all day long and had just gotten dressed after getting ready for bed. She tidied the loose strands of hair of her unkempt hair with her right hand.

When her brothers poked their head into the kitchen, she talked to them in Vietnamese and laughingly shooed them back, but her mother came out and stood against the back wall near the kitchen

221

utensils and fixed herself a fresh mouthful of betel nut.

Marlin knew he could not spend the night with Lisa as he had in Saigon. It would be way out of line in front of his men, but he could feel himself melting in her presence.

"Sit down," she said.

He set his rifle against the table, pulled out a chair and sat down.

Lisa said, "I am glad that you finally came."

"I don't want to get you into any more trouble than you might already be in now," Marlin replied. "That's why I waited until it got dark, but you have to tell me what you know about Hoppy."

The danger of the situation did not appear on her face. She asked, "How are you feeling?"

He shrugged, cracked a quick smile. "It feels like I have been here a lot longer than I actually have been. Almost like I never left."

"Is your wound healing well?"

"Yes, I think so," he reflexively touched his crotch without looking down.

When Keats appeared in the doorway, Marlin turned his head towards him and said, "Ken, take a look around the outside and post two men in the back until we leave, just to be safe."

Ken nodded his head and turned the corner.

Marlin said to Lisa, "Why don't you sit down here and tell me all you know."

The single candle on the table cast shadows that crossed each other on the ceiling, danced in the corners and stretched along the walls.

"He is being held in a camp, a VC camp." She

came no closer.

Marlin removed a folded map from the visqueen binder and spread it out on the table. He looked into Lisa's eyes. "Could you show me on the map where this camp is located?"

She looked at the piece of paper before her. "I don't understand," she replied. "I've never seen a map like this before, only one of the world."

"Look here." He bent over the map and put the candle right on top of it; its lashing flame cast shadows across the wrinkles and folds. He pointed his finger at the Ben Luc bridge and held it there and looked at her. "See, this is where we are, at the Ben Luc bridge. This is the east fork of the Vam Co River." He drew his finger diagonally across the page. "On Highway 4 to the south is Tan An and to the north Saigon." Each time he called out a name, he showed on the paper with his finger where it was located.

When he finished, he sat back and looked at Lisa again and repeated his question.

She shook her head in bewilderment, but Marlin got the impression that she was not trying very hard. He looked at Thuy.

Thuy moved away from the wall and leaned over the table and spoke briefly in Vietnamese with Lisa.

After a minute in which Marlin watched the two of them exchange words, Thuy looked at Marlin and said, "She says that she could take us there; but she does not know how to explain how to get there."

Marlin shook his head, "Do you know about this camp, Thuy?"

223

"No, Lieutenant, but I was not brought up in this province. I am from up north."

"How about the Captain?" Kraus asked.

Marlin looked at his radio operator as if he were crazy. He looked back at Lisa. She seemed stubborn. He knew he didn't have the time to seek others who might know about a camp, nor did he want to let the local villagers know that he had any information about Hoppy.

Marlin looked at Thuy and said, "I don't want her going anywhere with us, Thuy." There was anger in his voice. He whipped his head in Lisa's direction, "Lisa, how would you go if you were to take us there?"

It was almost inconceivable that she could not describe the route to Marlin. He could read a map as easily as a book, even faster. As he studied her frowning face, other questions popped into his head. He wished that she would hurry and answer the first.

When she remained silent, he tried to calm himself and asked in a soothing voice, "Has this camp been there very long?"

Lisa straightened her back and replied, "The tunnels have, but now there are more soldiers from the north."

"How many?"

"I don't know for sure. I just heard that many arrive daily."

"Why are they going to the camp?"

"For the reason you told me, to attack Saigon."

Marlin had heard it so many times before from the C.O. that it did not impress him anymore.

224

"How do you know that Hoppy is with them?"

"There is an American prisoner with fair hair like myself who was recently captured in the Delta nearly a month ago."

Kraus said, "So they did get him across the river."

Marlin asked, "What do they intend to do with Hoppy?"

She shrugged her shoulders. "They say that as long as he is with them, the Americans will not attack."

Kraus piped in, "They've been reading fairy tales instead of tactical books."

"Shut up, Kraus," Marlin said out of the side of his mouth with his eyes still on Lisa. "Can you tell us where the camp is?"

"I cannot picture it in my mind."

"Then we will have to take you with us," Marlin stated as he clenched his fist and quietly thumped it on the table.

Thuy replied, "That is what she wants."

Marlin shrugged. He couldn't believe he was getting her involved. He wondered if it was a selfish decision that his men would see right through.

Kraus asked, "Sir, do you think she might be leading us into an ambush?"

Marlin stared at Lisa. Her eyes were so gentle. "No. I don't think so."

"But I heard some of these bitches have razor blades up their cunts, ready to cut it off if a guy sticks his prick in there."

Marlin jerked his head towards Kraus, "That is enough, Kraus. I know what I am doing. I've made my decision. That's an order."

225

When Thuy explained to Lisa's mother, the old woman began to weep in a high-pitched shrill monotone, the juices of the betel nut dripping down the sides of her mouth.

"How far of a walk is it?" Marlin asked Lisa, now upset with Kraus's statement and the screaming mother.

"Not far," Lisa replied.

"More than one day's walk?"

"About one day's walk."

"How do you know where it is?"

"The news is spreading through the village."

"Yeah, but how do you know where the camp is?"

"It is a recruiting camp for VC. After my second father was killed I was brought there for indoctrination, but I was released later on."

"How come it is still there?"

"It is not in one spot, but in an area. When you find it you will understand."

"You mean it has been there all this time and the Americans have not destroyed it."

"Wait until you find it."

"Well you can't go looking like that," Marlin said. "You're too easy to identify. We will have to get you some fatigues . . . Maybe the Green Beret's honey would have some fatigues."

"They would be too small for Lisa," Thuy said.

They all seemed to be eyeing her lovely body at the same time.

"We don't breathe a word of this to the Captain," Marlin said. "If his Vietnamese soldiers are as unreliable as the Captain says, Lisa's life could be in danger . . . Kraus," Marlin continued, "I want you to get some fatigues for Lisa."

He shrugged. "She could probably fit into mine. She would have to tighten up her belt and roll up the sleeves. She might pop some of the chest button, but hell, they weren't tailored for me either."

Thuy nodded his head, but the expression on his face was one of concern.

Kraus asked, "Don't you think you are going a bit too far, Sir?"

Beckwith hated when Kraus started "Sir-ing" him. He looked at Lisa and then at Thuy. "No," he replied. "I don't."

"I wouldn't be surprised if she got us all killed."

"No. Not Lisa." He knew he was ticking off Kraus again, trusting a Vietnamese. "I want to get on the trail at dawn."

The rumbling came first, like the shaking of the earth created by a large bulldozer working very close to the hootch, then came the light in the doorway along with the sound of an explosion.

The table vibrated, the candle fell over onto the map, dishes started rattling and the dried leaves on the roof began to sift through the rafter like dust as the ground trembled like an earthquake.

The weight of the radio broke one table leg and Kraus fumbled to catch it.

Thuy staggered to the door opening and pointed his finger back at the bridge. Whatever he was saying was inaudible. Lisa's mother tried to outscream the deafening roar of the explosion.

Marlin staggered towards the now flashing doorway, and looked outside to see the bridge in its final stage of returning to the ground in a huge ball of fire that showered chunks of metal in a mushroom configuration.

It was a kaleidoscope of color transpiring the night into strobes of senseless shadows and color.

Marlin thought of his men back at the bridge, but there was nothing he could do to help them now.

The fire turned from yellow to a glowing red and back to yellow, then began to flicker and diminish in intensity, the shadows to burn out, the ground to stop its shaking. Marlin found himself standing in the doorway with his legs spread, bracing himself against the jambs.

When the trembling stopped, he turned around and grabbed his M-16 which had fallen on the floor and at the same time said, "Let's go." He started running down the paddy dike without regard to being attacked. The rest of his patrol followed behind him, their rifles and ammunition rattling, their feet sloshing in the mud. They ran atop the rice berm to the road, turned left and came on line as they neared what was left of the bridge, every one of them panting.

Marlin glanced to see that the two bunkers on each side of the bridge were covered with shrapmetal with no signs of life coming from them. Keats ran down to Gatz's squad bunker and looked inside. There was enough light coming from fires in the grass and the wooden railing for Marlin to see well enough. He watched Keats speak into the opening, look up and give him the OK sign with his fingers.

Kraus had run to the other side of the road where the other bunker was and when Marlin looked over, Kraus was giving him the OK sign.

Surprised to discover that nobody was hurt on this side of the bridge, Beckwith ran as far as he could to where the bridge ended.

Kraus caught up to him and stopped right alongside. "Holy shit," he said.

The bridge ended in sheared, smoking metal. Across maybe fifty feet was the other side similarly sheared apart with girders, rails, support beams and diagonals dangling, like a giant dinosaur had taken a bite out of the center. The middle column that used to protrude from the water line was gone as well as the pier. All that was down there was the water flowing at its normal speed.

Marlin could see men on the other side of the bridge standing at the severed section, waving their arms.

Marlin turned around and pushed his way past Gatz and Kraus and ran back to the first bunker on the left. It was Gatz's bunker, and empty. Marlin was so confused he had forgotten that the squad had stood next to him on the bridge.

When he pulled his head out of the entrance hole, he could feel his leg throbbing. His leg was telling him to slow down, but Marlin did not have time.

Gatz said, "You better check the other side of the bridge, Sir."

Marlin whipped his head around and said, "Kraus, raise Hillerman on the radio and ask him what the situation is over there." He massaged his groin with his left hand as he hobbled to the other bunker and stuck his head inside. Castillo and

Spielberg were looking out the port holes upriver. Emmanuel was sitting on an ammo box holding his helmet, the new man, Bowen, had eyes shining like car headlights. Jaime Rodriguez had his rifle pointed at Marlin.

"You all right?" Marlin asked.

Rodriguez lowered the rifle barrel and spoke up, "Yes, Sir."

"Who is supposed to be on guard duty now?"

"We are, Sir." Spielberg answered.

Marlin's first reaction was one of relief, knowing that none of them were killed. Then he asked, "What happened?"

Spielberg shrugged his shoulders, speechless.

Marlin knew that if this squad was on duty, that the probability of any men in the other squads being on the bridge at the time of the explosion was less.

Kraus moved over to the Lieutenant, "Hillerman says the situation is statiscopic over there."

Marlin threw him a sneer at the rare slang. His own auctioneer.

Kraus continued, "Miracle, but they are all OK."

Marlin sighed, almost in disbelief. One little bullet could drive its way into a man's brain and a huge satchel charge could miss everyone. It confirmed his belief that there was no escaping a bullet if your name was on it.

Kraus held the radio receiver out to the Lieutenant, "The Old Man wants to talk to you."

"Son of a bitch. What does he want?"

Kraus half-chuckled, "That is for you to find out. It probably has something to do with the bridge."

Beckwith moved forward, grabbed the transmitter and identified himself.

"What the fuck happened to my bridge?" Bravo-six asked in a static, nearly inaudible tone.

Marlin thought of hanging up on him. "I can barely read you, Sir."

"I can read you loud and clear, three-six. What the fuck happened?"

"How do you know anything happened?"

"Every channel in the area is sending out mayday messages about it, except you."

"I haven't been able to raise you on the radio since I got back."

"What happened?"

"The middle column of the bridge is now missing. For all practical purposes, the bridge no longer exists."

"How many men did you lose."

"Zero."

There was another long pause in which Marlin just stared at the receiver. The Old Man finally spoke. "It is all part of this offensive coming up. I know it. I want you to prepare your platoon to move to Saigon."

"We are ready."

"Then I want you to wait there and await my orders to move out. I'll arrange for some type of transportation."

"But I think I know where Hoppy is."

"Beckwith, no fucking around now. I've been looking for him for the last month without any success. It is time to consider our main objective. There is the possibility that the MIA is dead and buried somewhere, and we can't waste our time any longer on him, especially under the circumstances."

Fuck Saigon, Marlin thought. He remembered his vow to never let up on Hoppy's trail if it ever got hot again. He considered Lisa's information as red-hot. "You don't even want us to check out a lead."

"Negative . . . Forget it."

"You just don't want us to sit here at this broken-down bridge. How about some patrols."

"That's different. I'm headed your way to take a look. Out."

Marlin handed the radio transmitter back to Kraus.

"What now?" Kraus asked with a confused look on his face.

The Lieutenant stood up and looked around confidently, "We move out on patrol . . . Everybody . . . Now."

Chapter 20

"If the Old Man knew you were going on a wild goose chase after Hoppy, he'd be chewing you a new you-know-what," Kraus said as he adjusted the weight of the radio on his back. The antenna slapped against the back of his helmet, sounding like an out-of-tune guitar.

"I'm still covering myself," the Lieutenant said. "He wants us to go out on patrols and that is exactly what we are going to do."

"Yeah," Kraus said, but he said it in a way as if he didn't believe him.

"Hoppy has nobody in the world who can help him right now except us. Congress can't help him. Protesters can't help him, the damn President can't even help him. Nobody else except us. And as far as I'm concerned, I'm fighting for us. Nobody else. We are all in this together and we may as well make it back home together, or die trying."

Kraus nodded his head. "What do you have planned?"

The cloud cover broke for a second, the moon shining its light on the two of them standing there at the end of the carved-up bridge.

"How about calling the squad leaders together so I can brief them?"

"Rodriquez and his men, Hillerman and Doc are on the other side of the bridge . . . I mean the river . . ." He said it like he was blaming Marlin, "And there is no way across. Remember?"

"Call up the River Rats and have them send a boat across to pick us up."

"Now? At this time of the night?"

"Now. At this time of the night . . . Holy shit, Kraus, sometimes I think I could do better with a woman secretary than with you. I can't give a command without you contradicting me or trying to make me do something else."

"I'm not trying to contradict you, I just don't want you to make any mistakes."

"Mistakes my ass. Save your mouth for selling cattle."

"What are you going to do? Bust my ass and send me to work in a PX." Kraus smiled.

Marlin shook his head with the tiniest smile appearing on his lips. Nobody was dead, just a bridge. Fuck the bridge. "Get moving."

Marlin realized that if the Russian River bridge back home near Petaluma had been demolished, the sirens would be blaring, police cars patrolling, ambulances ferrying the injured, the fire department standing by. Spectators would be swarming and stretching on their tiptoes to see over each other's shoulders.

Here, in Nam, nothing. If any of the locals came out to take a look they would be shot. Curfew had started at sunset. A few of the ARVNs could be seen stretching their necks above their compound wire, but they were not about to come out at night;

too damn dangerous.

Marlin scanned the hootches in the area and although he could see no faces, he was certain many a figure stood in the darkness of the doorways, eyeballing what was left of the bridge and wondering what the Americans would do to retaliate.

A lone dog, as skinny as a broom handle, wobbled to within ten feet of Beckwith, stopped, and stared for the longest time at what remained of the bridge.

The dog looked so sickly that Marlin wondered if it were rabid. No, he reconsidered, it is a breeder, like all the other dogs that lived to be older than six months without being eaten.

The dog finally turned around and walked back into the darkness of night, its hindquarters turned to one side as if it were trying to catch up to its front legs.

The sound of voices talking could be heard from Gatz's bunker. They were arguing, probably over who would carry what.

Beckwith stood alone listening to the sound of the water as it washed against the bank of the river. He was actually getting older and wiser in Nam, looking for people to kill.

Marlin sent Thuy and Gatz back for Lisa so that he would not have to send a PBR back for her once he crossed the river.

By the time they retrieved her and caught back up to him, Beckwith and everyone who remained on the south bank were aboard the idling PBR at the foot of the bridge, staring very carefully in the water, as if it now had the very power to blow them up.

When Gatz helped Lisa board and Thuy followed right behind, Marlin and Lisa joined eyes briefly and there was a wicked smile on each of their faces. It was the first time in public they showed a hint of feelings for each other.

Marlin was feeling kind of giddy. He felt bad about the bridge, but at the same time he thought it was kind of funny. He couldn't figure out why, maybe because he hadn't lost any men, maybe because the explosion was the largest he had seen so far.

When the PBR dropped them off on the opposite bank, the men filed up the hillside and headed for the bunker behind the tower where the other men in the platoon were.

When Marlin joined them, he said to no one in particular, "Tell the squad leaders to meet me in the bunker."

Marlin, Kraus, Thuy and Lisa joined Doc in the command bunker as Truskowski took up a position as sentry. Lisa sat on an ammo box next to Thuy. She concentrated on not moving or looking at anyone as the bunker filled with the bodies of the squad leaders.

Kraus sat on his cot and replaced the batteries in the radio. When he finished his job, he fine-tuned the radio and set it aside, then leaned forward and lighted a small candle atop a C-ration can. It provided enough light for everyone to see.

Gatz held his Bible to his chest, his back as

straight as an iron fence, and sat next to Kraus. Cox, Ivy, Rodriquez, and Hyde sat on the Lieutenant's bunk smoking cigarettes that they cupped in their hands. None of them had on their bandoliers or rucksacks, it was too cramped; but they were all armed. Doc left when he realized there would be no room for the Lieutenant inside.

What little was said was whispered. Maybe because they thought someone was going to get their ass chewed about the bridge, maybe because of Lisa. The squad leaders had no idea why she was there.

When Marlin entered the bunker, Ivy and Hyde went to move from his cot. The Lieutenant waved for them to stay put and sat down on the bottom step in the entranceway. Although he looked at everyone present, he asked Kraus, "Everyone here?"

Marlin knew the answer, but used Kraus's reply to get the meeting started. "OK. We are moving out tonight. Once we hoof it down the road a mile or two, we will rest until light and move on from there during the day."

"Where are we going?" Ivy asked.

Marlin looked at him sternly. "We got a lead on where Hoppy is located and we are going after him."

Rodriguez asked, "Why do we leave tonight?"

"The Old Man will be here tomorrow and probably stop us from going anywhere."

Marlin could feel a tension in the air, as if he needed to explain further. "Hey. If you were out there you'd sure as hell want us to come looking for you. Now forget everything else. We're going

237

after Hoppy."

Silence. The squad leaders looked at each other and knew that they had nothing better to do. None of them were about to make a suggestion. Sometimes even the most innocent actions proved to be fatal, whereas with the more catastrophic, like the bridge, everyone survived.

There was the sound of footsteps approaching the bunker from outside and all eyes turned to the entrance to see who it was.

Marlin got off the step, turned and knelt down with his M-16 pointed at the noise. He could see Truskowski waving the person forward and relaxed.

The sound stopped, then the face of the Green Beret appeared in the doorway. He smiled, looked at the ceiling of the bunker and said, "These damn things were built for midgets. Never could stand them."

"Come on in, Captain," Marlin said as he pointed his rifle away.

"Don't have the time," Captain Crystal replied. "I have to rearrange my living quarters. House is a mess after that explosion, real mess . . . Crazy nobody got hurt. I didn't even lose a chicken."

He looked around the bunker at the staring faces and when he came to Lisa, his head stopped and he said, "So the guys weren't fooling me. I'll be damned." He turned to Marlin, "I want to talk to you in private for a moment, Lieutenant."

Without looking at any of his men, Marlin stooped forward and made his way out of the bunker and followed the Captain a short distance, out of earshot of the bunker. When the Captain turned around and stopped, so did Marlin.

"You're fucking up this time, Lieutenant," he said it almost cheerfully.

"What's on your mind, Captain?"

"Word is spreading all over Ben Luc you are porking that young lady in there and sucking her for Intelligence."

Marlin took a deep breath and held it. He waited for some brilliant reply to come to mind, but the TV was blank. Static. Interference. He exhaled as he asked, "Who told you that?" as if it would make a difference.

The Green Beret shrugged. "Does it matter? It is front page news in gossip city. You better do something about her, and chop chop. The local VC will make an example of her for sure."

When Marlin stood there quiet, the Green Beret continued, "If you don't get rid of her, you'd better have her follow you around like a shadow, like I do my old lady. If not," he wrinkled his brow, "you could find her hanging from a tree one morning."

Marlin felt like a stream of rain water had dripped down his back. He shuddered and tried to hide his reaction by craning his neck. He replied, "Yeah, thanks, Captain. For the advice."

The Green Beret spat to one side. "No problem. Maybe that round in the groin took the edge off your judgment. Glad to hear you can still get it up, but I don't want you making a fool of yourself around here. Looks bad for all of us."

"You're right. Thanks."

"And if you need a ride somewhere, I got a jeep."

"OK."

There was an awkward silence. Nothing else could be added. Marlin had been caught with his pants down and he didn't want to pick them back up, but if he didn't, the consequences could affect more than his sex life. He knew the Captain was right.

"Remember. We're all on the same side, Lieutenant." The Captain turned around and walked away.

Beckwith didn't think it had been so obvious. He should have stuck to the damn whore house and paid his dues and walked away. Instead he had opened his heart to the woman and she had taken it.

Marlin returned to the bunker feeling stern and angry. The talking stopped when he sat back down and he quickly asked, "Any questions?"

"Resupplies . . . ammo?" Ivy asked.

"The Green Beret has all you want. Hillerman can arrange that."

When the conversation started to turn to wisecracks, Marlin dismissed them with the words, "We leave in one hour."

When the squad leaders filed outside, Lisa stayed seated.

Marlin looked at her and said, "He's right. I must be going nuts."

"What are you saying?" she asked.

"I'm not like the Captain. I can't stay in one spot and set up house. I'm on the move constantly. It would be impossible for you to follow me around."

"But I must go with you."

"I'll take you a ways, until I know where you are talking about. Then . . ." Marlin looked at Kraus,

240

"Go get me Thuy."

Kraus hurried out of the bunker, as if embarrassed to be listening to the conversation.

Marlin continued, "Lisa, it is not going to work out right. Believe me. I'm not going to be responsible for destroying your life, whether you want me to or not."

The talking stopped. There was no exchange of thoughts, feelings, no touching, no apologies or excuses, no insinuations or things taken for granted, just an uncomfortable silence.

Marlin started to fill his rucksack with his dirty underclothes, ammunition, toothbrush and socks. He saw the letters from home, grabbed them and stuffed them in his sack.

When Thuy returned, Marlin stopped what he was doing and said to him, "Thuy, I want you to take Lisa to the American embassy in Saigon. I want you to seek asylum for her."

Marlin looked at Lisa and could tell that she was shocked. Although her mouth was still closed, her lower jaw had dropped. The sparkling eyes had turned to glares. "Now?" she asked.

"Yes. Tet starts in two days. There won't be any fighting for the next week. It is the perfect time."

"But she could turn herself in here at the artillery camp," Thuy said.

"I don't want her around here. If they screw things up and send her home, she might become a VC target and we won't be around to protect her."

"But Saigon is so far away," Lisa said.

"That's the point."

"How about her mother and brothers?"

241

Thuy asked.

"Take them too."

"What will they do to me?" Lisa asked, her shock turning to fear as she mentally considered the leap into the future.

Marlin looked at her and felt her pain, even worse pain than when he had been shot. "What do you want them to do?"

She sighed. "To make things better . . . Like before I met you."

It hurt, but Marlin knew that he had it coming. This is not the way he had it planned either.

"I'm sorry, Lisa."

"What will they do to me?"

"Relocate you, hopefully in Saigon. You like it up there anyway."

"Will they send me to America?"

"I don't know." It was the first time her going to America had ever been mentioned. Marlin wondered if that had been her goal all along.

"Will I ever see you again?" she asked.

The wheels were smoking in Marlin's head. "I don't know. I'll try. You can always write to me and then I'll know where you are so I can visit."

"Visit?" she said. "I wish I had never met you. Can I go home and get some things before I leave?"

"Of course. Thuy will take you back."

"How will you know where Hoppy is if I do not show you?"

"You can take us close to the camp, not inside . . . You better get going now. We leave in an hour."

242

The platoon was strung out along Highway 4, waiting. They were resting on their helmets and against their rucksacks and smoking and talking, discussing the reasons for delay, watching the clouds move across the lighted sky and thinking about home or who would die next.

Lisa and Thuy had not returned yet. It was drawing towards midnight. Marlin was worried something might have gone wrong. He had heard no shots. If he had, he would have crossed the river and checked it out himself.

They were two hours late, arriving at one in the morning. Marlin sighted Lisa moving up the bank of the hill. Her face was cupped in her hands. Thuy was guiding her forward by the elbow.

Thuy looked nervous and frightened.

When they drew close enough, as Lisa was still weeping, Marlin asked Thuy, "What's wrong?"

When Thuy let go of Lisa's arm, she stopped. Thuy drew closer to the Lieutenant. "When we get back to the hootch," Thuy said. He looked at Lisa for a brief moment and saw that she was not going to stop crying. He continued, "Lisa's mother and brothers are dead." Thuy moved his forefinger across his throat and squinched his face.

"Fuck," Marlin replied; his stomach felt like it hit rock bottom. He was causing so much trouble when all he wanted to do was bring peace.

He moved towards Lisa and put a hand on her shoulder but she moved away from his touch and wailed into her cupped hands.

Thuy said, "She went stone cold on me. Hasn't

said a word."

"Is she going to be all right?"

"I don't know."

"Let's get moving."

As the platoon stood up, cigarettes were extinguished, packs rattled and rifles slung. Hillerman rode them like a herd of cattle and got them moving in the right direction.

Lisa drew to within a few feet of Marlin and followed. It seemed like all Marlin had been saying to her lately was, "I'm sorry," and he did not want to say it again.

The moon lighted the stage and they trekked in the direction of Saigon in the mud, cooled by the evening breeze, easy targets on the road but maybe too obvious to be fired upon. Once they were far enough from Ben Luc, when no lights could be seen anywhere, Marlin moved them off the side of the road and let them sleep in shifts until daybreak. At that time, he got them up and moved them out. It was no yellow brick road. When the sun rose, they reached a muddy fork in the road where it was obvious more than one truck had bogged down in the mud. Lisa pointed east.

Beckwith moved to her side and looked at her, seeking a smile, a sign of warmth, but all he saw was a face smeared with mud where the back of her hand had dragged across her cheeks to wipe away the tears, which even now were welling up in her eye sockets. Her jaw was set firm. She looked down the road and pointed, "You go all the way to Rach Kien and then on to Can Duoc. The road ends at Long Huu village. The camp is where the Vam Co

River meets the Saigon River, before the north fork. It is right between the two rivers."

Marlin had never reconnoitered the area. It was known as the Rung Sat district, or Jungle of Death. It was a swampy area that reached all the way to the ocean.

Beckwith looked at Lisa and wondered why she had not said so in the first place. It might not have saved the lives of her brothers and mother. It might not have changed anything; maybe it would have changed some timing, but not the facts.

"Can you make it OK from here, Thuy?" Marlin asked.

"We'll catch a bus to Saigon. No problem."

Marlin dug into his pocket and pulled out a billfold and handed Thuy some money. "Take this," he said.

Thuy took it without hesitation.

Marlin directed his men to start down the forked road, and as they passed, he looked at Lisa who now had her eyes averted to the ground. He looked at his men again. Willie and Cope were moving past and eyed him. Their gear rattled. Their faces were expressionless.

Marlin looked at Lisa and said, "Good luck." He went to touch her hand and she withdrew it.

He looked at her again and then at Thuy. Thuy spoke to Lisa briefly in Vietnamese.

Marlin turned and started to follow his men. He heard her talking to him behind his back. She said, "I love you."

Chapter 21

When Beckwith caught sight of Rach Kien, he ordered the platoon off the road into a strip of jungle that led to a line of rice fields about a quarter of a mile south of the village. Marlin did not want to pick up sniper fire as this area was sparingly patrolled by Americans and probably full of VC. Stealth was important, but at the same time he knew it would be impossible to walk past fields full of coolie hats unnoticed.

The Vietnamese workers never looked up from beneath their hat rims, they never stood up to watch them pass, but the third platoon knew that their every step was being watched, and in all probability, the news of their mysterious presence was being relayed ahead for others to take advantage of.

The men in the file wanted to draw closer together either for security or to talk. If it was up to them they would walk in a small circle, about the size of the killing area of one grenade. Marlin was forever spreading them out.

At the same time, Beckwith kept track of their every move. He was already out of range of the 105 artillery battery back at Ben Luc; another few clicks and the 155s would be unable to reach him. The eight-inch guns were as sure as guardian angels, but

Marlin hated like hell to call them in, just too damn big, like small Volkswagons hurled through the air; and the way he was headed would send those rounds flying right over his head. One round with not enough powder, or damp powder, could land on his own men. It wasn't worth the risk.

Dinner under the jungle awning. Marlin pulled out a can of ham and lima beans, a can of crackers and another can of apricots. The canned fruit was heaven-sent, but the dried-up old crackers stuck to the inside of his mouth and the salty ham and lima beans made him want to drink the Saigon River. The iodine in the canteen water stung his tongue and lined his mouth with a bitter taste that no amount of food could take away.

The only reason he ate was to unload some of the weight out of his rucksack. He kept the small roll of toilet paper more out of anticipation than necessity, placed the twin packet of gum in his shirt pocket for the night watch and removed one of the five cigarettes from the small packet of Salems and lit up. Such indulgence.

The break did nothing more than tighten up his leg muscles.

Past Rach Kien, Marlin could feel himself starting to limp; it just felt better when he did not bend his leg quite so high at the waist. He knew he would have no problems keeping up with the men, but his leg was definitely sore, ever since he ran back from Lisa's house to the bridge.

Skirting the perimeter of Can Duoc, they returned on the road and walked into Long Huu just as the residents were engaged in their afternoon nap, or so it seemed from the welcome they received. A haze from the cooking fires inside a couple of dozen huts hung over the village shaped in a large irregular circle with the thick jungle eating at its perimeter. The mud walls of the hootches were four feet thick and about as tall, strong enough to stop a small arm's round and nearly thick enough to stop a rocket-propelled grenade. The roofs were made of layered grass. There were no windows, only an open space between the walls and roof.

In the central plaza consisting of swept red clay, amidst half a dozen tall, shady rubber trees was a round water well.

Marlin approached the well and stopped the men for a short rest, scanning the dark doorway openings for somebody stupid enough to take a pot shot at him.

The few domestic animals moving about were a taxidermist's nightmare. You could play the piano on the dogs' ribs and pick your teeth with the chickens' legs.

Marlin twitched his nose at the smell of human excrement. They probably shit and bathed in the same water that the buffalos cooled their bodies in when not in the fields.

The kids were not much fatter than the dogs. They hung back in the doorways with their eyes about as big as their mouths, gawking. They were not like the kids around Ben Luc, always smiling and playing and joking with the GIs. These kids were dressed in faded rags, barely covering their midsection.

Some of women had no covering over their breasts, which under different circumstances would have at least drawn a whistle or catcall from some of the men, but now only cautious stares, like staring at the bare tits of death itself, neither provocative nor beautiful. The women stared back, not hateful or curious, just blankly. One woman turned her head and spat betel nut juice on the ground.

There was an obvious lack of men in the hamlet as there had been in the rice paddies on the way in. There was no doubt in the third platoon's mind where the men were.

A Vietnamese man probably close to sixty-five years old came prancing up to the well toting two full sacks of rice balanced on his shoulder by a stick. His white hair flowed over his shoulders and blossomed from his chin. His face was the color of a walnut with about as many wrinkles. Although his anatomy resembled a chopstick, he bent his knees to unburden himself from the weight and histrionically folded himself a slimy cigarette and gnarled on its end before putting a lighted match to its tip.

In a less remote outpost, Marlin might have been amused by the respectable-looking old man. Under the circumstance, he was cautious.

Cope pushed his shoulder away from one of the rubber trees, approached the papasan and lifted the sacks of rice with a grunt. He set down the load and looked at the Lieutenant in dismay and said, "It must weigh over 200 pounds."

The old man smiled. His legs were bowlegged.

Marlin finally said, "VC number 10."

The old man's smile faded and he spat to one

249

side, arrogantly defiant.

Beckwith said, "Cope, take the old fart up at point with you. If anything goes wrong, shoot the son of a bitch." He looked around for any of the villagers who might disapprove. They stared blankly.

Beckwith figured the whole hamlet staring like goddamn idiots were VC sympathizers probably wondering what they would find in his men's pockets once they were all dead.

When Cope pointed his rifle at the old man, the papasan ignored the gesture and walked back to his sacks of rice.

Marlin blocked his way, withdrew his pistol from its holster, cocked it with the snap of his left hand and planted the barrel on the man's nose. "I know you don't understand a word I'm saying, old man, but I'll make that the last cigarette you ever smoke if you don't follow my orders. I don't give a shit if you are a hundred years old, I'd rather see you dead than have one of my men scratch his fuckin' pinkie."

The old man's eyes, streaked with veins, stared down the blunt barrel of the pistol. He turned his head and looked at Cope, then walked over beside him. Cope tapped him with the barrel of the rifle to get moving.

The third platoon jumped to their feet without being told and left Long Huu with their eyes over their shoulders, their rifles pointed at the staring faces and feeling the vibrations of a stirred-up hornet's nest.

Over the millenniums, the marshes had become overgrown with vines that shot straight up out of

250

the boggy earth like a can of worms and made the walking painfully fatiguing. Each step had to be raised out of the sucking mud and then over foot-tall vines. Tanks could not penetrate the swamp. Trails could not be followed as they disappeared under the water. Only an infantryman could go there, and one with guts and determination.

Hordes of mosquitoes lunged from their mucky birthplaces as the platoon ventured forward. There were so many bugs that breathing had to be done through gritted teeth to avoid sucking the little buggers down one's throat. Howling monkeys tossed sticks at the third platoon and screaming parrots warned of their approach.

There was no breeze in the jungle. The air was stale and foul.

Towards dusk the platoon worked its way out of the thick swamps and reached a small hillock. Marlin started thinking about setting up camp. He was exhausted and he knew his men had to be as well. Suddenly the line of men in front of him stopped moving and he walked forward to investigate.

He came upon Cope standing over the old man who was sitting down and leaning back on one elbow with his head turned away. Cope had his M-16 pointed at the papasan and was telling him to get up.

Beckwith drew closer and observed the old man's shaking hands and knees. Marlin asked, "What's wrong?"

Cope was panting hard, and shaking.

The old man looked ahead and made a sign for everyone to go on without him.

"What do you think is the matter, Sir?"

"The way it looks. We are getting real close to something that this papasan does not want to face, especially with us around."

"Hoppy?"

"Maybe. Cope, stay put with the old man, I am going to send a scouting party ahead."

Beckwith moved back down the line of men until he came to Gatz and told him the plan. "Move ahead about a hundred yards or so and come back and report if you find anything. I'll decide what we do from there."

When Gatz took off, Beckwith moved back to his position in the platoon next to Kraus and gave the signal for his men to take a break.

Gatz had not been gone more than ten minutes when Cope came walking back to Beckwith with the same worried look on his face.

As soon as Beckwith saw him, he asked, "Where is the old man?"

"He took off."

Marlin jumped to his feet. "What? Why didn't you shoot him?"

"I turned my head for one second and he was gone . . . He just disappeared into the thickets. I didn't want to start shooting like a crazy man."

Marlin shook his head. "I wonder which way he headed? Fuck . . ."

When Gatz returned, all heads turned his way. He said, "I found something, Sir. You better take a look."

Marlin had the platoon follow him as Gatz led the way through the jungle for about fifty yards and stopped behind what appeared to be a rubber tree and looked down the hill.

It was not a village, but a camp cleared out beneath the jungle canopy so that it was not readily visible from the air.

Marlin could not tell how wide or long it was, but he had the feeling it was big. Vietnamese in T-shirts and sandals were walking around with small tin pans in their hands. Some were resting in hammocks under lean-tos, some cleaning their mess kits, standing around talking, walking to different shelters. Apparently they had just finished their evening meal. He could see armed guards around the perimeter, but he was still too far away to be detected. It looked like they could pull up stakes and be gone in a matter of hours as there were no permanent structures in the area.

Marlin spread out the platoon, with Hillerman and two squads on the far right and Gatz's and Hyde's squads on the far left.

"What now?" Kraus asked.

Marlin hoped the clouds would continue to billow overhead, hide the moon and open up its rain spout in torrents of showers.

In spite of the danger, he felt excited. He knew Hoppy was down there, everything else was right on.

"We'll wait until dark, then send down a scouting party to locate Hoppy. Pick up the eight-inch guns on the radio, Kraus."

"I don't know if we have gone too far, Sir."

"What do you mean?"

Kraus spoke in a whisper, "I mean that we might

253

be out of radio range for all the supporting elements. You know you just can't come on any radio channel and expect to broadcast all over the country on it."

"How far are you talking about?"

"Depending upon the conditions of the radio, the terrain, the batteries, at best we are talking twelve clicks; plus we are under a heavy cover."

"And we have gone about twenty."

"Exactly, and even the eight-inch cannons won't fire that far."

"Switch channels and see if you can pick someone else up."

"Roger."

Kraus tried all the artillery, medevac, and helicopter gun ship channels that he knew without success. He said to Marlin, "Maybe we had better head back, Sir."

"What are you talking about?"

"Well, we can't go charging down into that camp. It would be suicide. If they found us here, the same thing would happen."

Marlin became stern. "Keep trying, Kraus. Dip into your little book and start talking."

"Yes, Sir."

Marlin massaged his leg. It throbbed with each heartbeat.

When he heard some noise over the radio, he asked, "What do you have there, Kraus?"

"I got a Vietnamese station."

"Are you sure it is not VC?"

"They're speaking 'gook' language."

"That's as far as you go on that channel. Switch."

He thought of Thuy and wished he were along.

"But it might be an ARVN channel."

"Or NVA. Switch."

Kraus tried to contact the C.O. — the same man he had been trying to avoid all day.

"Three-six . . . three-six, this is three-five. Over."

When Kraus let up on the transmission button, he listened for a response but all that came over the radio was the sound of static.

"Three-six, three-six, This is three-five. Over."

More static.

"Try Skate Force," the Lieutenant said. "They might be in the air and hear us. Try 'em."

"OK. I already tried them once but I'll try again."

More static.

It was getting darker.

"Try all the frequencies again, Kraus. Raise somebody."

Then it happened; Marlin was watching the camp from his hiding place when he saw one of the soldiers pointing his finger in his direction and thrusting his finger at him and explaining to another soldier who was stretching his neck in the direction of the pointed finger.

The man straining his neck to see was shaking his head.

The old man from Long Huu was standing down there pointing his finger up the hill as well. Beckwith's gut feeling sank to his stomach. If that old fart started blabbing what he knew about the third platoon to the NVA . . .

Marlin grabbed ahold of a small branch on the tree in front of him, placed the stock of his M-16 in the cradle of his hand, let the branch steady his aim, sighted in on the old man and when the cross hairs were just a tad below chest level, he fired off two quick rounds that sent the old man to the ground.

The NVA regular with his arm as stiff as a board unslung his rifle and started to wave his arm in a gathering motion for troops to gather closer. A few scattered rounds were fired.

An NVA in uniform with a pistol on his waist and whom Marlin took as an officer, ran over, talked to the gathering soldiers, spread them out and shouted orders. The camp came alive with men running.

About thirty or forty armed soldiers started to beat the brush in the third platoon's direction with the rest of the camp behind them running for their weapons and apparently taking up a defensive position.

Marlin started rubbing his sore leg. "Here they come," he said to Kraus. "I hope the men are ready."

Although Kraus was making enough noise to be heard a long ways away, Beckwith let him continue talking. It was their only chance. They were outnumbered at least 20 to 1 and that was just the number of NVA that had been spotted. Once they started returning fire, the platoon could easily be surrounded and squeezed to death.

"Let them get closer," Marlin kept whispering to himself. He could not shout it out to his men, but kept thinking it.

The NVA coming up the hill disappeared in the

thick greenery but the sound of them thrashing became louder. They stopped talking to each other except for one voice that kept shouting out orders.

"Let 'em get closer," Marlin whispered as he removed two grenades from his thigh pockets and placed one at his side and pulled the pin on the other, squeezing the handle tightly.

Although he could not see the enemy now, he could hear them easily enough and they were getting really close.

Marlin looked at Kraus and gave him the whisper sign.

Kraus started whispering into the transmitter.

Then Marlin saw the face of an NVA soldier. The man looked in Marlin's direction as if he could hear something.

Marlin let the handle of the grenade fly, counted out "One thousand one, one thousand two." At that he lobbed the grenade into the air in a high arc over the soldier's head.

The soldier shouted and brought his rifle up to his shoulder.

When the grenade exploded, the concussion drove the soldier into the ground like the force of a sledge hammer. He disappeared from sight and at the same time the hillside exploded with automatic gun fire mostly going downhill.

Smoke arose from the line of the third platoon as the approaching NVA hardly had a chance to pinpoint the targets before they were riddled with automatic fire.

Kraus started to shout into the radio louder.

The NVA coming up the hill were pinned down

quickly; however the rest of the camp was just mobilizing. There must have been a battalion down there; probably close to 400 men.

Kraus was ready to push the send button when he heard a reply over the radio. "Identify yourself."

Kraus gasped, "This is three-five, Bravo Company with the Ninth Infantry Division."

There was the longest pause.

The reply came, "What's the problem?"

"We need help. Who are you?"

"We are Sticky Fingers."

"What are you?"

There was a chuckle over the radio. "I'm just a little ole spottin' plane doin' nothing but flyin' around up here ta draw fire, but my two buddies flying higher than a dog can tree a coon can give you just about anything you want."

Kraus and the Lieutenant looked at each other in an odd fashion. From the inflection of the pilot's voice it sounded like he should be milking a cow.

"Where are you located?" Kraus asked over the radio.

"South of Saigon here doing circles in the air looking for something to drop our load on before we go to sleep. Where are you?"

Firing from the camp was erratic, with most of the rounds still poorly aimed, but increasing in volume.

Marlin had already written down the coordinates on the plastic cover of the map in a black grease pencil. He kept pointing at the coordinates for Kraus to read.

Kraus did so and then asked, "How long will it

take you to reach us?"

"If I were a bird, about five minutes. In this little clonker about twice as long."

The sound of machine gun fire strafing the jungle made both the Lieutenant and Kraus duck for cover.

When it eased up, Marlin shouted out for his men to hear, "Help is on the way . . . Stay put." He did not stick his head up in the air to see how they were doing. He wondered how many of them were already dead.

NVA soldiers began to draw closer. Now they were running in full uniform with packs, pith helmets, rifles and bandoliers of ammunition across their chests.

Marlin's platoon settled down to firing in single shots instead of full bursts of automatic.

Marlin heard the thumping sounds of a mortar being dropped down a tube. Then another.

The first rounds were about a hundred yards short and fifty yards to the right. The sound sent a shudder through the platoon leader. He knew the NVA would just march the rounds up the hill and fire for effect when they were zeroed in. At that point Marlin would have to retreat, either that or be surrounded by the NVA and decimated by the mortars until not a man was left. He thought of pulling up roots, but he had to wait for the fighters.

A transmission came over the radio loud enough for Beckwith to hear. "This is Sticky Fingers, where do you want our ordinance?"

Marlin remembered how angry he had been with the C.O. the day the Captain had called in artillery around Marlin's position so that he could walk the woman prisoner and Hill out of the jungle safely. It was the day after Hoppy was captured.

Beckwith knew Hoppy was down there in the camp, and his next decision was tough. If he called the ordinance in on the camp, he might kill Hoppy along with everyone else. Hoppy, the reason he was even here.

If he waved the planes off, his platoon would invariably be annihilated.

"Where are they?" Marlin shouted to Kraus.

When Kraus shrugged his shoulders, Marlin said, "Pop a red smoke and tell them to lay it down on anything north of the smoke and to within a hundred yards . . . but keep it close."

The sound of the mortars clearing the tube sounded again.

Kraus got out the red smoke. He held it in one hand the the radio transmitter in the other.

Marlin heard the sound of a small plane overhead and looked up to see the long camouflaged body of a spotter plane streak overhead.

Kraus threw out the red smoke just as Marlin turned to tell him to do so.

The next burst of mortar rounds was only fifty yards short.

"Holy shit," came over the radio. "They're as thick as mountain mushrooms in an open pasture; looks like a little ant colony in one of them African movies."

Marlin grabbed the radio from Kraus and said, "But there are friendlies in the camp. Just put it on the hill north of the red smoke and about a hundred yards away. We're leaving."

"You're the boss," was the reply.

Then came streaking out of the sky at supersonic speed two jets on parallel courses that blurred between the openings in the jungle canopy.

Their sudden appearance did not discourage the mortar team from continuing their barrage. The next rounds came so close that Marlin and Kraus had to hug the ground for fear of being decapitated. One more adjustment and Marlin figured they would be landing right in his lap and firing for effect.

The NVA coming up the hill turned their heads skyward and aimed their rifles at the attacking planes, firing their rifles and sending racer rounds crisscrossing like fireflies in a windstorm.

The first jet opened up with its 20 mm machine guns, its barrels spitting out fire that strafed the hillside and sent foot soldiers flying in the air or running back down the hill.

The second jet was right behind the first and released two torpedo-shaped bombs that whistled and tumbled headlong towards the target at a screaming speed.

When the canisters struck the treetops, they exploded in a ball of napalm flames that licked like a tidal wave across the hill and into some of the lean-tos, tents, and tunnel entrances, lapping up men and exploding ammunition dumps with the speed of lightning.

The evening was aflame with a glow of death outlined now by the setting sun.

Kraus hollered, "Shake and bake the sons of

bitches. Shake and bake 'em."

As crude as it sounded, Marlin opened his mouth in a panting, half-baked smile and whispered, "Shake and bake 'em."

Chapter 22

Having released their payloads, the two F-4 Phantom jets climbed high into the sky, waved their wings in a farewell gesture and screamed into the darkening north skies.

On the ground where their bombs had exploded, flames licked from the equipment and tents and the tall trees created a consuming inferno. In spite of the recent heavy rains, the hill burned with the intensity of molten steel, consuming itself with explosions and more bursts of fire.

The area glowed with the intensity of floodlights as the NVA soldiers leaped, jumped and lunged over each other to save themselves and all of their belongings from being totally melted in flames. The annihilation of the third platoon became of little concern as they ran for their lives.

The spotter pilot's voice twanged over the radio like a farewell requiem, "You want us to come back with more of the same?"

Marlin grabbed the receiver from Kraus, "We're not sticking around. It is so damn hot where we are right now my eyelashes are curling."

"How about tomorrow?"

"Sure. If you don't have anything else going."

"Well, good. Glad to have satisfied customers.

Good luck."

"Same to you. And thanks."

Marlin took one last look at the burning camp. There were still too damn many NVA soldiers down there for him to reasonably overcome. They were forming into a group on the other side of the fire and in spite of the heat, still gathering their gear together and looking his way.

The Lieutenant didn't know if his platoon had enough ammunition left to kill them all. If he had some idea where Hoppy was so he could concentrate his attack, he might try it, but he didn't. No, it was time to back up, but not to give up.

When the firing quieted down, he signaled the men closer to him to come his way; they in turn signaled the others behind them.

Since Gatz was one of the first to crawl forward, Beckwith told him, "Go back towards the swamp where we just came from; but don't go more than a hundred yards now. Stop and I will join you at the point."

Marlin crouched down with Kraus kneeling right next to him and tapped each man on the shoulder as he passed his position. It was getting dark and the light from the fire in the camp was starting to die down. Marlin physically touched each man to make certain that none were left behind.

Ivy came forward with a man over his shoulder. There was blood dripping from the man's hair as well as from his finger tips that dangled near the ground. Marlin could smell burnt clothing as well as burning flesh. Marlin noticed that the back of the man's fatigues were still smoldering.

"Who is it?" Beckwith asked as he could not see the face slung over the back of Ivy.

"Zipper. We got his machine gun and ammunition as well as Kramm's rifle."

"Kramm?"

"Right. Truskowski is carrying him behind me."

"When you can't carry him any longer, have someone else relieve you."

Ivy shook his head.

Truskowski came by at a trot without stopping. Marlin looked at the load he was carrying. Kramm's body seemed so relaxed, it just wobbled like it was all flesh and no bones.

Once all the bodies were counted, Beckwith followed the column until it stopped. Before he moved forward, he said to Jaime Rodriguez who was pulling up the rear, "I want you to booby trap half a dozen claymores during our retreat."

Jaime knew what he was talking about and nodded his head.

The Lieutenant then said, "Remind me to have you walk point tomorrow when we come back. If I forget."

"OK, Lieutenant."

Then Beckwith quickly moved forward down the stopped column. He thought of returning to Long Huu, but the NVA would probably be waiting for him back there. He thought of the swamp, and as much as he dreaded it, realized it would be the safest place.

By the time they reached the back side of the hill, it was pitch-black.

Beckwith took over the point position from Pri-

265

vate Spielberg. With an M-16 in his right hand, Marlin moved his left hand in front of his face no more than six inches away, palm outward. Although he could barely see its outline from that distance, he had to protect his eyes from the dangling branches.

Half an hour of frantic sloshing and the weary leader stopped by a particularly large tree trunk, waited for the men behind to catch up and guided three of them into its upper branches. So pleased with the sudden solution, he scrambled ahead to direct more men into the less perilous treetops.

On his third stop, when he took hold of one soldier's arm and pulled him in the direction of the tree, he heard Gatz's voice whispering, "I seen him, Sir."

Breathing heavily through his nose, Marlin commanded, "Get up the tree, Gatz."

The squad leader wondered if the Lieutenant had heard him. He pulled his arm back and explained further, "I seen Hoppy. I'm sure of it."

"Good," Marlin panted, "but tell me about it in the morning or whenever we get out of this alive. Right now, find yourself a limb to hang from for the night. That's an order."

When Gatz stepped to, Marlin proceeded to place the remaining troops in similar trees, taking a head count as he did so.

He had Ivy and Truskowski hide the bodies of the dead men in the bushes at the base of the tree that they were to climb.

With the last man in place, Marlin said to Kraus, "Now it's our turn."

The Lieutenant shimmied up a nearby tree with tenacious grappling as the weight of his rucksack threw him off balance. He had to squeeze between the narrow limbs and constantly strain to free his equipment. Higher in the tree a bit of moonlight filtered down through the branches to illuminate his close quarters. When he found a suitable notch, he stopped, whispered for Kraus to take it, climbed a bit further and stopped at the next wide limb; he then removed his rucksack and tied it off to the tree, removed his flak jacket and sat down on it with a sigh of relief. He placed his rifle and the ammunition sling on his lap and leaned against the limb with just the thought of falling out of the tree making him alert.

As the glow of the fire over the hill died and the sounds of ammunition caches exploding quieted, he heard the sound of one claymore mine exploding; about ten minutes later he heard another. The sounds made him feel good.

Soon the North Vietnamese soldiers could be heard searching the perimeter of the marsh. They were probably just a tad more afraid to enter the stinking water than the third platoon was to leave it. Maybe because the aerial attack had been so conclusive, the NVA did not form a line and search as thoroughly as they should have.

Overhead flares ignited, they did not penetrate the darkness of the jungle. If the North Vietnamese troops used trip flares in the right spots, it might have been a different story and the whole third platoon would have been as obvious as a brood of monkeys in a banana tree, but they didn't.

Marlin listened with the attention of an orchestra leader to the sounds of the jungle, trees swaying, trunks creaking, the slight breeze sending the leaves fluttering, animals skittering and slinking across the wet jungle floor.

Soon the sounds of his own men could be heard and it irked him. The sounds of canteens being opened, C-ration cans hissing when stuck with the P-38, mess kits scraped with spoons, cans hitting branches before splashing into the water. Marlin wanted to stand up and scream for everyone to shut up, but it would be more preposterous than his own men's actions.

He removed the starlight scope from its case and scanned the vegetation on the ground. He saw something moving in the bushes. It appeared to be a person crouching in the open, bent over, with no rucksack. At first he thought it was one of his men who had gotten down from the tree, maybe to relieve himself. He lowered the scope and stared at the darkness in the direction he had been looking. Nothing. He looked through the scope again and the figure repeated its movement, in the exact same spot. Marlin removed his eye from the scope, shook his head to dislodge any fantasies, waited a while longer and looked again. It could have been a tree stump, it could have been anything; but it looked so much like a real person. It was there moving back and forth, but it never really went anywhere, only the black dots of its outline.

After a while, Marlin came to the conclusion that he was seeing things. When he admitted that to himself, he realized at the same time he was totally exhausted. He removed his waist belt and tied his right arm securely to the tree limb, leaned back against his flak jacket and drooped his head onto his chest.

The mellowing sounds of distant bombs and artillery exploding lulled him to sleep, but he never really lost consciousness of the movements in the jungle. It was like only half of him slept, the other half watched and was aware the entire night.

He was already awake before he opened his eyes at dawn when a mosquito buzzed his left ear. Like a slow-moving fan, his hand chased it away. When another mosquito made a dive for his inner ear and struck home, sounding like an alarm clock, Marlin sat straight up and worked the index finger of his right hand into the ear and stopped the buzzing with maximum pressure.

Relieved, he removed his finger and wiped it on his pants. He looked down the tree and saw Kraus awake and swatting mosquitoes. Marlin whispered, "Kraus."

Kraus stirred and turned his head up. "Yes, Sir."

"Get down."

Kraus had his head tilted so far backwards that he lost his balance and started to slip from his resting place. By the time his feet were clearing the branch, he reached out to catch himself, but crashed through the lower limbs and landed in the water with a splash. He came up sputtering and flaying his arms to stay afloat.

Marlin just shook his head. If the NVA were still waiting to open fire, now would be the time.

Nothing happened. Marlin slipped into his gear,

and slid down the tree, taking the radio with him. "You OK?"

"Yes, Sir."

"First time in weeks you did what I told you without bitching."

"Yes, Sir." Kraus had nothing more to say.

"Fuckhead . . . Let's get moving."

The rest of the platoon had gotten down from the trees when they heard Kraus.

Marlin took a head count again. All were identified.

The bodies of Kramm and Allen were starting to get stiff, but neither Truskowski nor Ivy complained nor looked for help. When the spotter pilot returned, Marlin would ask for help to take care of the bodies.

The platoon stopped at the top of the hill behind the camp and took a breath while Rodriguez's squad moved forward to survey the camp just like the night before.

During that rest period, Beckwith found Gatz in the column and knelt beside the sitting black man who was reading his Bible and asked, "Gatz, what did you tell me you saw last night?"

Gatz folded the Bible shut and said, "I ain't no fool, Sir, but I seen Hoppy . . . I know it was him."

"Why are you so certain?"

"It was like he was a wild animal or something. His hands and feet were tied together and two men were carrying him on a long stick."

"How do you know it was him?"

"I seen his blond hair, his blond hair mostly. It was straight and long. The man was as white as a sheet, not brown like the Vietnamese. It had to be him."

"He was alive?"

"He wasn't walking, but they hadn't buried him neither."

"Good work."

When Rodriguez returned to say that the camp was totally abandoned, the platoon moved to the same spot where they had been pinned down the night before.

Smoke was still rising from the roofs of the collapsed lean-tos, the remnants of tents still smoldering as well as the ground itself. There were bodies everywhere. All of them in different degrees of crispiness. The air smelled of spent gunpowder and cooked flesh. Craters where ammunition caches had been detonated were still hot, but for the most part, there was nothing of danger, either alive or dead. The NVA had moved out under the cover of night.

At first Marlin was very cautious. Then as he did not take on any sniper fire or see anything that might be of danger, he started to spread out his men. He sent a squad in each direction with instructions to look for a trail on which the NVA might have fled.

A single shot rang out and Marlin fell to one knee. The sound of automatic fire followed and then the scream of an American.

Men from the platoon started to run towards the scream.

Marlin ran past the smoldering poles and lean-tos and jumped over barrels and just to where the jungle began to turn green again, came upon Jaime

271

Rodriguez standing with his rifle pointed towards the ground, thrusting its barrel forward.

Marlin ran up and looked down at the bodies of two NVA soldiers. It was obvious the one on his back was dead as his chest was blown away. The other NVA knelt before Jaime with his head bowed forward. He had a gash out of his right side that looked like it had been caused by an explosion. It was already turning green. He had no new bullet holes.

"What happened?" Marlin asked.

Jaime explained, "These two sons of bitches tried to bushwack me, Sir. I got one of them. Should I finish off this one?"

"Negative."

Jaime jerked his head towards the Lieutenant. "I ain't carrying this son of a bitch."

"He might know where his friends are headed."

"Shit. He don't know any English."

"Then we will find someone who can interpret for us." Marlin thought of Thuy and regretted that he was not along.

Gatz ran forward. All heads turned to watch him as he said, "I found it, Sir."

"What's that?" Marlin asked.

"The trail."

Gatz was smiling a wide streak. He had just lifted another tuff of hair and was two shy of his goal of a dozen.

It was obviously the getaway route as it was newly trampled down and littered with equipment and clothing.

Lieutenant Beckwith did not want to follow it

directly, as the North Vietnamese regulars would probably set up an ambush or litter their trail with booby traps as he had done the night before; so what he did was crisscross the path, or when possible to avoid making it twice as long, followed a parallel course.

With the monsoon season raining itself out, as the day progressed, the skies cleared and the unrelenting equatorial sun bore down on the third platoon. Temperatures under the helmet liners were twenty degrees warmer than the outside temperature, hot enough to nearly scramble a man's brains. The clay ground dried up like a sponge and the horizon of rice paddies stretched out into mirages of licking flames that seemed to set the world on fire.

Marlin looked for the pith helmets of the advancing NVA unit but all he saw were mirages of elephants in single file transforming into waves of water breaking onto the shores of foreign lands, bamboo reeds waving in the breeze to palm trees on an ocean beach.

He would look away, but in no time his gaze seemed to be fixed once again on the horizon, once again hypnotized by its fantasies. It didn't make sense, but he wasn't alone.

The sweat started in the underarms, then down the back and around the collar, soon soaking the entire shirt. So much so that when a man stood up after a rest, the steaming outline of his butt was left in the hot clay.

"Clean your rifles, that means M-60s too." The M-16 had a great reputation for the speed of the bullets and its rapid fire, but take the tiniest rock and stick it in the chamber, the tiniest piece of straw and jam it behind the bolt and the rifle would jam after the first round.

Just thinking about it made Marlin nervous.

At the next break, Marlin's sat down on a rice paddy, removed his boots and then the socks as carefully as if they were a bandage. What he stared at made him wonder how his feet continued to walk. The skin on the toes was alligatored like a dried-up asphalt roof, as white as a newborn baby's skin, with lines of dirt between the toes as clear as veins. He massaged his toes, removed a fresh pair of socks from his rucksack and placed them on his feet.

When he laced his shoes back up, he gave an order for the rest of his men to do the same.

Within minutes they were wet again from the sweat and the rice paddies they had to cross. The men became sluggish and argumentative. They complained about the heat, the lack of water, the taste of the water they did have, the inevitable death at the end of the trail, the length of the walk, the food, the weather, about each other, about the time in country, about the futility of the war.

All the usual kidding done was now taken seriously.

The prisoner was in bad shape. The wound in his side had drained a great deal of blood and all the walking did little to rejuvenate his spirits. He had nothing to carry but himself, but he moved like he was going to keel over and die at any moment. Doc put a bandage on his wound, but the man would not take the salt tablets no matter what.

The spotter plane buzzed them in a clearing in the middle of the day. It was then that Marlin realized he had lost the trail of the NVA. He asked the spotter plane to try and locate them. A while later, Sticky Fingers returned with no good news, but with a medevac helicopter to take care of the two dead men. Sticky Fingers moved on.

Marlin's uncle's last words to him before he had gone to Vietnam were, "Don't volunteer for anything." Marlin thought of the advice and wondered if this was considered a volunteer or an AWOL. Captain Rice might consider it AWOL. His father might consider it volunteer. The men? They were just following orders.

Gatz sweated but his shoulders did not droop. His chest never buckled. He stood tall and moved forward, head erect, praying to himself.

Marlin lighted a cigarette and inhaled deeply. The smoke was as hot as the air itself, so he threw it away.

The earth began to rumble. It was the low rumble, not of an earthquake but the pounding of artillery in the distance.

Sometimes it was just hard to think, even harder to feel and almost impossible to care.

Back and forth across the paddies, clean the rifle, gulp the salt tablets, swallow the acidic water, smell the leeches burning, feel the heat waves. The ground had turned hot to the touch. Heat rose from the ground like the air above a gas stove burner.

There was never a cool breeze when the sun was the hottest. Sweat ran from their faces like feeder streams into a growing pond.

Marlin did not know if he really wanted to run into the NVA right now. He would probably not have a choice, but the men were just so exhausted, they were almost delirious.

By the time they reached the village of Rach Kien, they were all ready to pass out.

Chapter 23

The village was as baked as Beckwith's brain felt. With sheer relief he walked across a wooden decking to the front door of a Vietnamese market and eyed the rows of canned goods lining the shelves. He glanced back over his shoulder at his men stretched out in a column down the road.

Vietnamese children were cautiously encircling the men with baskets of soft drinks, pineapples and coconuts in their arms, smiling broadly, but shyly. Beckwith looked back at Hillerman and gave him the signal to take a break.

As the message slowly filtered back through the platoon, the men removed their helmets, packs and flak jackets, set them down in the shade of a tree or awning and collapsed against them, nearly ready to pass out with heat exhaustion. The kids drew closer.

When the Lieutenant left his rucksack and helmet at the front door, he walked into the small store. Kraus followed, steadying the radio on his back with both hands so that it would not crash into any of the canned goods down the thin aisle.

They reached the front counter where a small Vietnamese man in a breezy short-sleeved shirt stood with one hand on the cash register, smiling. When he spied the flock of kids starting to follow the Lieutenant into the store, he shouted out in Vietnamese and threw his arms about wildly. The children quickly shoved each other back out the front entrance and watched from the threshold as if they were about to start an important foot race and were vying for a better starting position.

"I'd like to buy a case of cold soft drinks," Marlin said. The walls of his throat felt like they were sticking together and the request came out in a raspy voice. He massaged his neck and ended up scratching a mosquito bite.

The storekeeper bowed slightly, turned to the left, walked half a dozen steps and pivoted into a large walk-in cooler. Soon he returned with a steaming-cold case of good old American pop.

Just the sight of it make Marlin smile and his mouth salivate. He was so damn hot, and there was so little moisture left in his system, the sweat was coming out in white lines of salt on his fatigues.

Beckwith paid for the drinks in piasters, grabbed a bottle and told Kraus, who was taking a bottle himself, "Pass these out to the men, and remind them to take their salt tablets."

As Kraus hefted the case, Marlin opened his bottle, took a long swig that quenched his thirst with pleasure. He couldn't drink it fast enough but when his throat started to burn with the liquid, he set it down, gasped for air, looked at the storekeeper and asked, "You speak English number one?"

The storekeeper shook his head eagerly and smiled, revealing a full mouth of crooked buck teeth. He turned to look at a small child's head that popped out between two curtains in a doorway to his left. The storekeeper shouted until the little face disappeared behind the waving cloth. Sounds of giggling could be heard in the other room.

"Well, good," Marlin said as he turned his head to one side and hollered loud enough to be heard outside, "Hyde . . . Hyde, bring in the prisoner."

The wounded NVA was in bad shape. He had lost a great deal of blood and his complexion had turned as white as his eyeballs. He looked dangerously dehydrated.

When Hyde let go of the prisoner's good arm, the man fell on the floor and leaned against the counter, holding his hand below the open gash in his right rib cage, panting.

Beckwith looked at the storekeeper and said, "Ask him where the rest of his North Vietnamese friends are going."

The storekeeper's eyes darted paranoidly around the store. Satisfied that no one was watching, he said, "This man is dying."

"And I want some answers out of him before he does."

"What do you want him to say?" the storekeeper said.

"Where did the rest of his outfit go?"

The storekeeper shook his head in disbelief, then started to talk to the prisoner in Vietnamese.

The prisoner acted like he was not listening, but replied in terse remarks, panting hard and acting like the words themselves were killing him.

The storekeeper said, "Your dying prisoner say they go to recruit more VC."

Marlin glared into the prisoner's eyes. The man

279

held his breath, tensed, fluttering, searching.

"He's lying," Marlin replied. Just the thought made him angry. Marlin's lower jaw jutted forward and his breath came out in spurts. He hit the NVA with the back of his hand which sent him choking and whining to the floor. Marlin looked around for something to hit the man with, but before he got too physical, he hollered, "GATZ . . . GATZ . . . get in here."

By the time Gatz arrived, Marlin was standing over the prisoner panting with rage. Marlin looked at Gatz and said, "The man knows about Hoppy and where his outfit is headed and refuses to talk. Loosen him up."

As a Christian, Gatz believed in the wrath and might of God. He was going to baptize the prisoner in pain. He glanced at the storekeeper and said, "The truth."

The tall black man was a psychological as well as a physical threat.

The NVA soldier withdrew and slid his back against the counter. The storekeeper rattled words at him.

Words were exchanged as Gatz stood over the man foaming at the mouth and waiting to drop on his chest and make a believer of the man.

Finally the storekeeper said, "To Saigon, to burn the American embassy."

The words startled Marlin. First he thought of Lisa. He had just sent her to the embassy. What the fuck did he do this time? Then he thought of Hoppy. He knew as soon as they reached the embassy, if they got that far, the NVA would probably kill Hoppy rather than risk losing him in a major battle.

"How many of them are there?" Marlin asked the storekeeper.

After more questioning, the proprieter turned and said, "He say about 300 men, maybe less after the plane raid last night."

"What about the American prisoner?"

"They will use him to stop the Americans from shooting."

Marlin looked at the prisoner and was not sure if he believed the last statement. Then he remembered last night. If Hoppy had not been a prisoner, the two Phantom jets would have razed the NVA camp instead of skirting its perimeter.

The storekeeper shrugged his shoulders.

The prisoner slumped over and lay on his side, now not even touching the wound from which blood was dripping onto the floor.

"How will they get up there?"

The prisoner did not know.

"When do they plan to make this attack?" Marlin asked.

The prisoner began moaning and twitching.

"When?" Marlin repeated himself.

When there was no answer, Marlin shook his head for Gatz to move away, then he withdrew his pistol, cocked it and said to the storekeeper, "If he doesn't talk, I'll shoot his nuts off." The cold drink that Marlin had sipped had gone right through him. Beads of sweat stung his eyes. He wiped them away.

The bucktoothed storekeeper said, "He is dying."

They both looked at the man who stretched out on the floor, heaved a final breath and stopped shaking.

Marlin thought he had passed out, but the store-keeper knew better. "He is dead."

Marlin nodded. "Bury him."

Holstering the pistol, the Lieutenant walked out the front door and sat on the threshold, drinking his soda and contemplating his next move.

Gatz silently moved past him and returned to his squad.

Half a dozen children stood ten feet away. One of them said, "Dai Wi." They did not come closer.

Three hundred NVA, going to Saigon, to burn the American embassy with Hoppy, but when? Son of a bitch. And I sent Lisa up there just yesterday.

He surveyed his men surrounded by the chattering kids. It brought him back to his present predicament. He needed more ammunition.

As much as he disliked the ARVNs, he knew that there had to be a military compound somewhere in the village, and along with it an American advisor.

Marlin finished his pop, set the bottle to one side, and slipped back inside to ask the storekeeper one more question.

The man was mopping up the blood where the dead NVA soldier had been lying. The body was gone.

The storekeeper acted shocked at Marlin's return.

"Where are the ARVNs located in town?" Beck-with asked.

When the man pointed down the road and explained it was only a short distance, Marlin asked,

"Do they have an American advisor with them?"

"Yes. Lieutenant Hensley."

"Thanks," Marlin tipped his helmet.

As Marlin walked out the front door of the store, he ran into Randy Emmal standing in the entrance, eyeing the shelves of food.

Beckwith said to Emmal with a frown, "We are on our own now, soldier."

The Lieutenant brushed past Emmal and walked over to Gatz and said, "Let's check out this ARVN compound down the street."

Gatz and Jesus followed the Lieutenant down the road a quarter of a mile to where a small bridge crossed a canal. The ARVN compound was right at the intersection.

An ARVN guard in uniform, bareheaded, wearing tennis shoes, sat on a stool under a small piece of shade at the entrance.

Marlin pointed at the gate. The Vietnamese stood up, opened it, and shouted something in his native tongue to his fellow soldiers inside.

When Marlin walked down a row of concertina wire and reached an open courtyard surrounded by a tall berm, a Green Beret moved forward to greet him.

Lieutenant Hensley was a blond-haired officer with broad shoulders, hefty chest and bulging arms. He had a sober, businesslike gaze to his blue eyes. He and the Lieutenant shook hands.

Beckwith asked, "Do you have a radio?"

"Of course."

"Big enough to reach Ben Luc?"

"I talk to Captain Crystal just about every day."

"Good. Can I use it?"

"It won't even cost you a dime."

Lieutenant Hensley led the way into a radio shack that made the Old Man's radio room back at base camp seem small. There were three banks of radios, receivers and speakers along the wall.

When Marlin saw it he said, "Holy Christ, you could reach China with that equipment."

"If I knew someone there I might give it a try." The Green Beret picked up one of the transmitters and within seconds had Captain Crystal on the radio. Hensley handed the receiver over to Beckwith, who identified himself and asked for Bravo-six.

"Of course, three-six. He has been looking for you. What the hell are you doing up there?"

"You'll find out soon enough."

"It'll be a few minutes."

"That's OK." He didn't even want to talk to Captain Crystal.

After Hensley handed Beckwith another pop, they all waited in an awkward silence.

In no time Bravo-six was on the horn. "What the hell are you doing in Rach Kien, three-six?"

When Marlin explained about the NVA camp and the sighting of Hoppy and the plane raid, Bravo-six asked greedily, "How many KIAs?"

Marlin knew it was the Old Man's soft spot. "At least eighty, maybe a hundred. Bookoo burned bodies. We couldn't count 'em all." He knew he had scored points with the company commander. He decided to make his request immediately.

"Bravo-six. I want to continue following them."

"What are you talking about?"

"I think I can get Hoppy back. Give me 24 hours. That's all and I'll have him back."

"How many men to do you have left . . . I want to rephrase that question. How many men did you lose?"

"Two."

Beckwith took a swig from the soda bottle as he waited the answer.

"OK, three-six. I'll give you 24 hours. No more. You are out of our operational area so I can't give you any transportation or means of support. That means no helicopters and no artillery. You might be able to round up some from the advisor in your area. I want you back here by sunset tomorrow or holy hell will come down on me, and by the time it gets down to you, you'll wish you were the prisoner of war."

Marlin smiled, "Thank you, Sir. You won't regret it."

"I hope you don't either. What did you do with the two KIAs?"

"They have been taken care of already. They're in Saigon."

"Roger."

"Out."

Marlin sighed, looked at Kraus and the Lieutenant and said, "24 hours."

They heard the sound of a horn honking outside and looked out the firing ports to see a long gray bus stop at the bridge.

The door of the bus flew open and out stretched sticky-fingered Randy Emmal holding onto the handrail on the stairs and waving at the compound.

When Marlin led the way outside and drew close enough to hear, his rifleman said, "This guy volunteered to take us wherever we want to go, Sir."

The smiling driver wore sunglasses with slicked-down hair and a Hawaiian luau shirt. Lieutenant Beckwith looked inside the bus and saw half a dozen civilians scattered about staring back at him. The bus had torn leather seats and smelled of rotting fish, but what the hell, it was shady inside and a hell of a lot better than walking.

"It is already ours," Emmal explained with outstretched arms. "He doesn't care."

"Sold," Marlin said.

Marlin got off the bus and asked Lieutenant Hensley for more ammunition which was quick in coming. Gatz, Willie, Emmal and Kraus helped load it aboard.

When they were ready to leave, Beckwith thanked the Green Beret, wished him well and jumped aboard.

The bus driver returned to the store where the rest of the platoon was still resting. When it stopped along the line of strung-out men, the Lieutenant got out and signaled the platoon to get aboard.

The men stood up, pushed the kids back, finished off their sodas, wrestled with their gear and moved forward.

While Marlin made a head count as the men squeezed through the door, he was reminded of the insanity of this war. The platoon could just as easily highjack a civilian bus and ride to Saigon as they could fly there in a helicopter. Nobody ever really questioned what was going on because nobody knew

286

what was happening. There was no SOP. Ninety-five percent of the time Intelligence did not know where the enemy was or how many there were; the other five percent of the time they were usually wrong or too late to make a difference. The war was one of ingenuity, survival, and luck.

Hyde asked, "Is this a charter going to Las Vegas?"

"Just get aboard," Marlin said.

By now the civilians inside the bus had gathered together in one group. The third platoon took over the rest of the bus, slinging their gear on the floor and opening all the windows.

"Where do you want to go, Lieutenant?" Emmal asked.

"Saigon."

"Sounds fine to me." Emmal sat down across from the driver, stretched out his neck towards the man and said, "Saigon."

The driver jerked his head backwards, curled his chin and shook his head as if Saigon were not part of the plan.

Emmal laid the rifle on his lap and pointed the barrel right at the driver. Emmal clicked the safety on and off and repeated "Saigon," clearer this time.

The driver looked at the clicking sound, quickly shifted into gear and started driving.

Beckwith felt safe. It was daytime. The bus trip had not been planned so the local VC had no time to booby trap it; which Marlin doubted they would do anyway because the bus driver probably paid them a fat tax just to drive the roads safely.

Within minutes half of the men were asleep with

their heads resting on the back of the seats or on their chest, some sprawled out on the double wide seats.

Marlin sat in the middle of the bus and watched. He wondered if he was screwing up again.

If he relayed what he knew about the NVA size and movement to Intelligence, he would probably be pulled from the mission. Sure, whoever took over for him would probably stop the NVA, but they would have little regard for Hoppy's safety. Hoppy would probably be killed along with all the NVA and possibly never identified. Marlin had come too far to let that happen.

It took the bus nearly two hours to reach the outskirts of Saigon. It slowly came to a standstill in a long line of traffic of cars, carts, and motorcycles bottlenecking at what appeared to be a roadblock about a quarter of a mile ahead.

"This is as far as we go," Beckwith shouted. "Off the bus."

As the troops woke up, Marlin made sure they got their share of the M-16 and M-60 ammunition, more grenades, a box of which was white phosphorus, LAWs, claymores, M-79 ammunition. They all dug into the ammunition boxes like they were Christmas presents.

Sergeant Hillerman checked to make certain no ammunition or gear was left aboard. He was the last one off.

"We kill bookoo VC for you," Emmal said to the driver before the door slammed in his face. The driver spun the bus around and headed back down the road with the civilians aboard stretching their necks out the back window.

The platoon walked through the column of cars, past ox-drawn carts and three-wheel Lambrettas. Horns were blowing and the chatter of impatient Vietnamese filled the air. Caged ducks squawked, chickens clucked, dogs barked.

At the front of the column stood the Military Police, one officer and three privates. The creases in the officer's fatigues were still visible, but his arm-pits and chest were streaked with sweat. He was shaven and free of caked mud.

Beckwith walked right up to the First Lieutenant and greeted him.

"Where are you headed, soldiers?" the MP asked.

"Saigon. On special assignment."

The MP curled his lips like he did not believe Marlin but waved him through anyway. He was too busy checking the Vietnamese I.D.s to worry about Americans.

The sound of ammunition clanking made Kramm sound like a street vendor. As he passed them Kramm asked the three MP guards, "You didn't search us for weapons."

They ignored him.

As the third platoon proceeded on foot in the late afternoon, other American soldiers waved to them from roadblocks, from passing trucks and behind concertina wire enclosures. Insults were exchanged freely.

Marlin was confused. In eight hours would start the Vietnamese New Year. Fighting would stop, but what the hell was a battalion-size unit of North Vietnamese soldiers headed for Saigon to burn the American embassy, and how the hell could they get there with roadblocks all over the place. It didn't make sense.

The more friendly troops he passed the more he began to feel duped by the wounded prisoner. The NVA regulars were probably still sloshing their way through a swamp somewhere. Maybe it would take them all of Tet just to arrive at the embassy. By that time, Marlin would probably be back in Ben Luc. The thought angered him.

Saigon grew like a small hill, with the outskirts of the city containing the dense slums of plywood and cardboard shanties like poker cards stacked against each other.

The smoke from cooking fires that hung in the air at chest level slowly crept between houses and combined with the smell of open sewers and rotting nuoc mam. The point element kicked up dust that swirled above the open gutters of stagnant water and eventually returned to stick on the perspiring skin of the men in the rear of the column.

As the platoon maneuvered through the slums, Marlin gauged their safety according to the activities of the locals. If the women performed their everyday chores in a carefree, relaxed manner, if the kids were outside playing and laughing, he continued cautiously.

When the avenues became devoid of activity except for the decrepit wandering of stray animals, he abruptly changed directions until he was absorbed into the local population again.

The shacks grew to small adobe houses to two-story houses with red slate roofs. The streets became wider and straighter; Flood drains appeared at the corners and the back yards broadened as the hedgerow grew in height. Street lights appeared like fruit dangling from trees.

Beckwith found a city park to wait for the security of night before he moved closer to the embassy. The men ate their C-rations and rested, cleaned their weapons and smoked, read old letters from girlfriends and chatted with each other.

As darkness blanketed the city, the civilians disappeared from the streets and the houses lighted at the windows. A few candles flickered. Beckwith waited well past curfew until the electricity was turned off, then rallied his men and moved them along one side of the street in a long file, keeping to the doorways.

Their equipment rattled and their heels clicked on the pavement.

Phan Ngu Lao street paralleled the train yard and it was there that the sound of an automobile with its headlights out could be heard in the distance moving towards them.

Marlin moved the platoon onto the railroad tracks and between the boxcars. As the vehicle passed, he saw it was the Military Police — probably making their rounds.

The platoon proceeded down the tracks until they reached the deserted train terminal. They crossed a wide boulevard, past the bus station and then across Dien Hong Square in the central market.

The lights in the Tu Do area could be seen glowing above the darkened homes in the foreground, as curfew was later in that area.

Marlin hid in a doorway, took out his map and flashlight, slipped a rain poncho over his head and squatted down. He ran his finger on the map over the area they had come from in a big curve and ran his hand straight beyond where they were to go. The American embassy was only four blocks away, one block short of the Saigon River.

He hoped that Lisa and Thuy had completed their business and were long gone.

He turned off the flashlight, worked his way out of the poncho, and motioned the platoon to follow. He'd make it to the embassy and find out.

Chapter 24

When Marlin turned the corner from Cong Ly onto Cong Tru, the American embassy loomed towards him like a ghost at night. It was only three blocks away and smack in the middle of a street that dead-ended at a white fence surrounding the vault-like building.

Marlin unsheathed the starlight scope for a closer look and mumbled to himself as he eyed the monolithic building. It had no windows, only leaf-shaped slits in the concrete face which he guessed was an outer shell over the actual structure. After counting the lines of unbroken concrete that ran the length of the building, he concluded it was six storeys tall. A solid white cement fence surrounded the embassy garden, behind which grew forty-foot-tall tamarind trees.

It was not a pretty building, but definitely bold and arrogant-looking—in contrast to the lavish French-style homes that ran down both sides of Cong Tru, with ornate porches and decorative cornices and landscaped gardens with trees and fancy wrought-iron fencing spread out over half-acre-sized lots.

There were no NVA soldiers near the embassy

nor signs that they had arrived or would do so shortly.

Beckwith cursed the memory of the prisoner who had steered him this far. Bullshit, he thought. That son of a bitch died and I didn't even get a chance to kick him in the nuts.

He decided to draw closer, set his men up in a safe place and enter the embassy to find out if Thuy and Lisa were there, at least to put his mind to rest about their safety. Then in the morning he would return to Ben Luc.

He waved Keats to keep moving down the street, and followed. When he got to the last street before the embassy, before he crossed, he stopped at the corner to look around and listen. It was awfully quiet.

The street lights were a novelty. They certainly made walking easier, but at the same time made him and his men easy targets.

The embassy foyer was glowing with overhead fluorescent lights. Marlin could make out the helmet of an American soldier moving around the lighted area. Marlin didn't want the guard to challenge him, take a pot shot at the platoon or call in the MPs. He wanted to set his men up first, then take a scouting party into the embassy. He looked at his wrist watch and saw that the dials were barely illuminated. It was 2:30 in the morning.

The fact that the embassy was not heavily guarded kind of surprised Marlin, but then again, it was in downtown Saigon, near Tu Do street, and really not much of a military takeover. The embassy was not prepared to stop an all-out assault.

There was a three-storey French colonial mansion at the end of the block on the left-hand side. It was centered on a huge lot with a full back yard lined by a hedgerow. Beckwith studied the windows to see if anyone was watching. All the lights were out and none of the curtains were drawn back to one side. He hoped the occupants were asleep.

The garden would make a good spot to set his platoon in. They would be out of sight and still be able to watch several different approaches to the embassy in case something happened.

He moved the platoon across the street and down the block until he got to the house and stopped at a small white picket gate. He raised the locking mechanism and pushed in. As the gate creaked open he walked inside. There were flower beds around a cement patio with lounge and easy chairs and a lunch table. He turned and motioned Ivy and his squad who were nearest to come forward, then pointed his finger and whispered, "Move across the lawn and set up along the hedge on the far side of the garden. Spread your men out every five feet and make sure you can see up and down the street. I don't want anyone sneaking up on us from behind."

Ivy tipped his helmet and motioned his men to move around the Lieutenant and across the crisp grass. Beckwith sent the fourth squad to the end of the garden and the second squad right behind them. When Hillerman showed, he sent him to the far side of the fourth squad. Beckwith sent Rodriguez and his men to the left, up against the house. Beckwith would stay near the gate.

The men got on their knees and started to make themselves comfortable. They removed their ruck-sacks and set them aside, stretched out on their bellies on the damp grass with their heads right up against the bushes and their toes digging into the grass. Pouches of ammunition were laid alongside within easy reach.

From Marlin's vantage point, he looked to his left across the intersection at the white fence surround-ing the embassy. He scanned to the right at the corner house across the street with an equally large garden, then scanned the houses up the street which became smaller the farther they got from the em-bassy. The tall tamarind trees cast huge shadows along the houses on both sides of the street. The sweet smell of the flowers in the garden reminded Marlin of a funeral parlor.

Once the men were settled in place, Marlin made his rounds, checked to see the men were not too close together, briefed the squad leaders on the next move, and told them to keep an eye peeled for Hoppy if any NVA were spotted. Gatz and his squad would make the reconnaissance patrol with the Lieutenant to the embassy.

It was a perfect ambush sight. However, every time Marlin looked at the house next to him, he felt nervous. There were just too many windows on each floor and he felt eyes were looking at him from behind the curtains.

If the NVA regulars ever took over the house they could lob grenades down on the platoon and wipe them out in a matter of seconds.

He moved to Rodriguez's position and said,

296

"Jaime, I want you to go in the back of this house and make certain that there are only friendlies inside."

Jaime looked to where the Lieutenant was pointing and nodded his head. Up a short stairway was a double door, the outer one being screened. Jaime gathered up his squad, crouched over and moved up the stairs.

Marlin looked at his watch again. Five minutes had passed. They were three hours into the Vietnamese New Year. Marlin looked through the bushes across the street for movement as well as down the street in front of the embassy. The visibility was excellent, but nothing was moving.

Marlin would wait for Jaime to return before he crossed the street into the embassy.

Rodriguez and his squad no sooner disappeared through the back door, the hinges squeaking, when Marlin heard the sound of footsteps moving down his side of the street. He listened for a moment and realized the sound was not coming from shower clogs or tennis shoes, but leather boots, the kind the NVA regulars or a GI would be wearing.

If the sound were made by an NVA soldier, he could either be flank security or a point man. In either case, if the soldier stepped on the third platoon by surprise and alerted his comrades behind him, the whole momentum of the battle could be turned before it even started.

Beckwith looked down the line of men and saw Gatz kneeling behind his men with his ear perked to the sound and his eyes riveted on the Lieutenant.

Marlin ran his index finger along his throat.

Gatz set down his rifle and removed a long K bar knife from its sheath. The knife was large for most men, but in Gatz's huge hand it looked small.

He listened for a moment, then slowly duck-walked into the hedgerow.

The whole third platoon waited.

The clicking footsteps died and in its place was the sound of rustling bushes. Soon Gatz returned from the shrubs, this time dragging a body by the back of its collar. The head was turned awkwardly to one side and nearly detached from the shoulders. Blood was still pulsing from the neck gash. Gatz moved the body onto the grass and returned to his squad to retrieve his rifle and return the K bar to its scabbard. He said nothing and looked at no one.

No sooner had Marlin sighed in relief than he heard more footsteps. He held his breath and peered through the bushes and stretched his neck forward and saw movement across the street. He counted two men as they walked out of the darkness of a shadow and into the light of a street lamp. Two others followed, hugging the garden fence.

By the time Marlin grabbed a hold of Kraus's shoulder, he knew they were NVA soldiers. There was no way of identifying them as the ones occupying the camp he had raided the night before, but they were certainly NVA soldiers. It was their size, the shape of their helmet and packs, the way they carried their rifles. They were such lovely targets that Marlin had to hold his breath to stop himself from yelling out to open fire.

The NVA soldiers dribbled out of the darkness like drops of rain and kept a few yards apart, moving with more speed than caution. The point man was fifteen feet ahead of the others. Marlin counted ten of them.

As more came into view, Marlin grew more anxious at the thought of blowing them away. He glanced down the line of his own men to make certain they were alert and ready. When he looked back across the street, he saw Hoppy walk out of the darkness.

Startled, Marlin whipped the starlight scope up to his eye and gazed at his lost platoon member. Looking through the starlight with the aid of the street lamps turned everything green and brighter than day. Hoppy had his hands bound behind his back, his head drooping forward, barefeet, bareheaded, with black pajamas on, his blond hair caked with mud, a terrible, long gash on his swollen cheek. There were probably a dozen men in front of him and none behind.

The NVA point element was beyond Marlin.

If Marlin had his men commence firing on the NVA regulars too soon, possibly enough of them would not be in the ambush's killing zone. If he waited too long, too many of them might pass his position, escape his ambush and come around and attack him from behind.

If he started too soon, Hoppy might be mowed down. If he waited too long, Hoppy might get away from him again. It was a delicate situation.

He pulled a grenade from his pocket and looked down the line of his men. They all had their rifles to their shoulder and were aiming down the sights. He knew all they were waiting for was the signal to commence firing. He hoped they saw Hoppy as easily as he had, but he knew the odds were against it. Castillo could probably not even see that far.

Beckwith got to his feet and crouched behind the hedgerow.

Suddenly the screen door of the house slammed shut and Marlin looked up to see Spielberg walking tall down the stairs, totally unaware of any NVA soldiers.

Marlin heard a shout in Vietnamese from across the street. At the same time he tossed the fragmentary grenade as far as he could throw it. It hit the house across the street, bounced to the ground, rolled and exploded on the pavement.

It tossed three men into the air and lighted up the surprised faces of half a dozen other NVA soldiers standing close by.

The whole third platoon opened up with their weapons on automatic. M-60 machine gun fire streaked tracer rounds at waist level along the line of NVA regulars. M-16 fire, grenades and LAWs blasted the opposite sidewalk as the NVA soldiers dropped like dominoes.

Marlin kept his eyes peeled on Hoppy and tried to pick off some of the NVA nearest him with well-placed rounds. Two NVA regulars dropped. Four or five other NVA regulars crashed through the front door of the corner house and dragged Hoppy along with them.

"Gatz." Marlin screamed as green tracers streaked through the bushes over his men's heads. A grenade exploded to the back of them and a rocket struck a tree that cracked in the middle and crashed against the house.

By now Rodriguez and his men had found cover behind the hedgerow and were slinging lead across the street.

"Gatz." Marlin hollered again.

Within moments, Gatz and his squad came crawling on their bellies up to Marlin's position.

"What's that, Sir?" Gatz asked. Overhead flares lighted the black man's face streaked with sweat that dripped from his nose.

"Gatz . . . Hoppy is across the street."

Gatz stretched his neck to follow Marlin's finger as it zeroed in on the corner house.

The surprised NVA soldiers who had sought protection in the gardens and doorways had been quickly chopped to pieces. The few remaining who fired from cover were quickly ink-blotted as their muzzle flashes pinpointed their hiding places.

As the firing died, Marlin moved to the gate and looked to the right. He saw a line of NVA regulars crossing the intersection two blocks away.

"Ivy . . ." Marlin hollered.

"Yo!" came a scream from the back side of the garden.

"They might be circling around the block and coming your way. Stay put."

"Yo."

"Gatz . . ." Marlin said, "four of them took Hoppy into the front door. You and I are going inside. Kraus, call Hillerman on the radio and tell him he is to remain here with the rest of the platoon and lay down covering fire so we can cross the street." Gatz licked the beads of salt from his lips.

No sooner had Kraus relayed the message than Hillerman was there couching beside Beckwith. He was panting and fidgeting.

Marlin had his eyes fixed to the houses across the street.

The returning fire was coming from a few windows in the houses that were now starting to go up in flames. The street was littered with bodies.

One NVA regular fired a single shot from behind a tamarind tree. Marlin lobbed a grenade at the tree and when it exploded, the firing stopped.

When Marlin looked at Hillerman, he gave him the thumbs up sign and explained the plan.

Hillerman asked, "What do you want us to do here?"

"Just lay down a base of fire to cover us when we cross the street."

"But while you are in the house?" Hillerman was justifiably scared.

"They know you are here and will probably try and sneak up on you or surround you. If they get near you, kick the shit out of 'em."

Suddenly Marlin heard the whining of a speeding automobile engine and looked up to see two vehicles pull up the front gate of the American embassy on Vo Di Nugy street. The leading vehicle was a pickup truck and the trailing vehicle a yellow taxi. What confused Marlin was that the occupants were not in the NVA uniform. They were armed Vietnamese in civilian clothes. They scrambled from the two cars, crashed through the front gate of the embassy and ran towards the foyer. When the guard on duty called a halt and opened fire, the Vietnamese cut him down and ran past him firing their rifles.

Two Vietnamese guards ran from the building, out the front gate and down the street without being fired upon. They disappeared from view around the first corner.

Unbeknownst to the third platoon, the VC and NVA were launching the largest offensive of the war, attacking every American base and every town and city in Vietnam. Eleven battalions, 84,000 men, hit Saigon, and if Beckwith had to guess, they were all headed for the American embassy.

Marlin was stunned. The American embassy was actually coming under attack.

He watched through his starlight scope as NVA troops in a half crouch ran down Hans Nghi street, directly to the left of the embassy. If other troops were doing the same to the south, the embassy was being surrounded. Didn't seem like 300 NVA troops, but some of the NVA soldiers might have gone to different targets within the city.

Some truce, he thought. They're all over the place.

The city was on fire; thick, black puffs of smoke rose like a puffing volcano from the different quarters cutting out the moonlight as the city exploded with flames and the sounds of firing.

Ivy started firing from his position and green tracers filled the yard, now coming from behind.

The truck and taxi out front went up in smoke and flames. Firing broke out atop the embassy building and small flashes of fire could be seen coming from between the slats on the different floors. The firing was sporadic, probably coming from automatic pistols. Whenever the single flash of a muzzle sparkled from the embassy, it was quickly fired upon by a fussilade of green tracers.

Rockets blew holes into the side of the embassy. The cement on the face of the building began to crumble as rounds ricocheted off its side.

A fire started at the right front of the building about two storeys up.

As far as the Lieutenant could reckon, he had slowed down the attack on his corner of the street, but the NVA regulars were popping up all over the place.

He looked across the street at the embassy building slowly being surrounded and said to Kraus, "I wonder if Lisa is still in there?"

It was the first time the Lieutenant had mentioned the girl in his conversation, and even under the circumstances, Kraus was mildly shocked. "I don't know, Sir."

"Damn . . . I got to go after Hoppy first. By that time, reinforcements should be here to help out the embassy. It has to be that way."

"Yes, Sir."

"Kraus," the Lieutenant hollered as he looked across the street at the corner house, "cover me."

Chapter 25

Hoang Tran silently stared out the window, his tall posture taking on a slight slumping of the shoulders. The military commander of the North Vietnamese troops stood next to him, peeking out the window as he held the curtain to one side and spoke, in an angry tone.

Hoang Tran barked back at him.

The three NVA soldiers who stood with AK-47s at the ready neglected their primary job of guarding Hoppy. They were fidgety and nervous, trying to speculate out the window as well.

Hoppy knew that the two officers were arguing about the ambush they had just triggered, probably wondering how many Americans there were, what would be the Americans' next move, what would be theirs.

Hoppy sat against a wall a good eight feet away from them. He thought of trying to escape down the stairs, eyed the doorway furtively, but his ankles were tied together so he could not take a full stride and his hands were bound similarly. A futile attempt at such a dangerous moment would be suicidal, especially with the guards so keyed up to kill. He didn't feel strong enough to handle another beating.

Hoppy inspected the room with the freedom of not being watched. There were the bodies of a porky Vietnamese man and his two children on a throw carpet to his right, near the bedroom door. The man had been killed when he had barged into the living room demanding an explanation for their intrusion. Hoang Tran had shot him in the chest with his pistol. The curious children showed up later and were shot by the NVA regulars.

He pressed his bare feet to the wooden floor and shimmied his shoulders up the wall. When he got to his feet, he snuck a glance over his captors' shoulders out the window at the rooftops glowing with pockets of fire, surprisingly close. Smoke billowed in clouds skyward and the sound of artillery rounds striking their targets shook the house. When the light from a flare careened towards the ground, Hoppy saw the outline of a few American soldiers crouching next to a set of stairs across the street. He knew them right away as Americans—it was their rounded helmets and bulky figures, so much larger than the NVA regulars.

He had a gut feeling that the Americans were leaving him behind again and the depression that overwhelmed him was heavier than the depression the previous night when the camp had been raided and his hope of freedom had been crushed. The depression was the deepest, emptiest and most useless feeling he had ever experienced, and each time it overwhelmed him, it seemed to grow more intense.

His head slumped forward on his chest and his body shivered with fatigue, feeling like the blood had drained from his veins. The feeling of aloneness was painful.

The first time he had felt that way was when the NVA had stuck him in the hole and covered him with the bamboo lid. At that time, he felt like he was going to drown, alone, without any of his family or friends knowing about it; and he was going to die by drowning in his own urine. Since then, the same deep depression came and went, sometimes for no apparent reason; and when it did, it immobilized him.

He was emotionally and physically exhausted, yet his mind refused to accept his imprisonment. Like in the past, he tried to avoid the depression by transferring his thoughts to other matters, pretending. It usually worked, but his emotions were getting all mixed up and had little to do with the way they used to act. The pretending made him feel better until he was awakened to the situation by a jab from one of the soldiers. The depression sunk in like a knife and made him want to pretend all the more. It was driving him crazy.

At least he did not feel the pain in his face anymore where Hoang Tran had slashed him with the knife his second day in captivity. His face burned from the wound with a numbing intensity. He could feel the maggots growing there and sometimes touched his face and removed the small white eggs, but there were so many of them and so deep in his wound that he did not like to pick at them. It made his face swell and hurt even more. He tried to coexist with the maggots, removing them only when they crawled up to his eyes; that was going too far, even for him.

Hoppy looked at Hoang Tran who pointed out the window across the street where the initial firing had come from. Hoang Tran pounded his fist into his other hand as he hollered at the commander. The commander gruffed and pointed out the window, this time in the opposite direction.

Hoppy could not understand the conversation, but he could tell they were undecided and scared.

The three soldiers fidgeted with their AK-47s. For some reason they were not returning the fire. They wore their ammunition belts across their chests like Mexican bandidos and chattered quickly to each other.

Hoang Tran and the Commander were deep within their argument, and the thought made Hoppy feel a bit of energy. He loved to see them miserable, like the previous night with their camp burning. Their fear fed his humor.

Hoppy heard the downstairs front door crash open and footsteps chase through the lower rooms, lurching forward, silent, spreading out, coming together, the sound of doors opening. He felt relief and fear at the same time.

"Try upstairs," came a voice in English. It sounded like the voice of Lieutenant Beckwith.

Hoppy's heart started pounding so hard at the voice of an American so near that it felt like it was going to choke off his throat.

He knew that there was no way for Hoang Tran to escape now without a fire fight, and he knew that the Americans would win. They had to.

Two of the guards took up their places on each

side of the door. The one on the left removed a hand grenade from his ammunition belt.

When Hoppy thought of shouting out, before he did so, he looked at Hoang Tran who was pointing his pistol at Hoppy's face and glaring at him. Hoang Tran knew what Hoppy was thinking.

Hoppy was silent. Just like he had been when he was first captured. He saw it all again. Ankle-deep in mud, rain pouring down on his head, the sight of the NVA regulars in the treeline, his arms flying up in the air like they were attached to a string and he were a puppet.

He felt like the same coward he had been back then; even now. In spite of all the beatings and torture, he felt like he had not grown in courage.

When Hoang Tran had held the pistol to his face once before and threatened to blow his brains out, Hoppy had spilled his guts out, telling him everything he knew about everyone in his platoon. It had not helped out the North Vietnamese that much strategically as Hoppy did not really know that much, but it had made him feel like he had not only betrayed his platoon, but had shit upon them at the same time. He didn't want to do it again.

There is a fine line between being a coward, a fool and a hero. It just depended upon where the dice stopped, what numbers came out on top. Hoppy decided to go for it and started to scream at the top of his lungs. He wanted to holler something intelligible, but it just came out as a scream. At the same time, he cringed, bringing his shoulders up to his neck.

When he did not feel a slug or powder burns, he opened his eyes to see Hoang Tran still pointing the pistol at him, but now it was shaking. Both soldiers at the door started firing their AK-47s through the closed door and downward.

Hoang Tran signaled the third soldier to silence Hoppy.

Hoppy wanted to knee the guard in the groin as he came at him, but he had no strength. The soldier brought the butt of his rifle in a whirl against Hoppy's face and hit him in the jaw with the metal butt before Hoppy could even move his hands up to protect his face.

Hoppy felt the whole side of his face explode. Teeth shattered in flakes and pieces and landed atop his tongue and in the recess of his throat. Blood flooded his mouth.

He spat and choked and felt with his tongue the ragged edge of his molars and eyeteeth. When he finally opened his eyes, he was on the ground looking into the face of one of the murdered children. For a second he stared at the face, with its non-blinking eyes, its mouth open and still wet with drool, taking on macabre shadows from the flickering fires casting shadows through the curtained window.

Suddenly, the guard set his rifle aside, grabbed Hoppy around the throat and started to press with his thumbs against his Adam's apple.

A tremendous explosion shook the room, which made the NVA troopers at the door fire even faster.

It did not distract the guard on Hoppy's throat, who started to pound Hoppy's head on the floor as he squeezed with his finger tips, pressing even harder with his thumbs.

Hoppy groped at the man's hands, but futilely.

Hoppy moved his hands to the man's chest, felt an American-made grenade on the ammunition suspenders, cupped his hand around it, and ripped it from the clip. Hoppy's head was spinning, little white dots appearing, but he pulled the pin from the grenade while squeezing the detonation lever and opened his eyes to read his captor's reaction.

The guard reacted by releasing his grip and looking between his arms to where the sound came from. When he saw the grenade without its pin, he sat upright on Hoppy's belly and snatched at the grenade, but only half-heartedly, like he did not really want the thing.

Hoppy moved the grenade to one side, just slightly out of reach. The guard rolled from Hoppy and started to crawl away on all fours back to the door where Hoang Tran and the Commander were standing.

Hoppy displayed the grenade in front of Hoang Tran's eyes, even in the dark room, showed so much white that they nearly glowed in the dark.

Two of the guards charged out the door with their rifles blazing on automatic. The returning fire was phenomenal, the tracer rounds passing right through their bodies.

When the noise and sounds of firing quieted, Hoppy opened his eyes to see he was still alive. He looked up for Hoang Tran. His body was across the room and ripped to pieces. So was the body of the Commander and one of the soldiers. The bodies of the other two soldiers were missing.

Realizing he was still holding the grenade, Hoppy got up on his knees and hurled it through the open window. The explosion shook the room.

He leaned against the wall and studied the picture around him. There were blood and bullet holes sprayed all over the walls, smoke was still rising from the furniture as well as just hanging in the air. He spat blood and teeth on the floor.

He looked down at his own body and saw his clothes were intact. He felt his body with both his hands, first his legs to make sure they were still there, then both his arms, his head. He was still all together, no new wounds.

He heard someone charging up the stairs, a noise at the door. He looked up to see Lt. Marlin Beckwith in the doorway with his rifle aimed at him.

As they stared into each other's eyes and the recognition sunk in, they both sighed. Hoppy collapsed on the ground.

Marlin looked over his shoulder and hollered down the stairs, "Doc, get up here. He's OK."

Marlin ran over to Hoppy and picked up his head in his hands. Hoppy's eyes shown with gratitude.

"You OK?" Marlin asked, as he looked at the maggots on Hoppy's cheek in disgust. Hoppy's mouth was so sore from the broken teeth he just shook his head.

"Doc, get up here," Marlin called again.

Doc and the rest of the squad came bounding through the doorway. The men headed for the windows and knelt so they could look outside. Doc went to Hoppy.

In all of Doc's months working in Nam, he had never seen anything like Hoppy before. Doc had seen many a man blown apart, but Hoppy was rotting away. Doc laid Hoppy's head back down on the ground and searched through his pouch for morphine.

Beckwith ran to the window and looked outside again. Overhead flares were lighting up the embassy. As the NVA tightened the grip around the building, they concentrated their fire on the entranceway where the muzzle flashes of small arms fire were glowing. He looked up and down the street.

"Son of a bitch," he said. "I don't see any American replacements coming."

Beckwith turned his head back to see Doc giving Hoppy a shot. Then he looked at Gatz. "Gatz, you better stay here with your squad and keep an eye on Hoppy. I'm afraid if we try and move him he won't make it. I'm going to move the men across the street and evacuate the embassy, if at all possible."

"Don't be no fool, Sir," Gatz replied as he fired out the window.

"No choice." Beckwith replied. "Kraus, raise Hillerman."

While Kraus got on the horn, Beckwith watched Hoppy and just shook his head. What a mess of a man, but he was still alive and in a way Marlin had accomplished part of his mission. It was all coming together.

Kraus handed the mike to Beckwith.

"This is three-five," came over the radio.

When Beckwith explained the plan, he concluded with, "I want you to move the platoon across the street to my position. I'll meet you at the front stairs."

"Roger."

313

"Be careful, Three-five. We'll cover you coming across the street."

"Roger. We're on our way."

Chapter 26

If courage could be measured by the glassful,
each man in the third platoon filled it to the rim in
his own way. Not a man amongst them fell below
the common degree of hero. Sure, they were all
afraid to die, but more afraid to die cowards.

Marlin ran down the front stairs, jumped over
the handrail and crouched down as he glanced up
and down the street. There were a few North Vietnamese soldiers skirting from house to house in
both directions, but they seemed more interested in
surrounding the embassy itself than engaging Marlin. He looked at the long run across the wide
street and had a feeling the NVA would change
their plan as soon as he made his move.

Marlin heard the rattling of weapons and looked
over his shoulder to see Ivy's squad and Rodriguez's
men darting across the street. Gatz and his squad
opened fire from the second storey windows and
laid down a steady base of fire into the garden from
where Ivy and Rodriguez had run.

The sound of enemy machine gun fire rattled
from across the street and green tracers filled the
air over the heads of the advancing Americans.
When the two squads made it across the street, they

dropped to their bellies to low-crawl closer to Marlin's position.

Kraus and Marlin still had their rifles pointed at the garden across the street. When two NVA soldiers came running through the gate just behind Sergeant Hillerman, Marlin and Kraus joined Gatz in mowing them down.

Salvador Castillo, who was the first man to reach the Lieutenant, pushed his glasses back on the bridge of his nose and said, "Where are you going, Lieutenant?" His head was darting back and forth.

There were street lamps along the road, lighting up their position as well as the NVA's.

"Take out some of those lights, Castillo," Marlin said as he pointed to the street lamps. "There's too much light if we are going to make a move."

Castillo pushed his glasses to the bridge of his nose again, aimed his M-60 at the nearest light across the street and plinked it out. He shot out another further to the left and by then Emmal stood up and knelt behind the staircase to shoot out the lights down the other side of the street.

As the platoon grew in deeper shadows, Marlin looked at the cement wall surrounding the embassy. It was about six feet tall, and as it was painted white, seemed to glow in the dark. Marlin did not want to waste time jumping over it. He knew some of his men would have a hard go of it weighed down by the flak jackets, helmets and ammunition. If anything went wrong halfway over the wall, they would be easy targets.

Marlin saw Spielberg with two LAWs slung over his shoulders. "Spielberg, get up here," he hollered as he waved his arm forward.

316

Spielberg stood up, crouched as he ran forward, stopped and knelt down on one knee right next to the Lieutenant.

"Blow a hole in that cement wall with your LAW," Beckwith hollered.

Spielberg removed the LAW from his shoulder, pulled the retaining pin, and popped the two sections open, which made the sights snap up in place. He clicked off the safety, sighted on the wall and said, "Tell me when!"

Marlin looked behind Spielberg to make certain no one was lying in the back blast zone. Satisfied, he patted Spielberg on the shoulder. "Now."

The recoilless rifle spewed out more fire to the rear than forward, but the rocket flew at the wall, hit it solid and tore out a hunk of cement large enough for a water buffalo to leap through.

Satisfied, Marlin knew there was only one more thing he had to do before he made his next move. He looked back and waved Hillerman closer.

When Hillerman came up, the Lieutenant said, "Sarge, leave your radio with Gatz."

Hillerman ran up the stairs and disappeared inside the door just about as quickly.

While Marlin waited, he got two more white phosphorous grenades from Emmal as he had already used up his; he waited for the Platoon Sergeant to return while he eyed the hole in the wall, as well as the street in both directions, weighing the grenades anxiously in each hand.

When Hillerman appeared at the front door, Marlin popped one of the white phosphorous grenades as Kraus readied a smoke grenade. They threw them both into the middle of the road at the same time and even before they popped, both had the pins removed from two more grenades and had them on their way. When the green and red smoke mingled with the white phosphorous hair strings of cover, Marlin started his men moving forward.

When the momentum was going forward, he joined the ranks right after Rodriguez's squad.

As they ran through the smoke, Marlin heard Kraus holler out, heard an M-16 sliding across the pavement and heard Kraus fall to his knees, grunt, and then the radio crash.

Marlin stopped, turned and searched with an outstretched hand like a blind man would cross a street, waved his men to continue forward, and searched for Kraus. When he felt something, he reached down and took hold of Kraus's shirt and raised him to his feet.

"You all right?" Marlin asked.

"Yeah," Kraus replied as he stood up. "I just tripped over something."

Kraus could not find his rifle so he just limped his way forward through the smoke with the Lieutenant pulling him along by the arm.

Ivy's squad was already behind the wall by the time Beckwith could see the opening. Somehow Castillo got separated from his squad and came wandering over the broken cement and nearly tripped on a piece of protruding rebar. Hyde jumped what remained of the wall like Surfer Joe and Hyde's men followed close behind Hillerman.

Kraus and the Lieutenant were the last ones in.

Once behind the fence, the platoon returned fire at a small element of NVA regulars sneaking up the street towards the house they had just moved from.

Marlin spread the men out along the opening in the wall until everyone was accounted for. He counted fifteen men in all. Then he turned his attention to the embassy building.

He was afraid that some of the trigger-happy Americans inside might mistake him and his men for NVA soldiers, so he shouted out to two Marine guards visible in the entryway.

When the Marines acknowledged their presence with an arm gesture to come forward, Marlin signaled Spielberg to get going and soon the platoon filed past the two Marines, who had dropped to their bellies and were firing like maniacs.

The platoon crouched in a tight circle under the overhead lights and Marlin screamed, "Spread out . . . Spread out."

Hillerman pointed for Ivy and his squad to move up the staircase. Rodriguez and his men knelt behind a row of flowerpots and Hyde's squad went to the rear of the foyer that ran the width of the building.

There were four dead Vietnamese lying in pools of bloods on the cement walkway. The bodies of three dead Marines were pulled back beyond the flowerpots.

Marlin slid his back along the white wall until he reached the side of one of the Marines who looked up from his sights and said, "The other sons of bitches got past us."

"How many?" Marlin asked.

"Two. I think."

Sporadic fire was coming from the second and third storeys of houses across the street; still no NVA regulars had snuck up to the cement wall to fire through the leafed openings.

Marlin looked over to the corner house where Gatz was still located and thought he heard some firing coming from it. They were probably holding off those NVA soldiers that had been following him. He hoped like hell they would not be surrounded.

"Kraus, how is Gatz doing?"

"They're returning some fire; but they're OK."

"Keep in contact."

"I will," Kraus hollered.

Suddenly the fluorescent lights popped and darkness enveloped the foyer.

The rooftops across the street started to light up with the flash of muzzle fire and so did some of the windows from the second storeys of the houses across the street a couple of hundred yards away. Not a bad target, but Beckwith chose to save his ammunition in case they charged. By now he figured help was on its way.

Whenever the Marine fired, the muzzle flash momentarily blinded Marlin. For all practical purposes, his night vision was gone. He could have tried to keep one eye closed, but then his sense of depth would have dissolved. With so many obstacles around, that would be as treacherous as losing his night vision.

"Satchel charges," Marlin said to himself more than to the Marine. "Sappers running around the city throwing satchel charges into windows and doorways, setting the city afire." He looked at the Marine again and half screamed, "Are there any Americans in the building?"

The man got up from his belly and leaned against the wall next to Marlin. "Most of them are one. They don't spend the night here." The Marine's face was streaked with sweat but his cheeks formed a wry smile, like he was enjoying himself.

"You seen a French Vietnamese girl with a small Vietnamese interpreter running around here?"

The soldier puckered up his face and hollered, "If I had, I might have shot them."

When Beckwith acted startled, the soldier said, "Nope. They friends of yours?"

"Yes."

"Just because I didn't see them don't mean they're not here. I work the day shift. Those dead Marines were working the night."

"How many civilians are in the building?"

"Fuck if I know. They come and go all the time. Maybe a dozen. Maybe two dozen."

"Where are they?"

"They bed downstairs, but when the firing started, they all headed for the roof."

"I'm going to gather up all the civilians and move them out of here. The North Vietnamese regulars have this place surrounded and I have a feeling they won't be satisfied until they turn this building into a bowl of dust."

"When you head upstairs, take out those two gooks that got past us. No telling what damage they will do . . . We'll stay here and try to hold the others off if they try and jump the wall . . . How many do you figure are out there?"

"There were supposed to be 300 headed to the embassy, but I'd say about a third of them got here."

The Marine gave Marlin a dirty look like he could take on that many by himself.

"There must be some reason they are just settin
down a base of fire. Got me?" Beckwith asked.

The Marine emptied his magazine into a window
across the street. The firing stopped.

"I'll leave a squad with you," Marlin said.

"Suit yourself, but if I were you, I'd hurry."

Marlin turned his head and when he saw Rodri
guez, he said, "Rodriguez, you and your squad sta
here with the Marines."

Rodriguez nodded his head.

The Lieutenant ran over to Ivy and said, "Ther
are two armed North Vietnamese in civilian clothe
somewhere in the building. I want you to take 'em
out, but be careful because Lisa and Thuy could u
there as well, plus some other American civilians
Get going up the stairs."

Ivy stood up and signaled with his head for hi
men to follow him. They took off up the stairs righ
behind each other with their rifles at the port, thei
equipment rattling. The rest of the platoon wa
right behind them.

On the first floor, tracers were streaking acros
the hallway. Papers were strewn in the corrido
paintings shot off the wall lying broken on the floo
fire extinguishers foaming from bullet holes. Puffs o
smoke ignited in the wall where bullets struck
There were no dead bodies in the corridor and i
was too hot for the platoon to check out for liv
ones.

"Fuck this floor," Marlin said from the protection
of the cement staircase as he waved Ivy upward.

The second floor was about as bad as the first
The NVA machine guns seemed to have found th
building itself a desirable target.

322

By the third floor, the firing seemed to slow down ut it was on this floor that Ivy hollered, "There's a re down the corridor."

The hallway door was off its hinges and the men ooked down the long corridor. The fire was coming ut of a room that faced the front of the building, pparently the last office on the right. Flames were cking out of the room and lashing down the corridor. Smoke was seeping down the hallway.

Marlin wondered how much time he would have) find the survivors, if any, and get them back hrough the smoke and flames. He thought of leav-ng a few men behind to try and put the fire out, ut he decided against spreading himself any thin-er. He'd just work faster.

On the fourth floor landing, they came upon the odies of two American civilians in light tanned uits. They were lying face down, with small hand-uns within easy reach. The backs of their heads ad been blown apart.

On the fifth floor, Newsome, who was leading the harge, swung around the stairs to the next floor vhen the sound of firing opened up from the floor bove. Newsome's body buckled with the sound and omersaulted backwards, his rifle rattling as it slid lown the stairs.

Quickly Ivy removed a grenade from an ammuni-ion pouch, pulled the pin, let the handle fly and fter holding it for a split second, threw it to the anding above. By the time it exploded, he had nother grenade in his hand with the pin removed nd lobbed that one upstairs as well. With the sec-nd explosion, he bounded up the stairs three at a ime and came upon the body of one dead NVA soldier.

Newsome was bleeding from the chest and throa
He was dying and Doc was not there to tend hir

"Who Do," Beckwith said. "Stay with Newsom

At that, Who Do set his rifle against the wall ar
removed a bandage from his pouch and tried
treat Newsome for a sunken chest wound, but B
had already stopped breathing.

Ivy knew there was one more NVA around ar
he bounded around the stairs, listening to the cli
of heels ahead of him.

There was the sound of a door opening and the
the sound of screaming.

Ivy pulled himself around the bannister with or
hand and as the door swung closed, with his oth
hand fired his M-16 on fully automatic through th
closed door. He emptied the magazine, replaced
with another, then ran to the top of the stairs an
kicked against the door. It moved heavily. H
shoved harder and by the time he got it halfwa
open saw that there was a body on the other sid
holding the door shut. He laid his shoulder into th
door and pushed it completely open and looke
around the back of the door to see the dead NV
regular.

Ivy wiped his brow and sighed.

Marlin jumped through the open door onto th
rooftop and from that vantage stared at the smo
dering city. It reminded him of pictures he had see
of the 1906 San Francisco earthquake. The entir
city seemed to be on fire. Smoke bellowing in larg
clouds, flames coming on line and licking the sk
red. The wind had picked up, swirling smoke an
flames and bringing with it added heat from th

ining fires. There were the sounds of small arms
re and rockets exploding, artillery and mortars
acking the air. The city was a living inferno.

There were half a dozen civilians huddled around
e vent duct holding onto each other. When they
w the Americans, they still huddled close together
nd stared in fright.

Marlin spotted Lisa at the same time she saw
im. She stood up and ran towards him with her
rms out. She threw her arms around his neck and
ugged him. He responded by patting her on the
ack and pulling her arm loose. "Lisa, we have to
et out of here . . . Where is Thuy?"

She pointed to the wall and Marlin saw a lone
oldier on his belly hanging over the side of the
uilding with a pistol in his hand, firing.

"Thuy," the Lieutenant shouted.

Thuy rolled over on his back with the pistol still
eld tightly in both hands. When he recognized the
.ieutenant, he shouted out, "Dai Wi."

As Thuy stood up, tracer rounds surrounded
im, penetrating the back of his helmet, which
olled forward off his face. At the same time Thuy's
gs buckled and his shoulders slumped forward as
e toppled like a tree, hit the ground on his helmet
nd rolled over to one side.

Marlin ran towards him, slid across the roof be-
ore he became a target himself and pulled his
riend back a ways from the wall. A pool of blood
ollowed behind. Marlin did not bother to turn him
ver. The bullet had blasted through the back of his
ead and taken out a large hunk of bone. Marlin
laced the helmet back over the exposed tangle of
rain, removed Thuy's dog tags from around his

neck, removed the pistol from his hand. Thuy h:
been a hard-fighting soldier whom Marlin h:
grown to respect and love. Marlin hefted him ov
his shoulder. The Vietnamese felt light. Marlin w
going to take care of Thuy's body as he would h
American friends. Bring him out for a proper buri
or die trying.

As Marlin trotted across the gravel rooftop to t
group of civilians, he saw Lisa looking at the de:
body of Thuy but there was no time for him
speak comforting words. Instead he said, "We ha
to get off this roof. There is a fire downstairs th
will cut us off from escaping at any moment."

"But they will kill us down there," one of tl
women said. She was hysterical. She had her arn
pressed to her chest, her knees brought in front
them.

"The helicopters will come and pick us up," a:
other woman said. She was standing, her che
bulging forward. Her curly hair twisted and h:
cheeks were too full, hiding sunken eyes. Even
the dim light it was obvious she wore too muc
make-up, especially on her red lips. She continue(
"My name is Dolores Track."

Marlin replied, "Dolores, any chopper that com
near this place will be blown out of the sky. Th
NVA regulars have this place surrounded. They a:
probably just waiting for such a target . . . Th
only way you will escape from here is out the froi
door."

"What will we do then?" one of the men askec

"The problem is getting out of here. I think the
are more interested in this building than in us."

Just as he spoke, he heard the sound of mortar

ing dropped down a tube. Mortars started to ex-
ode. The first two hit in the front garden down
storeys and the last one on the far right corner
the roof.

One of the men said, "They won't listen."

"Follow us," Marlin said.

A second and third mortar exploded in the same
ot as the first and Marlin knew it was not time to
gue. The roof trembled with each explosion.

"Hillerman, get them moving."

Hillerman hefted one of the hysterical women to
r feet and that was enough to get the other civil-
ns moving. They were reluctant to follow, but
th the mortars exploding, obviously did not want
be left behind.

The mortaring stopped. Marlin listened for the
und of more being dropped down a tube, but
stead heard only a rumbling sound, seeming to be
ming from the direction where he had set up the
mbush.

Just before they entered the staircase, Marlin
ve Thuy's body to Truskowski and crawled over to
e side of the building with Kraus right behind
m.

They lay on their bellies watching.

"Kraus, see if you can raise Gatz on the radio.
e might know what's going on down there."

Kraus tried to raise the second squad leader on
e horn without luck. He knew something had to
wrong because they were too close to have any
pe of transmission problems.

"Can't get him, Sir."

Marlin watched under the flickering light from
res as the sound of the rumbling grew louder, then

he saw a tank approach. Reinforcements finally a
rived. Son of a bitch. He watched it for a secon
until it stopped right next to the house where Gat
his men, Doc and Hoppy were still holed up.

It moved its turret towards the entrance of t
embassy. Marlin saw the insignia on its side, t
bright red star of the NVA army.

"Fuck," he whispered. Maybe that's what th
have been waiting for.

Gatz was in a perfect place to take out the tan
"Get a hold of Gatz," Marlin said again.

"I can't," Kraus repeated. "He is not answerin

Finally Gatz opened up firing. Grenades explod
around the tank and what looked like a LAW ric
cheted off the tank's curved sides and blew up
the air.

The tank turned its turret upon the house, fir
a tracer-marking round and followed with a hi
explosive that ripped out nearly the entire botto
floor of the house and sent it streaming down t
block in flaming balls of garbage.

Quickly the tank turned its big gun back on t
embassy and blasted a hole in the side of the wa
large enough for a freight car to pass through. T
building shook on its foundations as smoke ro
from the roof.

Then it started to raise its gun to the top floc

Chapter 27

Marlin looked down the side of the building and could see tracer rounds firing from the foyer and headed across the street. Apparently the Marines and Rodriguez's squad were holding their own, had not taken on the tank as a target as of yet, nor vice versa, which was just as well.

The cannon on the tank kept rising, as if it knew exactly where Marlin was. Marlin crept back from the wall and when he was safe enough from ground fire to stand up, sprang to his feet and raced back to his men who were still surrounding the civilians in a haphazard manner.

Trains of flares popped overhead, and when some of them landed on the roof and continued to burn, they emitted a sulphur smoke that drifted like fog and further contaminated the air.

Coughing started with the women and quickly spread to the men.

Marlin made a quick count of the civilians — ten of them, eight being American and two Vietnamese. Of the Americans, two were men. Beckwith counted his troops, ten, including himself.

He glanced back at the door they had come through and saw puffs of smoke creeping under the sill.

He brought his hand to his mouth and made one hacking cough and said to no one in particular, "Let's get moving before that fire cuts us off," and he jerked his arm in the direction of the door.

At the mention of the word fire, one of the women went hysterical, which brought the fever of the other civilians one degree higher. A few of the ladies dropped to their knees and started to pray while some of the others just cried. The two American men acted more composed, but showed little inclination to follow Marlin's order.

The platoon had come to a standstill.

Beckwith looked at Hillerman and shouted, "GET THEM MOVING," making every word deliberate and pronounced.

Hillerman looked more confused than afraid. He moved towards one of the women and without touching her, shoved his rifle at her. Instead of moving, she fell to the ground, sobbing. Hillerman helped her to her feet.

Beckwith grabbed a hold of Lisa's hand and said, "I want you to stay close to me." She looked up into his eyes with adoration. Her cheeks were wet where she had wiped away the tears, but her eyes sparkled as she blinked.

He squeezed her hand and then released it.

"Dai Wi," she said, "I love you."

"I love you too, Lisa. I just don't know what to do about it . . . and now is not the time to discuss it."

The words made her lift on her toes and stay there except for some slight bouncing motion. "It will be all right then," she said. "Love will take care of us."

Marlin glared at her in disbelief and shook his head. How could one person be so naive? He looked at his M-16 and knew what would take care of him.

Hillerman started to create more anger than co-operation from the civilians, who were trying to explain their important positions to him and how they were not to be pushed around.

Finally Marlin raised his rifle above his head in his right hand and fired it once into the air. After the initial startled responses, the civilians grew quiet as they withdrew from him in horror.

Beckwith said, "I want your asses shaking down those stairs or I'll throw you off this damn roof."

They were all shocked, realizing the Lieutenant might be a bigger lunatic than the NVA. One of the women said, "You'll be sorry you ever said that, Lieutenant."

A tall man in a light suit stepped forward and pointed a small pistol at Beckwith. It was shaking in his hand, but he seemed determined to use it. "We are not prisoners of war," he said looking about at the other civilians for backing. "You can't order us around like that. If you try and force us, I'll shoot."

Fosdale had his M-16s pointed at the man's rib cage and was eyeballing the Lieutenant, waiting for a nod to blow the sucker away.

Marlin hadn't come this far and taken all these risks to start blowing away Americans. He looked at Kraus and just curled his lip and nodded his head.

Kraus kicked at the man's hand, catching him right in the wrist bone and making the pistol fly to one side.

As the man nursed his hand, Fosdale retrieved the pistol and placed it in his pants.

Marlin continued to shake his head as he pointed his index finger at all of them, "You do what I say or next time Fosdale will get his way . . . Get your asses moving." He waved the butt of his rifle at them. "Now!"

They followed his orders.

Ivy ran back to the door and held it open while Keats led the way down the stairs. The Lieutenant and the civilians followed, then the rest of the men.

As soon as Beckwith entered the staircase, he wondered if he had made a mistake. The thick smoke inside made him cover his mouth with his hand and sift air through his gritted teeth. He could barely see. His eyes were burning and his skin felt like it was being skewered over a barbecue. With each step the smoke grew thicker and the temperature more scorching. All that could be heard in the staircase was coughing and moaning. One floor down, the hallway door flung open and Who Do stepped into the staircase with the body of Newsome over his shoulder. From the way the body was dangling, Marlin knew he was dead. Smoke rushed into the hallway and Who Do contributed to the sounds of agony.

Mortars exploding on the rooftop started shaking the stairs and bannister and Marlin wondered how long it would take for them to work their way down.

"Is there a rear fire exit down the hallway?" Beckwith asked Who Do.

"I don't know, Sir." Who Do began to hack as he brought his clenched fist to his mouth.

Marlin feared if the smoke got so thick they could not see and the civilians started passing out, they might all get trapped and die in the flames. To look for another exit would take time, but it could save them all.

The adrenalin that had been feeding Marlin's blood extra energy was diluting and he could feel the fatigue of the heat and of the long tension. He carried his rifle over his shoulder and held onto the handrail not only for balance, but to guide him downstairs. Lisa took hold of his free arm, embracing it with both of hers.

From the fourth floor landing, Marlin looked over the side and could see flames licking up the staircase. Son of a bitch, he thought.

When Ivy stopped halfway down the stairs, grabbed hold of the landing rail and steadied himself as he coughed, Marlin made up his mind and hollered, "Get back up here, Ivy."

Marlin opened the doorway to the fourth floor hallway, twisted his arm around to nearly sling Lisa inside and held it open for the others to pass through. He counted as they passed and when the last man was inside, Marlin followed, let the door shut behind him, and leaned against the door coughing. Most of the civilians were lying on the floor.

When Marlin caught his breath, panting, he said to Ivy who was only a few feet away and coughing,

"Take Keats with you and run down the hall and see if there is a fire exit at the other end."

Marlin already knew that there were no external fire ladders as he had not seen any from the outside, but he was hoping there could possibly be a rear staircase.

Then he realized who would have the answer. He knelt down beside one of the coughing women, took her by the arm. At the touch, she stopped coughing, withdrew her arm and glared at the Lieutenant in fright.

"Is there a fire exit down the hall?" he asked.

"Of course," she replied, as she pointed at the backside of Ivy and Keats on the run.

Marlin just shook his head at his own stupidity. "Let's get moving down the hall," he said. "Hillerman, . . . Move."

As the civilians got to their feet grumbling and wheezing and groped forward, Marlin opened one of the office doors overlooking the front of the embassy and walked to the outside wall and looked through the leafed slats of cement. Lisa and Kraus were right behind him.

"What are you looking for?" Kraus asked.

The tank still had its cannon aimed at the embassy. It fired again. The building shook. The women shrieked.

"Son of a bitch," Marlin replied. He looked up and down the street. Fires and tracers everywhere. "Still no damn reinforcements," he said. "You'd think somebody would come to the aid of the American embassy . . . somebody." He just shook his head.

He turned around and scooted Lisa out of the room, saying, "Let's go."

By now everyone had disappeared from the hall and Keats was waiting near a drinking fountain, holding the door open.

Marlin pushed Keats ahead as he ran inside. The staircase was unfinished cement, narrow, steep and unlighted, with every sound echoing, and the rumbling and firing outside adding to the garbled sounds of coughing and footsteps on the stairs below.

When Lisa and Kraus passed through, Marlin set the hallway doorstopper in place and ran to catch up.

On the third floor, smoke was seeping under the door, but not nearly as much as in the central staircase. Marlin chose not to open the hallway fire door. He could see enough smoke through the door window to know it was worse that the floor he had come from.

They caught up to the slow-moving train of people and slowed down.

By the second floor, the air was growing purer as most of the smoke was rising. Marlin stooped to pick up a lady by the arm who had just plopped on the stairs.

"Come on, lady, we are almost there."

She coughed and said, "I'm holding you personally responsible for anything that happens to us, Lieutenant. This is insane."

"Yes, it is," he agreed.

Marlin looked over the bannister to a landing area where the men and women were spreading out against the walls. It was lighted by a single bulb on the inside wall. Ivy was leaning his weight onto the panic hardware to a wide metal door which would open to the outside garden.

"Don't open that door, Ivy," Marlin shouted.

Ivy held his weight away from the door and asked, "Where should we go, Sir?"

"Just wait a minute."

Marlin let go of the standing lady and made his way through some of the civilians who were sitting on the stairs. Lisa and Kraus were right behind him. Marlin ran to the hallway door first and looked through the glass. There were not as many tracers streaking across the hallway as when they had first entered the building. It actually looked safe.

"Go check out Rodriguez," Marlin told Ivy.

As Marlin held the door open for them, Ivy and Keats slinked forwards. As soon as the door was shut, they started to trot, leaping over the trash and watching in the direction of the front street.

The tank must have fired another cannon shot at ground level because the hallway disintegrated in smoke and flying cement.

Marlin opened the door and hollered for Ivy and Keats. He waited a moment, heard them coughing, then saw them staggering back his way.

Marlin shook his head as he realized if Rodriguez and the Marines were still alive, they were on their own. He patted Ivy and Keats on the back as they ran past him back into the staircase, then he closed the door and looked to the windowless fire door that led to the outside garden. He knew the tank was

ight across the street and probably the only thing
that was stopping it from blowing the door off its
hinges was it did not know that he was behind it.

Marlin hushed the civilians and military, had the
light turned off and when the coughing turned to
muffled sounds, slowly squeaked open the back door
a crack and looked outside.

The wall around the embassy in front of him was
nearly gone. Either the tank had blasted away a
large section of wall with its cannon or the NVA
soldiers had destroyed it with their rockets and hand
grenades. In either case, there was a large opening
exposing the tank, several NVA regulars hiding behind turned-over vehicles and chunks of wall.

There was the gardener's shack no more than a
hundred feet out front and to the right. The area
behind the shack still had the wall intact; the shack
itself was not much to hide behind nor did Beckwith believe they could all make it that far without
suffering major casualties. If the tank turned its
guns on them, he would have been better off leaving the civilians on the roof; at least by now they
would be dead.

As he watched, he saw some troop movement
behind the gardener's shack. He had the feeling it
was Gatz, but as he made out the outline of the
soldiers, recognized them as NVA.

He looked at the house where he had left Gatz
and Hoppy. A huge chunk of its facade was ripped
away, exposing bare timbers, some of the furniture
falling out of the room on the second floor and
fragments of wood, curtains and rugs dangling.

Son of a bitch, he thought. There was the possi-

bility that one well-placed LAW could take out th
tank from here, but it would have to be such
perfect shot that Marlin did not want to take th
chance. He was just too damn far away and to
much at risk. If he could get closer, he would try
but he was surrounded and cut off.

As he wished Gatz could be of help, he looked
back at the corner house and saw a man in th
black outfit of a VC standing at the top of th
exposed staircase. It took him a moment to identify
him, but again it was his height and blond hair
"Holy shit," Marlin said, "there's Hoppy."

When Hoppy looked across the street, he saw th
embassy building glowing with fires seeming to b
licking from every floor.

He looked at the city in the background and saw
it was turning the horizon red. The burning infern
seemed to be sucking the air from where he stoo
as if it were a huge vacuum trying to suck him up.

Hoppy could hardly believe his legs would support him as he walked down the stairs. Doc ha
given him a shot that had taken away the pain
almost completely. He had not felt so painless physically since his capture. He felt good, but what he
saw still overwhelmed him.

The first body he saw was Gatz leaning against
the bannister with his arm torn apart, blood dripping from small holes in his face, his clothes actually smoldering where they had been shredded by
flying shrapmetal, but somehow still holding his Bible in his good arm.

When Hoppy stopped by his side, Gatz made a grunting sound.

Willie's helmet was blown off his head and hanging around the back of his neck, the strap still round his chin. There was a hole in his forehead that cracked open his skull. Hoppy walked around the body and came on Wilson, who was blocking the stairs. Wilson looked like he had been flipped backwards down the stairs when he took a burst of metal in the chest. Hoppy stepped over his body.

Cope lay at the landing, parts of his body scattered around the foyer, a small fire burning on the back of his fatigues. Hoppy stepped on the fire and put it out.

Three LAWs were on the ground near Cope. One of them was blown apart just like an M-16 a couple of feet away, but the other two LAWs seem in working shape. Hoppy picked up both of them, staggered to the exposed face of the house, and leaned against what remained of a wall.

The tank was only a matter of feet away, across a short lawn and on the other side of a white picket fence. It was parked broadside and enveloped in a cloud of smoke from its last firing. It fired its cannon again and the whole tank actually lifted off the ground.

Hoppy looked down at the LAW and knew what he had to do, but he could barely remember how to open it up. He fidgeted for a second with the ring attached at one end to a pin and at the other end to a strand of wire that was tied around a hole in the plastic case.

He leaned back against the wall, almost in frus-

tration, and at the same time saw movement to th
right. When he fixed his gaze on the movement, h
realized it was his image in a fragment of mirro
broken and perched against the wall.

He drew closer to the image as if he were hypn
tized. The first thing he noticed about himself wa
he was out of uniform. As he drew closer to th
mirror, all he recognized of his old self was his hai
the color anyway; the hair was ratted and dirty an
much longer than it had been in months. His fac
was swollen and there were maggots dropping to th
floor from the festering gash in his cheek. His othe
cheek was bleeding from where the soldier ha
knocked out his teeth. He tried to make a grinnin
face to see his teeth, but his cheeks would not pu
out. He spat blood to one side and looked agai
He wondered who he was. He made an agreemen
with the face in the mirror about what he would d
next. He stopped a surge of emotion from explod
ing into tears as he squeezed his lips tight.

Leaning against the wall, he tried to open th
LAW again. When he finally popped the pin,
seemed to open itself.

Hoppy grinned inside. He knew what a terribl
shot with a rifle he had been in boot camp. H
remembered what his drill instructor in basic train
ing had told him, "You might be too stupid t
shoot straight, but you're not too dumb to shoc
back." The memory warmed him.

He moved the LAW to his shoulder and expose
himself around the wall as he aimed at the broad
side tank. He could not stop shaking, but when th
sights crossed the tank, he pressed the firing button

The round flew at the tank, hit the rounded turret, ricocheted to the right, flew about fifty feet into the air and blew up.

Hoppy could not believe that he had missed.

He just couldn't believe it.

Although there were NVA soldiers in front and to the sides of the tank, they were too occupied protecting themselves from the concussion and the back blast when the tank fired to see Hoppy.

As he fidgeted to open the second LAW, he looked up at the tank again. It was starting to move its turret his way.

Hoppy hurried to open the second LAW. Having performed the task once, it came easier this time and in a split second was ready to fire.

He aimed at the tank, but was shaking even more this time and started to squeeze on the trigger and stopped. He knew he was going to miss again. The thought of retreating entered his mind but he discarded the thought quickly. He knew he could not live with himself if he did it again.

He lowered the LAW from his shoulder and tucked it under his arm like it were a rifle with a bayonet and ran closer. He jumped off the landing steps and ran across the lawn littered with debris. He could feel his feet opening with wounds, but still there was no pain.

The cupola's hatch on the tank flew back and out popped an NVA soldier who grabbed hold of the machine gun mounted atop the tank and swung it in Hoppy's direction. As the man grabbed the handles of the gun with both hands, Hoppy fired. The LAW struck right above the tracks of the tank, burrowed its way inside.

At first Hoppy thought it was a dud. Nothin
happened. The machine gunner atop the cupol
opened up on fully automatic into Hoppy's ches
but as the rounds entered his lungs, the tank e:
ploded, sending the machine gunner atop the cu
pola flying into the air, and creating a huge bom
that mushroomed before Hoppy's very eyes. Hopp
got to see it all before he was blown to bits.

Chapter 28

Beckwith caught his breath as he watched the man whom he had fought so long and hard to rescue disappear into a certain death. Hoppy had sacrificed his life for the platoon instead of vice versa, another ironic ending to the twisted war in Southeast Asia.

Marlin felt a wave of sorrow, admiration, hate, and relief almost simultaneously as the concussion slammed the door shut in his face and shook the building like a tremendous earthquake.

As dust and fragments of cement rained from the walls and bathed the staircase in dust, screams from the civilians echoed through the room. When the building stopped shaking, the screams turned to coughs and the firing outside slowed to the patter of a dying rain. The hallway light had been knocked out and in the darkness Marlin groped for Lisa, found her hand searching for his, felt its warmth even in the moment of terror, gave it a squeeze and felt it respond. He stood up, released Lisa's hand and kicked the panic hardware on the door with his foot. Light flooded the room as clouds of dust swirled to the outside. Marlin ran forwards beyond the threshold and fanned his M-16 from side to side. Finding no nearby targets, he signaled for his men to come forward.

The two squads streamed out the doorway in low crouch, restraining coughs in their search f the enemy. The roof of the garden shack was fire and the NVA soldiers who had so recently be stalking about were now fleeing, and easy targe for the revengeful platoon.

"Get 'em over to Rodriguez," Beckwith shouted Hillerman who was standing in the doorway, awe by the disappearance of the tank and the hole had left in the attack. "Move it!"

The overhead flares had thinned out considerabl but beyond the burning city, in the direction of th Saigon River, the horizon was just barely aglo with the new day.

The explosion from the tank had ripped deep into the street block, having further reduced th trees to deadfall and the homes to windowles crumbling structures, but the tide of the attack ha definitely reversed.

Ivy approached the Lieutenant with his helmet i his hand, "Look at this, Sir?"

As Marlin looked at the crater in the helmet tha had sheared the camouflage cover and was dee enough to drink a martini from, he said, "Hell, th bullet didn't even break through the metal. N even close. Get moving."

Ivy put the helmet back on his head and wit drew.

Kraus came closer to the Lieutenant with th radio in his hands instead of on his back. He sai "Lieutenant." He was pointing to a hole in the mid dle of his receiver.

"Son of a bitch. You OK?"

"Yes, Sir. The batteries absorbed the bullet . . . but the radio doesn't work worth a fuck now."

"Who can you pick up?"

"Nobody. It's useless."

Marlin shrugged, and instantly looked at Kraus in a new light. Without the radio, Kraus was no longer his right-hand man. "Kraus, get the civilians moving and stay with 'em until things cool down. I don't want any of them running for it or causing any more trouble."

"Yes, Sir," Kraus said as he stood up with a rifle he had picked up somewhere along the line, threw the radio to one side and ran for the civilians. The women were beyond the stage of arguing with anyone. As the Lieutenant eyed them, Dolores stared back and glared with hate.

A couple of NVA troops ran across a blowout in the wall, looking like they were trying to retreat more than attack. Marlin's men plucked them out like chickens.

Sweat ran from Marlin's face like rain water and mixed with the dust to sting his eyes and face. He reached for his canteen and opened it as he brought it to his mouth and gulped down the tepid water. He was so thirsty his throat felt like it had constricted. He could feel the water land in his empty stomach.

Lisa drew closer to Marlin and grabbed ahold of his shirttail. He turned his head to look into her tender eyes, then scanned the wall surrounding the embassy, afraid that some sniper might be crouched on the other side ready to take his revenge. He held

345

the canteen out for her, but she shook her head.

Hillerman, Fosdale and Kraus herded the civilians against the wall and yelled at them to keep moving. The civilians acted tensed, indignant and ready to panic.

When Marlin was halfway to the entryway, and the first of his troops were already disappearing amidst the rubble of the foyer, he felt Lisa stumble behind him, turned his head to see her falling and offered his hand.

As she accepted it, she dropped to her knees. When Marlin pulled her to follow, she felt like dead weight. He stopped and saw that she had rolled onto her back and her eyes were closed.

He stopped, bent down, lifted her in his arms, and ran forward, every so often looking down at her face waiting for her eyes to open, all the time expecting her to stir in his arms. When he set her body against the wall in the foyer, it slithered to one side and curled up in a ball.

He dropped to the pavement and stretched out her lithe body on the decking. He saw her chest was bleeding, a large stain of blood was over her heart.

She was dead.

There was no time for sorrow, only for revenge.

Keats knelt beside the Lieutenant, looked briefly at Lisa, then said, "It looked like the tank made a direct hit on the foyer, Sir. I don't know how the hell Rodriguez survived."

Marlin looked around at the blocks of cement

346

blown from the walls and ceiling that littered the entranceway, and it was from behind them that Rodriguez waved to the Lieutenant.

As Marlin nodded his head in approval, he asked, "How are they?"

"Castillo lost his glasses and took a round in the shoulder, but the others are OK. One of the Marines is dead."

Marlin grunted and wondered if it were the soldier he had been talking to. It didn't matter if he knew him, especially now. On the spot Marlin decided they would make their stand here. He couldn't move aggressively with the civilians and he had too many bodies to care for.

"OK, Keats. Let's set up here and make sure there are no more KIAs. This is it."

Marlin looked back at the body of Lisa, alone, dead, taking on dust from a war she didn't even want to live with, in love with a man who didn't have the time to love her back. Marlin felt himself enveloped in a cloud of failure, but he could not indulge in the emotion, not in the midst of a battle to save his own life, and the lives of his men.

The fury that raged within his soul would have to wait for a better time to find a release; possibly by that time it would no longer be as strong.

He looked back at his men; some of them firing, others looking for targets or bandaging their wounds or their buddies.

Marlin looked to the cement wall and beyond at the burning houses in the neighborhood.

The NVA seemed to have lost interest in the embassy. Marlin was worried that they might be consolidating for a final attack. With so few of his men able to fight back and so little ammunition remaining, he spread the word to start firing on semiautomatic. He could probably withstand one major attack, then it would be time to fix bayonets and gouge out eyes. He anticipated the climax.

Within half an hour four armored personnel carriers from the Twenty-fifth Infantry Division came slowly rumbling down Vo Di Nguy. They came single file with infantrymen guarding the flanks, the lead track firing a fifty caliber machine gun and silencing what little resistance remained. Every so often the lead track stopped, changed places with the one behind it, and the file proceeded. When the enemy fire became strong, another track would pull up from the rear with a 106 recoilless rifle mounted aboard. When it fired, it disintegrated its target.

A photographer with two Nikons over his shoulder and one to his eye came closer to Beckwith, snapping pictures, circling the tracks, snapping at the soldiers standing around, going over to some of the dead NVA littering the sidewalk.

The civilians were taken away and soon Marlin heard himself saying, "Let's gather up the dead and wounded."

Gatz was found perched against the back wall in the corner house, bleeding like a dripping sponge, blabbering, holding onto his Bible. He was evacuated by helicopter along with Castillo and a few of the civilians who were scratched up.

Hoppy was found on the roof of the house he had been hiding in. What was left of him was placed in a plastic bag and like the bodies of his

348

dead friends, placed in the garden where the ambush started, lined up in a row. They numbered twelve in all.

Their story never would be told. How they fought for each other, alongside of each other, with each other and only for each other. What they wanted from life and what they would miss the most, what they would like to tell their fellow Americans. Just silent heroes to a little-known battle in Vietnam.

Lisa was placed alongside of them. Since she did not have a family to bury her in Ben Luc, Marlin requested that she be buried in Saigon, and could only hope they'd honor the request.

The tracks took Marlin, his eleven remaining men, and the KIAs back to Ton Son Nhut Air Force Base. After a few days of manning the berm against a possible ground attack, the platoon was flown back to Ben Luc in helicopters where the bridge was already being rebuilt by the Army Corps of Engineers.

The Old Man was pissed-off, but what else was new?

Beckwith took his men out on an ambush the first night back. He just wanted to get away from it all, far away.

He got himself way out on the middle of the rice paddies, a good mile from the road and the same from the black line of the jungle, set out the claymores, bracketed his position for the artillery and then just settled in for the night.

It was so still.

He looked through his starlight scope and scanned the rice paddies. Any VC who would venture to crawl all night just to get to his position would have to want to die.

Marlin looked back at Lisa's hootch. It hadn't changed, but at the same time he felt like he took a round to the heart himself. It didn't come out in blood or show on his face, but it grew around his heart in the form of a thick crust, like wrinkles on an old man's face that would never go away. She had shown him love and hope and even a bit of heaven in this country, and now that she was dead, everything she meant to him disappeared as well — innocence, trust, love.

Kraus crept closer to the Lieutenant, stopped and whispered, "You know what, Sir? That damn Hoppy was a hero. That's what he was."

Marlin looked up at the quartering moon. It seemed to be winking at him.

Marlin thought of the men who had died up in Saigon. They were tough, skilled and courageous. He was proud to have fought with them. He was proud of them, but still they were dead and he loved them so much he figured they had to be in a better place than he was.

"They all were, Kraus. They all were."

ACTION ADVENTURE: WINGMAN #1–#6
by Mack Maloney

WINGMAN (2015, $3.95)

From the radioactive ruins of a nuclear-devastated U.S. emerges a hero for the ages. A brilliant ace fighter pilot, he takes to the skies to help free his once-great homeland from the brutal heel of the evil Soviet warlords. He is the last hope of a ravaged land. He is Hawk Hunter . . . Wingman!

WINGMAN #2: THE CIRCLE WAR (2120, $3.95)

A second explosive showdown with the Russian overlords and their armies of destruction is in the wind. Only the deadly aerial ace Hawk Hunter can rally the forces of freedom and strike one last blow for a forgotten dream called "America"!

WINGMAN #3: THE LUCIFER CRUSADE (2232, $3.95)

Viktor, the depraved international terrorist who orchestrated the bloody war for America's West, has escaped. Ace pilot Hawk Hunter takes off for a deadly confrontation in the skies above the Middle East.

WINGMAN #4: THUNDER IN THE EAST (2453, $3.95)

The evil New Order is raising a huge mercenary force to reclaim America, and Hawk Hunter, the battered nation's most fearless top gun fighter pilot, takes to the air to prevent this catastrophe from occurring.

WINGMAN #5: THE TWISTED CROSS (2553, $3.95)

"The Twisted Cross," a power-hungry neo-Nazi organization, plans to destroy the Panama Canal with nuclear time bombs unless their war chests are filled with stolen Inca gold. The only route to saving the strategic waterway is from above—as Wingman takes to the air to rain death down upon the Cross' South American jungle stronghold.

WINGMAN #6: THE FINAL STORM (2655, $3.95)

Deep in the frozen Siberian wastes, last-ditch elements of the Evil Empire plan to annihilate the Free World in one final rain of nuclear death. Trading his sleek F-16 fighter jet for a larger, heavier B-1B supersonic swing-wing bomber, Hawk Hunter undertakes his most perilous mission.